KIDS ARE CHANCEY

5

I0586507

KIDS ARE CHANCEY

5

KAY DEW SHOSTAK

August South
PUBLISHING

KIDS ARE CHANCEY
Copyright © 2017 by Kay Dew Shostak.
All rights reserved.

This book is a work of fiction. The characters, incidents, and dialogue are drawn from the author's imagination and are not to be construed as real. Any resemblance to actual events or persons, living or dead, is entirely coincidental.

Printed in the United States of America. No part of this book may be used or reproduced in any manner whatsoever without written permission except in the case of brief quotations embodied in articles and reviews.

ISBN: 978-0-9991064-0-2

Library of Congress Control Number: 2017909079

SOUTHERN FICTION: Women's Fiction / Small Town / Railroad / Bed & Breakfast / Mountains / Georgia / Family

Text Layout and Cover Design by Roseanna White Designs
Cover Images from www.Shutterstock.com

Published by August South Publishing. You may contact the publisher at:
AugustSouthPublisher@gmail.com

To the Shostak kids
Robert, Ryan, and Lizzy

You are my best stories

Hey y'all,

Just a quick note from me, Patty, to say thanks for coming to mine and Andy's wedding earlier this month. Wasn't the reception at the Lake Park just beautiful? Something about dancing in a wedding dress. Even seemed to chill out Anna and Will some. Maybe it was that they were actually already married, since they'd eloped, or maybe it was because she's, well, you know. But things were pretty tense those days before the wedding and even during the wedding. However, they did seem to get along better when the dancing started.

Speaking of tense, let me apologize for Diego Moon showing up and getting all upset at Mr. Peter. Why, everyone knows nothing was going on with Mr. Peter and Jordan Moon. For crying out loud, have you seen Diego Moon? Besides Mr. Peter is like a duck on a June bug about getting his bistro opened and can't think of nothing else. Sooner he could get Jordan and Diego back together and her back in New York with her little girls, sooner he could open his new place up.

Just between you and me, I'm excited about the changes on Main Street. Mama says she's got things figured out for me and Andy to let Carolina have her bookstore back. Working with Carolina is fun, but maybe you've noticed she's not real decisive? Yeah, I like that Andy doesn't spend time talking or thinking about things, he just does them! But Carolina's real sweet, bless her heart.

Hope you stayed at the reception long enough

to hear that Ms. Laney told everyone she's having a baby! Sure surprised a bunch of folks. Guess that'll keep her from being jealous of her sister moving up to Laurel Cove. Them are some mighty fancy houses up there. Wait, does that mean Carolina is on her own with the B&B and the bookstore? Hmm, hope she gets better at making decisions. Maybe she'll ask Savannah. LOL

Gotta go. We're leaving on our honeymoon this weekend and I still ain't packed. I'd like to say I'll miss you and Chancey, but you know I'd be lying!

~ Thanks, Mrs. Andrew Taylor

Chapter 1

"Some would say it's poetic justice. That you got what you deserved."

Oops, did I say that out loud? Apparently so, since my sixteen-year-old daughter Savannah is staring at me, unblinking with her head tilted *just* a bit. Yeah, there we go, hand moving to her hip and chin tilting up ever so slightly. Alert sirens and red lights flashing in my head can only be dimmed with rapid retreat. "Not that *I* think that. I think he's crazy, and you're right." Smile just a bit and turn slowly away. There, now I'm safe to roll my eyes.

Must be the heat that got to me. Our AC unit died yesterday, and the house is hot. Open windows let in a little breeze, but by this time of the afternoon, the breeze isn't even refreshing. "Want a piece of lemon in your tea?" I ask her.

"Sure." She sits her glass on the counter beside mine. "When's the air going to be fixed? My room is like an oven."

Her room under the eaves holds all the hot Georgia air that rises from the rest of the house, and the tiny half-windows don't let in much breeze at all.

"FM says 'no time at all,' that's all I can tell you. If you get a better answer out of him, let me know. I'm going out to the deck." When I called Jackson yesterday morning (was that just yesterday?) to tell him the air wasn't working, he was already south of Atlanta. He'd left super early to beat the Monday morning traffic. Jackson, my husband, is an engineer who works with railroads. No, he doesn't drive trains, he's a civil engineer working with tracks and roads. He's heading up a big project in South Georgia, so he'll be there most of the week. Heck, most of this year. He said to call FM, an older friend who's lived his whole life in Chancey, and get an idea of who to call. So I did.

Well, FM knew a guy. A guy who's been doing air conditioners since they were invented. A guy who'll fix us right up. All I know is that in Marietta, in my beloved suburbs, I didn't have to know a guy. I just had to look up a website, call the number listed, and everything would be okay. No standing around talking about how 'the guy' used to play on this part of the river when he was a kid, or hear how he and FM played football against each other in junior high, or listen to his woes about his grandkids going bad. Give me a guy in a uniform with a name patch, those disposable footies he puts on, who just hands me a bill when he's done. Oh, and since our rush job is a "favor" for FM, we get squeezed in between his "real" jobs. I do not need to have a relationship with my repair guy, but apparently that's how it's done in Chancey.

When I accidentally sold our home back in the Atlanta suburbs, there were lots of things I hated about moving to a small town. And this part of small town life wasn't even on that list.

"And he's probably just doing it to get back at me." Back on the deck where there's a merciful breeze, Savannah sets her glass of tea on the table and flops into the chair across from me.

"FM?" She's interrupted my private soliloquy on small town repairmen, so it takes me a moment. "No. Ricky?"

She stretches her legs out to prop them on the planter at the edge of the deck. Missus planted it with pink geraniums last month for the Mother's Day brunch we hosted here at the

B&B, and they are loving the heat of June. Bunches of pink flowers with white centers crowd each planter. However, as the flowers die, handfuls of petals fall onto the deck, and I have to keep sweeping them up. Of course, compared to the work the garden in the yard is, give me geraniums anytime. Savannah's foot taps one of the flower heads, and a small shower spreads pink beside the planter.

"Yeah, Ricky," she says, adding, "but I really don't care."

Then quit talking about it! Okay, I did better that time and didn't say it out loud. Savannah's high school boyfriend hit the ground running at Georgia State, where he's enrolled in summer classes and working on building up his legs for football. Apparently, he's the toast of the town and is slated to be the starting quarterback in the fall due to a couple injuries and some bad grades on other players' parts.

Now, supposedly just as apparent, all that glory should've been additional feathers in Savannah's cap. She was planning on attending games as the star quarterback's girlfriend right up to this past weekend, when Ricky came home with Miss Georgia State on his arm. Not sure she actually has that title, but she should. She's stunning, poised, and smart—majoring in pre-med and helping Ricky ace his classes. He surprised everyone by coming home and then showing up with her in church on Sunday. His girlfriend Charisse looked like a woman beside Savannah. Of course, thanks to a viral YouTube video, everyone around here remembers lovesick Ricky pouring out his soul to cold-hearted Savannah at Valentine's, while at the same time burning down the town gazebo. So, like I said earlier, poetic justice.

I hear voices inside the house, but before I can get up, FM steps out onto the deck. "Carolina, got some bad news. That part Earl needs he can't find at the junkyard. Looks like he's going to have to buy a whole new part."

Standing up, I point FM to the chair at the end of the table.

"Sit there. You look hot, and it's in the shade. Let me get you some tea." In the kitchen, I speak louder. "So why would we want a part from the junkyard, anyway?"

"Well, it'd be cheaper. That's what Earl's been doing, having his wife call the local junkyards and checking their inventories."

I pour his tea but take a minute before I go back out. I'm breathing, in and out, real slow. Okay, I'm good now. FM is the very salt of the earth, even though he's married to the devil. Okay, Missus's not *actually* the devil. Anyway, I don't want to upset FM. "But I told you, we're good with doing a whole new system. We knew that was a possibility when we bought this place last summer. It was figured into the final closing costs. We have the money sitting there in the bank, just waiting for the system to conk out."

"Thank you, honey." he says as I hand him his glass. "But no need to throw away good money. Earl is going to check with some other places that might have it. 'Course that'll mean adding a trip a bit farther away, but he says it'd be worth it. Good tea, Carolina. Real sugar. I can always tell. Missus makes hers with those saccharine pills and Splenda. Leaves a bad taste in my mouth, but it's better than that unsweet stuff some folks'll drink." He leans back. "So, Savannah, you get to talk to Ricky's new girlfriend? She's real smart. Bet you and her would be good friends if you end up down at Georgia State next year. That's still your first choice, right?"

"No. I never seriously considered it."

FM raises an eyebrow. "What? You were all excited about their theater program! Yeah, I remember you talking about it. Right, Carolina?"

Oh, no, not going there. "Wait, back to the air conditioner. We don't have air because Earl is scouring the Southeast for a used part?"

FM nods. "Lucky it's not too hot yet."

Savannah stands up. "I'm going where there's air conditioning. Call me when ours is fixed." She stomps past me and into the house.

FM sniffs. "She seems right out of sorts. We didn't even have air conditioning when I was her age. Shoot, I wouldn't have it now if Missus had told me she was getting it put in. I was good with a couple window units when the heat builds up in August."

"Well," I say, "we have a business to run, and it's getting up into the eighties this weekend."

"Want me to set up a couple window fans in the guest rooms? Which ones are booked?"

"No, I want a new unit!" I pause to calm down. Everyone in this crackerjack box of a town thinks our B&B, Crossings B&B, is their own private project. They all know what's best. "Sorry, FM, but I want it replaced. Does Earl even do new units?"

"Of course he does. He just doesn't fly right into replacing good things for the sake of making things fast. You want it done right, don't ya?"

FM looks so sincere, so helpful. I stand up and walk toward the kitchen door. I'm not made for confrontation. That's why we have a B&B in the first place. "Sure. You know best. I've got to go." Sitting my empty tea glass on the counter, I shake my head.

Time is the most precious commodity in the suburbs. Here, it's money. Sanity is in short supply both places, but at least in the 'burbs, crazy is air-conditioned.

"Please tell me that was *not* Earl Shurbett's truck I passed leaving here," my friend Laney yells as she waltzes in the front door. At the door into the kitchen from the living room, she stops, leans against the doorframe, and takes a huge breath. She pushes her big dark sunglasses to the top of her head, corralling her mass of hair back from her face. "Was Earl here? What's broken? Call and fire him right this minute."

FM yells from the deck. "We are not firing Earl. Everything's under control."

Laney looks out the French door to the deck, then she holds her arms up so that her blue caftan floats around her. "Lord, it's hot in here! The air is broken, isn't it? How am I supposed to work here? Let me call Shaw. He'll get someone to take care of this." She pulls her phone out of the depths of the blue silky fabric swirling around her and punches it twice as she yells, "Should've known if Earl was here, you weren't far behind, FM." With flattened eyebrows, she shakes her head at me. "Can't believe you let him call Earl." Then into the phone, "Shaw, Carolina's air quit. Call somebody to fix it. Love you."

She punches the phone once more and plunges it back into the folds of her muumuu. "Here I am all ready to work, and this place is an oven. Why didn't you tell me the air quit?" She opens the fridge and pulls out the gallon pitcher of iced tea.

"'Cause they called *me*. I called Earl. It's under control," FM yells again from the back deck.

Laney takes the glass I hand her from the cabinet and pushes it against our ice dispenser. Under its noise she whispers, "Earl can't fix nothing. Shaw knows a guy."

Great, another guy. "Want lemon?"

"No," she spits. "What is it with everyone suddenly wanting to put lemon in iced tea? Some Yankee plot, I'm betting." She puts the pitcher back in the fridge and sashays out to the deck. She's always sashayed, but these caftans she's taken to wearing while pregnant take it to a whole new level.

"Hey, FM. So, when's Earl figure the air will be back on?"

"Directly. That is, unless you just messed things up calling Shaw. Who's Shaw gonna call? Terry? He calls Terry, and you might as well throw the whole system down the hill into the river."

Laney sits in the chair where Savannah sat earlier, and I just lean against the railing. "Who's Terry?"

"Some fool kid who doesn't know a hammer from a wrench. Just knows how to send out bills."

Laney primly sips her tea. "Unlike Earl, who never has to send a bill because he never actually fixes anything. Earl should actually send out checks to folks for having to listen to all his stories."

"Quit fussing with each other," I say. "I just want it fixed. Laney, have you quit over at the Charming House B&B yet?"

"Law, yes. They ain't ever gonna open. Besides, they're too bossy with me in my delicate condition. Can you believe I didn't even know I was pregnant? And climbing all those stairs they have and using all that cleaning stuff? Besides, they were too bossy."

We were shocked when Laney made her announcement to a few of us at the double wedding two weeks ago. She had only figured it out when she fainted and had to be taken by her new employer to the hospital over in Collinswood. She and her husband Shaw then went to see a doctor specializing in births for older mothers. Although apparently she'd blissfully sailed unaware through almost six months of pregnancy, and everything looks great for a healthy baby at the end of the summer.

FM stands up. "Well, I better be going. Anna wants flank steak grilled with veggies tonight for dinner."

"How's she feeling?" I ask as I sit back where I was earlier. Although she's twenty-five years younger than Laney, my daughter-in-law Anna, who is also FM's granddaughter, is having a rough pregnancy. Even though we knew about Anna and Will's bundle of joy first, it was just as surprising because we found out about the baby in the same conversation in which we learned they'd eloped. Before that, we didn't even know they were dating. But, honestly, it's too hot to think about all that. "Strange to have two babies in our little world on the way, isn't it?"

Laney takes a long drink and nods. "I'm just thrilled it's only one baby for me and not twins this time, like with the girls. That was seventeen years ago, but I still remember how awful it was. Did you know the older you get the more likely you are to have twins? I was a nervous wreck until we had the ultrasound and found out there's only one in here." She pats her stomach.

FM shakes his head. "Those ultrasounds are amazing. Did you see the picture of the last one Anna had made?" he asks me.

"Oh, yes. I saw it." I add under my breath, "*Everyone* saw it." As he turns to leave, I speak up, "You have a good day, FM. Tell Missus we said hi."

"Sure thing. Me and Earl will be back in the morning," he yells as he walks through the house to the front door.

"Earl Shurbett." Laney dismisses the man with a wave of her hand. "Wait'll you see Terry Minns. Good-looookin'!"

I shake my head. "I don't care what he looks like as long as we get some air. The house is unbearable until after midnight. Savannah's room is an oven, and she's more unbearable than the heat."

"What did she think of Ricky's Charisse? That was about the prettiest woman I've seen in a long time. Didn't just being with her make Ricky look older, too?"

"Going away to college does that to kids. I remember how old Will looked first time he came home. They change."

"So glad I'll have my new little one by time the girls go off to school next year. He'll be a year old by then."

"He? Did you say 'he'?"

"Shoot! Yeah. Don't tell anyone. Gender reveal party is Friday, and then everyone can know. The girls don't even know yet. Shaw either."

I give my friend a questioning stare. "I thought you didn't know."

"Right, like I'm not going to know something that important. Although I said I didn't find out so folks wouldn't keep asking me." She grins. "A boy! I'm so excited. Shaw's going to die."

A quick little breeze blows over us. Conversation stalls as we both lift our heads to feel it. Laney finishes her tea and fluffs her caftan to stir the air around her legs as she stands up. "Well, I'm going to take the laptop home and get things sorted out there where it's cool. I don't even have to ask if you've kept up with everything."

"Well, not as good as you do it. My system is more, um, more relaxed." I stand up and stretch. "Since it looks like the air's not going to be fixed today, guess I have to do some of the stuff I've been putting off. Like cleaning."

"How are things at the bookstore?" she asks as we walk inside.

"Good, I guess. Kind of waiting for Gertie to go home before I get too involved again at the bookstore. Patty and Andy leave this weekend for their honeymoon. Figure Gertie will go home then, but still not sure what she's doing with the store or when she's going home."

Laney speaks up from the office where she's gathering stuff to take to her house. "You know, you could just ask her. She *is* staying in your B&B."

"I guess. But then what if she says she's not leaving?" Gertie Samson is a force of nature all her own, and the sooner she leaves Chancey the better for everyone. Me, her daughter, Patty, and her new husband. Did I mention me? Especially me.

Laney comes back into the kitchen with a big red leather satchel slung over her shoulder. "Carolina, you beat all I've ever seen for not wanting to actually know what's going on around you."

Shrugging, I pick up her purse before she can and follow her out the front door. At her big black SUV, always new since her husband owns a dealership, we put everything in the back seat. Before she puts the car in reverse, she rolls down the window and lowers her sunglasses to cover her eyes. "And in case you think I didn't notice, you are also intentionally trying to ignore what's going on with both Savannah and Anna. Good job changing the conversation, but just because you ain't talking about them doesn't mean everyone else isn't." She rolls up the window and backs away.

Shoot.

Chapter 2

"You've got a problem with your air? Shaw asked me to stop by. I'm Terry Minns."

"Sure." I push open the screen door for the young man. "I'm Carolina. It just stopped working. It's old, and when we bought this place last summer we knew it was on its last leg. Do you do whole replacements of systems?" I leave the wooden door open as the morning air outside is cooler than the air inside the house.

He grins. "Now, no need to get ahead of ourselves. Let me take a look." He nods up the stairs. "Thermostat there, right?"

I nod and he walks up the steps.

"Saw your sign out front. So this is a B&B? I've never stayed at one. Folks say they're really fun."

"Yeah, people seem to enjoy them." I wait at the bottom of the stairs, and he joins me back there in a minute.

"I'm going to go out and take a look at the outside unit, then I'll give Shaw a call. Let him know what I find."

"I'm, well, my husband and I, are the owners. Shouldn't you let me, us, know?"

"Yes, ma'am. If you want. When does your husband get home?"

"He's not today. He's out of town."

"Oh." He steps to the front door. "You want me to give him

a call?" Turning around he pulls out his phone, then waits for me to give him my husband's phone number. He finally looks up at me when I don't say anything.

"*I'm* the one who's going to write the check. You might not want to dismiss me so quickly."

"Sorry, ma'am. Wasn't thinking." He tucks his phone back in his pocket. "I'll let you know what I find." He lets go of the screen door and turns around.

He's not even off the front porch headed around the side of the house before I have Laney's phone ringing. To her hello, I say, "Terry's here. He's a bit of chauvinist. Wants to talk to *my husband.*"

"Oh, ignore that. He's young. Isn't he cute?"

"Not that cute."

"Get over yourself. You know you're going to want him to talk to Jackson, right?"

"Of course, but he was rude about it."

"You're just lucky Shaw let him off work early to come check things out. Supposed to get even hotter this weekend, and I see we have guests."

"I know. Well, if he gets this fixed, he can be a raving sexist. He works at the dealership? Thought he was an air conditioner repairman."

"Not sure what he does. His father is Shaw's best sales-man. Will knows him. Mike Minns. Glad he got there so ear-ly. Don't mess with that Earl anymore, and ignore FM if he complains. I've got to get dressed. We're going shopping for nursery furniture. It's so much more fun to have a baby when you have money."

We hang up, and I watch Terry come from around the side of the house and walk to his truck. He is cute, in a country kind of way. His hair is a little shaggy, but it's mostly curls. He looks strong, and I guess he's around twenty-five? He sets something on the seat of his truck, closes the door, and turns toward the house. Of course, catching me watching him. Like he needs help thinking he's God's gift to women. He heads up the sidewalk, and I step out onto the porch.

"Hey, Miss Carolina, I've got what I need. Should have you fixed up in no time at all."

"So what's the problem?"

And he goes into some description of something that I immediately block out, but I had to ask, right? "Okay, thanks. Um, you said you'll let Shaw know, too?"

"Yes, ma'am. If that's okay?"

"Sure. His wife is my business partner."

Plus, that means I can have Jackson just call Shaw for the details, since I didn't really listen.

He yells over his shoulder as he reaches his truck again. "Hey, so Will Jessup is your son? Works at the dealership?"

"Yes. Laney says you work there, too."

"Yep, me and my old man. So Savannah is your daughter?"

"You know Savannah?"

"She came over to see Will. She sure is pretty. Tell her Terry said 'hi.'" He waves as he climbs into his truck. He is grinning entirely too big.

Wonder what Savannah was doing at the dealership? Back inside, I close the wood door to block out the growing sunlight and the heat it brings. All day the past couple days, I just go back and forth between opening up the windows and doors to let in cooler air, or closing them to keep out warmer air. I think it's just six one way and a half-dozen the other.

So, now we have two guys working on the air, and I have absolutely no faith in either of them.

Walking back towards the kitchen, a reflection flashes across the living room and I turn to look out the front window. Susan's car door is just swinging open, and she makes for the back yard without even looking at the house. Guess she's look-

21

ing for a bit of garden therapy (and not a minute too soon, my garden is looking bad.)

"Hey there," I say from the back deck. She's pulling on gardening gloves and just throws up a hand in the air at me without lifting her head. She looks tense. "Want some coffee?"

She says "no," but still doesn't turn around. Cradling my own cup, I walk out to the edge of the plowed section. In the spring, when I stupidly thought I was bored one week, I got Susan's husband Griffin to plow me a big garden area. Big. Then I dumped a bunch of plants from Walmart's clearance rack into a couple rows and decided I would never be so bored that I would like gardening. Luckily for me, Susan was just at that same time moving away from her massive garden, and she said she'd take care of mine. (This coincided with pretty much the same time I started going back to church. Coincidence? Don't think so.)

Barefoot in the cool grass, I watch her pull weeds for a minute. She appears to be working off anger or frustration, so I give her some time. If I didn't know how hot it was going to be in my house in a couple hours, I could enjoy this beautiful morning. The sky is clear, trees completely leafed out, bugs and birds singing their gentle summer songs. Wait. That's not a bird or the bugs. Susan is crying.

I sit my cup in the grass and pick my way through the rocky dirt to where she's kneeling beside my sprawling tomato plants. "Susan, what's wrong?"

She rocks back and then stands up. "Those idiots that bought our house have completely stripped the backyard. Everything is gone. All the flower gardens, even the pond. It's a bare wasteland, and they are having sod laid down. A big old lawn of grass. It's awful."

"No! Oh my goodness. Your yard was amazing. Flowers all the time, and the benches, and the pond. What did they do with all the plants and stuff?"

She wipes her forearm across her face. "I heard they had a back hoe over there, so I went there this morning to see if I could get some of the plants if they didn't want them, and it's all gone. The workers didn't speak much English, but they said it was gone, and when I looked around the place, they're right. Nothing left. Nothing." She walks out of the garden, and I pick my way out following her to the steps of the deck, where we both sit down.

"Were the new people there yet?"

"No. We just met the husband at closing, and he was in a big hurry. I offered to show him, or his wife, around the property sometime, and he said they would call. The sale went through so fast, we didn't have time to meet them. Just wanted them to know what all would be blooming and how to take care of it all. Guess they decided that was too much work, just strip it all out and plant grass. No explanations needed then."

"Well, you have your new yard to work with."

"Not really. The developer landscapes all the yards in our part of Laurel Cove, and then you just pay to maintain it. I'm not sure we belong up there." She reaches out and squeezes my hand. "I miss being able to pop over and see y'all. Shoot, our new driveway is longer than the road to your house was from our old house."

I nod, but don't say anything. She's not invited me over to even see the new house. She and Griffin are running in different circles all of a sudden. His new job has him working long hours, when before he only seemingly worked part-time from his one-man office. Plus, he and Grant have taken up golf, so we're not even seeing as much of Grant around here. They only moved a few miles away, but it feels farther. I'm sure once they get settled . . . okay, I *hope* once they get settled, it'll get better.

She jumps up, "Look at me! I have to get home and shower. Wednesdays we have lunch at the clubhouse." Then she holds out her hand midair. "I know! Come with me. Come to lunch today at the club. I'm trying to get friendly with the ladies there not only since they're our new neighbors, but many of them are supportive of the events at the Lake Park."

This perks me up. "I have wanted to see the Laurel Cove clubhouse. Are you sure it's open to anyone?"

"Yes, when you're with a member. And I'm a member. Come, it's beautiful, and besides, Laney said your air is out? I promise the club will be nice and cool." She begins walking toward the side of the house. "I'll meet you there a bit before noon."

Still sitting on the steps to our deck, my mind wanders over how strange this whole exchange has been. Susan wasn't here more than fifteen minutes. She's always been high energy, but this was almost manic. I stand up. Well, she does have a lot going on right now. I dump the bit of cold coffee left in the bottom of my cup over the deck railing, and as I lay my hand on the door going inside, I freeze.

What in the world will I wear?

CHAPTER 3

Nothing worse than trying to get dressed nice when you are sweating buckets. When I got into the shower, the house was still comfortable. Now, between the steam from the shower and running the hair dryer, the bathroom is like a sauna. And the bedroom is no better since the open windows are welcoming the morning sunshine along with the growing heat.

My hair is short so it doesn't usually take long to dry, but I can't seem to get it dry today. It is either damp from the shower or full of sweat. I'm no longer sure. I'm trying to grow it out, and, well, it looks like I'm trying to grow it out. Like an experiment or something. Of course, I'll get in the air-conditioned room, and it will dry then. Nice and bushy. Or I could gel it all down, and pretend I wanted it to look like this. Only problem with that is I don't have the cheekbones, expressive eyes, or little waist that works with that hairstyle. I'd just look like, well, like a drowned rat.

With bright red lips.

I bought this lipstick because it said it would last all day. Now I know why, it dyes your lips. Even stung a bit when I put it on, and now it won't come off. And I've rubbed it so much, the area around my lips are now red. Plus, I got some of it on the white skirt I was going to wear, so now I'm back to pulling things out of the closet.

Black. Black is always good. Plain black dress. Plain black sandals. I just need to get to the car, turn on the air conditioner and drive around for an hour until it's time to meet Susan. Plus, I need to get out of here before FM and Earl show up. Let them figure out whatever part it was Terry put into his truck and took with him.

In the car, I turn the air on full blast and settle in to send some texts before I drive off. Bryan is at the lake taking swim lessons. He can already swim, but as he wants to be a lifeguard, he needs some additional training. He rides his bike there, and then he and his friends stay most of the day. Susan has a fully running snack shack opened there, and she let us open accounts so the kids don't have to take money. It's awesome. I text him where I am going, knowing he won't see his phone until lessons are over. Susan also put in lockers so things can be left secure. She's done a lot in the short amount of time she's been managing the Lake Park.

Savannah texted me that she's helping Peter at the bistro today. MoonShots kind of evolved with Jordan moving back to New York and Peter taking over the space with his bistro idea. He's supposed to open soon. Savannah stayed at Laney's house last night and says she'll be home later to see if the air is working. I text her back where I'm going. No, scratch that. She knows more people up in Laurel Cove than I do, and she may forbid me going to the club for lunch. Just a smiley face to her.

Ignore FM's text. Ignore Shaw's text. Tell Jackson he needs to talk to Shaw. During all this, Patty texts me to come to the bookstore sometime soon. I answer her "okay." There's air conditioning there, and I do want to see how it's looking.

Use to be my cell phone felt like a leash, and I resented it. Now that I'm good with texting, it feels so freeing. And yes, I'm now on Facebook. But we'll talk about that later.

By the time I get downtown, I'm feeling much cooler. There's a spot around the corner coming into town, so I slide in there. Getting out of the car, I feel dressed up and think I might like this slicked-back hair idea. Better than being bushy, right? Around the corner, I look in the windows of Peter's newest endeavor, not sure he has a name yet. Maybe Chancey Bistro? But then I'm not that creative. Heck, we had to have a contest to name the B&B Crossings. Peter's trying to soften the modern lines of the MoonShots, which are known for being clean and straightforward, with hard lines and cool colors. He's added all kinds of shelves, I see. Just watching through the windows is good enough for me. Peter and I have a natural attraction, and well, I am looking good today. No need to get anything started.

Savannah sees me and comes outside. "What did you do?" She walks right up and puts her hand on my head. "Is that gel? Gross, mom."

Andy is walking up the sidewalk from the direction of Ruby's. The big goofy grin he always wears is bigger and goofier. "Hey, Mrs. J. Love the look. Like that old video of that guy singing that song "Addicted to Love" with the chicks all in black, slicked back hair, and really red lips." He gives me a thumbs up as he opens the door to the bookstore/flower shop.

I jerk away from Savannah's outstretched hand. "I'm going out to lunch. Don't touch me."

"Is the air fixed?"

"Not yet."

She crosses her arms and leans against the building. "Why can't you call someone? It's just air conditioning. I can't believe I'm basically kicked out of my own house. It's summer. I'm supposed to be able to relax and sleep in. This is the stupidest summer ever."

When her voice chokes up a bit, I look closer. Her eyes are shiny. "Are you okay?"

She bounces off the brick wall and throws her arms up. "I'm fine. Just fine. Go to your lunch." Slinging open the big wood and glass door, she goes inside, and I feel the blast of cool air. Peter waves from behind the counter and then turns to opens some boxes behind him. If I chase Savannah in there, she won't tell me anything and will most likely make another mean comment about my hair. Sugary, false compliments roll off a Southern girl's tongue like the icing fountain covering Krispy Kreme doughnuts. But with her mother? No such luck.

I'll go somewhere someone might lie to me and tell me I look good. "Hey Patty. Hey Shannon," I call as I open the next door.

"Hey Carolina. You're all dressed up today. Going some-where fancy?" Shannon is arranging a bouquet in the front window. It's a big spray of gladiolus, and she's making it even bigger. One look behind her tells me why. The bookstore side is worse than ever. Andy has turned it into a full-blown junk store. Guess Shannon's hoping to block folks from seeing it from the sidewalk. She and I meet eyes and roll them together.

Patty is behind the book/junk store counter, on which Andy has laid out his haul from Ruby's. Muffins and butter and nap-kins cover the space. What space is not already covered with, with stuff, that is. Open boxes of stuff, old displays draped with stuff, stuff in piles, and stuff stuffed on top of all that stuff.

"You do look like those women in that old video. Your hair is cool," Patty says. "Want a muffin?"

"Thanks, but no. I'm headed out to lunch with Susan."

"Thought maybe you were finally coming down here to start working." Gertie's voice carries from the back of the huge space where it's dark.

"Oh, hey, Gertie. Didn't see you back there."

"So, when are you coming down here to start working again?" The woman lumbering out of the darkness seems larg-er than ever. She has on purple jogging pants and a pink shirt. Her iron gray hair is cut short, and she huffs out a deep breath as she sits down on the couch. The only empty spot I may add. (See above sentence about stuff. Applies to the couch, too.)

I reach to run my hand through my hair, but there's nothing there, so I pat it and explain, "I'm not sure about having time to work here. Susan is busy with her new job, Laney has the baby coming, Missus is, well, busy with something or other, and I kind of need to run Crossings. B&Bs take a lot of work."

"Not the way you run yours. I'm staying there, so I see how little you actually do. It's more like an old-fashioned cat house where folks show up, take care of business, then leave money on the bedside table."

"Gertie! It is not. Why would you say that?"

"I can't not speak my mind just 'cause it ain't pretty. 'Sides, you promised to help out."

"Well, that was when it was a bookstore and not a . . ." Darn. Wouldn't it feel good to just speak your mind? Especially when it isn't pretty.

Gertie waves one arm at me. "Like a junk store? Yep, that's what my new son-in-law has done to this place. But they'll be gone on that honeymoon next week, and we're getting rid of all this stuff. Like I told you."

Andy walks toward his mother-in-law, mouth half-full of muffin. "Now wait a minute. This is all good stuff. I just need some time to get it arranged. Placed for customers to see it in its proper light."

Gertie struggles up off the low couch. "Son, that's what you been saying since I came to town over a month ago. I have some ideas, and you'll like them. You go on your honeymoon and get me a grandbaby started, and when you get back I'll have things all fixed up. A big ol' surprise for y'all. Carolina, let's you and me take a step outside," she says as she walks toward me.

"But it's hot out there," I whine. However, she tucks her hand around my upper arm and steers me out to the sidewalk.

Out there she looks me over. "Naw, your place ain't like a cat house. Think you just being all tarted up made me think of that."

Great, now the mountain thinks I look like a prostitute. "What do you want, Gertie?"

"I want to ask you real nice-like to run the bookstore for me after next week. I've got men hired to take all this junk to a new space, and Andy can run his very own junk shop. I been watching, and he can't help himself. And he's right, some of this stuff is good stuff. He just don't know how to put all in place, but I got him a new partner and it's going to all work out."

"Who's this new partner?"

Gertie frowns. "Now don't you no never mind about that. You'll find out when you need to know. I told you this much so you'd know you wouldn't have to sell the junk. You can play bookstore like you wanted to in the beginning. And no worries because I'm getting you a surprise helper, too."

She leans back, folds her arms across her big, soft chest, and grins. "I'm not real fond of surprises 'cept when I get to surprise other people. Then I enjoy them right good." She pulls open the heavy door. "You go on off to your big to-do and we'll talk later." Then, sticking her head back out, she adds, "And I'm deducting last few nights from my bill seeing as there ain't no air up at your place. You need to get that fixed."

The door closes and I'm left facing one of those dancers in the Robert Palmer music video in my reflection. Except her hair is beginning to pop up in little sticks, her full, high cheeks have slid down under her chin, she's gained thirty pounds (maybe more, but it is a reflection so hard to be exact), and her feet are in flat Target sandals that make her ankles look like melting ice cream cones.

Cool. Let's go to the country club.

Chapter 4

"Wish I was brave enough to wear my hair like that. Makes your eyes look huge," the woman next to me says. For the second time. She's wearing a flowing, soft, orange silk shirt over white slacks. She has on jeweled sandals and blonde hair in loose curls. But then, so does most everyone else here.

Lots of white slacks, jeweled sandals, and blond hair. My black dress sticks out, and my dark, slicked hair, well, it's different. But no one is acting like it's a bad different. They seem to like it. And not how Southern women say they like things. You know, it comes off fake or mean, but in all honestly it's neither, because it actually means nothing. It's just what we do when we meet someone. Compliment 'em. Or we do the sarcastic "Love that (hair-do, dress, necklace, etc.)," but we make our eyes real big and add to the side, "Bless her heart, she don't know better."

Even Susan said I look good and added that I was taking over Laney's role as fashionista, since she's pregnant and wearing caftans 24/7.

"So tell us about Crossings. Susan says you and your husband moved here to open a B&B. How exciting to run your own business!" the blonde across from me and next to Susan says. "I always wanted to run my own business, but with Ran-

dall's job being so hectic and the kids having such full sched-
ules, it just never seemed the right time."

Susan adds, "And Carolina's helping get the bookstore
downtown running."

When several pair of eyes light up, I jump in. "But we're
undergoing a shift. Don't come until after next week. It's kind
of a mess right now."

The woman on Susan's other side sighs. "Must be nice to
have two things to work on. Who knew retirement meant Jim
being as busy as he was with his job, and me sitting at home
like before. He's on the golf course practically every day, and
now he's taking on a part-time consulting job with his old
company. I thought we were going to travel."

My neighbor with the orange silk shirt agrees. "I know!
My husband always said he wanted to travel when he retired,
we just never talked about what we meant by 'travel.' He's
booked a kayak trip in South America. I don't swim and have
never camped. He didn't even ask me if I wanted to come. He
told me to go wherever I want, and we'll go somewhere later
in the year together. Then he mentioned backpacking in Cam-
bodia." She shudders a bit.

"Guess I'm used to that kind of thing," the heavyset lady on
the other side of me says. "My husband is a big hunter. Hunting season always meant him practically living at his family's
hunting lodge in South Georgia. We've lived most our life in
Chicago, and I thought moving here would mean he wouldn't
want to go to the lodge so much, or at least wouldn't need to
spend so much time there. Wrong! He's there more. And here I
am stuck in the mountains of Georgia in a much too big house.
I'm trying to learn to play golf. Anyone else taking that begin-
ners' class?"

Susan nods at me and lifts her empty iced tea glass. "Carolina, let's get some more tea, and I'll introduce you around."
After excusing ourselves, we walk toward the wall of win-

dows looking over the green lawns leading to the golf course. "See what I mean? I don't fit in up here."

"They all seem nice," I say. "Honestly, I mean that. They do seem nice. Kind of, well, lonely? At loose ends?"

Susan nods. "I know, I keep getting that feeling, too. Seems about half the folks up here are just here for the weekends. But a lot, like most of the ladies here on Wednesdays, they've moved here lock, stock, and barrel. Did you ever see that movie *Stepford Wives*?"

"I read the book. Don't think I watched the movie, though. Why?"

"Feels like that here. Not that the men are making robot wives to replace their real ones, but that the men are all just fine with living here, but the women not so much."

We turn from looking out the windows and watch the women. There are about twenty sitting at four round tables. Most of them are quite a bit older than me and Susan, but surprisingly many look to be not too far from us, late forties, maybe early fifties. "What about kids? Many folks have kids up here?"

Susan shrugs. "Some. Darien Academy attracts most of the ones with kids up here. It's pretty exclusive and hard to get into. Those families are really wrapped up in the school activities. I didn't realize how much until we moved here." She lowers her voice, "The school people feel like a cult. A very well-dressed cult." She laughs and shakes her head. "It's going to take some getting used to."

I'm trying to get used to thinking of Susan living here. She's right, it doesn't fit. The ladies seem nice, but it feels kind of hollow. We walk to the long table set up with the iced tea, water, and coffee.

One of the ladies from our table is there, and she turns and motions at me. "This is Carolina Jessup," she says to the lady beside her. "She runs that B&B, Crossings, somewhere downtown, right?"

"Yes, we're up on the bluff overlooking the river."

Susan takes my glass and fills it. "It's their home, too."

"I can't wait to see it." The new lady holds her hand out to me. "Hi, I'm Aggie Pierson. I organize these little lunches. So glad you could join us. Are you like Susan, born and bred in Chancey?"

"No, we've not even lived here a year. Moved from Marietta last summer."

"Oh, us too! Our son got into Darien and our daughter was going off to Duke for college, so we decided to just up and move. We *must* get together."

She had grasped my hand with both of hers, and as she leans toward me, my mouth opens and words spill out. "Why don't you all come for one of our wine and cheese afternoons at Crossings?"

Aggie leans back, but tightens her grasp. "All of us? Wonderful." Then she drops my hand and turns. "Ladies, ladies," she announces. "Carolina has invited us to her delightful B&B right down in Chancey for one of their fabulous wine and cheese afternoons." As the ladies clap, she whirls back to me. "When should we come?"

"Fridays are when we do the wine and cheese."

"Friday is perfect! We'll be there." She tucks her arms under mine and turns us both to the room. "Everyone, I'll get the details and send out an email. Thank you so much, Carolina. And I hope you know you are now an honorary member of our little lunch group here. Please join us any Wednesday."

Susan moves into my line of sight on the other side from Aggie, and as she lifts her newly filled glass to her lips, she smiles at me. She slowly shakes her head as her grin grows.

Wait, did I just invite all these ladies to the B&B?

"Jackson, I don't know who to trust. FM swears by Earl, and Laney swears by Terry. And they all talk like I know what they're saying. I keep saying to just put in a whole new system. That I don't really want to use parts from a junk yard. No one is listening to me."

I pulled over to the side of the road to answer when Jackson called me three times in a row. These roads are too curvy for me to talk on. Our signal that we need to talk right now is to call two times in a row. He didn't give me time to pull over before he called three times. I ducked into a little patch of gravel in front of a tiny, falling-down house with a huge tea rose bush beside it. The bush looks bigger than the little old house and is absolutely covered with tiny pink roses. Sitting here with the window rolled down, the smell is intoxicating. I'm hoping no one lives here or tries to pull in, since there's not room for more than one car to turn around.

"I can't help it that they are both saying different things are wrong. They are both so sure they know what they are doing. And just as sure that the other one doesn't."

Jackson continues to tell me what everyone has said, but I'm not really listening to him either. I just want air conditioning. The money is sitting in the bank for a new system. Finally I interrupt him. "Okay, I've met both men. Earl does drive you crazy with all his stories, but he's actually in the business. I'm not sure Terry is, I think he's a mechanic at the dealership. Can't get a straight answer about that from anyone. So I choose Earl, but you have to tell him. I'll deal with Terry and Laney and Shaw. Love you and talk to you later. Hopefully the house will be cool by time you get home Friday."

I don't tell him that I've invited the lunch ladies from Laurel Cove for wine and cheese. I need to think about that some more. But right now, I want to smell those roses up close. Laying my phone on the passenger seat, I climb out of the van and curve over to the rose bush on my way to knock on the door, although it doesn't look like anyone lives in the leaning house.

The air is thick with heat, the buzzing of bees, and the smell of roses. But the rose smell is fresh, not heavy like a perfume. There's a hedge between the rose bush and the door, and it adds its old, musty smell. Both are deep and green, the tiny leaves and the smell, as I brush my hand along the hedge branches. These two bushes together are like a book. There are stories here, and I close my eyes to hear them more clearly. When I open my eyes, there are two eyes looking at me through the rusty screen door. The woman is scrawny and old, reminds me of a wet chicken in how unprotected she appears. She has on an old house dress, like I've not seen in so many years. And an apron over that. They both kind of hang on her and her gray hair is pulled back, but it wisps around her wrinkled face.

"Ain't that about the prettiest rose bush you ever seen? My mama planted it there 'fore I was born."

"It is lovely. I just had to get out of my van and see it. And smell it." I offer my hand, but she's still behind the rusted screen so I end up just waving a bit. "Hi, I'm Carolina. Kind of new to Chancey. I've never even noticed your house here, but then I haven't been on this road more than a couple times."

"I'm LaVada. You want some roses to take home? Let me get my scissors."

Before I can say anything she's gone into the darkness, and I'm left with the bees, sunshine, and roses. Then she pushes the screen door open and bustles out. She moves pretty good, but as she steps onto the gravel and dirt which is uneven, she grasps onto my arm and leads me past the hedge to the back-side of the rose bush.

"They smell up a house real nice. I get a bunch ever other day and put them all around my house until they're gone. I clip from the backsides so the front don't have no holes. Used to take them around to the neighbors and such, but not many folks left now. So I'm right pleased to share them with you."

At the bush she hands me the scissors. "Take as much as you want. You'll see it won't make a dent, and besides, it's the backside."

With two loaded branches cut, I thank her and she laughs. "Why, sweetie, that's not enough to make it worth bringing the scissors out. Let me have them scissors."

I hand them to her, and she proceeds to load me up with an armful.

"Really, that's plenty, Miss LaVada. I don't know where I'll put them all. Let me help you back to the door."

"Well, I am getting tuckered out. This is usually my nap time after I've spent some time with the Lord and had my lunch. But today I just knew something fun was going to happen, and then I look up and there you are!" She laughs, and I can't help but laugh with her.

"I'm so glad you think I'm something fun."

"Oh, but meeting new folks is the most fun ever. Getting to find out where they've been and wonder about where they're going. You said your name is Carolina. Are you from Carolina?"

"No, ma'am. I'm from Tennessee. My folks just liked the name, I think. I've never heard your name, LaVada? It's pretty."

"I don't know where my parents got the name. Think Mama just thought it sounded pretty. We used to not put so much thought into what folks was called. Besides, once you name a baby, it just kind of settles and becomes everyday, haven't you thought that? People work so hard to pick the right name, and then just like that, it's just a name." She pulls on the screen door. "So might as well pick a pretty one."

"Might as well." I shift the flowers, so I can hold open the door for her. "It was so nice to meet you. And thank you for the roses."

From the other side of the screen she smiles, "Anytime. You just come get you some until they are gone. I'd love for you to meet my granddaughter. She lives here with me and is just about the sweetest thing God ever made. She's at school today, but come sometime of a morning. Then I won't be needing a nap, and we can visit." She steps away, back into the cool darkness of her home, and I wave before I turn for my car.

I lay my bower of pink roses on the passenger seat and maneuver the car back out onto the blacktop. I drive off the mountain with my window rolled down and the radio up loud on a classic rock station. I'm honestly surprised how much I enjoyed my day in Laurel Cove.

And when I get to the first stop sign and tilt the rearview mirror to look at myself I have to agree with the lady at the luncheon. My eyes do look huge.

Even better? They look happy.

CHAPTER 5

Good news? I fired Terry.

Bad news? Jackson fired Earl.

Yeah, our wires got crossed, and now no one is working on our air conditioner. We are guyless.

However, I'm on my way to fix that. I pull up in front of FM and Missus' house and park illegally, if that's really possible in Chancey. Walking up their sidewalk, activity at the old house next to theirs catches my attention. It's one of the two between their house and their son Peter's. The young family looks to be moving out. I could've told them restoring an old house is not for the weak of heart or wallet. It sounds romantic, but it's not. If you disagree, you've never done it. Try it. Just once.

The screen door slamming pulls my attention to the porch in front of me. Missus' voice comes from its depths. "Heard you were all dolled up yesterday. What for?"

"Oh, hey Missus. I had lunch with—wait—I'm sure you already know who I had lunch with and where. Is FM here?"

Missus steps out to the edge of the porch, to the center of the steps I was planning on walking up. Because of the way her arms are crossed, I stop where I am.

She uncrosses her arms to plant them on her hips. "Do you know what Anna is planning now?"

"No."

Missus sighs and her hands drop to her side. "Me either. But something's going on. I can feel it. Why do you want to know if FM is home?"

"Jackson accidentally fired Earl. I need to get him back."

"I'll tell him."

"And that'll fix it?"

Missus turns to go back inside her house, but she doesn't need to yell for me to hear her say, "Earl will do anything I ask."

"Really? Why?"

She turns around, one hand on the door handle. Her light blue sleeveless shirtdress, catches the light and shimmers. It's only a couple shades off her silver hair, which also catches the light as she bends her head. "Earl and I have a history. That's why he and FM are such good friends, FM likes to keep an eye on him. You know, keep your friends close, but your enemies closer?" She smiles a bit. "I'll put on some lipstick first, but I will take care of this for you."

While my mind argues with whether she's pulling my leg or just losing her mind, nothing comes out of my mouth. And then she's gone. I always thought as people got older they settled down, got boring. Wrong again. I turn back the way I came.

Things are busy on the square this afternoon. Next door there's all the activity of the family moving out. Lots of buzzing around the old MoonShots, which is now Peter's bistro. There's a group of kids doing something in the gazebo, and the front door of the museum is standing open with people milling around it. Probably some meeting of something or other. Small towns are all about meetings. The weekly newspaper has a whole column dedicated to who is meeting where and when and what they're going to discuss. What's crazy is it's the same people in that meeting that were in a meeting yesterday about some other topic. There's not enough civic-minded people to fill all the committees these people think they need. It's practically a full-time job just avoiding being put on a committee. Sometimes I forget which groups I actually belong to and fail to show up for a meeting. Then sometimes I *don't* forget, and still fail to show up for a meeting.

I'm gaining a reputation for being undependable.

Finally.

A horn honks. A big white box truck is trying to park in front of the house next door, but there's no room. I scoot down to my car and move out of the way. In my rearview mirror, I see the driver wave. As I slow for the stop sign at the end of the block, I take in the library passing on my right. The gray block building should be one of my favorite places in town since my hard-earned master's degree, which is only a couple years old, is in Library Science, but I kind of burned my bridges there. The head librarian hired me, made me start hating books, and then I quit. She's not someone that takes lightly to being called hateful, arrogant, and small-minded. And that is not just my opinion. It's fact.

Such a shame, as librarians are usually my favorite people.

I use the intersection to turn around in, and as I'm doing that I see the chalkboard in front of the museum says the meeting today is of the Chancey Preservation Society. I do not know what the Preservation Society does, and I will not ever know, because asking that question is as good a way to find your name on their rolls as there is. I wave at the couple of folks I know standing out front, and then go back down the street I was just on and turn to drive down Main Street. I'm not really cruising, but would like to see what's going on in Ruby's, the bookstore and flower shop, and Peter's bistro without having to talk to anyone.

Okay, I'm cruising.

Ruby's looks closed. Gertie and Patty are in the bookstore. Shannon is talking to a lady in the florist's. Peter has bunches of people in his place, and I decide it's safe to check it out.

41

Plus, I'm wearing khaki shorts and a blue T-shirt. No red lips or slicked back hair today. I pull into a parking place across the street and then take a walk over. As the sun begins to slide behind the mountains, a coolness tries to push at the afternoon heat. Soon, it'll be cool enough to go back home, but for now... I know when MoonShots opened Diego put in a whole new AC unit, so it'll be nice and cold.

Peter has done a lot to undo the modern coffee shop look. Diego Moon is one of his partners, so he has a vested interest in taking off Peter's hands the barely used equipment put in only a couple months ago. Plus, Diego seems a tad embarrassed that he put all the money and effort in to essentially exile his cheating wife from New York. Jordan couldn't get out of Chancey fast enough. According to Facebook and TMZ she's back to being a loving mother and wife and looking gorgeous doing it. She's saying she was at the resort at Barnsley Gardens, and I'm sure they're loving the advertising, but everyone knows the truth, thanks to our little spring tornado that got us Atlanta TV coverage. Can't say I really miss Jordan; she was pretty high maintenance for a friend.

The counter remains and the glass shelving at each end of the counter, too. Also left are the tables and chairs, which are stacked along one wall. I miss having MoonShots coffee, but it never felt right having a chain like that here. They are leaving one coffee machine, but stressing that it won't be MoonShots beans. However, unlike Ruby's, we will be able to get coffee to go, and that solves my biggest coffee issue in Chancey.

The new rustic wooden shelving units are placed around the room, and judging by the boxes stacked everywhere, some stock has come in.

"Carolina! So good to see you," Diego yells as he enters from the back room. He's the most beautiful man I've ever seen, and I'm disappointed he stays upstairs in Jordan's old apartment now instead of up at Crossings like he used to.

"Isn't it all coming together?" He's Colombian, and he uses a lot of energy when he's in a good mood. He opens his arms like a ringmaster introducing ladies riding elephants. "This bistro idea could become big for us. Maybe it's the next thing after coffee shops."

Peter comes up behind him and rolls his eyes at his partner's enthusiasm, then smiles. "Hey. What are you up to?"

"Wanted to see how things are going. And trying to stay cool."

"Oh yeah, Dad said your air is out. He didn't talk you into using Earl, did he?"

I hold my hands up. "No, do not tell me anything bad about Earl, or that you have a guy. Earl is now my guy."

"Okay, but let me know if you change your mind."

My eyes close and my heart drops. Shoot. I *thought* Earl was my guy. Never mind. I look up, smile, and ask, "Is Savannah around?"

Peter and Diego grin at each other and then me. "She's around," Peter says through his grin.

"Around where? What's going on?"

Diego shrugs. "My nephew is here. Alex. He's my sister's son. The sister that lives in New York. Ah, there they are." He points out the front window with his chin, and I turn in time to see a tall young man open the door for Savannah to walk inside. She has one of Ruby's baskets in her arms.

"Hi, Mom. This is Alex." She lifts her head, but it's at an angle and to the side. And not because Alex is standing to her side, offering me his hand to shake. It's because that's what girls do when they are being coy. I just never have put Savannah and coy in the same sentence. Her head is cocked, her eyes slant upward through her eye lashes, and she's not exactly batting them, like Scarlet in *Gone with the Wind*, but she's not far from it. Her smile is soft, lips barely open, and as he steps toward me, she sighs.

43

I do not roll my eyes as I hold my hand out. "Nice to meet you, Alex. I'm Carolina."

Shaking my hand, he says, "You're Savannah's mother? Ruby up at the café was asking if I'd met you yet."

I just bet she was. "Yes, Ruby likes to know everything going on. So you're from New York?"

"Yep."

Diego interjects. "Yes, ma'am. Use some manners."

Alex nods at his uncle and says the requested words, but his heart isn't in them. And the little look he shares to the side with Savannah tells the rest of us in the room exactly how old we are.

Savannah steps to the counter and sets the basket down. "Here's what Ruby has made so far. She says these should be easy to wrap up and sell."

We all gather closer as Peter lifts out cookies and shares them with us after breaking them in half. "I only had her make chocolate chip and snickerdoodles today. She also says she'll make a toffee shortbread."

When I turn to hand Savannah part of my snickerdoodle, she's looking up through her lashes again. Alex is tall and thin but not skinny, with dark hair, longer than the boys in Chancey wear theirs. He's looking down at her, and I realize the heat in the room is despite the completely functioning air conditioning. I've seen this look directed at my daughter many times. However, I have never seen it returned or even acknowledged. Well, looks like Ricky showing up with Charisse on Sunday is no longer an issue. Thank goodness Alex doesn't live here, or the biggest issue might be standing right in front of me.

Peter pulls the checked towel over the rest of the cookies. "Alex is going to give me a hand with opening the bistro. He's going to live upstairs."

What now?

Diego clears his throat and moves behind the counter, but I

get my question out before he can dart through the back door. "With you, Diego?"

With a big grin (which doesn't look very genuine to me), he turns and spreads his arms. "He's here for some education about business, before he starts college in the fall. He's going to live upstairs this summer. I have to go home."

Peter's eyebrows are high, matching Diego's, and they both shift their focus to the young man in question. The young man meets their looks with a shrug, saying, "Why not. Gotta be somewhere."

Savannah, however, giggles. *Giggles.* And yep, bats her eyes ever so quickly for half a second.

This summer just got very long.

Chapter 6

Earl's truck is in the driveway when I get home. It's old with a faded red paint job and a foot-high flame painted down the side, which is also faded. Pretty easy to know when Earl is around. Opening the front door, I pause, hoping to feel a chilled breeze, to hear that quiet hush of running fan, and to experience the stillness of a sealed room. Having the windows open is nice for a while, but it's so noisy and you have to close them if it rains and it just makes the house feel so, so alive. Okay, that sounds like a nice thing, but really? Is it?

Our house feels alive. Shoot.

"Earl?" I yell. He answers from the kitchen.

"In here."

Earl is a big man. His clothes are baggy, along with his skin. He has gray hair sticking out underneath his truckers cap, and it flows down his face in a thick beard. He seems clean, just disheveled, and well, baggy. He's leaning on my kitchen counter eating a sandwich. Before I can say "hi" or he can tell me my AC is working (fingers still crossed), he says, "This is the last of the ham."

Oh. "Oh," and that's all I can say or think. "Oh." Wait, there's more. "Is the air fixed?"

He chews and nods, as he leans over and reaches for his

glass of iced tea. "Almost. Needed to get some supper, since I've got more to do." He leans back against the counter.

"I guess I need to go the store and get some more ham. So, you're good here?"

He chews and nods.

"You think you'll be done tonight?"

Now he chews and shakes his head. "Hard to say," he says, and then takes another bite and goes back to just chewing.

My car keys are still in my hand, and I hold them up. "Well, I'll be back." And I walk back through the living room. I came home to make Bryan a sandwich, which I was going to take to the Lake Park. I was also going to make myself a sandwich, grab the book I'm reading, and go have supper at the park, too. But now I need to buy lunchmeat. If only we still lived in the suburbs where I had my pick of meals to go. Every fast food choice, along with a deli in every grocery store where I could have sandwiches made to order.

It may be healthier doing your own cooking, but the extra work could kill you. I never had to think about food so much when we lived back in Marietta. A glance at the clock in the car tells me I'm just about to miss the deli closing. So I bounce over the track crossing and hurry down the hill. At the Piggly Wiggly, I scatter gravel pulling into the parking lot too fast. Another thing, gravel parking lots are so unforgiving on car paint jobs and nice shoes. Who knew to be thankful for paved parking lots?

The store has that air-conditioned feel: sealed, quiet, un-alive. It's great. Pulling out my buggy, I can see the deli area is dark. Shoot. Packaged lunch meat it is. Now that I've missed the reason for hurrying, I can take my time. Everything in town is dead by this time of the day in Chancey. Oh, it's only six-thirty, in case you thought I might be whining without rea-son. Back in the suburbs, folks are just now making their way home from jobs in Atlanta. Here? Things are already quieting down. Meetings at churches or the civic meetings all start at five, six at the latest. School evening activities start at six. Even when Jackson isn't on the road, getting to things by six is hard for him.

At the register, I put the few things I've collected onto the conveyor belt and move up to the card reader. "Hey, Danielle."

"Hey, Mrs. Jessup."

I put my head down and dig in my purse, because Danielle can't scan groceries and talk at the same time. Laney says when Danielle checks her out she pretends she's having a conversation on her phone to keep the cashier scanning instead of talking.

"I hear Terry is fixing your air conditioner," Danielle says, holding my head of lettuce in her right hand. "He's good. He's cute, too, isn't he?" She's in her late twenties, but she acts younger. Her dad is head usher at the church. She and her two sisters sit on the front pew, just like they did when they were little girls, Susan says. After their mom died when they were in elementary school, their dad told them to sit there and behave while he was doing his ushering duties, and I guess he never told them any different. All three are in their twenties now.

"No, Earl's working on it." *Although "working" may not be the best word to use.*

She scans the lettuce. Picks up the package of ham and says, "Really? But Terry had to cancel a date with Sissy to work up there tonight. Sissy was real upset. She's been trying to get Terry to take her out forever." Her hand holding the ham drops to the belt, before passing over the scanner panel. "Oh no. He couldn't have lied to her. Could he?"

All I can do is stare at the package of ham and choke out, "I don't know."

After a pause to consider the possibilities, she scans the ham and picks up a bag of chips. "Maybe I should call her."

And she lays down the chips and reaches into the pocket of her pink smock, pulling out her phone.

"Please, Danielle. Can you do that after I check out? I really need to get Bryan some supper."

She shifts her gaze from me to the counter in front of her and laughs. "Of course. Silly me." She quickly whips through the rest of my things while I stuff them in the plastic bags at the end, then load them in my buggy. I pay and am headed to the parking lot when she hollers at me.

"Mrs. Jessup?"

I turn around.

"I'll let you know about Terry. You know, whether he's working up at your house or not, if you'll give me your phone number."

"Thanks, but I'm headed there right now." I wave and push through the automatic doors to the outside warmth.

You know, if I was here on vacation that would all seem real cute.

Okay, I hated the idea of my son, my young, innocent son, dating that girl Brittani with an "I." Find that I'm hating this even more.

Bryan is sitting across from me at the picnic table. He's wet from the lake and has a towel draped across his shoulders. His friends Grant and John sit on either side of him in the same posture, all with heads down, water dripping from their hair, not saying a word, just eating. John and Grant had brought sandwiches since they all have a lifeguard training session tonight when the park closes. Bryan and Grant are tanned already, John is fairer, so he's the lightest of the three. Usually these three are laughing and goofing around, but not now. They chew and listen. Listen to the laughs from a blanket down beside the water. There's a familiar redhead on the blanket with a high school boy I don't know. The laughter from the blanket is hard to take, but even worse is the silence, because that's when they are making out.

Yep, my son has been dumped by the skank.

And I thought I wanted to tear her eyeballs out when they were dating.

When I got here, the boys were out on one of the floating docks. They saw me and dove in, since John and Grant were waiting to eat until Bryan's food showed up. I fully expected them to head off to their own table, so my first clue things weren't normal was when they sat down with me. That was odd. Then them not saying anything, just opening their food and eating. Finally, I looked for the source of the laughing and saw that girl. When my eyes widened and my mouth opened to speak, Bryan shook his head, adding, "Mom. It's nothing."

Grant caught my eye as he slowly nodded. John mumbled something I couldn't hear.

I know my food seems awfully dry, so I can't imagine how Bryan is getting anything down. But they all do. Of course, feeding teenage boys is pretty much like trying to fill up a running garbage disposal with Jell-O. I try to not make it noticeable as I watch Brittani and her new friend get up and go into the water. She has on a tiny, royal blue bathing suit, and he's got his hand around her waist. Wish I'd put wine in my water bottle.

When did this happen? Bryan and she were together this past weekend. I may not be actually on the inside with what is going on, but they sat together in church and were in our basement playing video games Sunday night. (I get a lot of laundry done when they're down there. I'm not spying, I just seem to coincidentally always have a lot of laundry to do when my kids are alone with members of the opposite sex in the basement.)

Bryan stands up and collects his trash. I give him mine, and he moves off to the garbage can. Grant's eyes are glued on me, and as soon as Bryan is out of earshot, I meet Grant's look. "What happened?"

Grant lifts his hands up and makes an explosion with them. "She just showed up here with Adam Schecter. She didn't break up with Bry or nothing."

"No way!"

John nods. "It's crazy."

Bryan walks up, and John covers a little loudly, "Class isn't for a half-hour. My phone is dying, or we could play games."

"Go sit in the van and plug it in." I pull my car keys from my pocket and hand them to Bryan.

He looks up as he takes them. "But we're wet."

"Not that much. Just sit on your towels." They walk off, and I finish my chips and water. Brittani and the boy, Adam, I think they said, are out in the water. Seems like all the teens in the water are avoiding them. If she did dump Bryan as unceremoniously as Grant says, maybe she's being shunned.

Shunned? Maybe I've read one too many Amish romances.

Speaking of which, where is my book? I pull it out, then stand to set up my foldout chair, which is much more comfortable than the picnic table bench. It's hard to decide which way to face. Half of me wants to be able to keep my eyes on the two in the water, other half wants to turn away and forget that girl ever existed.

Facing the water, I can glance over the top of my book and see them in the water, and also see their blanket.

Really? You thought I might look the other way?

This is the South, y'all.

"You are not going to believe this. So then she and her new guy, Adam something, are leaving and she sees me, darts over and hugs me! Hugs me right there in front of everyone. Thank goodness Bryan was busy with his class over on the other side of the swimming area."

Laney is being appropriately shocked at everything I'm telling her. When the folks in the baby store they're shopping in asked her to please quiet down, she went outside to talk to me. Sometimes it's good to have a friend who will be outraged loudly and often.

"Listen, hon, I've got to go back inside. Store's closing soon, and I need to pay. I can't wait to show you everything. Shaw is being so sweet. Like I said before, it's so much more fun having a baby when you have money. Let's meet at Ruby's in the morning, 'kay? I'll call Susan, too. Better go, bye!"

We hang up, and I look down at my book. I think I've read all of two pages since I've been here. First I was busy watching Brittani, then the guys came back, and I got to watching their class, then Brittani left and hugged me and that took a while to process, and of course, share. Jackson was eating and couldn't seem to work up the outrage deserved, Savannah is headed this way on a tour of Chancey with Alex, so she didn't want to talk. Susan didn't answer. Missus, I was afraid, would dash up here with a gun. So, even though I knew Laney was out shopping, I called her.

Before I even find my place on the page, Savannah comes up behind me.

"Hey, Mom." She has on different clothes than earlier. A light pink sundress with green rick rack along the top and bottom. She told me it was too "cutesy" when her grandmother sent it from a shop in South Carolina. Too "southern belle-like," she also said. "You remember Alex?"

"Hi," he says as he walks out a little in front of us toward the lake. "So, you swim in the lake?"

Savannah and I look at each other. "Yeah, I guess," she says.

I ask, "Do you have a lot of lakes in New York?"

He turns around, pushes his sunglasses up into his thick hair, and shrugs. "Maybe in the state, but I'm from the city. We have pools. And the Cape, of course. Lakes are good for skiing and sailing."

Savannah flips her hair back. "I don't really like swimming in the lake. Kind of dirty."

I just roll my eyes, but of course she's not looking at me.

Alex turns around, looking up toward the sky. Savannah and I both look up to see what he sees. The sky is a deep blue as the sun moves farther down it, but that's all I can find to look at.

He puts his hands on his hips and turns around again. "These tall trees. Where are their branches? They aren't dead. They are green at the tops."

Even though Savannah and I both now know what to look at, we still don't know what to look at. "You mean the pine trees?" I ask.

He motions around us. "These are pines? But they don't have branches. We have pines, like Christmas trees. They aren't skinny like this."

There's that saying, you can't see the forest for the trees? Well, suddenly I'm aware of the dozens, no hundreds, of tall, skinny pine trees around us. We are literally surrounded by cinnamon-colored trunks that soar into the sky, but only have greenery at the top—lush, long pine needles. However, like Alex pointed out, no lower branches.

He points up high. "You can see where the branches were. But they've fallen off. Was there a storm?"

Savannah puts her sunglasses back down on her face and shrugs. "That's just how they are. Big, tall trees. Pine trees. They're everywhere."

Alex is still staring up and slowly turning around. "Fascinating. I know where I've seen them now. On the golf courses on TV. At the Masters." He looks at me. "That's in Georgia, right?"

"Yes. In Augusta."

He grins. "I thought they had cut off the limbs to make room for the golf course. Thought that was ingenious, but I had no idea this is how they are. Look how they sway with the wind."

Okay. They're pine trees. "Most folks here hate them because with big storms they do fall over. And, well, they grow everywhere."

"Not where I live. And not just where I am in the city. I've never seen them except on TV."

When I look to make eye contact with my daughter and grin at his enthusiasm over plain old pine trees, she's busy. Her eyes, hidden a bit behind her sunglasses, are glued on Alex, and she looks a little drugged. As she callously dragged around boys' hearts through the years, I'd wondered when she would find hers in jeopardy. She's dated guys, and even really liked some, but she's never had that look. That look of obsession. Guess I should be glad we got to put it off this long, but Alex looks like what they call a player. I don't see his heart getting dragged anywhere.

Alex walks down to the lake. I thrust out a hand to grab the tail of Savannah's dress, but it slips through my grasp. And there she is, following him. He didn't even have to look around. He knew she'd follow.

Yep, this summer is getting longer by the minute.

Chapter 7

"*She* invited everyone. I didn't do it!" Susan makes clear, pointing at me as I walk in the door at Ruby's.

Laney is draped in a long, voluminous, white top with white capris and a heavy gold necklace, long lacey gold earrings. Her dark hair is held back by a wide gold band. She looks like a goddess descended from Mount Olympus. She's perched, almost lounging, on one of the stools at the rear counter. Oh, and her sandals are gold, too.

Susan is seated in a booth and talking over her shoulder to her sister. I slide into the booth, facing both women, and ask, "Who did I invite, and where did I invite them? And why are you sitting over there?"

Laney stretches out one leg. "My sciatic nerve is giving me fits. I'm just stretching it out before I sit down. You invited all of Laurel Cove to wine and cheese at Crossings? Shouldn't you run that by me first? I am the manager, you know."

Susan looks at me and tightly smiles, then mouths, "Sorry."

"Okay. So now you know. And it's not all of Laurel Cove. Just the ladies at lunch. Say, twenty?"

Susan nods, and I look up as Libby carries a coffee cup over, sits it down, and pours. "You needing a warm up, Susan?" Libby splashes a bit into Susan's orange fiesta ware. "I thought that clubhouse up there was going to open up some nights to non-members. It'd sure be nice to have a fancier place to go out to sometimes. Must be nice to be members up there."

Susan stays tanned year round, so it's hard to see when she blushes, but she's blushing now. This move up for her and Griffin has definitely caused some hard feelings around town. It's always been a "them" and "us," but now that one of the "us" has become a "them," no one is sure how to deal with it. Folks who've never appeared to have a mean bone in their body seem to have found one. And it's a bone they want to gnaw on.

Laney comes down off her polished chrome throne. "Excuse me, Libby," she says as she stands at the end of the booth. "Think I'll sit here by my sister," she says. She stares at Libby until she turns to fill other cups around the restaurant. Laney's face is also red, out of anger, not embarrassment. Laney grimaces, getting turned around in the seat, and her stomach lightly rubs the table. "*I'll* give you and my newly hoity-toity brother-in-law hell for moving up to Snobville, but nobody else is. Who does Libby Stone think she is?"

"Don't. It's fine." Susan sips her coffee. "But it would be nice to get some muffins." There's an edge to Susan's voice I don't recognize.

Laney does a double take, too. She says, "Right," but it's weak. Almost like a question.

Did Susan just give her sister an order? That's what it sounded like to me. And obviously to Laney, too. Laney lifts her hand and waves at Libby. "Can we get some muffins?"

Libby shrugs and says, "Sure."

Our table is quiet, and we are all looking at the marbled top of our antique kitchen table, not a reproduction, but one that's been here in Ruby's since Susan and Laney were little girls in Chancey. Libby sits down a blue plate with an assortment of muffins, all studded with blueberries.

"That one is cream cheese with blueberries. That yellow

one, lemon with blueberries and glazed icing, and the dark one is whole wheat with carrots, blueberries, and pecans." Libby barely gets the word "pecan" out before she's gone.

Keeping my voice low, as I reach out with my knife and cut the muffins into, I say, "Is it really that big of a deal you moving up to Laurel Cove?"

Susan's voice matches mine in volume. "I told Griffin it would be. He said I was exaggerating."

"Men don't understand these things," Laney says as she struggles to lean over to reach for a muffin. "Forget it," she says flopping back. "Just put half of one of them on my plate. I've felt so good, I forgot about this part at the end. I won't get as big as I did carrying the twins, hopefully, but I am seventeen years older. Sleeping is awful." She takes a bite of the blueberry-lemon muffin. "Okay, so how many will there be Friday?"

"This whole wheat one is much better than it sounds," I say. "Big chunks of pecans. What do you think, Susan? Twenty or so?"

Susan nods. "I'll see if I can't get a kind of firm count from Aggie. She's coming over to the house later."

Laney looks at her sister, but just as she opens her mouth, the front door opens. She turns to see who is coming in. "Oh, its Missus."

Missus nods in our direction but goes straight toward the back counter. She talks to Ruby, then comes to our table, but she doesn't sit down. "All yours have blueberries, too."

"Here, sit down. Don't you like blueberries?" I say as I scoot closer to the wall.

"Oh, I don't have time to sit. And I do love blueberries, but, well, Anna doesn't. And you know how Ruby is. If she's on a kick, we're all on that kick. She doesn't have a single muffin left without blueberries."

Laney laughs. "Well, tell Anna she'll have to eat blueberries, or have a piece of toast."

"But she wants a muffin. A muffin from Ruby's." Missus is worrying her hands, almost wringing them, and about the same time, the three of us watching her realize she's really worried.

"Missus, are you okay?" I ask.

She looks at me, and her eyes well up. "I'm just so tired, let me go talk to Ruby." She walks back to the counter again, and I watch her.

"Wonder why she's so upset?" I ask as my eyes drift back to my table companions. There I'm met by stern looks. "What?" Laney growls. "What? You saw Missus. Your daughter-in-law is running her ragged. You need to tie a knot in that girl's tail. She's not the first girl to be pregnant, and she has a lot to be grateful for. And if you can't do it, then Will should. He can't let his wife act like that."

Susan agrees. "That's right. Everyone is talking about how demanding Anna has become. Even Peter is avoiding her."

"Peter is not avoiding his niece. He wouldn't do that." I pop the last bite of the whole wheat muffin into my mouth. "She young, she's in a new place, newly married, and pregnant. She's scared. Missus is just for the first time having to deal with another female being around. She's been top dog for a long time. Probably do her good."

Laney rolls her eyes. "So you're not going to talk to Anna?"

"Not on your life. I'm not thrilled about being a mother-in-law so soon anyway, no way am I going to be an evil one. Missus doesn't need me to fight her battles."

Laney lifts her chin and her big gold necklace catches the light from outside. "One more question. Why aren't you panicking about having such a big group of people at Crossings Friday afternoon?"

I wipe my hands on my napkin and shake my head as I scoot out of the booth. When I have laid a five dollar bill on the table and hung my purse on my shoulder, I look at her, then Susan.

"Maybe I'm excited about them coming over. Maybe I'm changing. See y'all later. I've got to go talk to Patty."

Remembering to smile, all the way to the front door, I leave Ruby's, but I just walk a few feet and wait. I know that wasn't a very good answer about why I invited all those Laurel Cove ladies to Crossings, but it's the only one I've got. And, believe me, I've been asking myself the same question ever since the invitation left my mouth.

Missus comes out the door, head down. "Hey Missus," I say softly.

She slides her face up, so she can look down her nose. However, it only stays there for a moment. "Oh, it's you. Good, I need to speak to you. Walk with me over to the gazebo, out of view of the gawkers in Ruby's." She has on a lavender skirt and blouse, very crisp and fresh looking, but I notice her hair looks smashed in back, like she hasn't teased it up to its normal height. And her lipstick, well, she isn't wearing any. She's wearing heels, but they have scuff marks on them and, whoa, I knew something was wrong. She doesn't have gloves on. She's not even carrying them folded in her belt. She's rubbing her hands as we walk, and I wonder if she even realizes her hands are bare.

Petunias fill the ground around the gazebo and the hanging planters in the gazebo. Purple, pink, and white, along with some striped ones in dark purple and white. Their scent is light, so as we walk up the painted steps, I walk first to push my nose into one of the baskets to sniff. Missus ignores the flowers and takes her seat on one of the wooden benches at the edge. When I turn, she's holding her hands up.

"Oh, I seem to have forgotten my gloves. How odd."

"I noticed that. Are you okay?"

She cuts right to the chase. "Anna is impossible. Complely impossible. I wouldn't say that to just anyone, but this affects your life as much as mine. Has Will said anything?"

"No, I think they get along fine. Maybe it's just you and her."

"No. She's become a prima donna. She's running FM ragged, and I won't have it. They should move back with you."

I shake my head. "But you built the rooms just for them." Still shaking my head, I add, "Maybe you just need to be more firm."

She tips her head toward me and raises an eyebrow. "Really? I need to be more firm?"

"Okay, maybe not. But I'm sure it will be better once the baby comes."

"Probably. But mostly because FM and I will be dead, and she'll have run of the house."

"Missus. It's not going to kill you. Just try and be more, well, don't let her run over you and FM. She's really a sweet girl. We know that."

"Have you talked to Will lately? He might have a different opinion."

"I do not want it to seem like I'm trying to come between them. I won't. I can't."

"Fine." She stands up and tugs where her gloves would normally end. She flutters her hands, looks down, and then sighs. "Peter was such an easy child. He still is. Anna has to argue with every word that comes out of my mouth." She turns and marches down the steps. "Forget I even said anything, Carolina. I'll take care of things." Without a wave or a look back, she continues down the sidewalk toward her house.

Aw, bless her heart, Missus has a teenage girl living in her house.

I bet it makes her family housing General Sherman during his March to the Sea look like a cakewalk.

CHAPTER 8

"Are they rebuilding the funeral home?" Jackson asks as he comes through the front door late Thursday evening. Then he stops, pauses, and curses. "Air still isn't fixed?"

I'm stretched out on the couch with a fan blowing on me. "Nope. Aren't you regretting coming home a day early now?" Lack of a permit put a halt on the project he was working on south of Atlanta, so he called it quits for the weekend and headed home at the end of the workday. Tomorrow he's working from home, then will head back down to the jobsite, permits (hopefully) in place, Monday morning.

He drops his suitcase and briefcase and leans over the back of the couch to kiss me. "You look awfully comfortable." He pulls at the neckline of my sleeveless gown and takes a peek.

"Stop, we have guests, well, a guest," I say with a laugh as I grab at his hand. He folds his arms on the couch back and lays his forehead on them for a moment. "What's the excuse with the air now?"

"Excuse? Earl needs an excuse? I don't think so, he just says, 'It's not done. Should be soon.'" I ruffle Jackson's hair, and he looks up to smile at me. I sigh and smile back. "Maybe he'll give you better answers. I've tried, some, to act like I know what he's talking about, but I really believe he and FM just think I'm cute for trying."

He stands up and grins. "Well, you are awfully cute. That short hair makes your neck look sexy. Why don't you come help me unpack?" He waggles his eyebrows at me as he picks up his suitcase.

I get up from the couch. "Want some water? I'll bring it up. What did you say about the funeral home?"

"There's a new building there. Not as big, though. No signs saying what it is. Are the kids home?"

He's already at the top of the stairs, so I wait until I'm almost at the top to answer him. "No. Savannah is staying at Jenna's and Angie's until the air is fixed, and Bryan and the guys are all at John's house. Our only guest is Gertie, but we have folks coming in tomorrow. I'm wondering if I should call them and tell them we don't have air. All week I've been counting our blessings that the air didn't go out on the weekend. I had no idea it could *possibly* still be out *this* weekend. It's ridiculous."

Closing the bedroom door behind me, I watch my husband sit on the bed to take off his shoes. He looks tired. Traveling wears him out, but I don't think it's as tiring for him as sitting behind a desk in an office all day. I climb on the bed and move behind him to massage his shoulders. I'm still mystified where my resentment of him went. Only a few weeks back I couldn't work up any compassion for him at all. For anything. Now, I not only can't work up any resentment, I can't imagine why I would want to. Marriage is weird.

"Mmm, that feels good. Don't get me too relaxed." He lays back, and I snuggle up to him. We lay there for a minute, and then he raises up on the arm I'm not pinning. "If I'm going to be this hot, let's do something to make it worthwhile. Then we can take a shower to cool down."

I busy myself unbuttoning his shirt while he kisses my sexy neck. Giggling, I compliment him, saying, "You always know how to make lemonade out of lemons."

He growls and laughs. "I do love lemonade!"

"What in the world is going on down here?" I yell as I stomp down the stairs. Early morning light fills the house, but it's *very* early morning light. Jackson is right behind me. I tried to not wake him up, but the loudest shouts from downstairs happened right as I opened the bedroom door so he sprung up from the bed and followed me out the door.

"Laney? What's going on?"

She meets me at the bottom of the stairs.

"I'm just lighting a fire under Earl. Threatening him with bodily harm if this place isn't cool by 3 pm today. I sent Terry up here again yesterday, and Earl ran him off. I don't know who Earl Shurbett thinks he is. I'm the manager of this establishment. Who I hire, stays hired!"

"But do you have to do it so loudly? And so early?" Jackson pleads from above me on the stairs.

"Oh, hey, Jackson. Didn't know you were home. Sorry. We woke y'all?"

Earl comes out of the kitchen to join the discussion, Pop-Tart in hand. "I didn't wake nobody. You're the one doing the yelling. Hey Carolina, you're out of cinnamon Pop-Tarts. I don't eat them chocolate ones. Too much like a dessert."

Jackson is still standing on the stairs behind me. His mouth is hanging open as he stares at our air conditioning expert.

"And you must be Mr. Jessup. Good to meet you. Shoot, if I'da known you was driving up last night from south of the city, I'da had you pick up the part we need in McDonough. D'ya come through McDonough? FM says you been working down near Bainbridge. Shoot, you're probably working on that train line down there, Georgia Southern or something, aren't you? My brother-in-law worked on that line for years. He's kind of a train nut, too. I should tell him to come stay here sometime. So, guess we could have you pick up the part in McDonough when you go back next week. Save ya a delivery charge." He finishes his soliloquy about the same time he finishes his Pop-Tart, so he turns back into the kitchen.

Jackson still hasn't closed his mouth and now his eyes are squinched up. "What is he talking about?"

"See?" Laney says with a wave of her hands and nod of her head.

I mimic her in every way. I nod my head, wave my hands, and say, "See?"

Jackson takes a deep breath. "Yeah, I see. Thanks, Laney." He pats me on my back as he moves past me down the stairs. "Me and Earl are going to have a talk."

In the kitchen he opens the back door and holds it open as he says, "Mr. Shurbett, Earl, can we have a word outside?"

As soon as they leave the kitchen, Laney and I dash in to look out the window. I mean, make coffee.

When Jackson comes back in, the coffee is done. I pour him a cup, so he can join me and Laney.

"Thanks," he says, then he takes a sip as he sits down at the kitchen table with us. "We'll have a new unit tomorrow."

"Praise the Lord!" Laney exclaims. "Some men like Earl are going to have to be dragged into the modern age. His wife rules the roost at their house, maybe that's why he won't listen to a woman on the job."

Jackson grins and shakes his head. "I thought you were exaggerating, but he's a handful. Didn't want to listen to me, either. But, finally, I called our old AC company from down in Atlanta. When he saw I was seriously going to have them do the job, he suddenly had a quote for a whole new system. Kept saying he was trying to 'save us a buck' and I appreciate that, but enough is enough." He grimaces at me. "So, no air today and one more night."

Laney stands up and takes her cup to the sink. "We'll just give our guests tonight a break on the cost, and the wine and cheese will be outside. By that time the back deck should be in the shade, right? It might be a tad crowded."

"Oh, yeah, those ladies I went to lunch with up in Laurel Cove?" I say with a look at Jackson. He nods, and I continue. "Well, I invited them for this afternoon."

"That's a great idea. Sounds like folks who could really advertise for us." He also stands and then leans to kiss me on top of my head. "I'm going to try and get some work done this morning, and then I can help get ready."

He leaves the kitchen, whistling. We can hear him whistling all the way up the stairs. Laney pulls her hair back and bundles it into a clip she pulls from her pocket. She smirks at me. "See how much easier life is with a bit of sex every now and then? I'll be in the office making a grocery list for this afternoon. Holler if you need anything else handled."

I'm not sure what she thinks she handled. But if sex makes life easier, so does letting Laney think she's right. And I'm all about easy.

CHAPTER 9

"Okay, I'm not complaining. Really. Just asking. Weren't these wine and cheese things supposed to be just for our guests?" Jackson asks as we survey our deck and yard. "I understand about the ladies from Laurel Cove, but the rest of them?"

"They all have some kind of connection with the B&B, if you think about it," I say, pointing through the crowd. "Gertie is our guest, and I'm sure she invited Patty and Andy. Then Missus is kind of a partner here, so she brought FM and Peter. Peter probably mentioned it to Diego, and so Alex came with him and, oh yeah, you haven't met Alex yet, have you? Oh, boy. You are not going to like who followed *him* here."

I give him a minute to realize it's his daughter at Alex's elbow. She's not instantly recognizable because she looks so pleasant. So smiley and cute in another sundress from her grandmother, which she derided as too "froufrou and silly" as she pulled it from the box sent by Etta. It's sky blue eyelet, off the shoulder, with a wide ruffle around the top. Her shoulders, neck, and a lot of her chest are bare. It's not clingy at all but fluffs out to where it ends, at the beginning of a mile of leg. It's actually not that short, but her legs are so long, it looks too short. And if I think it looks short, you can just imagine what her daddy is thinking.

"Where are her pants?" Jackson asks. "Who did you say this guy is? Where did she even get a dress like that? It's not her."

"His name is Alex, and he's Diego's nephew. He's staying here this summer. And *your* mother sent her the dress."

"He's staying here?" he practically yells.

"No," I hiss. "Not here, here. But in town. Jordan's apartment."

"But she hates the dresses Mom sends."

"Until she decided being a Southern Belle was a good idea."

"Savannah a Southern Belle?" He shakes his head as he watches the two of them. Then a small "Oh" comes out. After a pause, he nods. "Oh, she likes him."

"Yeah. She likes him." I walk away. There's really nothing else to say.

There are a lot of people here, from Laurel Cove, from town, and our guests for the weekend are fitting right in. It's two men from Nebraska who were in Atlanta for work and used the opportunity to spend the weekend chasing trains up here in the mountains. They are both married, but one is a true flirt who finds all the women here better than a train on the bridge. He has a group around him laughing and talking. The other gentleman is chatting with Peter and Diego. Gertie is lecturing on Chancey history to another circle of people, and Missus is correcting her at the end of every sentence. Why can't Missus just let her alone?

"This is a great idea, Carolina," Aggie Pierson says coming up the steps onto the deck. "You should charge money." She turns around and waves her empty hand toward the river. "And what a great view. Thanks again for inviting us."

"You're welcome. You were so nice to include me in on your Wednesday lunches. So how did you come to be in charge of that group? Have you lived in Laurel Cove long?"

Aggie looks to be in her mid-fifties, and her blonde hair is shoulder-length and straight. Like with a straightener straight. She has on black capris and a teal sleeveless shirt. She has a big smile and, my favorite part, lots of laugh lines. Her face naturally rests happy. She is athletic-looking, not like she plays tennis or runs or anything specific, just muscular and strong.

"Yeah, we have. Moved there fifteen years ago so our kids could go to Darien Academy. My husband worked from home, so it was a no-brainer for us. Plus, we love hiking and the lake activities. It's home now."

"It sure is beautiful up there. I hope Susan and Griffin are as happy there as you are." Of course Susan is here, and it's interesting to watch her handle this meeting of her two worlds. Aggie follows my eyes to also watch Susan for a moment.

"I hope they like it, too. However, we moved here from Colorado, so we didn't have to figure out how to live both up on the mountain and down in town. Plus, with two kids in Darien, we were so immersed in the school activities."

"Where do your kids live now?"

Aggie clears her throat and looks down as she says, "Both went to college back in Colorado and they live there now. Our daughter is expecting our first grandchild."

"Oh, we're expecting our first grandchild, too!" I point to Anna, seated in a chair near the picnic table. "That's Anna, our daughter-in-law."

"I think I met her. Seems she's having a rough pregnancy?"

"Yeah, she is."

Our conversation lags as we both look at Anna, who looks miserable. She's washed out, sweaty, and deflated. FM is sitting with her. She has a glass of ice water and is in the shade, but that doesn't appear to help. "Poor thing," Aggie says.

"Yeah, poor thing. She's not due until December. When is your daughter due?"

"October. A Halloween baby. Well, I think I should get the

carpools started back up the mountain. Thanks again for inviting us and letting us tour the rooms. It's charming."

"Any time."

"Oh, everyone is invited any Friday?" she asks.

Laney hears her and steps into our conversation, a glass of sparkling cider in tow. "I think so. This is fun, and there is nothing like this in Chancey. I know Laurel Cove has little events like this all the time, right?"

"Yes, and it really does create a nice community feel."

"Like Chancey needs any more community feeling," I say with a smirk.

Laney laughs and adds, "Okay, community feeling with wine. I should've said that."

Aggie and Laney toast each other, and Aggie says, "I can't speak for the rest of the ladies, but I know I'll be coming down to Chancey more." She looks around and takes a deep breath. "This feels good. Now, to get all my ladies back home. Some of them are a little too enthralled with your Midwestern gentleman. He's got a couple wrapped around his little finger, and," she raises one blonde eyebrow, "those two have husbands at home!"

She walks off toward the crowd around our newest guest, and Laney leans against the back of the house where we're standing. "I'm exhausted, and we still have the gender reveal party tonight."

"Go sit down, or even better, go on home and get a little rest. We'll take care of cleaning up."

"You sure? Thank goodness Mama is doing everything for tonight. I just have to show up. Y'all are coming, right?"

"Absolutely. I've never been to your Mama's house. I'm looking forward to it." I lean closer to her and whisper, "And don't worry, I'm wearing pink to throw everyone off."

Her eyes sparkle. "A boy. Still can't believe it. It'll be so different. So fun." She pushes away from the wall. "Okay, I'm going home. I'll see you tonight." She steps toward the door and then looks back at me. "That Aggie? Did y'all talk much?"

"Some. Why?"

She shrugs. "Nothing really. I like her. Reminds me of when I met you. I just knew we'd be good together, you know?" She winks and then lumbers into the house.

Sure, it's warm outside at the end of June in Georgia. And it's been warm all week inside our un-air-conditioned house. But a different warmth moves over me and through me.

Is this what it feels like to belong?

CHAPTER 10

"My husband isn't home."

The small woman at the door doesn't say "hello." She doesn't smile. She's barely opened the door and looks like she will close it if we give her the chance. *That's* why I brought Laney.

"Honey, we didn't come to see your husband. Just to welcome you." Laney shifts the bag of muffins into her other hand, and with the hand closest to the door, pushes it slightly. Like the wind blew it. "I'm Laney, and this is Carolina. She lives right up the hill, across the railroad tracks. You know, Crossings B&B?"

Last night, the gender reveal party went off without a hitch. Incidentally, the only person there Laney hadn't accidentally told that the baby was a boy, was Shaw. Hence, he was the only one not wearing fake-out pink. Anyway, Jackson and I saw lights on in Susan's old house on our way home. So, here Laney and I are bright and early on Saturday morning taking a look. With muffins in hand, of course.

My new neighbor swallows, sighs, then opens the door. "You can come in. We're just getting unpacked."

"Oh, bless your heart, just for a minute," Laney and I say at the same time as we step inside.

There are a few boxes, but other than those, everything

looks to be in place. Well, if this is *everything*. Sparse is the word that comes to mind. Sparse and cold. Susan's warm wall paints, golds and greens and blues, are all gone. Every wall is covered in the same off-white. It smells new and fresh, but feels cold. The furniture is worn and brown. Brown fabric, brown wood. Brown.

Laney walks farther in than I do, and she looks out the back window. "I see the garden is gone." She falters a bit, but then swirls around and smiles. "But the lawn looks beautiful. Much easier to maintain."

"Kyle likes a clean place. He's not one for a bunch of bushes and flowers. K.J., come say hello."

A boy of about five comes down the hallway. He has very short hair and bright eyes. He's wearing shorts and a pair of cowboy boots, which makes me grin. "You look like my boys did when they were little. Cowboy boots all the time. Oh, and who are you?"

Behind K.J. a little girl comes down the hall. The woman says, "That's Katherine. She's three, and Kevin, the baby, is taking a morning nap."

Laney is absentmindedly rubbing her belly. "Oh my, you sure have your hands full, um, wait. Maybe it's just pregnancy has ruined my brain, but I don't think I got your name."

"Kimmy. That's why all the kids have "K" names, you know since me and Kyle both start with a K." She smiles, but her lips don't part and she's still standing with her hand on the door knob.

She and both kids continue to stare at us, so I motion toward the bag Laney still holds. "We'll just leave you the muffins. They're from Ruby's, down in town."

Kimmy nods yes, and then the back door opens. A girl opens the door. She looks to be in junior high. She has medium brown hair that just reaches the tops of her shoulders and the light-colored eyes like the rest of the family. She's startled to see us, but Laney pretends she doesn't see the hesitation and reaches out to shake the girl's hand. "Hi there, I'm Laney. We just came over to welcome y'all to Chancey. What grade are you in? My girls are in high school."

The girl takes a moment staring at Laney, then grins. It feels genuine, and not cold at all, unlike everything else here. "Hi there," she strides over toward me to also shake my hand. "I'm Zoe. Should be in seventh grade, but we're homeschooled, so I'm really ahead of a regular seventh grader."

"Well, hi, welcome. I'm Carolina, and I live up at the B&B on the hill. We don't want to keep y'all. Just dropping off some muffins."

Kimmy still stands beside the door, and she speaks up. "Thanks so much. We're still getting settled." And she pulls the door open wider. "It was nice to meet you."

Zoe turns her back on her mother and rolls her eyes at me and Laney, then darts over to K.J. and Katherine. "C'mon kids, let's go finish up your rooms. Dad wants them done when he gets home." As she turns them and prods them down the hall, Laney and I walk back to the door. At the door Laney stops and asks the young mom, "Zoe? What happened to the 'K' names?"

Kimmy, small as she is, corrals us outside and then as she slowly closes the door, she shrugs. "Zoe is Kyle's. Not mine." The door shuts, and Laney and I are left in the hot, morning sun, blinking.

We turn down the driveway, and at the road turn to walk back to my house. We're both thinking for a moment, then I say, "Don't you hate when you try to get your questions answered, and you end up with more than you started?"

Laney lifts the hem of her long pregnancy top, then bends over to wipe her sweaty face on its tail. "Nope," she says as she drops her shirt and stands up. "I love it. Folks don't want to just come right out and tell you who they are, then they are asking for me to try and figure it out. And in this case, I know just where to start, or should I say, with whom to start?"

"Laney, you kill me how you say stuff like that like it's normal. Maybe these folks are just more private than you are used to."

"Really? Privacy to me is just another word for 'I've got something to hide.'"

"So, let me guess. Zoe is now your new best friend."

"Carolina, don't be silly. I can't have a twelve year old for a best friend."

At the crossing, as we leave the shade-covered road and walk up to my house, the bugs get louder. It's even hotter without the shade, and our talking fades. Laney stops beside her car and pulls her keys out of her pocket. "I am going to need a mother's helper with the baby, you know. That Zoe looks to have lots of experience with kids."

"And besides, if she's on your payroll, she has to tell you what you want to know, right?"

"Right."

"Laney, I'm joking."

She laughs and presses the key ring to make her doors unlock. "Well, I'm not. You should know better than anyone, Chancey is an open book. You want to live here, there are certain costs." She slams her door, and I can't see her through the dark-tinted SUV window.

Well, at least Zoe will be getting paid to spill her guts. That's better than most folks who move to small towns get.

Wait. Earl's truck. It was here when I left, but it's gone now. Afraid to hope, I climb the porch steps, open the screen door, then pause before turning the handle on the wooden front door. When I push it open, I'm met with cold air. Not just cold air from a mountain night, no, genuinely artificial cold air. Thank the Lord!

Jackson comes out of the kitchen. "Hey there—air is fixed."

"I know. Now why couldn't he just do this at the beginning of the week? Was Earl still grumpy this morning?"

Jackson sits on the chair beside the window, where his coffee cup is. "Yeah, don't think I've ever handed a check that big to a more unhappy guy. He kept saying, 'It's what you wanted, but I think I coulda fixed the old one. It's a shame, but it's what you wanted.'"

I laugh and stretch out my arms above my head. "This feels glorious. Any more coffee?" I ask as I turn around and see the light still on and the pot half full. Walking towards the pot, I talk louder. "Met our new neighbors."

"Oh, yeah. What'd you think?"

Back in the living room with a full cup of dark, almost bitter, old coffee, I sit on the end of the couch near Jackson. "Kinda odd. Real stand-offish. Like that'll work in Chancey. All of them have K names. Husband is Kyle, son is K.J., figure Kyle Junior, daughter is, um. Shoot. Let's see, baby is Kevin and the wife is Kim. No, Kimmy. Then there's this older daughter, not the one I can't remember, but she's junior high age, and her name is Zoe. The mom told us point blank she belongs to her husband and not her. Zoe seemed at least a little warm, and Laney has already decided to hire her to help her out with the baby."

"So what brought them to Chancey? What's the husband do?"

"Didn't come up. But they homeschool, did find that out. Although, only Zoe looked old enough to be in school. Oh, and Laney did some checking around, and it looks like the county bought the land where the funeral home was. Not sure what the building is that's going up, though. Although, I'm sure she'll find out something quick."

Jackson stands up and heads to the kitchen with his empty cup. "I'm going on over to the baseball field. They're having a work day there to get ready for the Fourth of July tournament.

75

Told Griffin I'd be there as soon as I squared Earl away and we had cold air flowing. What are you up to today?"

"This place. I put off cleaning because it was too hot. And with the windows being open so much, the dust is an inch thick."

"Griffin says Susan has some kind of family picnic thing set up at the Lake Park tonight. Everybody brings their own food and drinks. I'm good with that, if you are," he says as he comes back to the living room from the kitchen.

"Sounds good to me. I saw a flyer about it, but forgot. Wonder what folks here did before the Lake Park?"

Jackson stops beside the front door. "That's right. We didn't even live here this time last year. We were still in Marietta. That's weird," he says as he shakes his head at me. "I should be home in a couple hours. I want to move that woodpile away from the house today." He steps out, pulling the door behind him. But just before it closes, he comes back in. "Forgot something."

I had just stood up, and he comes to me, grabbing my upper arms in his hands. "Used to make fun of how your mom and dad never part without a kiss. Your dad always makes a big show of it, and I thought it was kind of dramatic and silly. But. . ." He kisses me. "Who am I to make fun of something that so obviously works?" He kisses me again, just a little peck this time. Then pulls away. At the door he looks back at me and grins. "See you later."

He's right. I've been in the car, ready to go somewhere with my mom, and she's gotten out of the car when she realized she hadn't kissed my dad goodbye. I cringe remembering how agitated I would get at her. And usually by time she got back to the front door, Daddy was standing there, hands on his hips, exclaiming that he "didn't get a kiss!" Oh, how that all embarrassed me. How country, how silly, how over-the-top.

As I head up the stairs to change into an old T-shirt and

shorts to clean, a smile starts in my chest and pushes out all over my face. Guess me and Jackson are going to be all country and silly and over-the-top.

It's about time.

CHAPTER 11

"We're getting a dollar store. Did you hear?" Laney and Susan's mother says as I help her carry stuff from her car to the picnic at the Lake Park.

"Here? In Chancey?"

"Yes, ma'am. Set to open July Fourth weekend." Mrs. Troutman's accent is softer than a lot of the old accents around here. Not softer as in not as thick, but softer in that it's slower and there's an extra beat on most words. It's an old Atlanta accent more than a Georgia mountain accent, and it's so lovely. Listening to her talk makes my blood slow down. I smell peaches, and my skin relaxes.

"Oh, so it's not the new building where the funeral home was, I guess. No way that could be open in a week."

"No, that's some county building. I was so much better informed when Griffin didn't work so many hours. Now getting a hold of him takes an act of congress. It's going in that empty place beside the China Palace. Down from the grocery store. Well, looks like Susan's got a right good crowd here."

We stop in the pavilion on the lake side. Tables are covered with baskets and bags and boxes, and people are everywhere. The sunshine is as thick as the humidity, and there's not a breeze to be had. Laney waves at us from a picnic table to our right, so we head that way.

"It's entirely too hot for me to be out here," she says as we walk up to her. "Now that you're here, I can get in the water instead of having to save the table." She stands up and then pulls off her cover-up. "Look at my maternity bathing suit. Isn't it cute? Let me say once again, it's so much better being pregnant when you have money."

"Well, in my day, not having money was *not* the reason we didn't buy such things as maternity bathing suits. It was more about having some decorum." Mrs. Troutman busies herself pulling things out of the bags and baskets we carried from her car.

Laney rolls her eyes and pulls her messy bun of hair through a visor. "C'mon, Carolina, let's get in the water."

"Oh, Laney, I didn't wear a swim suit. There's too many people here."

Mrs. Troutman, looks at me, and with a raised eyebrow, says, "Thank you."

"Mother."

"I'm just agreeing with Carolina. There are just some places a woman doesn't show everything she's got. Especially when she's carrying a child."

"But I do like that bathing suit," I say. When I was pregnant, the tent style was in fashion. Well, not exactly in fashion, but you know what I mean. Now, women wear clothes, and bathing suits, that accentuate the fact they are pregnant. Or, as Mrs. Troutman would say, "Show everything they've got."

Laney holds her hands out and twirls around. The body of the swimsuit is dark blue and the bodice is the same blue, but with little white stars on it. The wide halter tie is bright red, which matches the ribbon on her straw visor. She slides on her big sunglasses and strikes a pose. Big or small, Laney owns it.

I can't help but laugh and even admire her. And out of the corner of my eye, I see her mother smile, too.

Laney then turns and struts down to the water. Her mother's

smile turns into a little laugh. "Lord knows how I got a girl like that. She never did have a shy bone in her body."

"But that's what makes her Laney. Did you always call her Laney? Or is it a nickname?"

"I named her Elaine after my best friend in elementary school. However, Scott and Susan called her Laney from the very beginning. By time you get to the third child, you just don't worry about the name so much."

"Hmmm, someone just said something like that to me recently. Don't remember who."

"Thank you, darlin', for your help. Glad I didn't have to make two trips."

"You're welcome. I'm glad I forgot my sunglasses in the van and saw you in the parking lot. Oh, and thanks again for inviting us to the gender reveal party last night. Your house is so cute."

"It's old, but it's comfortable. Now that I'm alone, it's all I need."

"Well, enjoy the day," I say with a wave, walking towards our table which is closer to the water. I pull and lift at my knit shirt to try and get some air. But there is no air. The sun lays on the green water like a blanket. There aren't pretty sparkles or flashes of light in the water sprays from kids going off the high dive. Everything is flat and heavy. My shirt is sleeveless and my shorts made of light cotton, but the air is so thick it feels like I'm wearing a tight sweatshirt and heavy jeans.

Slumping down at our table, I look around. Women not swimming are all that's left on the shore. The water is full of men and kids and a few young moms who look good in their swimsuits. And there's Laney, arms draped over a neon green noodle.

I have to ask myself—what looks sillier? Her big old pregnant self in the water, or me sitting here sweating beside the lake?

"Hey, Carolina."

"Hey, Anna. How are you, sweetie?"

"Hot and tired." She sits beside me. "Wish I could go swimming."

"Well, honey, why can't you?"

She looks at me like I just asked her why she can't pick up this picnic table and throw it in the lake. "Look at me. I'm huge."

"You are not. You're barely showing. Look at Laney, she's expecting in a few weeks."

"I know. Look at her."

"I am. She looks really happy. And cool."

"Puh-leeze," Anna huffs and stands. "If she wants to swim looking like that she should do it in her own pool. Not out in public. I'm going home. It's too hot out here. Tell Will to find a ride home."

I don't say bye, I don't turn to watch her leave. She is Missus. Except she might be meaner than Missus. Yet...

Yet, there's this little voice inside my head reminding me that she said exactly what I had been thinking about Laney. It sounded so much better in my head than out loud.

With a sigh, I turn around on the bench and begin opening the bags I'd carried our picnic in. First kid, or husband, of mine that shows up gets to go out to the car and carry the cooler in. I would've brought it when I went back to get my sunglasses, but I saw Mrs. Troutman trying to lug everything she'd brought. Jackson had come earlier and brought the floats and football and chairs, which are set up around our tables.

Will comes up not long after I've unpacked. "Hey, where did Anna go? Where are the towels?" he asks.

He's dripping wet and his long boardshorts hang low on his hips. Well, where his hips should go. He's built like his dad, tall and thin. So is Savannah. Bryan is more like me. Shorter, with a little more, um, cuteness. Yeah, that sounds right. Cuteness.

Anna's attitude rubs off on me. "Maybe I didn't bring you a towel? You aren't really my responsibility anymore. And your wife went home." I pull a towel off the stack on the other side of me. "Here."

"Thanks. I'm starving."

"Maybe I didn't bring you a sandwich."

He grins and then comes up behind me before I can say he's too wet to hug me. While secretly smiling, I'm sprinkled from above. I look up to see him standing over me shaking his wet hair out on me. "Stop it, you goofball. Go get the cooler out of the van if you want to eat. Lunchmeat is all in there."

"Sure, van locked?" he asks, but I'm already pulling the keys out of my shorts pocket.

"Yes. I'm parked way on the right-hand side. Third row I think."

He pushes the red button on my key fob. "No problem, I'll just keep pressing this until I get close enough for it to kick in," he says as he begins to jog off.

"Or you could just look where I told you to," I yell.

Have to admit, the water he dripped on me feels pretty good. Maybe I should look into getting a new swimsuit. Okay, I should look into getting *a* swimsuit. I mean, I probably have one somewhere, but I can't recall it at this moment.

Will apparently began the exodus from the water to the picnic tables. Kids go scurrying by; close on their heels are the dads. The teenagers are still out on the platform dock they've claimed. The ones with the high dive and the slide are usually covered in younger kids. The one in the middle doesn't have any fancy equipment, but it has the teenage girls laying out, so that's the one the teenage boys favor.

With my back to the lake, I don't see Savannah make her way to the table. She stands to the side and has her arms crossed around her bare waist. "Do you have enough for Alex to eat with us?"

"Of course. I have plenty of lunchmeat and an entire loaf of bread. Where is he?"

She looks over her shoulder and tosses her head. "Over there."

I see him at the center of a group of young people walking up the hill toward the pavilion. "I don't think the concession stand is open tonight."

"I told them. Most of them want to leave. Alex wants to stay." She looks undecided for a moment, then turns to jog after the group. When she catches up to them, she eases up behind Alex and lays her hand on his upper arm. He turns, and they talk for a moment. Then he smiles at her, turning all that charm he got from his uncle on, puts his arm across her shoulder, and they start back this way.

Will arrives at the table with the cooler, just as they do. Jackson and Bryan stop throwing the football and come to eat, too.

"Thanks for including me," Alex says. "A picnic sounds like a great idea."

In all the laughing and talking of getting the ham and turkey passed around, debating mayonnaise versus mustard, then spearing pickles and opening chip bags, I miss that Will isn't saying anything. He's devouring his sandwich, swallowing mouthfuls with big gulps of bottled iced tea. I wait for a break in the action, and since he's sitting beside me, I say under my breath, "You okay?"

He nods and puts a chip in his mouth. "Anna isn't feeling good."

"And she wants you to come home."

He looks at me for a moment before he nods. "Yeah."

I don't even try to hide the snark in my voice. "You can't help her feel better. She just hates the idea of you here with your family having fun." Okay, I'm going to blame that on the heat.

Jackson looks up, the heat in my voice catching his attention. "What's going on?"

Will stands up. "Nothing. Thanks for supper, Mom. You know buffalo turkey is my favorite."

Bryan tilts his head up. "But you said we'd dive off the high dive together."

"Next time," Will says as he digs his T-shirt out from the pile of towels and clothes. "Sorry," he adds, with a grimace at his brother.

I growl. "But how are you getting home? Anna said for you to find a ride."

He slides on his flip-flops and looks toward the parking lot. "She's here. She didn't leave. She's giving me a ride. Bye, you guys. See you later."

"If Anna says it's all right," I spit, and then regret it. Can I blame that on the heat, too?

He shrugs at me, then lopes off toward the parking lot. I'm hotter than ever.

Alex, Savannah, and Bryan are chewing and looking down at the table. Jackson is trying to get me to look at him. He says my name a couple times and even waves his hand. I will not look at him. I'm mad and I deserve to be mad. I've done everything possible to be nice to that girl, and she's ruining everything. For crying out loud, she's just having a baby!

"This spicy turkey is really good," Alex says. "Thanks again for inviting me."

I look at him and choke out. "Anytime." Out of the corner of my eye, I see Bryan push an Oreo onto my paper plate. Turning my head towards him makes him snatch his empty hand back and look straight ahead with a silly, innocent look.

"Cheering me up with a cookie?"

He slides his eyes in my direction and says through a half-closed mouth, "Did it work?"

Savannah giggles, and I join her. Alex and Jackson laugh out loud and just like that my bad mood is gone.

I swear it used to be easier to hold onto a bad mood.

When we are all stuffed with double-stuffed Oreos, Griffin and John come by to pester Bryan into the water. (When I was growing up, we couldn't swim for thirty minutes, or was it an hour, after we ate. Now I realize that was so the parents could relax and didn't have to worry about someone drowning. It had nothing to do with letting food digest. Stupid Google means kids today know better.)

Jackson and I are sitting in our fold-out chairs watching the water and the swimmers when Peter comes up and sits at our picnic table. "Did you hear we're getting a dollar store?" He's not in picnic clothes. He's wearing a gray dress shirt and dark gray slacks. "Can you believe it? A dollar store." He leans back against the edge of the table and holds his hands up. "Just my luck."

"So, isn't that a good thing?" I ask. "Oh, but your bistro? I didn't think about that. But that shouldn't really be competition."

Jackson asks, "Where they building it? Is that the funeral home building?"

I pat his arm. "No, that's the county doing something. It's going in beside China Palace and Piggly Wiggly. But I don't think it will bother your business. You wanted to do more specialty stuff, right?"

He leans up, plants his elbows on his knees, and runs his hands through his hair. "Of course, but the special stuff won't pay my rent. I was going to have things you need more regularly at good prices. But I can't compete with a dollar store." He clinches his fingers as they run through his hair this time, and pulls. His hair stands on end for a moment, then he shakes his head, and it falls back in place. "This sucks! Can't I get a break?"

Jackson and I look at each other. Peter is usually so calm. So laidback and pragmatic.

"Hey guys," Susan says as she flops down on the bench beside Peter. "How can something I don't have to do anything for be so much work? Everyone brought their own food and drink. Shouldn't that mean it would be easy? I haven't sat down since I got here. Or eaten."

"Want an Oreo? Or you can make a sandwich," I say pointing at our cooler.

"I *will* take an Oreo." She twists around and pulls the cookies out of the plastic grocery store bag. She pulls up the sticky opening, takes two, then holds them out to the rest of us. Jackson and I say no, but Peter takes two.

Jackson asks, "What's kept you so busy?"

Susan sighs. "Well, first we ran out of toilet paper in one of the bathrooms, then Janie Shelton's granddaughter got a bunch of ant bites, so back into the supply closet for first aid cream. And can you believe people just dropped their kids off here? Not teenagers, either. Elementary age." She rolls her eyes. "The Herefords, so not exactly a surprise. But I had to corral them while I tried to get hold of Marie. Of course, she wasn't answering her phone. She probably knew it was me. Or maybe there isn't cell service at the Dew Drop." She says all this around a full mouth of Oreo, finishing her cookie supper about the same time she finishes her rant. I've never seen her eat so fast. She, like, ate full bites and everything. No picking at it, little bit here, little bit there.

She opens the cookie package again and takes another two out. When she offers one to Peter, he holds up the one still in his hand. She seals the bag, then jumps up. "Need to take a walk around, see if everything's good." She sighs again as she strides off, but she's smiling.

Peter opines, "I don't think she's unhappy. She seems to be kind of reveling in this, doesn't she?"

Jackson and I both nod in agreement, but then I say, "I guess, but their whole life turned over in a matter of a few weeks. I haven't seen Griffin in I don't know how long. He's always working."

Peter turns to look back at the table Laney and Shaw and her mother share. "You're right. Griffin used to wouldn't have missed something like this."

"New home, new friends, new job," Jackson lists. "Hmmm, sounds familiar."

And I turn to him and ask, "Who?"

"Us! Just last summer."

"Oh, yeah. I guess so."

Peter laughs a bit and stands up. "Well, guess I better go figure out a way to deal with this dollar store thing. Wonder when it's going to open?"

"Hate to be the bearer of bad news, but it's opening July Fourth weekend."

"Already?" His mouth hangs open, then he closes it and his shoulders slump. "This truly does suck. I can't get a break." He walks off toward the pavilion, and Jackson and I are alone.

I reach over and hold onto his hand. "It has been an interesting year, hasn't it?"

"Yep," he says, but he doesn't look at me. "Do you see that?"

I follow his eyes out to the lake. On the teenager dock, the one in the middle without a diving board or slide, Alex is seated and there's a girl on his shoulders. Her long legs are laying on his chest and his hands are holding on above her knees. Savannah is in the group, but off to the side. She's watching, but something about the way she's sitting doesn't look right. She is hunched over her knees.

"She can't be that crazy over him, can she?" her daddy asks. "She's not one of those boy-crazy girls, right?"

"She didn't used to be."

He doesn't say anything else, but his gaze never wavers.

Mine does, and I look away from the center dock. Bryan and his crew are all around the high dive, egging each other on. Bryan starts up the long stairs, and I nudge Jackson. "Look, on the high dive."

Jackson sits up in his chair. "Has he gone off it before?"

"Nope," I say. "Think he'll dive, or just jump?"

"Don't know. Wish Will was out there with him."

I agree. Bryan isn't growing out of his awkwardness like both of his siblings did in middle school. He's active but not coordinated. At the end of the board he stands. And then he stands some more. The longer he stands, the more people turn their attention his way.

One of the teens on the next dock yells, "Jump!" and others join in his chant. Now everybody is watching.

In my brain, I'm also screaming jump. He has to follow through now, right? And he's a good swimmer, he'd be fine.

Jackson says under his breath, "Come on, buddy. You can do it."

Then, he doesn't. He turns around, walks the few steps back to the ladder, waits for those on the ladder to go back down, then he climbs down. He doesn't make it to the side of the dock before someone has already dashed up the tall ladder. Poor Bryan. And then the person up on the board is waving. Someone in a skimpy royal blue bikini. Oh, it's Brittani with an I. Sensing she holds everyone's attention, she takes three long steps and dives off the end of the board.

People talk about wanting to go back to younger days. How the good ol' days of high school were so good.

I wouldn't go back if you paid me.

Chapter 12

There's that saying that a mom is only as happy as her unhappiest child. Have you heard it?

Bryan didn't spend the night with his friends after the Lake Park picnic Saturday. He came home and went straight to his bedroom. Wouldn't talk. Didn't want ice cream. Said he was sick Sunday morning, so he didn't go to church with us. Spent the whole day in his room, except when he'd occasionally journey down to the basement to play video games.

Will doesn't have time to come talk to his brother because he and Anna are "fighting." He yelled on the phone at me when I called him after church. He yelled that he and Anna are fighting. Anna and Missus are fighting. Missus and FM are fighting. And that if FM didn't stop bugging him about how to make Anna happy, he and FM were going to get into it. Then he hung up. Yep. Hung up on his own mother.

Savannah stayed out late with her friends, coming home right before curfew Saturday night. She slammed the front door, stomped up the stairs, and slammed her bedroom door. She came back down the stairs Sunday morning just in time to go to church with me and Jackson. Repeating the same actions with the stomping and the slamming, just in reverse order. Not one word came out of her mouth on the ride there. However, upon climbing out of the van in the church parking lot, she was all sweetness and light. Butter wouldn't have melted in her mouth—until she realized Alex wasn't there. She came home, did her stomping/slamming thing and barricaded herself in *her* room. Sunday night she came out long enough to take a load of dirty clothes to the basement, where she and Bryan got into a screaming match.

So, having three unhappy kids, I should be miserable, right? Yeah, not so much.

Saturday night Jackson and I sat on the deck and had margaritas. We never do real drinks at home. We just have wine or beer. We laughed and played *our* music, no kids complaining. (They weren't talking, remember?)

We watched the moon rise, and possibly even did a tequila shot or two. Maybe. And stayed up to make sure Savannah was in before curfew. Don't worry, we had plenty of ways to make the time pass. (Imagine that winking emoji here.)

We enjoyed hot coffee out on the deck before church while we read the paper. The drive down the hill was peaceful, since I'd quit trying to get Savannah to talk. And while sitting in the pew, I kept working on worrying about my kids, but the sermon kept getting my attention and holding it. How odd is that?

Then after church, when Will yelled at me on the phone, I fully tried to be miserable about it. I honestly tried. But then Susan and Griffin called and asked if we wanted to go to brunch at the Laurel Cove clubhouse. It was lovely. Crystal and silver, hydrangea bouquets on the tables, adult conversation, and the best grits I've ever put in my mouth. See why staying miserable didn't work?

Then the afternoon was mild, with big, fluffy clouds and sunshine. Perfect day for reading on the back deck. The peace was interrupted by the fight in the basement, but by the time I got down there they "didn't want to talk about it." Savannah held back tears and retreated to her castle tower, and Bryan got back to his video game. I mean, I can't *force* them to talk, right?

Jackson and I had a relaxing Sunday night watching *Animal House*, which was on one of the movie channels. We laughed over the same things we've laughed at through the years. We went upstairs and chatted while he packed for the week. As I laid my head on my pillow, I again tried to concentrate on the kids and then, well, the sheets were clean. You know how hard it is to worry when you're lying on clean sheets?

Jackson's been gone about fifteen minutes now, and I'm stretching in those clean sheets. He had to leave extra early, so we didn't get up to have coffee together. But I can tell I'm too happy to go back to sleep. Of course, I'll have to deal with the kids.

That *is* kind of my job.

However, as the light brightens outside the windows, I remember how many mornings I've laid right here and been so sad. Sad. Mad. Depressed. Angry. Lonely. I have plenty of time for all those emotions when the kids get up in a couple hours. Right?

Besides, teenagers exist in a world centered on them. So, as far as mine know, I've been miserable all weekend right alongside them.

See? It's a win all around.

Thought I wouldn't fall back asleep, but I did. Despite the snooze button, it's still early when I come downstairs. My summer gown is white cotton with little pleats along the front, lace around the ruffle at the bottom, and pretty little lavender violets with sweet green leaves on it. Makes me feel so fresh and pretty. Sweeping down the stairs is like being in an old-fashioned fairytale.

Even the part where the mean ogre is waiting at the bottom. "Hi, Gertie." She's sitting on the couch with a coffee cup beside her.

"Been waiting on you. I have things to do, you know."

I walk behind the couch and into the kitchen. "I didn't know you were waiting on me."

"I didn't make extra coffee."

"I see that." Dumping the old grounds, I roll my eyes. When the wet grounds splash onto my new white gown, I curse under my breath.

"I heard that," the ogre says.

Finally with a new pot brewing and the front tail of my gown wet from me washing it out in the sink, I come back into the living room. "You're waiting on me?"

"We need to talk about the bookstore. We're going to do a grand opening next weekend in conjunction with the opening of the Dollar Store. You'll need to have it all set up for that. It'll be cleaned out of all of Andy's junk by this evening so you can start on it tomorrow morning bright and early."

Words don't come, so I turn around and manage to push out through gritted teeth as I re-enter the kitchen, "Coffee sounds ready." Clutching my cup in my hands, I'm breathing deep through my nose and letting each breath out slowly. I pour my coffee and return to the living room. I set my cup down, fluff out the front of my still-damp gown, and sit down in the chair next to the couch that looks out the front window.

Gertie holds up a hand. "Now don't go getting your panties in a wad. I felt—"

"Sounds great."

"Really?" Her brow sits heavy over her beady eyes, and her jaw hangs as she looks sideways at me.

A little laugh escapes me. "Believe me, I'm as shocked

as you are." And I am shocked. So much of the time here in Chancey I've been on the defensive. Like things were being done against my will, my wishes. For some reason I can't work those familiar feelings up. I feel… I feel *excited*. "I actually missed it. It broke my heart to see the books hidden under the junk. And… wait, what are you doing with all the junk?"

She pushes up off the couch. "Come see for yourself. I have to get down there now. Just look for me when you get there. Don't think you can miss Andy's new place." She pulls her pocketbook over her shoulder and starts to the front door.

"Patty and Andy got off on their honeymoon all right yesterday?" I ask before she opens the screen door.

"Yep. Got 'em all set up in one of the resorts in Jamaica where all you do is drink, eat, and make babies. I'm ready for a grandbaby." She takes a deep breath. "Lord knows though, this area here might be even better than some exotic island for making a baby. Look at your son and that girl, and then Laney. Her eggs can't be all that fresh. You aren't pregnant, are you?" She points with her head at me as she asks.

"No! Absolutely not."

"Okay. Just that flowy, flimsy thing you're wearing makes you look big. See you downtown," she says as she lumbers onto the porch.

Ever notice how some people just keep working until they've ruined your good mood?

CHAPTER 13

Susan picked up Bryan a bit ago to go take a golf class with Grant up at Laurel Cove. After the high-dive debacle, the Lake Park didn't sound like a good idea. Plus, he'll get to meet some of Grant's new friends. It took a while straightening up the house and getting dressed, but I'm finally ready to go downtown.

In my rearview mirror, I watch Savannah turn her car around and then drive across the railroad crossing and down the hill. The bistro is doing a "soft" opening this week, she informed me when she flounced downstairs earlier. "Flounced" is the appropriate word when your daughter looks like she's dressed to work a street corner. Her short shorts couldn't be any shorter, her hair couldn't be any straighter, and her lips couldn't be any redder. The vehemence with which she defended her styling choices says, loud and clear, that the battle for Alex is ongoing. The vehemence with which I attacked her styling choices says that I'm "old," "hopelessly out-of-style," and "hate my daughter." Which may all be true, but I do not need it shouted at me in my own living room this early on a Monday morning.

People say the way women feel about snakes is God's punishment for what happened in the Garden of Eden. I don't think so. He knew snakes were a breeze compared to raising teenage girls, the true divine punishment. After the show at our house this morning, I'm guessing he's still laughing.

As I pass Susan's old house, I see Kimmy putting mail in their mailbox. Stopping, I roll down the window on that side. "Hey, things still going good? Getting settled?"

Wouldn't have surprised me if she just nodded, waved, and turned back to the house. However, she closes the mailbox door and turns to lean in the open window. "Good morning. Yep, it's all coming together. Told the kids we'd come downtown today and get some of those muffins."

"I'm headed down to Ruby's, too. Plus, I'm going to be taking back over at the bookstore, and it's getting cleaned up. Hi, K.J.!" The little boy runs up and tries to see into the window.

His sister, the name I can't remember, also runs up, but luckily she's short enough I can act like I don't see her and don't have to say her name. "I'll see y'all at Ruby's, okay?"

Kimmy stands up and pulls both kids back. "See you there."

Maybe she was just tired the other day. She seemed right nice this morning. At the bottom of the hill, where all the daffodils were in the spring, a couple dozen American flags have sprouted. I see now what the seemingly random placement of hosta plants was about. Each bunch of hostas must have a flag holder in the middle and at some point last night or this morning, the flags were installed. The morning sun brings out the bright colors of the flags, and a bit of breeze causes them to slightly ripple. July Fourth is Sunday, so this weekend will be full of activities.

The patriotic decorating continues downtown. Red, white, and blue bunting graces the gazebo, and ribbons in the same colors are tied around the smaller, decorative light posts. American flags fly from the street lights at the corners of the square. The front window boxes on our building have red and white petunias in them. Comes in handy being in the florist's building. At Ruby's, she's stuck little American flags next to the plastic poinsettias that are still in her window boxes from Christmas, though they've now faded to light pink.

Then suddenly my head snaps up. Oh my word. She said I couldn't miss it. But, well, I never imagined. Main Street, which goes in front of the line of shops including Ruby's, the bookstore and florist, and Peter's bistro, dead-ends at a line of Civil War era homes. Big homes with deep porches, varied rooflines, and lots of windows. Houses small towns cherish and celebrate. Some of these in Chancey are cared for and restored, like Missus' and a couple more in the line. Peter's new home is the last in the line, off to the right when you have to turn. It used to be the eyesore in the bunch, but he's fixing it. Between his house and his parents' is the house the younger couple was moving out of last week. It sits center at the end of Main Street. They'd done some repairs, but these houses take a boatload of money to fix up and then monthly arrivals of boatloads of money to keep up. Well, apparently the latest money boat has arrived. The U.S.S. Gertie Samson is in port.

Neon green paint covers the wooden siding. Elaborate gingerbread trim I hadn't really noticed before is now bright purple. The front door and shutters are orange. Highway safety vest orange. The lack of taste isn't how I know its Andy's new place. Nope. Says so, in big letters on the roof. "ANDY'S."

A honk lets me know I've gawked long enough, so I pull into one of the angled parking spots off Main Street on the park side. Out of the car, I step back into the empty street to take a picture. Jackson is not going to believe this. Heck, why just share with him? On the sidewalk outside Ruby's, I add Laney and Susan onto the text and send it out.

Walking in the door, I tuck my phone in my skirt pocket. Laney holds her phone up. "Got your text. Come sit down. Can you believe that? I didn't send you a picture because, well, because I didn't want to look at it even a minute longer. And you should hear Missus."

Ruby's is buzzing, and it's an angry buzzing. Sure, our little town doesn't look like those postcard ones. We've been kind of proud that we're not artificial, we're a real small town where the signs don't match, with artificial flowers in some of the window boxes, and a boarded up business right on Main Street, but come on, there was a certain charm.

Libby brings coffee to the table, so I flip over my green cup. "How did she get it done so fast?"

Libby pours as she talks. "There was a full crew up there working when I got here at five. Barely light."

"Gertie told me this morning I couldn't miss it. She was right. Where's Missus and FM?"

Laney reads her phone. "Be here in a minute, she says." She lays her phone down on the table. "Oh, look, it's the K family." She waves. "Hey, Kimmy. Hey, kids."

Kimmy seems even smaller carrying in the bulky baby carrier. She looks around and points to the table near our booth. Zoe grins at us as she takes the younger kids, which she has by hand, to the table.

"Was that house that color before?" Kimmy asks as she kicks out one of the chairs at the table and deposits the carrier onto it. "Zoe, get an extra chair," she calls over her shoulder and flips her hair. Kimmy's hair is fairly limp and non-descript. Wonder what color she calls it on her driver's license? It's not really blonde, not really brown.

"No," I answer. "Never a dull moment in Chancey."

She folds her arms and looks at us. "It's original? Interesting."

Laney throws up a hand at her. "You don't have to be nice. It's hideous. Hey, Zoe."

Zoe looks up from where she's unbuckling the baby. "Hi, Miss Laney. Miss Carolina." She lifts the baby out and puts him on her shoulder.

"You sure are good with that baby," Laney says.

Kimmy looks over her shoulder. "Is there a baby seat here?" Then she looks back to us. "It's so nice to get away from unpacking this morning. Is there room here in your booth for me?"

I scoot closer to the wall, and she slides in. I ask, "Are the kids all right there without you?"

"That's what Zoe is for. She loves being with the kids."

"Good, because Laney is wanting—"

"Wanting to tell you how much I like what you've done with the house. It seemed so cluttered when my sister lived there," Laney says while kicking me under the table. "Right, Carolina?"

I echo her "Right," but I have no idea why she's kicking me. I introduce Kimmy to Libby as she comes around with her coffee pot and a plate of muffins.

"Kids want muffins, too?" she asks and Kimmy just nods her head toward Zoe.

Zoe smiles at Libby. "Hi, I'm Zoe. Can we get three milks? What muffins do you think the kids will like?"

Libby looks back at Kimmy, but she's busy fixing her coffee and doesn't look up. So she says to Zoe, "Blueberry are good, and I have some strawberry ones with white chocolate chips."

"Okay, one of each of those. Do you have banana with nuts?"

"Sure do." Libby by this point has moved next to Zoe.

"Great, I'll have one of those. Kimmy, do you want me to order for you?"

"No, thanks. I'll just try one of these. I'm assuming the plate is for the table?"

"Apparently," Laney says through tight lips. Then she raises her head. "There's Missus."

Walking through the restaurant, Missus receives condolences, questions, and just shakes of heads from those who don't know what to say. When she reaches our table she stands at the end to make her pronouncement. She really should have a balcony. "I'd ask if you've all seen it, but it is impossible to miss. Which is the entire purpose, that woman says. I told you people when she showed up last fall, Gertie Samson is not to be trusted. Did you listen? Not at all. My husband said I was nursing an old grudge. You," she points at me, "welcomed her into the bosom of your home. She steamrolled over every objection, every caution I tried to lay in her way. Me, just me, left to protect our town from such complete disaster."

"Hi, Missus. This is Kimmy and these are her kids," I say.

Missus nods at Kimmy and then steps toward the seat left open for her beside Laney in the booth. "If they are your children, shouldn't you be sitting with them?"

Kimmy's mouth opens, but nothing comes out.

Missus waits, but finally looks away from her. "I've spoken to my lawyer, who also happens to be the town's lawyer. He's not offering much hope. We never finished the paperwork for any type of historic designation. Griffin was obviously too busy tracking down a power plant to bring to town for new jobs for him and his wife. Such a shame when people don't take their responsibilities seriously."

Laney squints up her eyes and shakes her head. "Now, that doesn't sound like Griffin. On the contrary. He's the most responsible person I know. Makes it kind of a pain to have him for a brother-in-law, but he always did a good job on the council."

Missus huffs. "Of course he did. Just look at that monstrosity he allowed in our town."

Kimmy shrugs. "If this Gertie bought the house, I guess she can paint it whatever color she wants, right? This is America. You know, Declaration of Independence and July Fourth, and all that."

I can't help but let a laugh slip out. Missus's face is turning red. Her eyes are bugging out. If she were to shout, "Off with her head!" I don't think I'd be surprised at all.

Kimmy looks down at her empty saucer and mumbles, "But I don't really know."

I catch Zoe's look, and she's rolling her eyes at her stepmother. Zoe sees me catch her, and she winks, then grins. I don't believe I've ever seen a middle schooler wink. And we all know I love a man who winks. Now, I love kids that wink.

When the baby, Kevin, starts to cry, Zoe lifts him to her shoulder and rocks him back and forth. He calms down for only a few seconds and then gets louder. Zoe continues rocking him, eating her muffin at the same time.

Missus' face is losing its redness, Laney's frown is deepening, and Kimmy is looking over the plate of muffins for her next selection. The rest of us watch her and wait for her to hear her baby. Surely she hears him?

Zoe stands up and begins walking with the baby still on her shoulder. The toddler girl—what *is* her name? – plops off her chair and comes to her mother's leg. "Mama, I don't like my muffin."

Kimmy reaches out to the plate on our table and takes the last muffin without even looking at us. She hands the full muffin to the little girl. "Go back to your table. This is the adult table."

Missus says, "I believe that was my muffin you just gave away to a child who still has virtually a full muffin at her place."

"You want her old muffin?" Kimmy asks. "She said she didn't like it."

K.J. has left the table, I realize, and is whirling on top of one of the stools at the counter. He stops it by hitting his hand on the counter as he goes by, and when the stool stops, he falls off, laughing. Zoe, walking by with the now-screaming baby, reaches down and grabs him by one arm. Still laughing, he climbs back up on the stool and starts the spinning again. The little girl apparently has decided she doesn't like her second muffin either, as she's tearing it into pieces, and then shaking her hands to get the pieces off. There are bits of muffin all around her on the floor and on the table.

Hard to believe, but this little family, new to our town, has completely caused us to forget Gertie's paint job. We are mesmerized by the little crew, and their mother is calmly eating her second muffin and drinking her coffee.

Suddenly Ruby appears at the counter. She stares at K.J., once again picking himself up and climbing on for another ride. "Who do these kids belong to?"

Zoe stops walking and looks at Ruby.

"That baby is not yours, is it?" Ruby exclaims.

Kimmy takes one more sip of coffee, then laughs and says, "Don't be ridiculous. Come on, kids. Time for story hour at the library." She gets out of the booth, ignoring that she's now mashing the bits of muffin her daughter threw in the floor, lifts up the carrier, and heads to the door where Zoe is waiting.

Zoe yells, "K.J., Katherine." (There, that's her name!) She sheepishly adds, "Storytime."

K.J. jumps off the stool and shoots by Ruby who's come out from behind the counter. Katherine grabs what's left of the two muffins in her hands, slides off her chair, and heads to the door; leaving a trail of crumbs like she's headed for the witch's house.

When the door finally closes on the newest Chanceyites, talk picks up again, accompanied by lots of rolling eyes and shaking heads. Ruby surveys the damage and then everyone's attention is grabbed by Laney's loud laughter.

Ruby turns towards our booth, eyes, elbows, and voice, all sharp. "You think this is funny?"

Laney eventually makes enough of a gap in her laughter to

explain. "I'm just hoping those muffins last long enough to get to the library and Ida Faye."

And as we imagine the gossipy head matron of our library with the K kids running around her, Laney is no longer the only one laughing.

"Okay, enough of this fun. Who wants to go check out the bookstore and give me some ideas? It probably won't be empty of all the junk yet, but we can take a look," I say, sitting on the end of the booth seat while Libby sweeps the floor around the messy table.

Missus perks up, not in a good way. "Do you think Gertie might be there?"

"Now, Missus," Laney advises the older woman beside her, "you know if you get Gertie all riled up she's only going to make it worse. She'll put a searchlight on the roof, or a flock of plastic flamingos in the yard." She then looks at me. "Of course I'll go, because you know, no matter what I say, Missus won't be able to keep her mouth shut, and I do love a Monday morning brawl."

"I do not brawl. Thank you, Libby," Missus says as she steps out of the booth and marches towards the door. Laney follows, and after I add a few bills to the pile on the table, I hurry to catch up. Hard to not notice Kimmy didn't leave any money. Of course, as a newcomer we would've told her it was our treat. Not very nice to not give us a chance to *tell* her how nice we are. Not very Southern, either.

Laney has on a yellow dress with daisy buttons at the neck. It is sleeveless and pure maternity wear. "Your dress is cute," I say as I fall in step beside her.

"Yeah, cute," she tsks and looks down. "Maternity clothes are for girls, young women. Not, well, not women my age. They have more business, or professional looking suits and such, just, well, just not in my size. So, I got a couple of these. Basically tents in pre-school colors. The long caftans got too hot, and those long swirling skirts are a pain getting in and out of the car."

Missus beats us to the bookstore. By the time we join her inside, she's searched the space and tells us, "Gertie isn't here. Just Shannon."

Shannon is short and reminds you of a fairy or an imp. She has wispy black hair all around her tiny face. She's short and her waist is really small, but her bosom is rather large. She's cuter in the whole than she is cute in her parts. Like, her face just doesn't uphold the fairy image. And her tiny waist looks too small in the shadow of her breasts. Her hair is cute, until you really think about just how black it is, which is kind of unnatural. I don't think she colors it, but it sure looks like a bad dye job. But she's a hard worker and a good florist. Could definitely have worse people running the business that shares space with my bookstore.

Laney walks straight to the couch and sits down. "It's hot out there. Looks like some of the junk is gone."

"It does. Hey, Shannon. Do you know where Gertie is? Has she said anything to you about Andy's place? Have you seen it?"

Shannon bobs her head as she arranges a small basket of carnations. "Oh yeah, I've seen it. And she thinks it's a hoot. So, don't believe you, or anyone," she adds a glance at Missus, "will be able to change her mind." Wandering over to the front window, I look down at the display I did a while back. The painted wine glass has been knocked over. The books have been laid on their sides in a stack and used as a pedestal for an old, green bowl. Inside the bowl are about a dozen boxes of playing cards and two dozen Bic lighters, still in their wrappers. A shudder runs through me. "Let's get out of here. Nothing can be decided until all this stuff is gone." I turn back to the door. "Shannon, tell Gertie I came by, okay?"

I hold the door open for Missus to march out of, and then

I wait for Laney to get up out of the depths of the couch and slowly proceed to the door.

"Do you think it's possible I could be bigger than when I was carrying twins?" Laney asks, moving past me.

"Surely not," I say out loud. Then add a bit quieter, "You're just eighteen years older."

"I'm going to peek into the bistro, and then I'm going up to your house to take a nap," Laney says.

"Why my house?"

"Well, that's where I work, right?" she says, as I let the door fall closed behind her. "If I go home, I might have stuff I have to do."

I follow the yellow dress, and the tense gray head bouncing at the head of our column, next door. There's still that quiet hush that I liked from MoonShots, the clean, new smell of new construction and paint. Peter has tried to make the space more homey and old-fashioned, but there's too much shine for him to cover up.

"Mother, welcome. Hey, Laney and Carolina." Peter greets us from near the front windows. He's standing behind a table with big jars of fresh lemonade, both pink and regular. There are slices of lemons in both jugs, and he holds out little sample cups to us. "Here, try this. So refreshing on a hot day."

Missus ignores his offering and walks on into the store. "Harvard education for you to play lemonade stand." She shakes her head in disgust as she wanders down the next aisle.

"I'll have some," Laney says, reaching out her hand. "Are those cookie samples, too?"

She and I both have a piece of a wonderful sugar cookie and a sip of lemonade. The place feels good. It does remind me of the bistro over in Canton where we had Anna and Will's rehearsal dinner. "This is nice. Oh, and there's the area for folks to sit down and eat. Have you figured out what you're going to serve?"

"Sandwiches. Hi, Carolina, Laney," Alex says from somewhere near the back counter. "I'm coming up with the menu."

Missus says clearly, even though we can't see her on the other side of the aisle. "That is *Miss* Laney and *Miss* Carolina, young man."

Alex laughs, clearly thinking she's joking. "See, I'm going to put it on this chalkboard, that way we can change it. Lots of restaurants in New York do it that way."

Coming around a center display of cheese straws toward his voice, I see him leaning on the counter writing on a pad of paper. Sitting on the counter next to him is Savannah in her short shorts, tight tank top, and her bright red lips.

Oh. You didn't think I won that battle this morning, did you?

She doesn't even look up at me. Just says, "Hey, Mom. Hey, Miss Laney."

Laney looks at me, acknowledges my rolling eyes, and then shifts her weight and leans her head way over to the side. "Y'all probably know all about advertising and such, right? I mean, Alex, you're from *New York* and all."

Now Alex's and Savannah's heads are tilting a bit right back at her. And their eyebrows are straightening out. Laney shrugs. "Silly me, I just don't get how this all works. I mean, look at Savannah with your lipstick and those shorts that don't cover good sense, I'd be a tad concerned about exactly what it is you're selling here."

My daughter gasps and scoots off the counter to stand next to Alex.

Alex stands up straight and looks at Savannah. "Um, well, Laney—"

"That's Miss Laney to you." Comes from over the next aisle.

"Miss Laney. We're not really open."

Savannah flips her hair at me and Laney, and tilts her chin up.

"She won't dress like that when we're really open, of course," Alex finishes with a grin at Savannah. "Right?"

My daughter's face goes red, and she flees to the back room.

Alex turns to follow her, and Laney turns in the opposite direction toward the front door. She's almost to the door when Missus says from whatever aisle she's in now, "Well done, Laney. Public shaming is the trick to raising kids, you know. Not near enough of it these days."

Laney raises a hand in a wave behind her. "Learned from the master. I believe that's the same line you used on me at the snow cone booth at the fair when I was sixteen."

There's a pause, then Missus says, "Thought it sounded familiar."

Peter, who'd followed us to the back of the store, leans toward me and whispers, "Hope it takes better with Savannah than it did with Laney."

"Amen."

He leans on the back counter, where Alex and Savannah had been, and looks around. "So, what do you think?"

"I like it. Reminds of places we go into on vacation or in tourist towns. Can't believe it's right here in Chancey."

"I know. I'm worried we won't have enough traffic. Especially now that the Dollar Store is opening. Nowadays those places sell cute stuff. But I'm thinking we'll expand on the food. Have sandwiches and maybe even do some takeout. I figure I can read a recipe as well as the next person."

Looking at the chalk board Alex left and the food items written on it, I ask Peter, "Do you like to cook?"

Missus joins us. "Yes, tell us, do you like to cook? Is that how you want to spend your days and evenings? Mixing up tuna salad and pitchers of lemonade? I imagine the return on investment for those items is astronomical."

"Mother, it's what I'm doing now. I don't know. Diego and I are trying some things out."

"I bought the newspaper because you earned a degree in journalism, but when you came back to town you chose to hang out in that crummy museum instead. For free. Now you have to play second fiddle to that Yankee, who already has one successful business. I told you we could buy him out if you wanted, if you sell your house and live upstairs. At least then you'd be a business owner. I just don't understand." Missus grits her teeth and starts toward the door. "A shopkeeper. A shopkeeper!"

Peter and I exchange grimaces, and then look at the door where Missus stands, waiting for someone to open it. Peter makes a dash for it.

"Here, let me, Mother." He opens it with one hand and touches the other to the small of his mother's back.

She turns around and lays a hand on his arm. "Forgive me. You know I will always be proud of you, but things are just not going as I'd planned. Anna, and that junk store next door to our beautiful home." She walks on out, and as she passes the windows, she looks reduced. Wrung out. Tired.

Peter lets the door fall shut and looks at me.

"Did she just ask you to forgive her?"

He puts his hands in his pants pockets and sighs. "Kind of shocking, isn't it? Anna is wearing her out. They really should not be living together. Has Will said anything?"

"He yelled at me yesterday on the phone. Said everyone was fighting. That even FM was getting on his nerves."

"Yeah, mine, too." Peter pours himself a small cup of pink lemonade. "He's become by Anna, the way he's always been about Mother. No. He's worse. At least with Mother he could fight it out. But with Anna? She can do no wrong. Don't be surprised if Will isn't moving home soon."

"Just Will? Without Anna? No."

We both are quiet for a moment. Only sound is the air conditioner kicking on. Peter crushes his little cup and tosses it in the wastebasket beside the table. "But you're getting your bookstore back, right?"

"Yep, looks like it. Do you know what hours you're going to be open yet?"

"Not really. You and Shannon making any changes? Guess we'll want to be a little more regular than Ruby's. Hey, Alex," Peter says as the young man comes in from the back room. His hair is messy, and there is actually lipstick on his face. Red lipstick.

Now it's my mouth that hangs open. My face flushes. He and Savannah were back there making out while we were right out here. And I've been in that stockroom, it's not that big. We were right here! Worst part? Her trampy outfit worked.

Peter grins, and Alex grins, and I leave.

There are just not enough convents in Georgia.

CHAPTER 14

Pulling out of my parking space, I catch a glimpse of Andy's new junk shop behind me. Of course, it's hideous, but... it fits? But how can it fit? It's purple and green, for crying out loud. At the end of the block I stop and take a longer look in my rearview mirror. No, no way it fits. Right?

Instead of turning up the hill for home, I decide to take a run by and check out the new Dollar Store. Pulling in the parking lot on the end beside the Piggly Wiggly like I usually do, I see the bright orange and yellow sign at the other end. There are a few cars in front of it, and I drive on through the gravel lot to that end.

Even in the noonday glare, the sign shines, and the interior lights are evident. Apparently, the electric is on. Still can't imagine how I hadn't noticed this part of the strip mall was empty, or even down here. But it has been a busy year. Turning around, I drive by again and park in front of China Palace. Might as well pick up some wonton soup while I'm here. Laney and I can have it for lunch when she gets up from her nap.

Inside is dark as they have thin, printed paper taped over most of the front windows. You can kind of see through it, but it keeps the place dark and cool. I step to the right to look at the lunch buffet. General Tso's chicken, fried rice, eggrolls, veggies and lumps of white meat in a white sauce, green beans, and then the fried dough balls rolled in sugar. Maybe I'll get some stuff to go along with the soup.

Back at the side counter, I place an order with the teenager there, and then sit in the chair in the corner beside the empty coatrack. Notice how smartphones make waiting so much easier? Used to be I panicked if I didn't have a book with me to read in case I had to wait somewhere, but now? Not so much. Bryan has checked in at the Laurel Cove golf course. Patty and Andy posted a selfie of them on a Jamaican beach. They already look pink, and I see someone has already commented "Sunscreen???" Peter's pictures of the bistro look really good. Good idea to have a Facebook page for the bistro. I should do one for the bookstore.

Yes, I'm on Facebook. Although I've not done a post yet, so I'm what they call a "stalker." I don't have a problem with that.

"Carolina. Hey." Anna stands just inside the door of the restaurant with a man I don't know. He has a short-sleeved dress shirt and tie on. He's about the same height as Anna, and he's looking around.

"Anna, what are you doing here?" I stand up and start to give her a hug, but she pulls back slightly, so I awkwardly touch the back of her arm. "You look good. How are you feeling?"

"Fine, thanks. We're here for lunch." She takes another little step back and holds out a hand toward the man. "Carolina, this is Mr. Kendrick. Carolina is my mother-in-law."

"Mr. Kendrick." We shake hands, and he nods, with barely a smile.

"Nice to meet you."

Anna speaks to the teenager behind the counter. "We need a table." She then looks back at me. "Mr. Kendrick is my boss.

He just hired me to work at the Dollar Tree. Work up to assistant manager."

Oh. "Oh. I didn't realize you were looking for a job. Congratulations."

Mr. Kendrick rocks on his heels and crosses his arms. "We are lucky to have found her. We always try to hire local people for all positions, including management, but sometimes it's not so easy. I didn't even have time to advertise."

One of the waitresses waves them toward the open table she's standing beside. I take a step back. "I'll let y'all get to lunch. Looks like my take-out order is ready. Nice to meet you, Mr. Kendrick."

He reaches out to shake my hand again. "You as well, Carolina. And please, call me Kyle."

They walk off, and I pull my billfold out of my purse to pay as I watch them get seated. Anna has on black pants and a blue blouse. She looks older than eighteen and doesn't look pregnant at all. Wait, Kyle? Oh my gosh, I bet he's Kimmy's husband. Yep, she said her husband's name is Kyle, and he looks like he fits that family perfectly.

See, a trip to town is never wasted. I'm bringing home Chinese food and gossip.

"'Bout time you woke up. Just hit start on the microwave to heat up your soup a bit."

Laney rolls into the kitchen just as I'm finishing my soup. "There's also some General Tso's chicken, but I was eating my soup first."

"Is there anything like the sleep of a pregnant woman? Man, my head hit that pillow and I was out. Um, the soup smells wonderful." She slides the bowl of brown, saucy chicken into the microwave and pushes some buttons. "I just collapsed on the bedspread in the Orange Blossom room. Don't you just love how the sun comes in there? You'd think it was too bright to sleep during the day, but not so."

She cuts up her wontons and then takes a spoonful. "That is delicious. So you checked out the Dollar Store?"

"How did you know?"

She raises an eyebrow at me. "The soup? I did a drive by, too. Looks nice."

"Guess who the newest employee is?" She just looks up as she eats and questions me with her eyebrows. "Anna. And guess who the manager is?" I don't even wait for raised eyebrows. "Kyle. You know, like Kimmy's husband Kyle?"

"Really? I guess we didn't find out why they moved here, or anything about her husband. Does he seem nice?"

"Well, he seemed like he, um, he seemed a little self-important? He's not quite as tall as Anna…"

"Oh, so he's one of *those* short men? Always trying to make you think he's tall? Puffed out chest, head tilted back, takes himself very, very seriously, and, obviously, you should, too?"

I simply nod. It's nice having friends you can count on to say all the impolite stuff you're thinking. "But he seemed nice."

She pauses with her spoon midair and rolls her eyes at me, then resumes eating when I get up.

"Ready for some chicken?" As I'm walking to the microwave, Savannah comes into the kitchen.

"What smells so good?"

"Brought home some Chinese. There's another container of soup and plenty of General Tso's. Get you a plate."

Laney stretches, and as she brings her arms down from over her head, she asks my daughter, "So you've set your cap for our new boy Alex?"

Savannah shrugs. "He's cute."

She's changed out of her short shorts and has on gray capri-length yoga pants. She's still wearing the tank top, but it's fine for wearing at home, especially without that lift-'em-up, push-'em-out bra she had on earlier. Teenagers having jobs is great in theory, and even in practice, I suppose. But since she has money to buy her own lingerie, things are harder to control. I get embarrassed doing the laundry.

"I'm going to eat on the deck," she says as she opens the door and scoots out there.

Laney shakes her head. "Gotta be hot out there."

"She probably figures it's not as hot as in here with you asking questions about Alex."

"Him having his own place is a problem," Laney says with a sigh.

"I know. And she works right there."

We eat for a minute or two, then Laney leans back. "Oh! Baby kicked. He must like Chinese food."

"Still can't believe you're going to have a baby. And he'll be here before we know it."

She feels around her stomach waiting for another kick. "It doesn't seem real to me either, and I've got him right here, kicking and rolling around. Shaw was really excited at first, but now…"

"What? He's getting cold feet? Who wouldn't?"

"I guess," she says a bit slowly. "But he's not great with kids. And now that I've been thinking about it…" She looks up at me and her big purple-blue eyes are shiny. "Neither am I. My mom pretty much raised the girls. She even moved in with us when they were born."

Patting her hand, I say, "But that was twins. So much harder. I can't even imagine having twin newborns."

"But she stayed until they went to school."

Oh. "Well, yeah, but…"

"But Mom's too old, now. She's worried about how I'll

do, and now she's got me and Shaw worried. And it's not fair to the girls. It's their senior year. Everything should be about them." She pushes her plate and bowl away. "This all seemed like such an adventure, but it's forever. I don't think I can do it."

Laney is always the one barreling through anything with the rest of us in her wake, holding on for dear life. Every time I see her these days as she gets larger and larger, all I can think is thank God it's not me. What do you say to the person who never needs cheering up, never needs a supportive shoulder, never has a doubt? Especially when I agree with her that she *should* panic?

"You know you. You'll be fine," I say with an extra firm pat of her hand. "Don't really have a choice, now, right?" She looks up at me and sighs.

"Well, enough of this moaning and groaning." She pushes herself up from the table and picks up her dishes. "I have some work to do on the books. Reservations sure aren't good for the summer, are they? We might need to look into some advertising. I'll see what I can find out."

"Here, just sit your dishes in the sink, and I'll take care of them."

"You sure?" she asks. "Appreciate you bringing lunch. I have crackers and an apple in my purse, but this is so much better."

Busying myself with the dishes, I avoid looking in her direction until she's heading down the hallway. Her bright yellow dress looks cheerful, and her hair looks good even after a nap. She didn't even have big black smudges from her mascara. Hopefully, looking good will lift her spirits, because, God knows, her good friend Carolina didn't help.

Savannah comes back inside and sits her plate on the table.

"Seriously? You see me standing here loading the dishwasher and you set your plate over there?"

She picks it up and brings it to me. "Here."

"Put it in the dishwasher. I'm really sure you can do it."

I know she's rolling her eyes, but I don't care. She bends down to slide it into place and then drops her fork into the basket. "Where's Bryan? He posted on Facebook he's at the golf course?"

"Yeah, he's taking some golf lessons with Griffin up at Laurel Cove."

"Maybe I'll go over there and look around." She wanders to the refrigerator, suddenly interested in the collection of papers hanging behind the odd assortment of magnets on it. "This stuff is old."

"Well, throw it away if it's for something that's already happened. Why do you want to go up to Laurel Cove?"

"Mom, this coupon expired at the end of the year. *Last* year. This one, too."

"So, shoot me. You could've thrown it away at any time." I squeeze out the dishrag to wipe the table. "Have you ever been up to the clubhouse at Laurel Cove?" I ask. Yes-or-no questions work best with reluctant witnesses. At least that's what they say on *Law and Order*.

"Of course. With Aston." She's still reading things from the front of the refrigerator.

"What's Aston up to this summer?" The boy's mother is a big executive in Atlanta and his stepfather is Bill Weatherman, who used to be my favorite author. Like they say about making sausage—meeting the author and seeing his mind up close kind of ruined his books for me. Aston is a bit too spoiled for my taste, but at least he doesn't have his own apartment.

"I don't know. He's traveling with his sister. She's modeling."

"So why are you interested in Laurel Cove?" I know, it's not a yes-or-no, but I don't have all day.

She pauses, but makes small noises in her throat like she's

working the words out. As I wipe off the counters, again, she finally says, "Thought Alex might like it."

I don't look at her, matter of fact I'm facing away from her, looking down at the counter. A very *clean* counter, I might add. If you try to look a teenager in the eye when having a serious conversation, they run like a scared bunny. Or they turn on you like a mama grizzly bear. It's probably best to quietly back away from them, but, yeah, where's the fun in that? "Alex seems like a nice guy." See, start with an open palm and a bowed head, show that you mean no danger. "But, I'm not sure he's looking to get involved."

She keeps reading the refrigerator, but doesn't say anything.

"He's heading off to college in the fall, right?" Back to a yes/no question.

I've turned part ways around, still trying to be non-threatening. Just an innocent conversation.

Savannah shrugs. "Yeah." Then she flips around to face me. "Guess if he's only got a summer here, I should probably see if he wants to go up the Laurel Cove one day this week. He does like golf, and I've always wanted to learn to play." Then she's gone.

As she climbs the stairs, she yells, "Thanks for lunch, Mom."

And I'm left in the kitchen looking at a refrigerator still full of outdated coupons and flyers.

Chapter 15

"Really think it looks good on me." I giggle at what Jackson says back to me through the phone. "I'll let you get back to work. Just thought I'd give you a quick call." Sitting at the mall, surrounded by thick green plants, the smell of new things, an iced coffee on the table in front of me, I'm happy.

There, I said it. I'm happy.

Also, I bought a bathing suit. And I'm *still* happy.

When Savannah and Laney left the house and Bryan called to say he was spending the night up at Grant's, I decided to come down to the mall. To look for a bathing suit. Almost felt like I was drunk or something. Excited about trying on bathing suits? And you're figuring I'm going to now say something about having lost forty pounds, and I have no idea how it happened! Well, I'm not. I might've even gained a pound or two recently.

It's been so long since I've looked at bathing suits, I had no idea there were so many to choose from. And so many ways to make me look okay. No, look *good*. My new suit is dark red and drapes or something, lifts or something, tightens or something which adds up to me looking good. There's an adorable cover up with bright green leaves and dark red flowers that matches it and looks like a dress I would wear anywhere. Of course, I then got some sandals to match.

I know I said I looked good, but did I say I'm happy? And it's not just about the bathing suit. Jackson and I are giggling on the phone again. The traffic here where I used to drive all the time is crazy. The thought actually crossed my mind that I'm glad it's not like this at home. Home! Chancey is my home. Pulling my purse up over my shoulder and picking up my bags and iced coffee, there's a lightness in my chest. I'm guessing it's happiness, at least that's what I'm calling it.

That blue time of a summer day, when the sky just won't go dark, is my favorite time of day. As a kid these late days felt magic, like the dark never would take over. Especially if there was full, or near full moon, like there is tonight. As I left the mall area and suburban Atlanta behind me, the cars got fewer and fewer, the buildings, too. Leaving the interstate, I drove past the neon sign of Applebee's and the bright-lit parking lot of the big Wal-Mart shopping center. Not so long ago seeing those lights in my rearview mirror caused a bit of panic to rise in my chest. Driving into the darkness of the hills and the big trees, which seemed to suck me in, was claustrophobic. Now there's a comfort, a familiarity. With my window rolled down, the warm air flows in bringing the sound of bugs and the smell of honeysuckle, and it brings back my childhood.

Didn't realize I missed it.

Didn't realize it could bring tears to my eyes.

On the last curve into Chancey, my phone rings. Probably the kids looking for me. "Hello."

"Carolina, its Beau. Beau Bennett. You got a minute?" Beau Bennett runs a hair salon out by the state route. She's also Brittani with an I's aunt.

"Sure."

"Listen, this stuff with Bryan has to stop. We're friends, and, well, honestly, you don't want to have my sister, Angel, calling you. She gets a little out of control when it comes to her kids."

"What are you talking about? Bryan? My Bryan?"

"See, I didn't figure you knew. Angel and Momma keep saying that of course you know. But I didn't think so. Boys can be so sneaky, like men. Stalkers are almost exclusively men, you know."

"Stalkers?" I pull over into the high school parking lot and shove the car into park. "Beau, what's going on?"

"Bryan is harassing Brittani. He keeps calling her, following her around at the Lake Park, leaving notes in their mailbox. I understand first love and all that, but he's obsessed."

"She did dump him, you know? No, wait, she didn't even dump him. She just started going out with some high school jock."

"Oh, Carolina, of course that's what he says, but they've been broken up for weeks."

"But she was at our house playing video games with him just last weekend. They were alone in the basement."

"Well, see, you've given them too much leeway. Guys become obsessed when they're allowed to get physical."

Happy feelings are leaking out of me like a sieve. "Me? Her mother practically had them married. You and her both talked about them being family. I kept a close eye on them in the basement. Besides, watching her at the lake on the blanket with her new boyfriend, it's easy to see who wants to get 'physical.'"

"Oh? So now you're stalking her, too? Getting off on watching her and her boyfriend since you and Jackson have been on the outs?"

"Are you serious? Jackson and I are fine. And that's gross,

just gross. You tell Brittani to leave my son alone. She's the skank, everyone knows it."

I can hear the anger boiling on the other end. "You did not just call my sweet niece a skank. Now I see where Bryan gets his crazy streak. Tell him to leave us alone and go stalk someone else!"

She hangs up before I can say another word. How did our call blow up like that? After a couple of deep breaths, I put the car in drive and pull through the parking area to the stop sign. Pulling out, I head up the hill toward home.

Wow, I sure hope Bryan *hasn't* been stalking Brittani. I mean, sure, it would make me look bad after what I said to Beau. I don't think he'd do that, but, honestly first rule of parenting should be, *Never put it past your kid to completely and totally screw things up.*

Susan's car is in the driveway when I get home. It's too dark for her to be out in the garden. She does often wait for the sun to go behind the mountain to come get some weeding and harvesting done. As I park, I realize she's sitting on the front porch.

"Hi," I call as I get out of the car.

She hollers "hi" back at me. She's slowly rocking and says as I get closer, "What a beautiful night. Came down to do a little weeding and was just sitting here watching the moon come up. Where've you been?"

"Don't be shocked. I went to the mall. Bought a bathing suit, believe it or not." I sit down in the rocking chair beside hers. "The boys still up at your house?"

"Yeah. Griffin finally got home, and they were all in the pool."

"Your mom said he's working a lot more with the new job," I say as I rock my chair into motion.

She sighs. "I'm beginning to think I took it for granted when he was around so much. Didn't think about him being gone such long hours, when I took on *my* new job at the same time."

"How are y'all liking everything? The jobs, the house, living in Laurel Cove?"

"Feels like someone else's life. Now Grant is talking about going to Darien Academy."

My shock is evident in how squeaky my voice gets. "You'd take him out of Chancey High? But you and Griffin both went to Chancey High."

She shrugs. "Think he just wants to fit in with the other kids in Laurel Cove. I need to have Bryan up more often."

"And Grant is welcome here any time. I'd really hate for him and Bryan to not be in school together."

"Me too. And I can't see it happening. I'm sure it's just a phase," she says as she stands up. "I left you some squash and tomatoes on the back deck. Gertie was out there and said she'd take them in." She walks down the steps, then turns back. I can barely make her out in the dark. "Gertie's right pleased with how Andy's place turned out."

"Yeah, that's what folks in town said. And I guess it kind of grew on me throughout the day," I admit.

Her voice coming from the darkness, Susan adds, "Hard to believe, but living in a place like Laurel Cove where the lamp posts have to appear to be made from sapling trees and the signs can only be dirt- brown or forest ranger green, a little neon orange and purple is a welcome sight." She sighs again.

I say, "True." Then add, "Laurel Cove will start feeling more like home soon, I'm sure."

She only answers with another sigh before turning to walk to her car.

Just as she opens her door and the interior light shines out, I stand up and yell, "Hey."

Susan stops and looks at me. "Hey what?"

As I yell to her, my accent gets thicker. "Guess you can educate us, sell us subscriptions to *Southern Living*, hook us on watching *Downton Abbey* on PBS, and shame us into not putting ice in our wine, but all in all—we're just a couple big ol' hillbillies that can't resist a place slicked up with shiny purple paint selling junk. We can appreciate Biltmore Gardens, but we're Rock City at heart!"

"You goofball!" she yells back at me and then bursts out laughing. Her parting shot she says out her car window before she backs out. "Wait'll Laurel Cove finds out they've let the Clampetts move in!"

CHAPTER 16

"Hey, it's Carolina. I forgot to ask you something last night. Call me when you get a chance." I click the red button on my phone to disconnect from Susan's voicemail. Completely forgot to ask her about Bryan possibly stalking Brittani. Maybe I can see if Grant has said anything. Tucking my phone into the pocket of my shorts, I step to the front window and open the curtains. Another sunny summer morning. Only three more days in the month of June. Summer just goes so fast. I have to pay attention or the kids will be back in school before I know it.

Savannah comes in the back door just as I enter the kitchen from the living room. "Good morning. You going in to work early today?"

She nods as she pours coffee into the cup she carried in from the back deck. "I'm helping Alex figure out the menu and then taking him up to the driving range at the golf course in Laurel Cove." She squats down to look at the cereal boxes in the lower cabinet. "We don't have any good cereal."

"That's because you quit eating it. I had to throw out two boxes that you opened and let get stale."

"You didn't tell me it was here. I can't look all the time." She pulls out a box of Cheerios and sets it on the table.

I'm not answering her accusation. She's happy, chipper

even, and I'm not messing with that. "I'll get the bowls. Grab me a spoon, please." I sit the bowls on the table, across from each other, and she brings the milk along with the spoons.

When she sits down, I ask, "So how do you think Bryan is handling his break up with Brittani?"

She shrugs one tanned shoulder at me as she spoons sugar on her cereal. "Okay, I guess. Why?"

I pour milk into my bowl. "I heard he might not be over her. May be kind of chasing her. Calling her, leaving notes for her. That kind of thing."

She shudders. "Oh god, I hope not. It was bad enough he dated her. But to stalk her, too?" She puts a spoonful of cereal in her mouth, but talks anyway. "She's a skank. Those are the kinds guys have trouble getting over, you know."

"Don't talk with your mouth full. And don't say 'god.'"

She holds a hand up as she exaggerates chewing and then swallowing. "Where does he leave notes for her now that school's out?"

"Yeah, exactly. He can't drive. Beau said he left notes in their mailbox. You haven't taken him by there?" I lift up a spoonful of cereal, but look at her.

She stares at me, then rolls her eyes. "So you think Miss Beau is lying?"

"No, that doesn't make sense does it? But if it's not Bryan, who could it be?"

She shrugs again, and while she reads the back of the box she starts smiling.

We eat in silence, then I realize she's humming. "So you really like Alex?"

That causes her head to lift and her eyebrows to straighten. "Why?"

"The smiling, the humming. You've not been very fun to live with lately."

"Whatever." She goes back to eating, but then lifting her

bowl with only milk left in it, she adds, "He does make me happy." She tilts the bowl to her mouth and drains it. Then stands up and puts the bowl in the sink.

"I saw how you made him happy yesterday. In the back room at the bistro? He was wearing most of your lipstick."

She grins and cocks a hip at me. "Just marking my territory. Lipstick is awfully hard to get off, you know. I've got to get ready for work." She darts out of the kitchen, humming louder now. Well, that's one out of three kids that is happier. Thirty-three percent success rate is about all a mother can hope for. Now, if I can just get Bryan more interested in golf than Brittani.

Sure, golf is expensive. But so is stalking.

Savannah is back downstairs and getting ready to leave for work when the doorbell rings. She opens the door, as I step into the living room from the kitchen and hear, "I'm Zoe. I'm supposed to meet Miss Laney here."

"Oh, hi Zoe," I say. "This is my daughter Savannah. Zoe's family bought Susan's old house."

Savannah waves and nods. "Oh, yeah. Don't you have a bunch of little brothers and sisters?"

"Yep. Well, only three. They're all half-siblings. Miss Kimmy's not my mom."

I lean against the back of the couch and inquire, "But she's your teacher for home school? Or does your mom do that?" Maybe she's just with her dad for the summer.

Zoe laughs and comes on in the door. "Not hardly. I pretty much teach myself. Mom and Kimmy don't like books or school, but they do like having me around to take care of things. So…" She shrugs and sets her backpack down. She looks around the room. "This is nice. I'd stay here. I mean, the bed and breakfast thing." Then she turns toward the door, where Savannah still stands. "Savannah, isn't this your senior year? Where are you going for college?"

My daughter licks her bottom lip before answering. "I'm not sure yet." Her eyes flick on mine, and we share a look of... confusion, maybe? Zoe talks like an adult. Her words, actions, and body are all solid. I've often read in novels the description of someone having "nut-brown skin," and here it is. She's only a seventh grader, but she seems to have more weight than a lot of adults I know. Not physical weight, but weight like she's really here. Solid.

Savannah rattles her keys and says, "Gotta go to work. Nice to meet you, Zoe."

Zoe smiles and says, "Nice to meet you, too. Have a good day at work."

As the screen door falls shut behind Savannah, I turn to Zoe. "So, you're meeting Laney here?"

"Yes, ma'am. Oh, looks like that's her pulling in now," she says, looking out the front door. "She's pregnant, right? Not just a large lady? Although she's a bit old to be pregnant, isn't she?"

"Yes, she's pregnant. It was a surprise." I suck on my teeth to keep a smile from breaking out. Laney is used to being the straight talking one of the bunch. Zoe might give her a run for her money.

I hold open the door and say, "Hey. Zoe's here."

Laney stomps up the steps. "Don't 'hey' me. I'm purr-tee mad." She brushes past me, well, as much as a 'large lady' in a bright purple maternity dress can brush past someone.

"Goodness, Miss Laney! What's got your panties in a wad? You come sit down." Zoe has lifted a pillow off the couch and is directing Laney to where it used to lay. "You sit right there and let me get you a glass of ice water. Here's a pillow for you to rest your neck on. There's no need for you to get all upset. Not in your delicate condition."

Zoe looks at me as she heads to the kitchen, purses her lips, and shakes her head. I go to sit in the chair near Laney. "Yeah, so what's got your panties in a wad?"

"It's not funny, Carolina." Then she lowers her voice. "And did Zoe talk this grown-up when we met her? Has she ever even been in your kitchen?"

"Got me," I say. "It is kind of odd. But whatever. What's wrong?"

"That doctor got my numbers back from the lab, and he wants me on bed rest until the baby comes. Bed rest! Have you ever heard anything so ridiculous? I can't be on bed rest."

"If it's for the baby you can. It's not like it's forever. And so what in the world are you doing here?" I ask.

"Here's your water, Miss Laney." She sets it on the end table beside Laney and then sits on the other end of the couch. "Doctor must've decided your blood pressure is too high. You have to take care of your little one. A boy, I hear."

Laney scowls and drawls, "You hear a lot seems to me."

"Yes, ma'am, I do. I listen."

I reach out and touch Laney's knee. "What does he mean exactly by bed rest?"

She takes a drink of her water, sits the glass back down, and then sighs. "Well, he said if I don't start getting off my feet, he's going to put me on bed rest."

I tilt my head. "Wait, so just rest more. He didn't actually put you on bed rest?"

"Not yet. But, we all know I can't just start resting. It's Fourth of July weekend. And the girls have to do their school shopping. We always go down to Atlanta for shopping. And we've not taken our vacation. This just isn't going to work for me. And I'm as big as a whale. This was not a good idea for me to be pregnant. Just not a good idea, at all." Her voice cracks, and she closes her eyes and lays her head back on the pillow at her neck.

Zoe and I meet eyes again, and I see an old soul looking

at me. We nod at each other, and I say, "Laney, honey, we're going to help you. Isn't that what you asked Zoe here for in the first place?"

The girl agrees. "I'll help any way I can."

Laney's head lifts. "Oh, I'll pay you. I'll pay you good. You're just so soothing. And, well, sugar, you seem so much older than you are. How old are you?"

"Twelve, but I like taking care of things and helping people out. God put lots of folks around me that need help, like my mom and Miss Kimmy and the little kids, so that I'd get lots of practice helping. I've never been paid for it, but sounds like a natural development, don't you think? After all, I want to be a nurse when I grow up."

"A nurse? Then it's like I'm helping your career path." Laney is already breathing slower, and her cheeks aren't as red.

I hate to throw cold water on this, but I speak up. "But won't Kimmy miss you helping with the kids?"

"Probably. But Daddy told her she had to get off her tail and take care of them. He's been after me to get a job, and now I've found one. Daddy says we all have to pull our own weight. However, I will need a ride out to your house. Found out you live outside of town a ways?"

"You sure seem to have found out a lot to have only been here a few days," Laney says again.

"I listen. And when I want to know something, I ask."

I stand up and say, "I'm sure between the girls all driving, Savannah included, we can work out getting you out to Laney's." I turn to face my friend. "Are you thinking you need her now, or is this for after the baby comes?"

"I'm thinking now. Shaw and my girls are almost worthless around the house. Zoe, you can start as soon as you want."

Inwardly, I roll my eyes at the thought of Shaw and the twins being "worthless," it's more like they quit trying years ago to please the queen. Laney always thinks her way is the only way, unless her mama's way is involved. And then her mama's way should be at least considered, out of respect. Shaw and the girls know they can't do things the way she does, so they don't do anything. However, this pregnancy and Zoe might be Laney's time for reckoning. As they say, her "come to Jesus meeting."

Zoe stands up and then reaches down to shake Laney's hand. "Thank you much, Miss Laney. I'll work real hard and do whatever you need. I need to get home, now, though. Me and Kimmy are taking the kids to the Lake Park today. You let me know when you want me." At the front door, she looks back and grins. "This is exciting, isn't it?"

We say "bye" and after we hear her run across the porch and down the steps, Laney laughs and says. "Is it just me, or does she just make you feel better?"

I look out the window and see the girl running across the railroad tracks. As she turns to look down the tracks, her face is in full view. Joy. That's what she exudes. Joy.

Hmm, didn't realize it was so rare.

Chapter 17

I know nothing about country clubs. I know nothing about golf. Shouldn't there be an age where you become comfortable being uncomfortable? When I was younger, I thought adults knew how to handle themselves. So… when does that happen?

Last week when I came here for lunch with Susan and her friends, I thought that was it. I'd gone in and had lunch and not embarrassed myself. Now I see that was a cakewalk. The dining room has a separate entrance with a striped canopy where Susan was waiting to show me where we were going to have lunch. Now I'm supposed to pick Bryan up somewhere at the club, and I'm lost.

First of all, there are lots of men on this side of the club. Men who look important, busy, focused. There are signs pointing to things and places, but I don't see any signs saying, "Parent pick-up" or even better, "Carolina, go this way." I've called Bryan's cell phone, but it went straight to voicemail.

I pull up to the stop sign and circle back into the parking lot. Back at the entrance, I turn right and pull up next to the dining room doors with the green striped canopy. Maybe a waitress or the hostess can tell me where I need to go. I'm not even thinking about how much I'd rather talk to a waitress than a man driving a golf cart in a pair of salmon-colored pants with little white turtles on them.

The quiet of the afternoon here on top of the mountain is so pleasant after being in town all day. The grass, golf club green, is inlaid upon a backdrop of dark gray mountains. The white of the fences and trim on the river stone buildings stands out like it's glow-in-the-dark paint when the sunshine breaks through the scattered clouds. There's a steady breeze, and that's the only sound.

Between getting ready for the Fourth of July festivities and Gertie's contractors at Andy's place, things were noisy downtown. Even inside the bookstore, things were noisy as Gertie's hired a crew to move Andy's junk out. Hunched over the laptop Gertie provided us, I stayed out of the way of the movers and entered all the book titles for a solid three hours. The movers' voices and banging of the junk became a dull background noise. But it was still noise.

Pulling open the door to the dining room, there is suddenly noise. Loud noise. Familiar noise which I look farther inside to find. Oh no.

Savannah stands near the door, against a table, and she's yelling. This is not normal. She's always the cool one. The one who doesn't care. Has "whatever" on a loop. As I step closer to the booth, I see who is causing this loss of cool—Susie Mae. And Alex. Susie Mae is sitting on Alex's lap. Worst of all? Susie Mae and Alex have an overabundance of cool. They are looking at Savannah how she usually looks at, well, me.

"Hey, y'all," I say as I step up and put my hand on my daughter's arm.

Savannah whirls at me, follows my eyes back down to the occupants of the table, then leaves. I wave at Alex and Susie Mae, as I follow her back outside.

"Honey, what's going on?"

"She is such a tramp. Alex was coming up here with me, but he came up earlier as I had to work. I have that whole work schedule thing, and he just comes and goes at the bistro whenever he wants. He was supposed to be up here putting, or golfing, or whatever, but you see what he's doing. She's such a sneak! I've had it with her innocent act." She grits her teeth and looks around. Her arms are folded and pressed against her chest. She tosses her head and stares at the door we just came through.

She snorts. "Where is he? He should've followed me out of there." She wills the door to open and for Alex to dash out and beg her forgiveness. But that doesn't happen. Honestly? Alex doesn't strike me as the begging sort.

"Honey," I begin. "I don't think he sees you and him as a real couple. I don't think he wants to be a part of a couple."

"Mom. You don't understand." She dismisses me with a wave of a hand, a roll of her eyes, and by turning her back on me as she pulls open the big wooden door. It slowly closes behind her, and I have plenty of time to follow her inside. However...

Really? Do I really have to explain why I turn in the other direction? I'll play twenty questions with a dozen men wearing a full 64-crayon assortment of colored pants and short-sleeved shirts than go back in that place.

Around the corner, I see there's no need to ask anyone anything. Bryan is sitting on a bench with Grant. They both have cans of Coke and are eating orange cracker sandwiches from little packs.

They see me, collect their stuff, and meet me at the end of the patio where the benches are.

"Want a cracker?" Bryan asks.

"Sure," I say. Both boys are sweaty and red-faced. "Looks like y'all got some sunburn today. How was the golf lesson?"

Bryan answers, orange crumbs flying from his mouth as he talks. "Okay. I'm not any good, but Grant is. Can you take us to the lake?"

"I guess. Is that okay with your folks, Grant?"

He shrugs. "Yeah. Dad's probably working late again, and Mom's at the Lake Park already."

"What about Susie Mae? I saw her in the dining room here."

Of course, I'm stupidly trying to get information out of middle school boys. I'm reminded of that fact when they both just shrug. As they are getting in the van, Savannah's car pulls out of the parking lot, and she heads down the mountain back towards Chancey. I stall leaving when I see Alex and Susie Mae leave the dining room and get in a car I don't recognize. Alex gets in the driver's seat, and when they pull out of the parking lot, they don't head down the mountain. They turn in the opposite direction. The direction of Susie Mae's house. Her empty house.

"Grant?" I get the attention of his reflection in the rearview mirror. "Do you have your swimming suit?"

Bryan answers. "He's just going to wear one of mine."

"I'm not sure you have a clean one. Maybe we should run by your house and get yours, Grant. I've never seen your new house."

Grant nods. "Okay. I can get my goggles, too."

I don't see if he nods again. I'm backing out of my parking space. Don't want to give Susie Mae and Alex enough time to actually get anything started before we interrupt.

Now what do I do? Grant has his bathing suit. His towel. His goggles. I've been given a tour of the house by an increasingly angry Susie Mae. Alex has the big screen TV on and is comfortable on the huge leather couch. He's got nowhere to go and all day to get there. Bryan has actually honked the horn at me, which should make me dash out of this elaborate glass and metal front door – which stands in front of an eight-foot-tall wooden door with more glass insets – and snatch my youngest child baldheaded. But I act like I don't hear the horn.

Susie Mae was embarrassed when we pulled up. She fell all over herself helping Grant get his things and was graciousness itself as she showed me the living room area. The anger built as I pushed to see "everything." Alex, completely cool, settled in like he owns the place. A good Southern boy, whose mama I could report to, would've excused himself and hightailed it down the mountain. However, Alex is perfectly fine waiting me out.

After all, how long can I pretend to ignore the honking?

Susie Mae slowly, deliberately (apparently she's forgotten I *do* know *her* mama), squeezes me out the front door. As I storm to the car, I glare at my son who is no longer even looking towards the house and me, he's just laughing with Grant and signaling Morse code with the horn.

"Stop that! Right now!" I yell, opening the van door.

His hand slides off the steering wheel. "You were taking forever. It's hot out here."

Starting the car, I also pull my phone out of my purse and dial Laney. When she answers, I step back out onto the slate driveway as Bryan exclaims, "Mom!"

I turn toward him and say, "Don't you dare touch that horn." Then say into the phone, "Hey, I'm up at Susan's."

"Oh my gosh, you're seeing it before I get to see it? How is that fair? You didn't think of including me in on the invite?"

"Wait! Listen to me. Susan's not here," I explain.

"Great idea. She won't invite us, we'll just show up and look around. I mean, she never locks her doors. I'll be right there."

"No! Listen to me. Susan's not here, but Susie Mae and Alex are. Alone. Well, they'll be alone once I leave with the boys."

She hardly even pauses, Laney always gets exactly what's

going on. Makes life so much easier when I don't have to explain things. "But isn't he supposed to be Savannah's beau?"

"Well, as much as another person can belong to another, I mean, I guess. Kind of. But that's not really the problem. It's that..."

"Oh, I know what the problem is. You take me to my niece right this minute."

I hold up a finger to the boys in the car and ignore their exaggerated looks of betrayal, then turn back to the house. Susie Mae has opened both big doors before I get there and meets me on the porch.

"You called my mother! Oh my gosh. I'm allowed to have friends over. I'm not a baby!"

I hand her the phone, and she begins to argue until she realizes it's her Aunt Laney. Her smugness drains away, and she only listens for a moment before handing me back the phone. Before I can say anything to Laney, Susie Mae has leaned back inside the house and is talking to Alex.

Lifting the phone to my ear, I hear, "It's handled. Now, tell me about the house."

"What did you say to her?"

"Doesn't matter. If Susan had told me a long time ago that Susie Mae was boy crazy, I could've helped then, too. Just takes one to know one. Now, the house?"

"Can't now. I'm taking the boys to the Lake Park. Thanks. I just wasn't sure what to do."

"Of course not. You think like a good girl. That's not really helpful in these types of situations. Call me later."

Maybe Laney should get one of those car magnets: "1-800-BAD-GIRL – When your daughter turns into a skank, we know what to do!"

CHAPTER 18

"We were coming down the mountain and there was an ambulance with lights flashing at Miss LaVada's house. You know, that little white cinderblock place with the amazing rose bushes?" I say all this while handing Susan the things the boys forgot as they jumped out of my van and ran straight for the lake.

Susan asks, "How do you know LaVada Webster?"

"I stopped one day to look at the roses, and she came out. Sweet lady. Didn't know her last name is Webster. Anyway, she had some kind of seizure, and they're taking her to the hospital and she was alone. Thought I'd go until her granddaughter can get there. Does she have other family around here?"

Susan shakes her head. "No, their son moved out west somewhere. Boys are fine here with me." She looks down at the towel in her hand. "That was nice of you to go by the house and get Grant's things. I figured he'd just wear one of Bryan's suits."

"Well, I, uh…" With the excitement of the ambulance, I hadn't had time to decide if I'd tell on Susie Mae. Kind of thought I'd let Laney do it.

Susan holds out a hand to stop my stammering. "Look, I know. I should've had you up to the house before now. Only myself to blame that everyone is curious." She shrugs. "Heck, I'da been curious, too."

Her face has gone from flushed, to splotchy, to hot-looking. Oh, wow. She's embarrassed. "No, Susan. It wasn't that—" However, before I can explain, she waves me on.

"Go on to the hospital. It's all good here. Thanks for bringing the boys!" She says all this as she turns and fast-walks into the pavilion.

Back in the van, without the boys and their noise, the tour of the house comes back to me. During the tour, I was so preoccupied with Susie Mae's situation—and the horn-honking—I wasn't paying attention. But now... Oh. My. Word.

The house was nothing like what I expected. I was picturing the big houses in Marietta where we used to live. The suburbs northeast of Atlanta are full of upper middle class people who have houses that show it. That's what I expected, but Susan and Griffin's house is way beyond even those. It was maybe the biggest house I've ever been in. And not only was there a pool, but a pool cottage. And a full outdoor kitchen. Wait.

What exactly is Griffin *doing* for the power company?

Having never been to the area hospital, I'm very surprised. Very pleasantly surprised. Our little hospital is so easy to maneuver. My first shock was parking right beside the emergency room – there's just a parking lot. With lots of empty spaces. I never spent much time in Atlanta-area hospitals, but I do know you pay to park in huge concrete parking garages and then you walk and walk and walk. Just to get to the outside doors. Then inside, walk and walk and walk, mostly because you're lost. They do things like paint the floor different colors for different departments, but, uh, seems like red would be cardiac, not green? And blue makes me think of baby boys, but not baby girls so that can't take me to the maternity ward, right?

So, surprised but happy, I park right near the ER entrance. And there's no meter or parking attendant, I guess that means parking is *free*? Really? I walk in, and there's a sweet lady in a pink sweater sitting at a little desk. Before I can tell her why I'm there, she asks. And calls me "honey."

"Honey, what can I do for you today?"

"My friend was just brought in, Mrs. Webster. I just wanted to see—"

The little gray-haired lady jumps up and waves me past the desk. "Oh, yes, we have Mrs. Webster in Exam Room 3. Let me take you right back there."

"But I don't need to actually go back there right this..." However, I'm following the pink sweater down the short corridor. She stops and knocks on the wall beside a beige curtain.

"Mrs. Webster? I have a friend of yours here. Oops, I didn't get your name, honey," she says as she turns to me.

"Carolina Jessup." She's pulled back the curtain, and I can see LaVada. "Hi, Miss LaVada."

"Oh, it's you. I thought I saw you when they were getting me in the ambulance. But then I thought if I was having a stroke I mighta imagined that! Come in. Come in."

Holding back the curtain for me to pass, the hospital volunteer (I see that on her nametag now), pats my arm and whispers, "I'll bring the sign-in sheet back for you to sign in. Supposed to do that when you first come in, but it'll be okay this time."

"Okay. Thanks, I'll remember next time."

She grins and squeezes my arm. "Thanks, honey."

In the bed, LaVada beams at me. "You are just the sweetest thing ever! Coming all the way here to check on me."

"Well, I wasn't sure when your granddaughter would be

able to get here." While I'm saying that, she directs me to the chair beside her bed.

"Sit there. Yes, my granddaughter was in class, and I wasn't going to give them her phone number until class was over, but apparently she's put it on all my emergency forms. Sweet girl. This is nice, now we can visit."

"How are you feeling? Have you seen the doctor?"

"It was just a spell. Got lightheaded and fell. Happens when my roses are in bloom." She sighs and rolls her eyes. "But tell me about you. What are you up to today?"

"Wait, why when your roses are in bloom?" I'm thinking maybe I need to get a doctor or nurse in here. She's not making sense, and isn't that a sign of a stroke? There's that tongue rolling thing, but… yeah, I don't remember what I'm supposed to look for with the whole tongue thing either.

"When the roses are blooming, I forget stuff. I get busy cutting them, finding enough containers to put them in, changing the water in the vases, and just sitting out there with them." Her cheeks turn pink, and she looks down at her hands, crossed on the white hospital sheet.

"You forget what kind of stuff?"

"Oh, eating. I had some tea and crackers last night, but this morning I forgot to eat anything. Just had my cup of tea, and I had the real stuff, not that decaf tea." She whispers the part about the tea. "Don't tell anyone, but I hide the real stuff."

At a knock on the wall outside the curtain, she says, "Come in," and a white-coated doctor pushes the curtain to the side and steps in.

"Like we thought, Mrs. Webster." It's an older doctor, and I'm surprised to see him in the ER. I usually think of young doctors manning the emergency room. He's portly and has lots of curly gray hair. His head is big, which fits his big nose, on which a pair of thick, black-rimmed glasses sits. When he takes LaVada's hand in his, it looks like Cinderella's tiny slipper resting on the prince's soft, overstuffed pillow.

She looks up at him and flushes, "Oh, Dr. Barsetti. You're so good to come check on me."

"Of course. When they call and say my favorite patient is heading this way, I jump right up, cancel all the appointments, and get here as fast as I can."

She points at me. "And look, this is my friend, Carolina. Isn't she pretty?"

He turns to shake my hand and grins at me. "Very pretty, indeed." He turns back toward the bed. "Where's Rose?"

"Here's Rose!" says a voice just outside the curtain. A tall, thin young woman steps into the cubicle and then around to the bed. "Nana. Did you do it again? I left you out bread for toast, and there are boiled eggs in the refrigerator. You can't forget to eat."

"Your blood sugar bottomed out again," the doctor says.

"Why do they have to bring me all the way to the hospital? I feel fine once they give me that stuff in the bag. I hate to bother everyone."

Rose leans over the bed and hugs her grandmother. "They know what they're doing. And if you hate to bother everyone, you're going to just have to remember to eat. But I'm so glad you're fine." Rose turns to the doctor. "She is fine, right? Can I take her home?"

He nods. "Yes, in just a bit. Everything looks good. Now, I have to get back across the street to my other patients." He reaches in and grabs LaVada's hand. "Eat! The roses will wait." He then gives a shoulder hug to the young woman, Rose. As he backs out, he stops in front of my chair. "And nice to meet you. Carolina, right?"

I push to get up out of the low seat and take his offered hand. "Yes. And nice to meet you, too."

He steps out with a wave of his paw of a hand, and the curtain swings behind him.

"Oh, I'm sorry. I didn't see you there," Rose says with a move in my direction and an extended hand.

"Sweetie, this is my friend Carolina. She stopped to see my roses. And now you get to meet my favorite Rose of all."

We shake hands, and I explain. "I was coming past your grandmother's house, and I saw the ambulance, so I pulled in to check on her."

Rose is tall and thin with smooth, long brown hair. She is covered with freckles, which stand out against her pale skin. "Thanks for checking on her, but she's good now."

Her voice carried warmth a minute earlier, but that is now gone. She's not exactly cold, but she's not gushing like most Southerners would be to someone concerned about their grandma. I didn't come here to be lauded as some kind of saint, but this is so off, I start stammering.

"Just wanted to make sure and find out what, you know, was going on? I mean, I don't need to know what's really going on, but how she was, or is. But it's all good now." Luckily, the pink sweater lady shows back up, darting inside the curtain and shoving a clipboard at me.

"Here. You came in at 3:40. Sign fast."

I scribble my name, and she's gone just as fast as she appeared.

Everything's good here, so I'm going to head home," I say as I lean around Rose to wave at her grandmother. LaVada rolls her eyes at her granddaughter's back.

"Ignore Rose. You're welcome to stay. Rose, be polite."

"No, I really ought to go. Glad you're doing well." I reach out to shake Rose's hand again. "Nice to meet you."

"You, too," she says. Taking a couple steps she encourages me right through the curtain, then she pulls it shut.

"Well, that was weird," I say as I head back to the doors

leading to the waiting room. "If I'd had to pay to park for that, I'd have wanted my money back."

In the car, I roll the windows down and turn the air on high. Even though I hadn't signed in, I had turned my phone off when I entered the hospital as per the sign on the door. As it chimes that it's come back on, I see that Laney has called. So, I call her back.

"Hey, I see you called?"

"Yep, just wanted to give you a heads up that we are booked solid for this weekend. Think we're going to need to come up with increased holiday rates and maybe add on some rooms."

"We are not adding on rooms. What's gotten into you?"

"North Georgia Mountains are a hot commodity now. I joined a Facebook page about what to do in the mountains this summer, and the interest in Crossings is off the chart. I'm putting up our own Facebook page tonight when the girls are home to help me."

"Aren't you supposed to be resting?"

"Zoe is a godsend! She's got supper cooking, she's unwrapped everything for the nursery, and is going to paint it tomorrow."

"Do not overwork the girl. She's only twelve."

Laney *pshaws* me. "Whatever. She's happy here. So, now, Susan's house?"

"Oh, well, it's amazing. More amazing than I imagined. Are you going to tell her about Susie Mae having Alex up there?"

"I don't know. See what I feel like when I see her. Back to the house, what's so amazing?"

I rev the car engine. "Listen, I've got to go. Talk to you later." I hang up because if I try and explain I don't like being on the phone while I'm driving, she'll laugh and argue with me and tell me to get that earpiece thingy. But honestly, I need *some* time not talking and seems like driving is the only time I get it.

And my phone rings. At the stop sign at the edge of the parking area, I look at it, and then answer my daughter's call. "Hey there."

"Mom, that stalking thing? It *is* Bryan. I'm going to kill him. You've got to stop this."

"But how did he get the notes over to her house? I thought we decided it couldn't be him."

"He pulls that innocent little boy crap and gets rides helping him deliver his stupid love letters. He's an embarrassment. I'm going to kill him."

"Okay, I'm going to the park to get him, and I'll straighten it out. How did you find out?"

"I mentioned it to Jenna and Angie, and they said they'd both given him rides out there. They thought it was cute."

"I'll be home soon. Are you home?" There's a special kind of silence on the phone when a person doesn't want to tell you something. "Are you at Alex's?"

"For just a minute. He wanted to show me something. Geez, Mom, don't be so suspicious."

"Ask him how he liked Susie Mae's house, after all he was there this afternoon alone with her."

This silence is the kind you get when someone is thinking.

"Gotta go," she says and hangs up.

This thinking like a skank has possibilities. Wonder if Laney's put up a Facebook page for that yet?

Chapter 19

July Fourth is on Sunday, and today is Wednesday. I am still not sure what we are doing.

Here's where you act surprised that the Jessup family has no traditions surrounding yet another holiday. We always managed to find something to do in the past, but I never really *planned* anything.

If my mom and dad were camping in the area, we'd go see them and do whatever fun things they came up with, eat whatever food they cooked, watch fireworks wherever their campground suggested.

If Jackson's parents were visiting, Etta would make some grand old-fashioned meal and we'd eat until we were stuffed. Hank carries a full firework arsenal with him (doesn't have to be July), so we'd let him put on a show for all of us. Not exactly legal, but Hank is a little fuzzy on fireworks law.

If we were alone, then one by one the kids would end up at some friend's lake house or pool, and Jackson and I would hang out and do chores around the house until it was time to decide on going to see fireworks. Then we'd decide it was too much trouble, and we'd get takeout or make a frozen pizza. Jackson might've grilled, but that would mean me having something on hand to grill.

Honestly, I never imagined folks had Fourth of July traditions. But here in Chancey? It's a thing. A real big thing. There's a parade mid-morning and then a softball tournament in the afternoon. In the park next to the softball fields, there are kids' games with sandwiches and homemade ice cream. There's a run/walk out at a big church near the highway. That's done really early in the morning, I think I heard. Everyone ends up at the lake towards Laurel Cove for a picnic dinner and fireworks. Of course, with the actual holiday being on Sunday, all the special events are on Saturday the third.

So, when I say I'm not sure what we're doing, that's not really true. Of course, we're doing everything on this schedule of events. I've been told that we'll be doing all this *several* times. Matter of fact, every time I say I'm not sure what we'll be doing, I'm given this exact rundown. And looks of incredulity that I have any doubts.

Looking at the paper I'm holding in my hand, I realize I apparently expressed my doubts one too many times. Missus is seated on the edge of my couch before I've even had any coffee. She's dressed in a red short-sleeved blouse and trim white slacks. Her shoes are low-heeled navy pumps. I have on shorts, a T-shirt, and no bra. So, I'm having to do that whole bit of holding my arms close to my chest and not moving too much.

"So, Carolina, you can see there, I've laid it all out. Jackson will give out ribbons at the race. These are those ridiculous participation ribbons for every living soul who manages to put one foot in front of the other for the whole two miles. As ridiculous as they are, it was the cheapest thing to sponsor and get Crossings on the sponsorship list. You and the kids will be running or walking and there"—she leans up and points at the paper—"I have which groups you will be in." Missus stabs again at the paper. "You'll also see the times you need to show up."

"Six-thirty? I need to be out there at the church at 6:30 a.m.? Why are you even involved in this? That's not your church."

"July Fourth does not belong to any one denomination or group. We all share in the responsibility to make this a memorable town event. I am on the committee, and we work at all events."

I screw up my mouth and mumble out the side of it, "Or find suckers to work for you."

She shrugs at my comment. "That's not attractive. True, but not attractive. Then after the race, the parade will be downtown, and Gertie says you're doing an open house for the book store. So you'll be there from nine until noon."

"Wait, Gertie and you are working out *my* schedule?"

She takes a deep breath through her nose. "When would you like to hold your open house? Is there another time you can think of when downtown will be full of people? Are the hours not to your liking? We thought a half-hour before the parade begins and then the hour or so afterwards. When would you prefer, my lady?"

Then she wrinkles up her face just before she takes the paper from my hands and studies it. "Although the softball games do begin at one. It works unless the organizers assign you a kids' game, which requires much set up. So, do not let them do that. Ring toss or pick-a-duck would both be good for you." She hands me my schedule back and tilts her head. "For goodness' sakes, do not let them saddle you with the cakewalk or face-painting."

"Where do they get the sandwiches and homemade ice cream?" I ask.

She points. "That's on the back. You need to bring two dozen peanut butter and grape jelly sandwiches on white bread cut in four pieces, diagonal. The ice cream is done by the senior citizens council. The older folks love competing over their family ice cream recipes. Plus, they're good to sit in the shade and visit."

"Of course. I'm making sandwiches."

"Do not be petty. *Everyone* makes sandwiches. Even *I* make peanut butter and jelly sandwiches for the Fourth of July. It's what we do." She stands up and heads to the front door.

I stand and follow her, my arms crossed in front of me, with the piece of paper held strategically in front of where my arms cross. I ask, "Then there are fireworks and dinner out near Laurel Cove?"

"Yes. Near the clubhouse there's a lake, and they allow everyone to set up on that part of the golf course to eat and wait for fireworks. You can park at the clubhouse or along the road. Laurel Cove began the fireworks and dinner to create goodwill with the town when they were first developing the community. Now, it's a tradition." She reaches for the door knob and sighs. "However, it feels much too much like the masters of the manor allowing the peasants to come up to the castle for a free show." She raises an eyebrow at me and adds, "But have you ever seen how expensive a fireworks show is? We'd all rather bow and scrape for the rich folks and their benevolence than pay for our own. Plus, it is a really pretty venue."

"And if they pay for the fireworks *and* dinner? Sounds like a pretty good deal," I say.

Missus sighs again. "They don't provide dinner. You bring dinner for your own family. And you can include Will and Anna in that since FM and I will be having dinner with the committee members. We always do a special thing for the committee members."

I shrug and step out onto the front porch with her. "Well, I can always just make another dozen sandwiches and take them." At this she stops, her hand on the porch post, and turns to me.

"Really, Carolina? You'd feed your family cold sandwiches

for supper on the Fourth of July?" She shakes her head and walks on down the steps to her car. As she opens her car door, she says loudly, "Are you sure you're Southern?"

Well, now that you mention it ...

Back inside, I pause to determine if anyone else is up. I have to talk to Bryan about his stalking of Brittani and I need to talk to Savannah, again, about Alex. But more than all of that, I have to get to the bookstore and see how things are there, since apparently we are having a grand opening this weekend.

Right now the only B&B guest we have is Gertie, and I know she's already left for town. (I waited upstairs until I saw her leave, which is why I haven't had coffee yet.) Barefoot, I go into the kitchen and pour coffee from the pot that just started brewing when Missus showed up. I take my coffee and list from Missus into the living room. Just those few minutes on the front porch told me it's already too hot to sit outside.

As Missus said, on the back she's written the items I'm responsible for bringing.

2 dozen peanut butter and grape jelly sandwiches on white bread. Cut in 4 pieces, diagonally. Smooth.

How insulting. Of course I'll cut them smooth, like I don't know to make them look nice since they're for strangers. Sometimes that woman can be downright demeaning.

At the bottom of the page, I begin my shopping list.

White Bread

Grape Jelly

Peanut Butter

Wait, should I use peanut butter with nuts or sm...

Never mind.

Dinner that night. What should I make? You know people will show up with freshly fried chicken and corn salad and a homemade cake or blackberry cobbler. It'll be a walking, talking magazine article. There'll be as much oohing and ahhing over the elaborate picnic dinners as the fireworks.

I know. Football hotdogs. I can wrap them up in aluminum foil, and they'll stay warm in a cooler. My stomach growls. Football hotdogs are a staple from when Jackson and I used to take the kids to the drive-in movie. One of the last drive-ins in the country was near our house, and we went whenever possible. Hmm, so wonder why we call them football hotdogs if we only took them to the movies? Guess my mom and dad named them that.

I add hotdogs and buns and onions to my grocery list, and before long it takes up the rest of the page on the back of my weekend duty list. There are still no noises from upstairs. So, with a look at the clock, I head upstairs to get dressed. At Bryan's door, I can hear him softly snoring. Guess I'll talk to him about Brittani later.

And as for Savannah, what am I going to say about Alex that I've not already said and that she would actually listen to? I'll talk to her about it later, too.

In Jackson's and my bedroom, I put on a pair of jean capris and an old T-shirt from Tennessee. It's bright orange, but has a small bleached-out spot at the hem on the side, where I got some cleaning stuff on it. Perfect for a busy morning getting the bookstore in order.

Pulling the heavy front door closed behind me, I can't help but feel good. New white tennis shoes, travel mug of coffee, and headed to a bookstore. *My* bookstore. I refuse to consider that my good mood has anything to do with not having to engage with any of my children this morning. Of course, at some point they'll wake up, but maybe they'll be totally different people when they do.

Hey, I can hope.

CHAPTER 20

"It's like Chancey has cornered the paint market in North Georgia," I say looking around the florist's and bookstore. "Andy's place is dripping with green, orange, and purple paint. Peter painted those old rusty tables and chairs and set them out on the sidewalk. And now this."

Shannon nods. "I wasn't too sure about it at first. I kind of liked the old brick walls, but Gertie said it had to be done. Now, I'm liking it."

Entering our front door this morning I was met by the smell of fresh paint. Imagining a redo of Andy's Place color scheme, I instantly felt sick to my stomach. However, my fear was for naught. Gertie is having every interior wall in the place painted white. The paint is high gloss, so it makes everything look brighter and bigger. The ceiling is an old tin ceiling, but it was ugly with rust and dirt. She's having it painted also, a soft blue. She calls it Haint Blue. Something about folks in the South saying that particular color on a ceiling keeps the ghosts, or Haints, away. Whatever, it looks really nice.

She moved the crew she had at Andy's here yesterday afternoon, and they are working up a storm. Shannon and I are cleaning things Gertie had moved to the center of the space. I've wiped the shelves and their belongings and cleaned the windows and the wide windowsills. Shannon has cleaned her coolers and work tables.

Now Shannon is pulling everything from underneath her counter and is throwing away more than she's keeping. Tossing another old Moonshots coffee cup, she says, "I think the new paint gives me energy. Knew all this junk under the counter needed to be gone through, just never did it."

"Who knew this place could look like this?" I say as I collect the dirty paper towels and rags. "Well, I guess Gertie knew. It's a little unnerving how she just steamrolls ahead, but…" I shrug and look around. "Who can argue with the results? Makes our furniture and shelves look old, though."

Shannon grunts her agreement from below her counter. When she stands up, she wipes her forehead with the tail of her shirt. "I'm getting hungry. Want to get some lunch?"

"Wow, it is after lunch," I say after I check my phone.

"Yeah, we don't have to stay here since we're closed. Want to go next door and see what the bistro is serving?"

She holds up her hands. "Like this? I came dressed to clean, not go out to eat. My mother would kill me if I went out on Main Street like this."

I look down at my old T-shirt, some dirt now added to the bleach stain. "Yeah, but it's Chancey, probably—"

Shannon waves at me. "Oh, doesn't matter for you. You're older and stuff."

"Older and stuff?"

"You know, married."

I roll my eyes. "Yes, I know. What do you want?"

"Oh, just ask Peter what he'd suggest. I'll go wash my hands and wipe off your coffee table for us to eat on." As she walks past me, she pulls out a ten dollar bill from her shorts pocket. "Here ya go."

With my purse in my other hand, I'm halfway out the door

before she yells from back near the bathroom. "Tell Peter I said hello."

Oh, that's what's going on. She's set her cap for Peter.

I'd warn Peter, but where's the fun in that?

It's hard to imagine I once thought I had feelings for Peter. We're friends, but we don't match. However, the whole thing taught me it's easier to walk away from marriage than I ever could've imagined. It's easy to take something for granted and make it not that special in your head. And once it's not that special, well, why stay?

The sidewalk is wider at the corner, and that's where Peter has set three metal tables surrounded by wrought iron chairs. They've been used up and down the street for events, and Jordan talked about painting them to use when MoonShots was here, but she never got around to getting them cleaned up. Usually they're stacked out behind the building, underneath the decking of the apartment upstairs, which is now Alex Moon's swinging bachelor pad.

The table and chairs are bright white, and the setup looks peaceful in the shade from a large tree, which is around the corner in the alley. Peter opens the bistro's front door and asks, "Like them?"

"I do. They look good here. I would've thought they'd look out of place, but they look nice." Walking past him and into the coolness, I ask, "Y'all are serving lunch today, right?"

"Absolutely. Alex has some chicken salad, and I think he said egg salad. "Right?" Peter calls out louder, as we walk toward the back of the store.

Alex lifts his chin and smiles from the back corner, where he's behind the deli station he's created. "Hello. Chicken salad has cranberries and blueberries, red and blue, in it for the Fourth, and the egg salad, well, I may have made a mistake with that." He grimaces and adds, "Not sure capers are that popular down here. Folks earlier kept asking what those salty, hard things were."

I laugh. "Yeah, I'm not sure I've ever had capers. I see them in recipes, but I'm not really much of a cook. So I just never made those recipes." I scrunch up my nose. "But I don't think I'd like salty things in egg salad. I like sweet pickle relish in mine."

Alex raises his eyebrows at Peter. "Told you. Seems people down here like things sweet more than salty."

Peter nods. "Think you might be right. I know when I first moved up north I couldn't figure out what was wrong with their tea. First, they kept serving me hot tea and then when I could get iced tea, it wasn't sweet. But I'd never made iced tea, so I thought it was a whole different thing. Plus, they kept pushing a bowl of sugar at me, and the sugar wouldn't dissolve."

Peering over the counter window, I look for the chicken salad. "So, what's in the chicken salad, besides blueberries and cranberries?"

"Rest assured, it's not weird. Just chicken and mayo, the berries mostly for color. And some slivered almonds," Alex explains.

"Almonds? Not pecans?" Peter asks.

At the same time, Peter and I say, "I prefer pecans."

"Okay, pecans next time. You know, pecans are used mainly in desserts back home."

Peter sits on the end of an upturned crate. "Get used to it. I'm still trying to find Italian beef like I got up in Chicago. And sausages? Don't get me started."

"I'll take two chicken salads. And what kind of bread are you using?" I ask.

Alex laughs. "That's another thing. I know someone in the mountains here has to make homemade bread, right? But hell if I know how to find out who. Think I'll have to go all the way Atlanta? Today I have the best wheat bread I could find at the Piggly Wiggly and some croissants, but they seem stale. They're marked fresh, but still…"

"We'll take the wheat bread, I'm sure it'll be fine. I know there's places selling homemade bread in Marietta, I'll put Laney on it. She loves finding stuff like that on her computer. Did you hear she might get put on bed rest?"

Peter laughs and crosses his arms. "Yeah, right. She was in here this morning with that Zoe girl. It's like someone has given her her own minion. Who is this Zoe?"

"She's the daughter of the manager of the new Dollar Store. His oldest. He and his new wife have three more little ones."

Alex says, "Oh no," and looks up. "Those brats that almost singlehandedly destroyed the store? Their mother lets them do whatever they want."

Peter adds. "Their mother was preoccupied with flirting with the deli guy."

"Oh, really?" I ask. "And what deli guy would that be?"

The one and only deli guy goes back to making our sandwiches. "It was awful. She hung out here and left the kids to race around the store pushing a stroller. They knocked stuff off the shelves and even knocked down the display there." He points to where Peter is seated.

"Yeah, I had that big picnic basket sitting here on this crate with all the things you'd want to take on a picnic, and when they rammed it, mother's plates broke. Hopefully, I can replace them before she figures out I had them."

Alex places our sandwiches in plastic containers as he shakes his head in disgust. "And she let them clean out the sample plate. They ate every piece of cheese and meat I had on it. Then they moved on to the cookie jar."

"They made a mess in Ruby's the other day, too. Can I get two lemonades?" I turn to Peter. "Did you know Anna is practically the assistant manager at the Dollar Store?"

He nods as he slides his eyes to glance at Alex and then stands up. "Here, let me ring those things up for you. I'll take them up front. Grab some chips if you want them."

"Thanks, Alex," I say and wave bye, snagging two bags of chips on my way up front. What did Peter not want to say in front of Alex? At the front counter, I lean his direction and raise my eyebrows.

He sighs as he begins punching the buttons on the electronic tablet in front of him. "Yes, I know about Anna working at the Dollar Store. Have you talked to Will since last night?"

"No. Why?"

Peter shakes his head and frowns. "Biggest fight yet." He presses his lips together and stares into the bag.

"About what? Who was fighting?" I whisper.

He finally looks up. "All of them. Mother gave Anna one of her famous to-do lists, and Anna tore it up. Right in front of her. Mother lost it. Dad got involved protecting Anna, then Will went on about how Anna thought her job was so important when it's just a shop clerk at a Dollar Store. So, you can imagine what my niece then had to say about him selling used cars."

"How did you hear all this?" I ask as I hand him money.

He hands me my bag and frowns even more. "Anna. She spent the night at my house."

"She *told* you she tore up Missus' list?"

"She was right proud of it. I've got to say, though, Will did come to the house and try to apologize. But she wasn't having it."

"Well, they'll work it out. Don't you think?"

He pushes the cash drawer closed. "Not sure about that. Will said he's moving home."

"Wait. My home?"

Peter nods.

"You don't think he was just mad when he said that? Just threatening her?"

"He didn't seem mad at all. It was this morning. He stopped by the house to tell her on his way to work."

"Oh, Peter. That's not good."

"No. I don't know what to even say to her."

I agree with him by shaking my head and then walking away from the counter. Peter comes around to hold open the door for me with my bag and two drinks. "I didn't want to say anything in front of Alex, as I figure everyone knowing might make it harder for them to get back together."

"Understand. Well, thanks for lunch. I'll let you know what Will has to say."

I took Shannon her sandwich and lemonade and carried mine back out to the tables out front. The shade feels good as I choose the seat in the darkest part of the shade. The street is still as only a hot summer afternoon can be. No bugs buzzing, no kids shouting, no breeze ruffling the leaves. My lemonade is sweet and cold. My sandwich is delicious, and while the dried cranberries add a familiar taste to the chicken salad, the fresh blueberries really make it different. Why hasn't someone else thought of this? I sit back and relax for a minute, but one look down the street in the direction of Missus and FM's house reminds me of Peter's story.

Wish I was surprised, but I'm not. Sad, but not surprised. I take a deep breath, then lean up to wrap up my garbage. I take it to the can beside the bistro's front window and throw it away, then I go back into the bookstore. I barely get in the front door before Peter is right behind me.

"Carolina. Um. I guess that paint, well, it felt dry. It was dry. Maybe the humidity?"

I turn around toward him. "What?"

Shannon bursts out laughing from the couch where she'd had lunch. "Oh no. Look at you!"

Peter tilts his head as if to look behind me. I look over my shoulder and see white on my jeans and all down the back of my bright orange shirt. "Are you kidding me?"

"We'll pay to have your clothes cleaned. I'm so sorry. It felt dry, I promise."

Before I can even close my mouth, my phone rings. It's a local number. "Hello?" I listen and try to explain. "I can't come right now, but I'll be there shortly."

After listening some more, I say, "Okay," and hang up. "Can anyone give me a garbage bag to sit on so I don't get paint all over my car? Guess I won't be going home to change. Officer Ramirez wants to see me out at Brittani's house."

Peter grabs my arm. "Is everyone okay?"

I dig my car keys out of my purse while I drop my phone down in it. "Nobody's hurt, but I don't know much. Except that apparently my son, the stalker, is out of bed."

Chapter 21

"For crying out loud, I know I have paint on my backside!" I launch my purse across our foyer and onto the couch.

Missus follows me into the house. She'd met me on the front porch when I got home. "Carolina, this is a mess. A real mess."

"Oh, believe me, I know it's a mess. I'm the one that had to see my thirteen-year-old son in the back of a police car."

Bryan speaks up from the kitchen, where he scurried as soon as we entered the front door. "Officer Ramirez just let me sit back there because he had the air conditioning on. Geez, mom."

I step to the kitchen doorway. "You get downstairs right this minute and bring me the cords to your Xbox, oh, and gimme your phone." I hold out my hand and watch his mouth open to complain. With the set of my jawline and steady glare, I convince him talking would not be a good idea. He puts it in my palm, turns, and heads down the basement stairs.

Missus hasn't followed us into the kitchen, but is sitting on the couch in the same spot she sat early this morning. Was that just this morning? Plopping down in the chair where I sat this morning, I ask, "So, how did you hear about my juvenile delinquent?"

"Honestly, I had no idea. I wanted to talk to you about your other son. He's moved back home?"

Other son? Oh, the good one? The one that's supposed to be working in DC and getting ready for law school? That son? My shoulders fall, and I look around the room. "I don't know. He's not told me if he has, and I don't see any of his stuff. But then I've not been upstairs." I shrug. "Maybe a break will do them good. They go from not even knowing each other to married and expecting a baby in a matter of months? It can't be easy."

"Life isn't ever 'easy.' However, I've done everything I can to help." Missus stands up and paces behind the couch. "Given them a place to live. Not interfered." (Mercifully, her pacing keeps her from seeing my eyes roll at that.) "Convinced Shaw to hire Will."

Now I jump up. "I knew it! You're the reason he moved here. You made this whole thing happen!"

She stops and looks down her nose at me. "Oh, yes, Carolina. I made your son sleep with my granddaughter. That was all me."

Shoot. She's right. "But selling cars? We could've helped him in law school, helped them live in Athens."

Missus shakes her head. "No. They need family to help them out. They don't need to live across the state, and then goodness knows where he would've gotten a job. Look at how badly they're handling their marriage. Imagine if they didn't have us nearby to help."

"I am imagining it. They would deal with things together. There would be no uncle's house to run to, no parents to just up and move back in with."

Missus tsks at me. "We see family differently. I see it as a support system, a help. You see it as a nuisance. I saw how you were with your mother and father."

"Don't you dare! I'm fine with my parents. Seems I heard it

was one of your infernal lists that pushed Anna over the edge. You want to boss everyone, but your granddaughter isn't used to being bossed around like that. *You* are their main problem!"

She pulls herself up and marches to the front door. "We should be working together to keep Will and Anna's family intact. Not tearing at each other. I believe in family."

"Oh, like I don't?"

Lifting her hands and shrugging, she says, "How would I know? However, I will say what I came to say, please send Will back home to his wife and unborn baby. I will make sure she's there to welcome him."

"How are you going to do that?"

"Reason, common sense, and… bribes. When you hold all the economic cards, you'd be foolish to not use them. I know when you calm down from your younger son's unlawful escapades, you'll see things my way." And she stomps out the front door.

"Mom, can I go to the Lake Park?" comes from the dining room doorway.

Pausing to get a grip on my anger, I turn. "No, Bryan, you may not go to the Lake Park. You may never get to go there again the rest of your life. Where's the cords?"

He slumps and shuffles up to me, holding out a bundle of cords.

I take the cords and step back. "I'm so embarrassed. What were you thinking? I told Beau no way you were stalking Brittani. No way. Did you think that would get her back?"

As serious as a heart attack, he looks up at me with wide eyes. "Yeah."

Exhausted, my eyes close and you can barely hear my voice when I say, "Go up to your room. This is not just some little thing. They called the police, Bryan."

He drags to the stairs and at first walks slowly, one foot in front of the other, up the staircase. Then he stops midway.

"The officer was nice. He showed me all the cool stuff in the car." His face breaks into a wide grin. "Hey, yeah, I want to be a police officer. That'd be neat. Can I have my phone back just to tell people? Just for a little while."

All I can do at first is stare. Stare at the crazy person I gave birth to. "No, Bryan, you can't. You're being punished."

He grins again and shakes his head. "Oh, that's right. Okay, later mom." And he dashes up the rest of the stairs.

Why *do* people keep having kids?

My phone rings, and I see its Jackson returning my phone call. "Hey. I got your message when I got back in cell range. Bryan was with the police? Is he okay? He was stalking Brittani?"

"Yeah, we're home now. Beau had mentioned it to me last week, I guess. But when Savannah and I talked about it, we decided he couldn't get all the way out to Brittani's house to leave the notes and stuff, so I was going to talk to Beau again."

Jackson huffs out a deep breath. "So he denied it to you?"

"Well, um, I never got the chance to ask him. Things are kind of busy here with the Fourth of July stuff this weekend. Plus, I didn't think it was him."

"So how was he getting out to her house?"

"Begging. He begged rides from everyone. All in the name of true love. Apparently, he has a very active imagination and has watched one too many teenage romances. Susan has even taken him by there. He's also, apparently, very persuasive."

Jackson laughs a bit under his breath. "He does come off as pretty cute and harmless."

"And I asked him in the car on the way home why he did it. He said there was a movie he and Brittani watched where the boy wouldn't let go. He said it's her favorite movie, and he thought that was what he was supposed to do."

"Okay, listen, I'll be home tomorrow afternoon. I have to hand some stuff off, and I'll do that first thing in the morning, then come home. Me and Bryan will go out to dinner. Just the two of us."

My next sigh comes through a smile. Parenting is hard work. And I can't imagine doing it with anyone other than this man. "Thank you. That'll be good." Then I laugh. "And wait'll you hear that I had to do all this with white paint all over my behind!"

"What? How did you do that?"

"I'll tell you tomorrow. Love you and drive safe. Go have one more nice solitary dinner before coming back to this nuthouse."

We hang up, and I pull myself up off the couch, which I put newspapers on before I sat down. I don't know how single parents do it. I feel about a thousand times better than when I first got home.

Oh, I forgot about Will maybe moving home. And Savannah and Alex, someone has to do something about that.

And then there's dinner. Wonder who's cooking?

Passing the mirror beside the coatrack at the foot of the stairs, I get a glimpse of the white paint on my jeans and shirt. I pause to take a longer look, and I don't even try to stop the laughter that blasts out. First things first—put these clothes in the washer.

Changed into shorts and a tank top, and standing in the basement at the washer, I hear someone upstairs calling my name. Then more talking. With the washer filling, I pour in detergent, add my clothes, then walk back up the stairs. At the top of the stairs, the door to the basement opens before my hand hits the handle. "Oh, hi."

Susan stands at the door, then steps back for me to come

up the last stair. "I'm furious at your son for tricking me into taking him up to Brittani's. I'm taking him out to your garden to get him busy, if that's okay with you?"

"Of course," I say. Rest of the country may give lip service to it taking a village to raise a kid, but in a small town in the South, it's a way of life. Adults will call out a kid misbehaving even if they don't know him, and if you object, you're the one everyone looks at. Took some getting used to when we moved here. Suburbs have lost much of that.

"Mom, I don't know what to do in the garden. It's hot out there," Bryan appeals to me, but Susan twists around to answer him.

"You should've thought of that when you were lying to me that you were taking Brittani a card since she wasn't feeling good. And that your mother knew all about it!"

"Bryan! You told everyone I knew what you were doing?"

Suddenly he looks like he would prefer the heat in the garden to the heat in the house. He drops his head and mumbles, "I'll get my shoes."

As he turns away, Susan smiles at me. "I should've known he wasn't telling the truth. Guess I've had too much on my mind to think straight. But I'm too busy to pull all those weeds out there, so I needed some kid to act up that I could put to work."

"Good idea. Have a seat," I say as I sit down at the kitchen table. "So, about your house."

She slumps back against the chair just as her bottom settles on the seat. "Yeah. It's something, isn't it?"

"It's amazing is what it is. Griffin must've gotten some kind of raise."

Susan nods. "He did, but we've also had the money from the sale of his grandmother's property sitting in our account. She split it up between him and his three siblings years ago, and we never spent it. Plus, the power company was trying to get rid of that house. It's sat empty since it was built by an ex-company official who left under bad circumstances. They offered us a crazy deal, and, well, Griffin's pretty competitive. Couldn't pass up being the local boy done good."

"I'm just figuring that out about him being competitive. Never realized it until lately."

We sit quietly until we hear Bryan dragging back down the stairs. As I stand, I say, "You know you have to show the house to Laney."

Susan grimaces. "I know. Griffin's champing at the bit to have a big party, but I have to have my family there before that. I keep holding him off." She opens the back door. "Meet you in the yard, Bryan," she says as she walks across the deck.

I look out at the jungle I created and pat my son's back as he walks past. "Daddy is coming home tomorrow night, and you and he are going out to dinner to talk."

He stops. "Okay, that'll be fun, but where will you be?" His eyes are innocent and full of light. Is he joking? Is he really naïve, or is it all a cover? Either he's really good at lying or… wait, evidence says he's really good at lying. And I remember something I heard once, probably in a political campaign or on *Dr. Phil.* "How do you know he's lying? His lips are moving."

Shaking my head, I push him on out the door. "Susan's waiting."

Savannah's honesty stings, but I'm beginning to see it beats the alternative.

Chapter 22

"You came in late last night," I say to Will from my seat at the kitchen table.

He nods as he pours a cup of coffee. He sets it on the table across from me, then collects a cereal bowl, the box of Lucky Charms, and the milk. After he sits down and pours his cereal, he looks up. "Oh, forgot to get a spoon. You done with yours?"

I look at my spoon, resting in the puddle of milk in the bottom of my cereal bowl, then look at him. "You'd rather use the spoon that I've already used than get up and walk five feet to the silverware drawer?"

He shrugs, sighs, then gets up to get a spoon. "Just seemed easier," he says as he sits back down.

"So, you came in late last night," I say again.

"Yeah," he manages before he puts a spoonful of cereal shapes laced with bright-colored marshmallows in his mouth and starts chewing.

"Were you with Anna? And if you were, did you get anything straightened out?"

"No, wasn't with Anna. So the answer to question two is also no."

Now, I know, like every parent knows, that the more questions I ask, the fewer answers I'm going to get. However, I'm no longer dealing with a snotty teenager, he's a man. A married man with a baby coming. So, I take a deep breath. "Quit ignoring me. Act like a man, not a boy. What is going on?"

His head jerks up so fast, there is milk trailing out of his mouth. He wipes it away with the back of his hand before he says, "Don't you think that's between me and Anna? It's enough that her family is all involved. You want to get involved, too, now?"

Part of me agrees with him. Part of me thinks he needs to talk. Part of me wants another bowl of cereal. After all, I do still have my spoon.

"Hand me the Lucky Charms," I say. I just want a bit to take the bran cereal taste out of my mouth. "Okay, what do you want us to do? Me and your daddy."

He eats for a bit, then says, "I don't know. She's changed or something. Acts like that job of hers is the greatest thing ever. It's just a dollar store."

He's totally dismissive. Think I see part of the problem. "Well, son, have you tried to look at it from her perspective? She's never had a real job, probably sees this as something to be proud of. That Mr. Kendrick seems to think she's doing really well."

That gets his attention. "You've meet this Kendrick guy?"

"Just for a moment, at the China buffet. Right after Anna was hired. Why? Have you met him?"

Will laughs and drops his spoon into his empty bowl. "No. Why would I go meet him? I'm busy. I have to work, remember?"

"Hey! No need to get all snippy with me."

He stands up and takes his bowl to the sink while talking. "Sorry, Mom. I did stay out too late last night. Went down to Marietta to hang with some guys from high school. Haven't seen them in a while."

"Who's back there now?" I ask.

He leans on the counter, "Just some of the regular guys.

Pete and Mike and some others I don't think you know." He straightens up and tucks his dress shirt in.

Another piece of the puzzle. His friends are moving ahead like they always planned. Pete has an internship with the governor's office, and Mike is headed to medical school. "I guess it was good to see them?"

He bobs his head up and down, but also sideways. "Okay, I guess." He leaves the kitchen. Heaviness surrounds him. He's never had to settle. Never been anywhere but at the top of the heap in grades, sports, life. I believe he'll rise to the occasion, that he'll find a way to see the good in being married to Anna and the baby coming. I do believe that, but I don't know how to help him.

Maybe I should talk to Anna.

From my purse sitting in the front seat of my buggy, my phone rings. I stop right in the middle of the aisle and grab for it. "Hi, Anna."

"I saw you called," she says.

"Yes, just wanted to stop in and see you, but didn't want to interrupt you at work. I'm over at the Piggly Wiggly. Do you have a minute? I could run over."

She hesitates, but manages to drag out an "okay." "Just come to the front door, and I'll unlock it for you."

While we've been talking, I've pushed my buggy to the front of the store. "Hey Danielle," I call to the cashier, which means she stops checking out the women in front of her, turns completely away from her register, and answers me.

"Hey, Mrs. Jessup. How are you? Did you get your air conditioning fixed?"

I shoot the lady now waiting on Danielle a look of apology.

"Yes, we did." I don't let her ask her next question. "But I need to run over to the Dollar Store. Just going to leave my buggy here for a minute." Me waving my hand and trying to stop her doesn't keep her from leaving her register and coming to look in my cart.

"Okay. Anything you want me to put back in the freezer? Reckon your deli meat will be okay?" She picks up a baggie filled with turkey breast. "I can take this back to the deli right now."

I take the turkey from her. "No, it'll be fine. I don't have anything frozen yet. Just go finish what you were doing."

She expresses her lack of understanding by sighing and reaching for the turkey. "It won't take but a minute—"

"No! Go take care of your customer. I'll be right back." And I whirl away from her to leave through the automatic door.

I trot and half-run down the sidewalk in front of the China Palace and stop to slow my breathing at the door to the Dollar Store. Anna is waiting, and she turns the key as she sees me approaching. "Come in," she says as she pulls open the glass door.

"Thanks, wow, look at this place." It smells new and clean. There are still boxes everywhere, but many of the shelves have merchandise on them. "Y'all have really gotten a lot done."

She closes the door and locks it saying, "Yes. And we still have a lot to do. You sure we can't talk about this later?"

I chuckle. "Where? Figured this was the only place we wouldn't have all those other people." She and I had a good relationship when she lived with us. Before we were related. Maybe I can get back there. I reach out and cup my hand around her upper arm, firm enough to show I honestly care, soft enough to not make her feel trapped, and bend my head to look in her eyes. "How are you? You look good. Tired, maybe? But with the new job and all…" As my voice trails, she jerks her arm away from me and pulls back.

"Of course, it's my job making me tired. Not being pregnant, or fighting with your son, or listening to my grandmother blab all day about everything I do. Y'all don't want me to work. You only care about the *baby*. When, in reality, my job is the *only* thing *not* making me tired."

"No, honey, I didn't mean it like that. I think your job is great. I think—"

"What's going on here?" Kyle Kendrick demands as he comes around the end of the far aisle. His stride is angry, and he looks bigger than I remember. "Anna, are you all right?" he asks as he comes up behind her.

"She's fine," I say. "We're just talking. I'm Carolina, her mother-in-law. We met the other day." I reach out my hand to shake his. He ignores it, but steps toward me. Putting himself between me and Anna.

He lowers his voice, but not in a soft way. "I've had just about enough of the bullying of my assistant manager."

"Bullying?" I exclaim as I step away from him. However, he quickly fills the space I just emptied and continues talking.

"I'd hate to have to take away the promotion she so deserves because of her family situation. Now, you need to leave."

Pulling my eyes off his angry red face, I look to Anna. She's smiling. Not at me, she's smiling at her boss. Like he's, I don't know, but it doesn't make me feel good. I speak up as I back towards the front door. "Anna, we can talk later. I'm not on any side, just want to help."

At the door, I turn away from her, and Kendrick, who's kept pace with my retreat, twists the key and jerks open the door.

He says, as I walk past him, "Anna knows who's on her side. And none of them seem to be related to her." He shoves the door closed, turns the key, then folds his arms, and glares at me through the glass.

Trembling, I race for my van and sit in the driver's seat. When I immediately lock the doors like someone is chasing me, I realize how shaken I am. Taking some deep breaths while closing my eyes, I try to relax. He really scared me.

A banging on window causes my eyes to fly open as I scream.

Danielle is standing there, wearing her Piggly Wiggly apron, shouting, "Mrs. Jessup, you forgot your groceries."

I nod and blow out a long breath before I open the door. "Thanks, Danielle. I'll be right there." She walks back toward the store, and the line of customers I'm sure she left waiting there.

Setting my feet out of the car and onto the gravel, I test them to see if they are still shaky. That was the first time anyone has ever come at me like that. He was truly angry. At me!

As I near the grocery store entrance, I finally sneak a peek in the direction of the Dollar Store and find it hard to believe what just happened. Then my stomach really drops.

The way Anna was looking at Mr. Kendrick? It was like he was some kind of knight in shining armor. And worse?

I've never seen her look at Will that way.

This is a mess.

Chapter 23

Gertie is in the kitchen eating lunch when I get home from Piggly Wiggly. She asks without looking up from her food, "You need any help carrying groceries?" After my encounter with Mr. Kendrick, Gertie's kind words make my tight shoulders relax. Then she adds, "'Cause your son is upstairs and you could call him."

She continues eating her sandwich and talking with her mouth full. "Bought this at Peter's place, and it's right good. Italian Beef, that good-looking boy called it."

Sitting my bags on the counter, I say, "Really? He called it Eye-talian Beef?"

"Yes, Carolina, he gets to name his own food, right? Speaking of naming stuff, you and Shannon need to get to thinking about what you're going to call the store. Got the painter for the sign coming tomorrow, so think on it."

"Tomorrow? I don't know. Never really thought about a real name. What's Shannon think?" I ask as I close the freezer door.

"Not much from what I can see. Look at this pepper, kinda sweet. He called it a cherry pepper. Right good." She pops the piece of pepper in her mouth, and then folds up the messy wrappings and puts it all in the white bag it came in. "You're coming to the bookstore this afternoon, right?"

"Yes. Is the painting done?"

Gertie groans as she stands up. Then puts both fists on her wide hips and straightens the rest of the way up. "You know, you and Patty working together didn't really work, and I told you I was getting you another partner?"

"Yes, you did," I say as I get out two slices of bread from the bag and place them on a saucer.

"Well, it was harder than I thought it was going to be. There are a bunch of folks don't want jobs. Leastways, not one selling books."

Layering turkey breast on my bread and adding lettuce, I ask, "Did you put an advertisement out or something?"

"Naw, just asked around. But I did find someone, and she'll be there this afternoon." She sways into the dining room. "Oh, and Carolina, did I tell you I'm moving out?"

"Out of here? No. You're going home?" I try to not sound *too* happy.

She stops and leans with her hands grasping the back of one of the dining room chairs. "No, made me a right nice place in Andy's Place. Got a bedroom and the kitchen. Porch out back. That way I can keep an eye on it and the kids."

My lunch forgotten, I walk towards her. "Are Andy and Patty going to live there, too? They get back from their honeymoon this weekend, right?"

"Yeah, but no, they're staying in the apartment upstairs of your store. I'll get them a house when they get me a grandbaby. Figure that place is so small, it'll be good incentive." She waves a hand at me as she lets go of the chair back. "Go eat your lunch and come down to the store straight away."

I turn back to finish my sandwich thinking of how Gertie has orchestrated everything. Wonder who she got to work with me. She's thought of every little thing it seems.

Well, except who's going to tell Missus she has a new next-door neighbor. A smile interrupts my chewing.

Oh, please, let me.

Hard to believe it was only a year ago, less than really, when we moved to Chancey. Driving down the hill toward town, the thick shade no longer hides just neat, big, old houses, it shelters the home of our friends – okay, maybe not actual friends, but people we know. At the bottom of the hill, I look out at the grassy triangle and know there are hundreds, maybe thousands, of daffodil bulbs waiting. I don't have to think about which way to turn, I do it automatically. And I can't remember what I was so scared of.

It's like a nightmare you wake from with heart pounding and fear in your throat, but then when you try to put the scene together, it slips away like egg white down a sink drain. You remember it being so real, and yet it's gone, leaving no evidence behind.

It's still a small town, and small towns are still not my favorite, but it doesn't feel as alien, or as scary, as when we arrived. In some ways I feel like a completely different person than who I was back in the suburbs.

Not sure if that is a good thing or a bad thing.

My phone rings as I pull into a parking spot across from the store. It's Laney, so I answer it as I turn off the car. "Hey there."

"What are you doing? Can you come for dinner tonight? We can swim and then eat."

"Um, sure. Oh, wait, no. Jackson is coming home. Did I tell you about Bryan stalking Brittani? I can't remember who I've told what."

She sighs into the phone. "You didn't, but Susan did. Said

she worked him like a dog out in your so-called garden yesterday."

"She did. Although he loved it. Left the house with him out there working this afternoon by himself, as hot as it is. Anyway, Jackson is coming home and taking him out to talk it all over, thank goodness. I can't get a read on the boy. I'm afraid he's smarter than Will and Savannah put together. Not that his grades show it. A different kind of smart."

"Okay, well, come over when Jackson leaves with the boy. Shaw says Will and Anna are having big problems. We need to talk about that, too."

"Oh! And wait until you hear what happened this morning on the Will and Anna front. Had a run-in with her boss, Kimmy Kendrick's husband. But, listen, I've got to go. Gertie is staring at me from the front door of the store. She's hired someone to work with me."

"Who?"

"Don't know. But I will by time I come over tonight. I'll text you when I'm headed your way, okay? Bye."

I wave back at Gertie as I climb out of the van. "I'm coming."

Gertie hollers. "Saw you pull up and wondered what was keeping you. I have things to do. Come meet Bonnie."

Bonnie? I don't know a Bonnie. I rush in the door and realize, oh yes, I do. I do know a Bonnie. She sat across from me at the lunch up at Laurel Cove Club House.

"Hi, Bonnie. Nice to see you again. So, you want to work *here*?"

Gertie rolls her eyes at me and says, "Well, that's a nice how-do-you-do."

"No, I just mean… that, well, I mean, that I'm surprised."

Bonnie laughs and says, "Well, not as much as me! When I came in to take a look at the bookstore—I know you said not to come down yet, but I couldn't wait—and Gertie here asked me if I wanted a job, I sure was surprised when I said, 'yes.'"

Bonnie is older than me, with blondish-gray hair and very nice clothes. And a very nice voice. She seems, uh, very nice.

Gertie nods her head and lumbers back toward the door. "You ladies are going to do just fine. Now, to get things settled up at Andy's place. Carolina, tonight will be my last night up at your house. Crossings, I guess I should call it. Got a load of furniture coming tomorrow for my place here. I'll settle up with you later, okay?"

"Okay, and…" As I look at her, my mind stalls. Gratitude swells up, and I'm not even sure what for. "Um, thanks. Thanks for… everything."

Gertie pulls open the door, looks back and me, and winks. I'm thinking having Gertie Samson on my side is not a small thing.

"What an unusual lady," Bonnie says after the door closes. She looks around. "So, this is your store. We are going to have such fun! Let's sit down and get acquainted."

She sits on the couch, and I settle in the chair across from her.

She says, "I know we sat across from each other at lunch, but we didn't really get to talk. I'm Bonnie Cuneo. My husband Cal retired nine years ago, and we moved to Laurel Cove for him to play golf and for me to teach at Darien Academy. I retired last year and discovered I do not like golfing enough to do it every day. This sounds like the perfect job for me. My kids are grown and live around the country, I love books, and can't wait to get to know Chancey better."

I grin. "Okay, you know my name. Well, my husband Jackson works for the railroad so he travels a lot. We opened a B&B, Crossings, like Gertie said. Our three children are, well, still at home, I guess. The oldest one graduated from UGA last month, got married, and moved back home just last night." All this makes me frown, and Bonnie reaches over and pats my knee.

She says, "Isn't it hard when they get too old for us to fix things?"

"Exactly. I just want to help, and, well, seems I've done everything but."

She stands up. "That's what this place is for. All our fixing we can't do on our children we're going to use here. Now, who does the flowers? Gertie says that's a separate business?"

"Oh, yes, Shannon is the florist." I stand and follow her to the middle of the room. "We've been closed for painting, but she's nice, very talented with flowers, young. In her thirties."

We both look around, and Bonnie laughs a bit. "Okay, I know I'm new here, but have you ever thought of combining the two businesses? Not on the books, but on the floor? Incorporate the bookshelves and the tables with the florals? Like some beautiful private garden." She wanders around, talking and thinking, while I follow her listening and smiling.

Bonnie is a fount of ideas, good ideas, and she talks and explains and lays it all out until I can't wait for Shannon to come to work. So I call her.

"Shannon will be here in about ten minutes. I'm going next door to get us iced coffees. What can I get you?"

Bonnie laughs again as she says, "I'll take one of those, too."

On the sidewalk, the heat is oppressive. Heavy like putting on a winter coat that's soaked with hot water. However, there's not the afternoon quiet I expected. There's music. A light jazzy sound, which grows louder as I get to the door of the bistro. There, sitting in the corner of their window is a speaker, the source of the music. Inside, the music is the same as outside.

"Great music," I say to Peter.

He points toward the back corner. "It's all Alex. Through my phone. It's okay folks can hear it outside your place, too?"

"It's perfect. And I got a new partner. Well, co-worker. Bonnie. She's got great ideas. I need three iced coffees."

Peter walks from behind the counter and shouts, "Alex, need three iced coffees." As he walks he turns back towards me and asks in a lower voice, "So, how's Savannah?"

"She's fine, I guess. Isn't she here?"

Peter stops and stares at me. Then he licks his lips, and I watch him search for words. "No. She's not here. She doesn't work here anymore."

"What? She quit?" I pull my phone from my pocket and notice she's not answered my last four texts. Now, that may sound alarming to you, but there are other parents, *lots* of other parents, to whom that sounds quite normal. So quit judging.

I text her again. "Where are you????" I know, seems like a phone call is warranted, right? But think about it, would she really answer that?

"Carolina," Peter says, and as he pauses, I realize he wants me to look at him. So I do.

"She didn't quit. I had to fire her this morning."

"What? You fired her?" I lower my voice when I see Alex at the counter with my iced coffees in a little tray. "Why?"

Peter pushes me into the nearest aisle. "She wouldn't leave Alex alone. Hung out at the deli area when she was supposed to be working and would leave when she wasn't working. Then, well, last night."

"What happened last night?" I don't want to know, but that's what being a parent is all about. Doing things and asking things you don't want to do or ask.

"She showed up at his apartment. And wouldn't leave. He had to call me."

"Why didn't you call me?"

He takes a deep breath. "She said she'd told you she was coming down here. That you knew."

"And you believed her?"

"Well, sometimes you don't really get involved with stuff." He holds out his hands at me. "I know it was a mistake now, but at the time... I mean, you know? Anna was at my house crying, and Alex was here with a, another girl, and she got upset. So, Alex was dealing with both of them. Savannah, well, she finally just left. Said she was going home. So..."

With a sigh, I turn around and walk back to the deli counter where I smile at the young man my daughter is enamored of. He's placing the last coffee in a cardboard tray. "Thanks, Alex. Sorry about Savannah messing up your date last night." I pick up the tray of coffees.

"No problem, Carolina. And it wasn't like it was a real date or anything. Just, you know, a girl."

I bite my tongue and make it to the front counter mumbling, "Just a girl. Just a girl."

Peter rings up the drinks in silence. As I start to leave, he says, "You know—"

But I cut him off. "No, I don't know. Obviously I don't know." I push out the door.

On the sidewalk, I stand still and let the sun wash over me for a minute.

Great. Just as I'm beginning to think our move to Chancey might've been a good thing, my children are facilitating a full-scale, scorched-earth campaign.

What Rambo did to that little southern town is nothing compared to the Jessup kids on the loose.

When you're carrying a tray of drinks, it's hard to be really mad and slam doors and stomp. Shannon has arrived, and she opens the door to the store for me. Bonnie meets me and takes the tray from my hands, and as she moves to the side, I see Savannah sitting on the couch.

While I'm making up my mind on what to say in front of Shannon and Bonnie, Savannah takes care of it for me.

"Peter fired me. Fired me!" she says as she wipes her nose

with the heel of her hand. She's crying, and her nose is running. She has on jean shorts and a loose muslin peasant blouse. She's wearing those winter Ugg boots, which are hot when it's freezing, so her feet have to be sweating, right? But never mind that.

I'm not giving in to her histrionics. "You went to Alex's apartment last night after I was asleep. You are not allowed to roam around like that. And carrying on at work? Sounds like Peter didn't have a choice."

She sniffs as she stands up and then takes one of the coffees from the tray in Bonnie's hands. "Thank you," she says in her snot-thickened voice. Opening a straw she turns toward me, new tears running down her face. "Of course you'd listen to Peter. Your old boyfriend."

Shannon yelps. "What?"

And Bonnie adds, "Oh my."

My daughter takes a long sip of my iced coffee while she continues to cry. I grab hold of her arm and pull her with me out the back door. When the door behind us closes, faster than usual due to me shoving it, I squeeze harder on her upper arm. "I want to smack you right now. Peter is not my old boyfriend, and he only got to tell me his side of the story first because you didn't answer any of my texts from this morning. Crazy mom that I am, I assumed you were hard at work and couldn't answer me."

I release her arm, take a deep breath, and reach for my drink. "Give me that."

We stand at the back of the row of businesses on Main Street. It's mostly weeds growing up around chunks of old black top. When Savannah's eyes look above my head, I remember we are now standing at the bottom of the metal staircase going up to Alex's apartment. More tears fill her eyes and begin to roll down her cheeks.

After a quick sip, I hand her back the drink, then I wrap my arms around her. "Sweetie, he's just not worth it. You've never been like this about a guy."

"I know," she whispers in sobs. "Do you think I love him? Is that why it's so awful?"

"No, I don't think you love him. I think…" What do I think?

She sobs on. "Everybody says it's because I love him, and if he just realized how much I love him, well, then…"

I chuckle a bit and lean back to look in her face. "Everybody? And these everybody's, why would they know? Are they in long-lasting, good relationships? Do they know what it means to be 'in love'? Honey, I'm glad you have friends to talk to, but honestly, they don't know any more about being in love than you do."

She jerks away and opens her mouth to say something, but stops. Then I see a bit of light in her eyes as she admits, "Okay, you might have a point there. But he drives me crazy. He's so different from the guys here, or even back in Marietta." She puts the straw back in her mouth and looks down at the ground.

"It's maturity, I guess," I say with a shrug. "Or maybe it's him being from the city? And he is older and has helped run a business. Plus…" I nudge her shoulder to get her to look up from her drink. "Plus, he's the first guy I ever remember not falling all over himself to be the object of Savannah Jessup's attention."

She smiles and looks back down. She sticks out a foot. "Why in the world am I wearing these boots? My feet are dying. Let's go inside."

We enter the business, and I'm surprised at how bright it is. Used to feel like a black dungeon, but with the shiny white walls and the blue ceiling, it really is like a different place.

Even my daughter notices. "Patty isn't going to believe how great this place looks." She lowers her voice. "Who's that new lady up front? The old one."

"Shh. That's Bonnie. Gertie just hired her to work with me. Patty's going to work at Andy's place."

As we near the front flower counter, she sighs. "Everybody has a place to work except me."

When I open my mouth, she holds a hand up. "I know. My own fault. Went a little crazy."

Shannon grins. "But it just feels so right at the time, doesn't it? I heard about your little midnight trip to town!"

I reach out my arm towards Bonnie. "Bonnie, this is my daughter Savannah. She's usually not this emotional."

Bonnie steps over to Savannah and puts out her hand. "Nice to meet you. And don't worry, I'm sure you'll find another job soon. And another boy."

Savannah's eyes brim again, and she turns away from us. Over her shoulder, she says, "Mom, can I take your iced coffee? I have to go home and get out of these boots." Her voice shakes, and she rushes out the door. It closes behind her, and I head towards it.

"Maybe I should go make sure she's okay to drive." But as I stick my head out the door I see her striding across the street, heading toward the gazebo. I wait until I watch her walk up the couple of steps. She sits on one of the seats there in the deep shade. Looks like as good a place as any to nurse a broken heart.

I close the door and turn around. Shannon is beside her counter. "Peter was your boyfriend?"

"Uh, no. She was just mad. It was around the time of all that ghost stuff."

She sighs. "Oh, good. Didn't want to break girl code and steal a friend's man. So now, about the business. Bonnie told me her idea of combining our shops, and I love it. We've already done a little mixing, and I think we can make this a really neat place. But what should we call it? Sign painter is coming tomorrow."

Bonnie brings a stack of books with red covers to sit next to a red, white, and blue arrangement. "I have to admit the thought isn't original. My friend, Mindy Lee, has a place in northern Illinois, town outside Chicago called Crete. Mindy's mother ran a florist shop in the next town over, and when she retired, she started doing flowers in a corner of Mindy's bookstore. Eventually they were pretty equal. They came up with an interesting name."

"What's the name of their place?" Shannon asks.

Bonnie laughs. "That's what I'm looking up on Facebook right now."

I haven't moved far from the front window, and I keep peeking out at the park. "Y'all think Savannah will be okay?"

Shannon just waves a hand in the air. "Those long legs of her's and her confidence? She'll be fine."

Bonnie shrugs as she looks at her phone. "And a little humility can be a good thing for a teenage girl. Here is it. Petals and Pages."

"Oh, I like that. Petals and Pages sounds perfect!" Shannon exclaims.

"Listen, I'm going to go check on her," I say as I pull open the front door. Outside I look both ways before jogging across the street. The park is pretty, all spruced up for the big holiday weekend. Wave petunias spill from containers on the edge of the gazebo floor. The stone paths are clean of any weeds or trash, and the flower gardens are full of blooms and bees.

Nearing the back of the gazebo, I hear Savannah talking. Oh, she's on her phone. Then she laughs. My heart actually skips, and I smile. She's fine. So, I pause and take another look at the shaded park.

Petals and Pages, or was it Pages and Petals? Oh, we could use the '&' sign! Petals & Pages. Oh, I like that even better. Wait, Pages & Petals. Hm, wonder which should go first. Shannon was there first, but... then I hear it.

"Sure, Alex, I understand. It was too distracting to work together anyway, wasn't it? Oh, you miss me? Really?" She giggles. "Want to go swimming?"

Still talking, she's up and skipping down the gazebo steps. At the bottom she sees me, but all she does is shrug and continue towards her car. Still on the phone. Tears dry. And a date planned.

Well, so much for a dose of humility.

Unless you're talking about me.

Chapter 24

"Think we have a name for the store," I shout to Jackson, who's out on the back deck.

"What? Give me a minute, I'm coming in," he shouts back.

At the kitchen sink, I'm washing my hands after chopping up two onions. Jackson comes inside and wraps his arms around me as I lean against the sink. I shut off the water and snuggle into his embrace. "It's good to have you home."

"It's good to be home. Now what are all these onions for?"

"Saturday dinner. I'm making football hotdogs to take to the picnic up in Laurel Cove." I point with my chin at the counter to my left. "And there's everything to make the two dozen peanut butter and jelly sandwiches for Saturday lunch that I've been assigned."

I turn around in his arms and lift mine over his head to rest on his shoulders. "So, Bryan showed you the garden?"

He kisses me before he answers. "Yes, he seems really in to it. Or is he just faking us out? I can't get my head around him stalking Brittani when he seems so, I don't know, so innocent?"

Patting his chest, I push him away a bit. "Exactly. That's your job tonight. Figure our son out and then tell me. And Will? I heard you making plans to take him to breakfast tomorrow?"

Jackson picks up a jar of peanut butter and seems engrossed by the label, but his frown isn't because the label says "extra-nutty." Although as I realize that's what it says, I frown, and curse. "Damn, I was supposed to buy smooth." I push him to the side. "Please tell me these other jars are smooth."

He steps out of the way, but watches over my shoulder as I look at the other three jars. "Sorry," he says. "Looks like all nutty. But nobody will notice."

I just roll my eyes at him. Has he *met* Missus? "So anyway, Will and you and breakfast?"

"Yeah, before he goes into work tomorrow. I'll be home after that, and you have me for the day. It'll be good to be home for a long weekend."

As I point to a sheet of paper hanging on the refrigerator, I say, "There's our weekend schedule, thanks to Missus. She wrote it all down for us."

He takes it down, reads it, and mutters, "So much for sleeping in." He holds it up and points at the word "smooth" written on the back. "Want me to just cross it out?"

"Like Missus doesn't have a copy somewhere."

"Well, I told Bryan to wash up and then we'd leave. I'm going to make a bigger effort to spend time with him. I didn't travel like this when Will was his age."

"Yeah, and look how that turned out. Did he say what time he'll get home tonight when you talked to him?"

Jackson shakes his head. "Not really. Just said he was going down to Marietta to hang out with some old friends from high school."

I groan. "Again? He needs to be spending time with his wife."

"Again? So he's been down to Marietta recently?"

"Yeah, last night. Came in really late."

"Hmm. Okay, I'll see what I can find out about it tomorrow." He starts out of the kitchen, but then leans back. His eyes squinted, he asks, "Should I even ask about Savannah? Is she at least a little bit happy?"

"No, don't ask. She's at the lake with Alex, whom she thinks she might be in love with. So she snuck out to be with him last night, but found him with another girl – not on a date, but just 'a girl' – and then she caused such a scene that Peter fired her." I snap my fingers. "And I completely forgot about her sneaking out, and I haven't even punished her for it. Bet she wouldn't fall in love with gardening. Hand me my phone," I say as I hold my hand out.

Jackson picks up my phone from the table near him and lays it in my hand, grasping it as he does and looking deep into my eyes. "So, you're saying all's good with Savannah?" Then he pulls my hand toward him with a laugh and wraps me up. "You are Supermom, holding all this together and opening a new business."

"Mom's opening a new business?" Bryan asks from behind us.

We pull apart enough to see him. I say, "The bookstore? Remember?"

Bryan nods and maneuvers around us to get to the refrigerator. "Oh, that. Dad, are we leaving?" He grabs a Gatorade and says just before he takes a big gulp, "I hear Savannah got a new job."

"How did you hear that?"

He burps. "Facebook."

"Where?" Jackson asks.

"The Dollar Store. Can we go now?" Carrying his bottle of blue liquid he moves into the living room.

"Wait, I have your phone. How do you know what Facebook says?"

He shrugs. "Brittani emailed me on your tablet." He plods out the front door.

Jackson pulls his keys from his pocket, his eyes squinting again. "Isn't Brittani who he's stalking?"

"I know! Go. Go see what else you can find out." He gives me a quick peck on the lips and follows his youngest son's path. I walk to the front door to wave and then remember this morning. Was that just this morning? Opening the screen door, I yell, "Oh yeah, and remind me to tell you why there's no way on God's green earth our daughter can keep her new job at the Dollar Store. Bye. Love you."

"I want your bedroom," I say to Laney as I lounge on her princess couch. I guess that's what you call it. It's a chair where the seat comes all the way out for your legs to extend on it. Like princesses have. Well, when they're not on their throne. Or in their fabulous canopied bed, like where Laney is resting now, the beginning of sundown shadows creeping across the sea green comforter.

Her and Shaw's bedroom is upstairs and stretches across the front of the house. It's actually three rooms: the bedroom, the master bathroom, and the sitting room. My princess chair, or lounge, as Laney calls it, used to be in the sitting area, but that is now the *infant* nursery. Not to be confused with the *actual* nursery, which is down the hall. I'd seen her house downstairs, but I'd never been up here. It's just as beautiful. All dark wood and white walls. You never forget you are in an old farmhouse, but it just doesn't feel old. The windows look out on the acres owned by Shaw's family, so it's all green and peaceful. We each have trays in front of us. Laney's is on the bed with her, while mine is on a TV tray beside my lounge. However, the plates on the trays are empty now.

"Your mother's chicken pot pie is delicious," I say as I stand up to gather our plates. "I'll take these downstairs. Should I come back up? Or do you need to rest?"

"Oh, please come back up. I'm not tired, and bed rest is so lonely. Angie is taking Zoe home in a bit." Laney's news for the day is that she's on bed rest for the rest of the pregnancy.

"Okay, I'll be back up in a few," I answer as I start down the hall. I stop when I hear Laney's voice again.

"Take your time asking Zoe about her dad, since you had the run-in with him this morning. Which you have yet to tell me about."

I smile and singsong, "I will!" Even in bed, she doesn't miss a thing.

Setting our plates on the white granite counters, I look around for Zoe. She comes through the garage door carrying a large casserole dish covered in aluminum foil. "Hey, Miss Carolina. Putting this French toast casserole in this refrigerator for them to cook in the morning. Miss Laney's mama has them all set for food. She and her friends have the garage refrigerator full!" She slides the white casserole dish into the bigger stainless steel refrigerator in the kitchen. "I'm trying to keep this one from being packed to the rim."

"You are a godsend, Zoe. How do you like working for Laney?"

The girl smiles. "It's a dream. My dad and Kimmy aren't all that reasonable. Neither is my own ma, if I have to be truthful. You can't ever seem to please them. Miss Laney thinks everything I do is great. Makes it easy to work for her."

I jump in. "Looks like Savannah got a job working for your father at the Dollar Store."

"Really?" Zoe folds her arms across her. "And that Anna is your daughter-in-law, right?"

"Right." I pause to let her think because it looks like she's doing some heavy thinking.

She finally lifts her shoulders in a shrug. "Some folks like working with my pa. And some don't. And he likes working with some folks, and some he don't."

"Well," I reason, "guess that's how most of us are."

She nods. "Yes, ma'am, except most of us don't let everyone know when we don't like someone."

"But your father does?" I ask.

She looks at me, light eyes staring right into mine, and says, "Seems you already know that, right? He didn't leave you wondering this morning, did he?"

That closes my mouth and causes me to take a deep breath before I nod in agreement. "No, you're right. He didn't leave me wondering."

"And, Miss Carolina? He doesn't change his mind." She looks out the window at the car pulling into the driveway. "Well, there's Angie. I'm going to go. Tell Miss Laney I'll be back around tomorrow when the little ones are laying down for their nap after lunch." She picks up her backpack and opens the big side door, but before she leaves, she looks back in. "And don't worry, Miss Carolina, it's not so bad. Dad never has liked me."

She grins and waves as she pulls the big door closed behind her. She runs down the steps and looks like a young girl heading off to a fun outing. Not a hardworking girl having to be the adult for two families. I look around at the sparkling kitchen. Shoot, she may actually be the adult in *three* families.

Coming through town on my way home from Laney's, the night sky still isn't completely dark even though it's after nine o'clock. I roll down my window and let the smell of honeysuckle waft in with the sounds of millions of bugs. Summer nights are the stuff songs are made of. Wish I remembered to enjoy them more.

The shops, including Ruby's, are all closed, but there are a few people in the park. Looks like some kind of meeting letting out at the depot, and folks are taking their time getting back into their cars. As I start to turn at the end of Main Street, I see FM walking along the sidewalk on this side of the park, the opposite side from his house. Pulling into a parking spot, I call to him.

"Oh, hey, Carolina," he says. "Where you been?"

"Went out to have supper with Laney. She's been put on bed rest."

He leans a hip against my car next to my open window. "I did hear that. When's she due to have that baby?"

"End of August, but guess her doctor says if she can only make it until the end of July he would like it."

He nods but doesn't say anything. It's almost like we are avoiding something, but I can't think what. Anna and Will, maybe? But what can be said about them that we haven't already said? The comfortable pause turns awkward. Well, at least it does for me. FM looks fine. So I blurt, "Did you hear Gertie is moving in next door to you?"

"You don't say," he says as he tilts his head toward me. "When?"

"Uh, tomorrow, I think."

"Now, that makes sense."

"Really? Why?"

He bends down to look at me closer. "Like she was going to stay up there with you forever?"

"I thought she might go home."

"Chancey *is* home to Gertie Samson. She mighta left when she was barely out of those teenage years, but it's still home." He straightens up and looks across the hood of my van towards his home. "Well, Missus has the porch light still on so I better get on home. Better get some lovin' before she finds out about her new neighbor!" He steps away from the van and winks as he laughs. "Don't come a-knockin' if the front porch's a-rockin'! Night, Carolina."

Now that he mentions it, my husband is home tonight, and we have our own front porch. I put the van in reverse and then head up the hill.

However, as I pull across the tracks, I see our front porch is occupied.

"There she is!" Bryan yells as he jumps up from his rocking chair. As I get to the steps, everyone on the porch stands up. There's Will and Jackson and Savannah and... wait, just my family? No love interests or nosy neighbors or police?

"What's going on?"

Jackson holds his hand out to me as I step up onto the porch, then he leans to kiss me. "Hey honey, we're just moving out to the back deck. Bryan has a surprise."

I pull back a bit and whisper, "A good surprise or a bad surprise?"

Savannah sighs. "It better be an amazing surprise."

Jackson puts his other arm around his daughter and guides us both towards the front door. He says, "What did I tell you about playing hard to get? Guys need to hunt a woman. Let Alex hunt you."

Will cocks his head and says, "I don't know. Sounds like Alex is pretty good at hunting."

Savannah punches his arm. "You don't know anything. You don't even know how unhappy your wife is. But she's finding *plenty* of people to talk to about it." Savannah darts out from under Jackson's arm and dashes through the front door.

"Like I care," Will says following his sister, until I grab his arm.

"Wait, Anna is your wife. You should care."

He shrugs, pulls out of my grasp, and walks toward the light of the kitchen.

With a sigh I look at Jackson. "How was dinner with Bryan?"

"Come on, I'll tell you later. Bryan's been waiting to show you something."

The overhead light in the kitchen is on and crowded around the sink are all three of our kids. As I get close I see what Bryan is doing. Lifting a paddle of ice cream from an old-fashioned ice cream tub. "Oh, delicious! I haven't had homemade ice cream in a million years. Who made it?"

Bryan speaks up, "Me. Dad bought the stuff, but I put it all together with a recipe from Google."

I stick my finger in the white drifts and take out a dip. "Where did you get the ice cream maker?"

Jackson looks at me. "It was sitting on the front porch earlier. I didn't notice it until Bryan asked me about it when we were leaving for dinner. Didn't you leave it there?"

"No, I've never seen it." Savannah and Will both shake their heads when I look at them. Savannah picks up the top bowl stacked on the counter. "Well, it'll probably poison us all, but what do I have to live for anyway? Give me a scoop."

Will agrees. "Yep, me too. Dying by ice cream doesn't sound so awful." And he picks up the next bowl. "What flavor is it?"

Bryan scoops as he talks. "Vanilla, but there are toppings over on the table. Oreos, chocolate syrup, strawberries. We're having an old-fashioned family ice cream party, just like the note said."

As I hold out my bowl, I ask, "What note? Like an ad in the box?"

Jackson asks, too. "Yeah, what note?"

Bryan lays down the scoop and sticks his hand into his back

pants pocket. "Here. This note. I found it in the ice cream maker."

I roll my eyes at Jackson. With my full bowl in one hand and the folded note in the other, I go to the table and sit beside Savannah.

I pile on some of all the toppings and take my first bite.

"It's really good, isn't it?" Will says. "Good job, bro."

Savannah agrees. "This is way better than the ice cream from the store."

With the note laid on the table, I unfold it with my free hand and then read the handwritten words: "Be happy. Eat ice cream. Quit fighting and remember you are family."

Surprisingly, tears rise up, and I sniff. "It's not signed," I mumble.

Bryan reaches for another spoonful of crushed Oreos and says, "Who's fighting?"

But his question is met with silence. Will's eyes are wide, and he's looking at the rest of us. Savannah's eyes match Will's, and then she looks back at her bowl.

Jackson only nods and reaches over to squeeze Bryan's shoulder. "Good job, buddy."

We all eat for a few minutes, then Will starts in on a story about something that happened at work on the car lot. We laugh and eat. And, basically, do what the note instructed.

Chapter 25

"How is it none of my kids give a hoot about gardening and yours are so into it?" Susan asks as we stand in the kitchen watching Bryan instruct Grant in what needs to be done in our garden.

Shrugging, both mentally and physically, I answer. "Maybe it's all new to Bryan. Grant grew up with your gardens."

"So, I've ruined them? I got my love from gardening from my mother and grandmother. They didn't ruin it for me."

"But did you *always* love it, even as a kid?"

Susan sighs. "Yes. Just a big, ol' dork. Anyway. You ready to go?"

We're headed down to Ruby's to get the day started. Although with Jackson home, I got up early for coffee before he left to meet Will for breakfast.

Last night was like a relaxing swim in a cool pond on a hot day for the Jessups. We laughed and talked and breathed. Oh, that reminds me. "Susan, do you know anything about this ice cream maker?" I walk over to the sink where the old teal plastic maker still sits.

"You mean like how to use it? Looks like it's just a regular old-fashioned one. Pretty straightforward to use, I think."

"No, do you know where it might've come from?"

She steps closer to it and looks inside it. "No, why?"

"Someone left it on the front porch with a note telling us to enjoy it and not forget we're family."

"Really?" She takes a closer look at it. "No, doesn't look familiar. But would have to be someone who knows what's been going on with y'all, right? Where's the note?"

Moving past her, I pick it up from the kitchen table. "Here it is. Recognize the writing?"

She shakes her head. "It's just printed, so harder to tell." She presses her hand to her stomach. "Let's go. I'm starving, and I've only had two cups of coffee."

We get in our separate cars which are still in the early morning shadows in the front of the house. The sun isn't fully up over the trees, but the heat isn't waiting on the sun to arrive. By time I get in the car, the back of my neck is wet with perspiration. I swipe my hand to dry it and then ruffle my short hair. I miss having enough hair to pull into a pony tail. My thick hair feels like I'm wearing a toboggan hat.

By time I park across from the shop, the AC in the car has me sweat-free. As I cross the street, I watch FM and Missus hanging red, white, and blue bunting on their porch railing. Everything downtown looks festive and ready for the holiday. Even Ruby has changed out her plastic poinsettias for bunches of blue roses. Plastic blue roses, of course. However unrealistic, they beat faded poinsettias for July Fourth by a mile.

"Hey Ruby," I say as the door opens, because Ruby is out from behind her counter and near the front door. Shocking, I know.

"I'm busy here, can't you see? Get you a table, and if you want coffee, pour yourself a cup. Get refills for that table back there, too."

The café is almost full, so I snag a table for me and Susan by placing my purse on the tabletop. "Where's Libby?" I say over my shoulder as I head towards the back.

"Doctor appointment. She's got hemorrhoids," Ruby shouts.

"Ruby! I don't think she'd want you talking about that out in public."

Ruby stops beside her next table and wags her head at me. "Then why did you ask?"

"Never mind." I pour two cups of coffee and take them to our table, but before I can sit down, Ruby yells at me.

"Take the muffins in the oven out. Sit 'em on the counter back there. And did you forget to get those refills?"

Susan figures out the situation as she comes in the door and says, "I'll get the coffee refills."

The hot muffins smell amazing and are oozing with blueberries. Risking my fingers, I pull two muffins out and put them on saucers for me and Susan.

Ruby stomps around the counter. "Out of my way."

I press against the side of the warm oven and let her by. Imagining myself invisible, I slide out the counter opening and into our booth, just as Susan sits down across from me and says, "Poor Libby. She's having surgery later this summer when her grandson gets back in school. Wonder if she's told Ruby she'll be out of work for at least two weeks, probably more."

"So, does everybody know about Libby's, uh, problems?"

Susan nods a bit and pulls one of the saucers towards her. "Oh, look at these. The berries are huge."

"Carolina! Come get this," Ruby shouts from behind me.

"Ruby, I'm eating. I have a job I have go to. Didn't come here to work, too," I yell back.

"Fine by me if you don't want the lemon curd I made for those blueberry muffins."

Susan and I stop, mid-bite, and as I put my muffin back on the saucer, I say, "Be right back."

Of course, I have to hand out the small bowls of lemon

curd to the other tables, but it looks well worth it. Smooth and warm and such a beautiful shade of yellow. And its looks have nothing on its taste, I find out.

"I'm becoming redundant saying each of Ruby's muffins is my favorite," I say as I settle back into our booth, "but this really is my favorite."

Susan nods and mmm's her agreement and spreads another bit of lemon curd on the piece of muffin she's eating. It must be good, she's eating whole bites again, instead of the bird pecking she usually does.

Before I take another bite, I hurriedly say, "I went out to see Laney last night. Can't believe your sister is on bed rest."

"Me either. How are you managing up at Crossings? Don't you have your wine and cheese thing this afternoon?"

I laugh and pick up my cup—which is empty. "Want a refill? Figure I'll just go get coffee instead of waiting for Sunshine to come back out here and wait tables."

Susan drains her cup, as I scoot from the booth while explaining, "Laney is directing her empire from her canopy bed. She's got Angie and Jenna making deliveries and Zoe setting everything up. Be right back."

One glance at Ruby tells me to pour my own coffee. She's cradling her cordless phone on her shoulder and talking, while scooping batter into muffin pans. Then I hear her say my name.

"Carolina! Hang up this phone."

She releases it by lifting her chin as my hand touches it. I make sure it's hung up and try to sneak back out without being stopped again. But alas, "Did you know it takes two, sometimes three, weeks to get back on your feet after hemorrhoid surgery? Talk about a pain in the butt," she growls. Then looks up, "Okay, that's funny. Pain in the butt. Oh, there's Libby. Thank God."

Libby races up the middle of the café. "Oh, I'm so sorry, Ruby. Just had to get some bloodwork done. Who knew it would take so long? Oh, bless your heart, Carolina, getting your own coffee." She rushes by me to get the coffee pot, and I just step back to let her pass. Once she does, I start back around the counter.

Almost made it.

Ruby calls, "Carolina. Might need some help from you. I was just on the phone with my daughter Jewel, who's coming later in the summer. She's going to leave her two teenagers here to help out for a couple weeks when Libby's out. I don't like teenagers, never have. Maybe I'll just send them up to your house to hang out since you seem to always have a passel of 'em up there. Isn't your coffee getting cold?"

"Oh, yeah. Okay." This time I do get all the way to my seat. I lower my voice. "Do you know anything about Ruby's grandkids? Couple of them are going to be here helping out while Libby's off."

"No, except Jewel was right wild when she was in school."

I nod. "Ruby told me that herself one time. So, what are you up to today?"

"From here I'm going over to Laney's to visit with her a bit. Then I have to go to Costco to restock the snack shack at the park. Figure I can get anything Laney needs from there, too. Oh, plus, well, I haven't told her yet, but I'm going to have a baby shower for her at my house. That way I can have all my family and our friends up there to see it at one time."

"Perfect, let me know how I can help. When do you think you'll do it?"

Susan wipes up the crumbs around her and brushes them onto her saucer as she answers. "Going to check with Laney this morning. This has been good to get to catch up, miss our mornings here. When did we get so busy? I want to stop in and see the shop with you before I go."

"Oh, and you can meet Bonnie. Gertie hired her, and she's perfect. From up in Laurel Cove."

Susan tilts her head as she says, "Bonnie? Oh, from the lunch group. So is Patty going to work at Andy's Place?"

I pause before standing up. "Oh, wait, I didn't tell you. Gertie made herself a place to live there. At Andy's Place." I can't help but grin. "She and Missus are going to be next-door neighbors."

"Perfect!" Susan exclaims as she stands. Turning toward the door she adds, "Looks like Missus found out." Standing outside on the sidewalk, Missus is motioning for us to hurry. She might actually be stomping her foot. Yeah, looks like she heard.

"Hey, Missus," Susan and I say in unison as we walk out of Ruby's.

"This is not to be borne," she says. "Simply not to be borne."

As I walk past her, I say, "Come on to the bookstore and we'll talk about it there."

Missus stands her ground. "If I wanted to talk about this with an audience I would've come into Ruby's. Privacy is still in order at times. Although many on Facebook have completely forgotten how privacy even works."

Susan grins. "Missus, everyone is going to know that Gertie lives next door to you. How private can something like that be?"

"Next door to *me*?" Missus turns to look at her house, and we watch her eyes travel to the side where the purple, orange, and green building nestles close to her tastefully decorated home. "Oh, good Lord. She's going to live there?"

"Yes," I say. "Listen, I've got to get to the store. Walk with me."

Susan starts walking and Missus sidles up to me, tucking my arm in hers. "The private matter is between us. Keep walking, Susan." As Susan moves ahead, Missus slows us down. Finally she takes a deep breath and says, "Anna wants a divorce. A divorce! Will has obviously given up on the marriage,

199

I mean he did move home, and now going back down to Marietta to see his old girlfriends."

That stops me. "What? Will doesn't have old girlfriends in Marietta. He never dated in high school, much. They're just taking a break. Things have happened so fast for them. Everyone needs to just chill out."

She centers on me by moving to grasp both my forearms. She looks into my eyes. "Anna has a lawyer. One with that godforsaken place she's working. She's being advised by that man she works for. That Kyle person. FM tried to talk to him, but it didn't go well." She lowers her voice even more. "I hear your talk with him didn't go well either."

I sigh. "Wasn't much of a talk, he yelled at me."

Missus tightens her grasp on my arms and presses her lips together.

I tighten my arm muscles to try and loosen her hands. "Listen, Jackson and Will went to breakfast this morning." I get one arm away from her by lifting my arm up to look at my watch. "When I hear from Jackson, I'll let you know what Will says. Maybe she's just trying to get Will's attention. You know, he can be kind of clueless when it comes to Anna."

She shakes her head and steps away. "Carolina, she's not playing games. That Kyle man has her mesmerized. It's like he's drugged her." She grabs my arms again, tighter. "Oh my God, do you think he's drugged her?"

Tugging away from her, I say, "No. She's enjoying being appreciated and working. Listen, I have to go. But I'll let you know what Jackson says."

Leaving her standing on the sidewalk behind me makes me sad. Missus is not someone who ever gets left behind. She's world-class at making mountains out of molehills, and I've laughed at my share of her antics, however...

However.

Susan sticks her head out the door of the store. "You better get in here." She pushes the door open wider, and I enter into chaos.

Shannon is screaming about glass, and Bonnie has her hands above her head and she's clapping while repeatedly saying, "Children! Children!" Kimmy pops up from behind a chair near one of the bookshelves and says, "Hi, Carolina. We love your shop." Then she turns to Shannon and yells, "Stop screaming, they have shoes on." And she flops into the chair with a paperback.

Zoe tiptoes past me with little Katherine in her arms. She rolls her eyes at me and says for their mother's benefit, "No, Kimmy, they don't have shoes on. Remember you said it was summer and nobody cares if kids are barefoot? Stay still, K.J. I'll come get you when I put Katherine down. Here, will you watch her?" she asks as she sits the toddler on Shannon's counter.

I place my hand on the little leg. "Sure. What happened?"

Shannon starts hyperventilating about glass and kids. Bonnie marches towards me preaching about manners and kids. Zoe struggles to lift K.J., who's almost as big as she is, while she explains something about Kimmy and kids.

Kimmy is quiet because she's reading her book. Yep, just sitting and reading.

Katherine, at my elbow, lets out a scream of "Down!" and that's all I really hear. And probably ever will, since I'm now deaf in that ear.

Zoe manages to get K.J. over to where I am standing. "Kids knocked over that table. Broke some stuff."

Bonnie announces, "I told them the children shouldn't be in here while we were moving things."

Kimmy does respond to that. "You know what the Bible says about welcoming the little children."

Bonnie turns with hands on her hips. "You are not quoting scriptures to me, are you? Thirty years in education, I saw too many parents like you. Then I couldn't say what I wanted to, but now…"

I interrupt. "But now you are in a place of business and you can't say what you want either." I make eye contact with Bonnie and try to calm her down. Then I walk towards Kimmy. "Kimmy, it would be best if you take the children outside while we clean this up."

She doesn't raise her head from the book. "Zoe. Take them to the park."

Zoe cheerfully says, "C'mon kids. Let's go to the park. K.J., hold Katherine's hand while I get the stroller.

Susan darts around me. "Let me get the stroller. You're Zoe? I believe you're helping out my sister, Laney."

Transferring Katherine from the counter to her hip, Zoe smiles and nods. "Oh, you're Susan. I've heard about your amazing house. Laney's right jealous. Says she hasn't even seen it. That right?"

Susan pushes the stroller around the scene of destruction and chatters to the baby who appears to just be waking up. Guess the baby's used to sleeping through pure mayhem. Susan's concentrating on the baby and not looking up, obviously hoping Zoe will drop her inquiry. But she's not met Zoe.

"It is kind of embarrassing that you've not had your family up there, but I get how sometimes we just want to keep things to ourselves," Zoe commiserates.

"It's not that," Susan protests. "It's just we've been real busy and, and other stuff. Want me to push the stroller across the street for you?" As she says this, she looks over at Kimmy, who is still engrossed in her book. Then she looks back at Zoe. "Guess their mom is staying here?"

Zoe shrugs and heads out the door with Katherine on her hip and holding K.J.'s hand. "Sure. So just how big *is* your house?"

Susan sighs, but follows behind her with the stroller.

The door chimes a couple times as the door closes, and as that sound disappears, I take a deep breath and ask, "So what broke?"

Shannon is disgusted. "That huge clear vase I use for displays *all the time*. And a stack of candleholders that were going to look great on the book display Bonnie put together over there. I had put them on the table until we got the scarf down on the shelf. *All* of them broke." She keeps slicing looks over at Kimmy. But Kimmy's not paying any of this any attention.

Bonnie has gone to the back to collect a broom and dust pan. As she comes to the front she also steals looks at Kimmy. "Thought I was done with out-of-control children when I left public school teaching."

Missus comes in, and you can tell she's been given the low-down by Susan outside. She also looks at Kimmy, but not in slices or stolen glances, oh, no. She's staring at her like a cat stares at a laser light. She stops only inches from Kimmy's crossed legs. "Ma'am, something must be done about your children."

Kimmy doesn't look up, just starts flipping her foot which is hanging in midair. The flip-flop, now in motion, grazes Missus' pant leg. (Missus has on the same color scheme as yesterday, except her pants are red, her top white and blue stripes, and her shoes navy.) Missus reacts by stepping backward.

She opens her mouth, but before anything comes out, Kimmy asks, "What kids?"

Okay, that throws us all off. After a glance around to see that no one knows what to say, I pick up the dust pan and walk over to where Bonnie is sweeping.

Kimmy not only doesn't look up, she pulls a hank of hair down towards her mouth and swings her foot harder. She speaks as if she's reading the words off the page in front of her. "My kids are across the street, playing in the park. They bumped the table, which was obviously overloaded. They were just excited to get over by the window where there's that children's area sign. However, I see there are no children's books there. Isn't that a little misleading?"

Bonnie pulls herself up tall. "It's just an idea. I, well, I haven't even run it by Carolina yet."

"I think it's a great idea," I say, then add, "unless we don't want to have children in here. Guess we need to talk about it."

Shannon dumps some big pieces of glass she'd picked up into the trash can. "We've never really had kids in here before." Under her breath she adds, "Kids that act like *these*."

Kimmy stands up and weaves her way past Missus. She never looks back, or up, as she walks to the door. "Carolina, that's a good book. I think I'll come back for it later."

We are all quiet, again leaving plenty of space for the door chimes to resolve. Bonnie, Shannon, and I start talking about the shop and what we want it to be and whether having children's books is a good idea.

Missus interrupts us. "Did you see her face?"

"Not really," I say, and Bonnie and Shannon agree. So I ask, "Why?"

Missus just shakes her head and turns to leave, once again causing the bells to ring.

Bonnie smiles as we watch Missus on the sidewalk. "Well, she seems like a nice lady."

"You don't know her," Shannon and I say together.

Shannon sweeps another pile of glass pieces into the pan I'm holding as she sighs and says, "And I have more bad news. There's a store over in Canton called Pages & Petals. It's one of those fancy paper stores. No books or flowers, at least not real flowers. I guess she makes flowers out of the paper, or paper out of flowers, something. I was telling my mother about that maybe being our name, but she knows that store because it's next to the Sally Beauty Supply store. She says we probably shouldn't name it something that's already in the area. Especially when it's not even close to what we sell."

Bonnie sighs. "Oh, that's too bad. I do have to agree with your mother, though. Guess we're back to square one."

"Not really," Shannon says. "Mom came up with another idea."

"What is it?" I ask as I sit on the couch.

Shannon leans on the arm of the chair where Kimmy was sitting. "Blooming Books. What do you think?"

I smile. "I like it. Maybe even more than Pages and Petals, or Petals and Pages. Blooming Books. What do you think, Bonnie?"

"Not that it's truly my place to say, but I do like it. Blooming Books. I think it lends itself to making a beautiful sign. If you decide on it."

"Look at what all you've done!" I exclaim as I sit up straighter. "With all the commotion, I hadn't noticed. You actually moved the shelves."

"What do you think? Anything can be moved back where you had it. We might have gotten a little ahead of ourselves," Bonnie says in a worried voice as her hands clasp each other in front of her.

I laugh and wave a hand in surrender. "Yeah, that's not really possible with me. I tend to let folks do what they want. One of my most favorite quirks."

Shannon laughs. "Told you, didn't I? Said Carolina will be happy if she doesn't have to make a single decision. Everyone in Chancey knows that. Peter says he thought she'd eventually get tired of it, but so far…" She holds up her hands in question.

Well, now. Personal quirks aren't nearly so cute when folks openly talk about them. I'm not laughing now.

Shannon frowns at my frown, then walks toward the windows asking, "Did you see what Bonnie put in the window space?'

I stand up and follow her. Maybe I'll make a decision just to show everyone how wrong they are. Maybe I won't like how she *decorated* the window.

Bonnie follows us and takes a deep breath before she speaks up. "I truly hope you're okay with this, but I lined up our first book signing."

"Really?" I ask, maybe a bit more sarcastic than I intended. "Without even talking to me?" I sniff at the thought and lean over to look at the window display I'm sure I'll find unsatisfactory. "All you have out are the Quilting Shop Mystery books by Barbara Trapp. We have lots of other mystery series. No reason to stick with just one. Unless…" I turn, all sarcasm wiped from my face by pure delight and I grab Bonnie's shoulders. "No way! Is Barbara Trapp is coming here? Oh, tell me you got Barbara Trapp. I *love* her books."

Bonnie just nods and I pull her to me in a hug.

Shannon smirks and I can hear her eye's rolling. "See, what did I tell you? She's easy and can't help it."

CHAPTER 26

"Oh, aren't you a sweetheart," I say to my husband as he presents a platter holding a mountain of peanut butter and jelly sandwiches. As I entered the kitchen, he presented it with a big "Ta-da!"

Setting the platter down, he adds more to "ta-da" about. "And I checked in both of the new couples. The ones from Atlanta are already out and about. They had a bottle of wine and were headed out to the bridge. The ones from Alabama are still in their room."

When he turns, I'm there to give him a kiss. "I just love coming home to you. However…" I hold up the Piggly Wiggly bag in my hand. "Smooth peanut butter."

"But I thought you said you didn't care what Missus wants."

I kiss him to perk up his frown, and in between kisses, I whisper, "Well, I felt sorry for her."

He steps back and holds me at arm's length. "Wait, you felt sorry for who? Missus?"

Looking around, I ask, "Where are the kids?"

He shrugs. "Will and Savannah are at work, and Bryan is, well, I don't know. I've been home just long enough to make these sandwiches, but haven't seen him. Where is he usually this time of day in the summer?"

"If he's here, and he better be here, he'd be in the basement," I say walking to the basement door. "Bryan? You down there?"

"Yeah."

Jackson gives me a lopsided grin. "Guess it's not ideal, but better videogames in the basement than running the back roads of Chancey stalking Brittani, right?"

I lift a half of a peanut butter sandwich. "Well, he is kind of grounded for all that," I say just before I take a big bite. The sandwich is good in a memory kind of way. And in a good-tasting kind of way. Jackson leans forward for a bite.

Around his mouthful, he says, "I thought you didn't believe in grounding."

"I don't. No reason for me to be punished along with a kid. But in this case it works. He's old enough that we don't have to be grounded along with him. Plus, his infraction involved being out of the house. I probably should've taken away the video games longer, but—"

Jackson laughs as he takes the last bite of sandwich I offer. "But again, why punish us? I like him working in the garden as punishment. Helps us and makes him unhappy."

"Except it doesn't make him unhappy." At the window I motion outside. "Look at it. Looks better than it has all summer. He was out there at the crack of dawn this morning. He even talked Grant into helping."

At the same time we breathe in and look at each other. I say what we're thinking, "Didn't Tom Sawyer or Huck Finn do that? You know painting the fence?"

Jackson nods. "Yes, yes he did. Convinced his friends it was so much fun that they begged to help."

We both look back outside. This right here is the problem with having more than one kid, you can't focus. And the one that seems easy can get away with pretty much anything. Again we have the same thought and say it almost on top of each other. "We have to watch him closer."

Jackson reached back toward the platter. "Now that I think about it, he did seem smooth at dinner last night. That sandwich was good. I don't know when I last had a PB&J. Share another half?"

"Yeah, might as well eat these since I'm going to make the right ones. Oh, I know, we can put these out for this afternoon at our wine and cheese time. The new couples know about it, don't they?"

"Yep, and Laney had two trays of cheese delivered earlier. They're in the fridge. But, wait, you never told me why you felt sorry for Missus."

"Oh, yeah. Didn't want the kids to overhear. First, how did breakfast with Will go?"

Now Jackson is looking around not wanting other ears to hear. "I think he's done. When I was incredulous and pointed out the wedding, which wasn't necessary since they'd already eloped, was less than a month ago, he just stared at me. Finally said, 'Yeah, that probably wasn't a good idea.'"

I'm shocked. "The wedding wasn't a good idea? What about the marriage? That was completely on them. We didn't even know about it." I grab another sandwich half and talk with my mouthful. "He told us they loved each other. They wanted to be together. Here. In Chancey."

Jackson picks up his own half of sandwich. "Well, he's re-thinking all that now. Guess being with the guys from high school who are moving on to grad school and stuff, plus the whole 'realness' of a job—a hard, long-hours job—is a little too real, I think."

"What did he say about the baby?"

Jackson puts his head down, and his swallow is more than PB&J stuck in his throat.

"What?" I ask, trying to get him to look up, but he answers without looking at me.

"He said, well, he said there are always couples wanting to adopt."

Silence fills the space between us, then expands to the space around us.

Finally, the silence feels empty, and I start with the first question in my head. "Have he and Anna talked about this?"

Jackson peeks up at me and sighs. "Don't think so. Honestly, I think he just said it because it would be the easiest thing, he thinks."

"Like he's thinking!" I blurt. "This baby is already a very real thing in two families. He thinks Missus and FM will just let it go? He's not got a brain in his head."

"Yeah, that's pretty much what I said. And, again, I don't think he's really considering it, but just trying to find a way for this to not have happened."

I lean back against the counter. "Well, news isn't any better from the other side. Missus says Anna wants a divorce and already has a lawyer."

Jackson's jaw drops, and his eyes widen. "Will doesn't know that, I'm sure. He'll be blown away. Part of the problem right now is he says he doesn't know Anna anymore. He thought she was sweet and easy to get along with." Jackson laughs and adds, "You'll love this. He said she's meaner now than Savannah."

"Oh, Lord," I say, then push away from the counter and open the fridge. "What wine goes with peanut butter and jelly?"

Chapter 27

It was a beautiful way to start off the July Fourth celebrations.

Once we all got out of bed.

Cheerleaders were walking together in the "Freedom 2 B 2-Miler" and they spent the night at one of their houses, so I didn't have to get Savannah up. Bryan was up and ready when I went to knock on his door, already chattering about running the whole way with some of the other guys and how he might go out for track in high school. I always took his good nature as proof that I was a chill mom. Now, I question everything about him. One minute I convince myself no thirteen year old could be that sneaky, that fake, and good at it. Then I remember—a teenager is a teenager is a teenager. You only trust them when, well, never mind.

The two-mile walk/run started at the big Baptist church out of town and looped around a lake and some low hills. It was early, so the sun sat low, making shadows that stretched across grassy meadows. Once the kids ran on ahead, it was nice and quiet. Didn't seem like two miles at all before we were back at the parking lot, where Jackson was giving out ribbons.

He was bringing my ribbon to the house so I could get right in my car, go home for a shower, and then get to the store for our open house. First thing I see as I come around the corner from parking my car behind our building, off the parade route, is Peter selling coffee on the sidewalk in front of the bistro.

"Peter, great idea putting the coffee out here."

"Good morning, Carolina. Mother said you were doing the run. How did it go?"

I puff. "Walk, I did the walk. And better than I anticipated. Pretty little road, and I'd never been on it. I'll take a large coffee."

He pulls the cup off the stack. "Going to be a beautiful day." He smiles and shakes his head as he watches the spout on his coffee maker. "Hard to believe I have a business here on Main Street. Always thought about this growing up. These buildings always looked so cool, but just got more and more rundown every year. Now look at *our* street."

He holds out my full cup, as in a toast to the street. I follow his motion with my eyes and do see the difference from just last summer. As he puts the lid on my cup, I ask, "Have you seen the inside of our store?"

Handing me my coffee, he points with his head toward our sign. "You mean Blooming Books?"

I turn to look as well and feel my spirits lift. "Oh, it looks great in the sunlight, doesn't it? Came by to see it this morning before the run, but it was still pretty dark." Gertie's sign painter did a great job with the store name in dark red, and then added baskets of flowers and books around it. In smaller words underneath the big bright, "Blooming Books," it says "Bookseller and Florist."

Peter agrees. "I'm having that guy make us a new sign next week. Think we're just going with The Bistro. We kind of missed the train to call it anything else since everyone seems to have named it already. Plus, it fits. Or maybe call it Bistro Market?"

"Oh, I like that. Better description of what you do, after all.

Well, I'll probably see you later. Good luck today!" I say as I lay a couple dollars on his table and head off to my shop.

I unlock the door, just barely beating Shannon to it from the other side. The smell of fresh paint, books, and flowers is one we should bottle. Taking a deep breath, I relax my shoulders and bless Gertie Samson. Again. Our store looks amazing. The mix of books and flowers looks so natural.

Shannon laughs. "Pinching yourself? I know, I can't believe this is our place either. I never bought into that interior decorating stuff much, but I'm a believer now. This whole thing never even seemed possible to me. Never occurred to me it could look like this. And yet Bonnie seemed to see it right from the very beginning."

"I agree. Had a taste of this when we decorated the guest rooms at Crossings, but it seemed more like it evolved out of a bunch of us talking and brainstorming. But this? Gertie knew what paint we needed, then Bonnie did the rest. Practically overnight." I turn as the bell over the door dings. "And there she is, our decorator extraordinaire!"

Bonnie takes a small bow. "Always wanted to be a decorator, but that steady teachers' paycheck, not to mention the benefits, was hard to pass up. And look what I made last night." She sets a big Tupperware container on Shannon's counter – well, guess it's *our* counter. We decided to only have one area to check out, and with everything having tags, shouldn't be hard to keep track and separate purchases.

"Flower cookies!" Shannon exclaims. "How cute, when in the world did you make them?"

Bonnie waves her hand in dismissal. "Oh, last night. They're made with sugar cookie dough in the tubes, so I ran over to Wal-Mart and bought all they had last night. And lots of colored sugar. And I have some platters to put them on in my car. Couldn't carry everything in."

When we get the cookies arranged and set around the shop,

it's right at nine o'clock, so I block the door open as I explain, "We'll block it open for a little bit until folks get the idea. Then when it starts getting sticky in here, we'll close it. Can't believe people are already setting up chairs for the parade."

Shannon says, "Most are the parents that had to have their kids downtown to line up, but every year seems we get more folks from out of town. Small-town celebrations are all the thing now."

I nod. "Our guests at the B&B said the same thing. Laney has made us a Facebook page, and it's already gotten over a hundred likes. She even paid to advertise on Facebook."

"You know," Shannon says with a wicked smirk, "Laney might be more help laid up in bed than gallivanting around town."

I laugh and whisper, "I wouldn't say that to her face."

Had to whisper because our first customers are coming through the door.

This is going to be fun.

"Sorry I'm just now getting here," Jackson apologizes as he comes through the shop door as the parade ends.

"Here, have a cookie," I say holding out the one I was getting ready to eat. "I've already eaten too many. Why are you apologizing? I didn't know you were even coming by here."

He leans to kiss me with pink sugar-decorated lips. "Miss your open house? Never!"

"Sweet kiss. Wasn't the parade great? Did you know Bryan was riding on a float?" I ask as I consolidate cookie platters.

"Yeah. I was supposed to tell you. Didn't I tell you?"

A look is enough to answer him. (Word to the ladies, if you get mad at your husband every time he thinks he tells you something that he, in reality, never mentioned? You're going to be mad more than is good for your health. Or marriage.)

He shrugs and says, "Meant to. Beau asked him last night when we ran into her at the park after dinner."

Okay. Now we're treading into dangerous non-communication territory. "Beau? As in Brittani's aunt? The Brittani that caused our son to sit in the back of a police car earlier this week?"

He senses the change. "Oh, honey, really? I thought I told you. Are you sure I didn't mention it? We had to go by the ballpark last night on our way home, and Beau was there. She seemed fine." He takes the empty cookie platter from me. "Can't believe I forgot to tell you. Besides, she said Brittani would be with the cheerleaders, so they wouldn't be near each other during the parade."

"Jackson! Doesn't that seem weird to you?"

I can see he's trying to figure out what should be weird, so I raise my hands in surrender. "Never mind. At least I knew where Bryan was." Then I add in a mumble, "When I saw him ride by on a float."

"Exactly," he says with a grin, then he looks past me. "Oh, and you must be Bonnie."

"Yes, I am. Good to meet you, Jackson. I'm so enjoying working with your lovely wife. Here, I'll take that empty plate. Making a stack of them in the back."

Jackson shakes her hand and then hands her the plate. "Well, Bonnie, Carolina has talked about how wonderful you are. The place looks amazing," he says.

"Thank you," she replies. "Our open house has gone well, I believe. Almost time to wrap it up."

"It's been so busy," I add. "Folks are in such a good mood. It was great to hear the band playing and all the sirens. Now on to softball and the kids' games." To Bonnie, I add, "I'm overseeing the duck pond. Missus says it's well within my scope of capabilities."

Bonnie speaks up. "Oh, and the fireworks up in Laurel Cove are wonderful. We really put on a show."

Jackson shouts to the back, where she's rinsing platters. "Looking forward to it. Nice to meet you, Bonnie. Thanks for keeping Carolina on track with the shop. I need to get going."

I bristle a bit at the idea I need someone to keep me on track, but I'm not going to be mad on such a fun day. So I turn to straighten up a stack of books in the window and ask before he leaves, "You and Bryan are heading out to softball field now? Nothing has changed about that, right?"

He shakes his head and leans over to give me a goodbye kiss. "Nope. No changes or I would've told you. Bye." He's serious.

I kiss him anyway.

Chapter 28

"What in the Sam Hill are we going to do with all these sandwiches?" Missus demands. She might as well have cussed a blue streak, the way everyone is looking at her. "This is intolerable!" she adds even louder, in case we missed the Sam Hill declaration.

The ballpark is just out of town. You travel about half a mile to the three-way intersection, where you take a sharp right up the hill to go to our house. (That's the corner where the daffodils bloom in the spring.) For the ballpark, you veer to the left just a little bit, going down a little rise, and not far on your right are the elementary and middle schools. The high school is farther down that road, on the left. Across from the elementary and middle schools is the strip mall with the Piggly Wiggly, China Palace, and the brand new Dollar Store. At the end of the strip mall where the Dollar Store is, there's a turn-off, down a little country road. At the end of that road is the ballpark.

There's a ball field, of course, and lots of space for another field to be built in the future. For now it's just open park area, where the kids' games are set up for the day. There isn't a real concession stand, yet. That's why seemingly every living soul in Chancey made two dozen peanut butter and jelly sandwiches. (No need to say that some of us made four dozen. No *need* to say it, but said it anyway.)

So, everyone coming to the ballpark drove right past opening day for the big celebration for the newest business in town, the Dollar Store. Right past the bright flags and loud music. Right past the petting zoo in the parking lot. Right past the big purple, blow-up gorilla. Right past the big grills billowing delicious-smelling smoke. Right past the signs saying "FREE Hot Dogs." Right past... oh, who am I kidding? We all stopped. Every last one of us.

The hotdogs were delicious.

Missus looks at us like she can smell hot dogs on our breath. Even the little kids gathered around my duck pond game look guilty. We're all keeping our heads down and our hot dog breath to ourselves.

Then FM comes walking up, eating a hot dog. "Hey, hon, got you a dog. Anna wanted me to bring it to you." He usually has better sense than this. He marches right up to his wife. "Got mustard on yours. Hey, what are ya going to do with all these sandwiches?"

Missus' lips are pressed into a thin line. "Anna sent me a hot dog? That *man* probably put her up to it. Give me the keys, I'm going down there right this minute."

FM pulls his hand from his pocket, and it's barely free before Missus grabs the keys. She storms off, and FM looks at me. "Carolina, maybe you should go down there, too."

"Can't," I explain with a gesture towards the duck pond, which is really a kiddie pool with plastic yellow ducks floating in it. Numbers are written on their bottoms. When a child lifts up a duck, he gets a prize from the corresponding bucket. Not rocket science.

FM shoves the last bite of hot dog in his mouth and comes up beside me saying, "Go. Go. I've got this."

"No. Why would *I* go chasing her? She's your wife," I declare as I solidify my position, gripping the edge of the table the pond sits on.

He shoves with his hip to come between me and the table. As he swallows, he clears his mouth, and says, "Anna and Savannah are there. Missus has a thing against that man, and it might be good for you to be there. I've got this. It's the duck pond, an above-average cat could do it." One last maneuver by him, and I'm completely out of the way.

"Okay, I'll go. Just to make you happy." I turn towards my car and stomp across the grass.

Besides, I think I saw a cotton candy machine beside the purple gorilla.

"Did you hit her?" Missus is yelling from the back of the store. The bright, clean store is full of people, but silent. Well, except for the yelling.

I race back towards Missus' voice, and as I round the corner, I see her facing down Kendrick and Anna. Savannah just shook her head from her post at one of the registers as I passed.

"He hit Anna?" I ask as I grab Missus' arm.

Kendrick lifts his hands in surrender. "Oh, yes. And Savannah and all my employees. It's a regular torture chamber here."

Anna closes her eyes and shakes her head. Then opening them back up she stares at me and her grandmother as she says, "This is so embarrassing. I can't believe I wanted to live here. That I wanted you both as *family*." She's practically spitting at the end.

I turn to Missus and whisper, still clutching her arm. "What is going on? Are you okay?"

She lifts her chin, but says quietly, "His wife. Kimmy. Her face. It was bruised."

Kendrick gets louder. "So of course I did it. Me, the monster." He looks at Anna. "Can you believe these people here? Lady, I have a business to run. Excuse me. Anna, can you take care of your…" He shrugs then throws out his hand in our direction. "Her? Them?"

"Of course," Anna says. To us, she says, "You both need to leave. I do not want you here." Then she follows her boss.

After a deep breath, I turn to face Missus. "Did Kimmy tell you he hit her?"

Her face is strange to me because it's full of confusion. I've never seen her like this. Maybe she's having some kind of stroke. "Missus? Are you okay?"

She shakes her head and straightens her shoulders. I watch her physically dismiss the confusion from her face. "Of course I'm okay. However, I remain convinced that man hit his wife. You saw how she was in the bookstore. Hiding her face, pulling her hair across it, never looking me in the eye. It's perfectly obvious." She turns to stare at the front of the store, where things are getting back to normal.

"But, Missus," I reason, "Anna wouldn't defend something like that? She must know him."

"Oh, she knows him all right and has decided to take his side at all costs." She shakes herself, and as she heads down the aisle she says something more. Sounded like, "Why do we do that?"

Following her, I ask, "Do what? Who?" But she doesn't answer.

We pause near Savannah's register. I look at my daughter, but she won't look up at me.

Kendrick is running one of the other registers and has the ladies there laughing. He says, "It's always exciting on opening day, isn't it?" Then rolls his eyes in Missus' direction. I don't know where those ladies are from, but it must not be Chancey, because they look at Missus and keep laughing.

Sometimes when you live in a small town, it's easy to forget how large the outside world actually is.

"Let's go," I softly say to Missus and open the door for her. The laughter behind us is hard to ignore, but we do it. We walk out to my car. I lean against the rear fender. Missus, of course, stands ramrod straight. "So," I ask, "What was that all about?"

"He's a bully, and I'm positive he hits, well at least *hit*, his wife. I won't have it in Chancey." Then she sees me, really sees me. "What are you doing here? Who is running the duck pond?" She turns toward her car. "I have to do everything for you people."

She drives off, and I watch her leave. Guess I should get back to my duck pond duty, but I seem kind of stuck here, unable to move. Having trouble imagining Kimmy being hit. I've seen the movies, the Public Service Announcements, the music videos, but a person I know? Yeah, I'm lucky, or blessed if you want to say that. I haven't been around women who were abused. Okay, that I knew about. I'm not stupid, I know it happens, but, well… I can't imagine it. I've never even been near a fist fight. People hitting each other, in real life, just isn't in my experiences, so it doesn't compute for me. Maybe Missus is wrong.

Pushing away from the car, I pull my keys from my pocket and sigh. Maybe Missus is wrong. In the warmth of the car, I shiver.

It doesn't feel like she's wrong.

Chapter 29

Now I remember why I don't get up at the crack of dawn and walk two miles every day. Dragging in our front door late afternoon, every muscle in my legs begs me to stop at the couch. Just for a little while. Stretch out and sink into the cushions, close my eyes and let go. But, no. Into the kitchen.

Thank God I'm doing something easy for the supper picnic. Football hot dogs. I pull out a pot and fill it with water, then put it on the burner. As it begins heating, I open two packs of hot dogs, nice hot dogs, not the cheap, skinny, red ones. But even these aren't appetizing since I had a hot dog already today. Hot dogs are not meant to be eaten often, as they lose their appeal rather quickly. Oh well, no choice now.

Just glad FM arranged to take all the leftover PB&Js to a homeless shelter over in Canton, or we'd have been eating those for dinner tonight, too. Above opinion on hot dogs goes for peanut butter and jelly sandwiches as well. And I had my fill of those yesterday.

Missus refused to discuss the Kendricks once we got back to the softball game. And while the duck pond game isn't mentally taxing, it'll wear your nerves to the stub. Little kids were never my favorite, anyway. No need to tell my children that.

Jackson yells as he comes in the front door, "Going to take a shower. I'm filthy. Be right down."

Hearing him pound up the stairs, I listen for Bryan to come in behind him. When I don't hear him, I step to the living room door. "Bryan?" I call his name again from the front porch. I'd call his phone, but I took it away from him. It's got a dead battery and is in the basket on top of the refrigerator. Shoot, I wanted him to load the car. Just when kids get old enough to actually be help, they are never around.

Back in the kitchen, I get out the container of chopped onions, the ketchup, and the mustard. Then I tear off sixteen sheets of aluminum foil, just big enough to securely wrap a hot dog.

As I dump the water from the pot of boiled hot dogs, I hear Jackson coming downstairs. He pops into the kitchen.

"Hey," I say, "Where's Bryan?"

Jackson picks a hot dog from the pot and blows on it before taking a bite, but apparently it burns his mouth because I can't understand what he's trying to say.

"What?"

"Um, good hot dog," he says as he takes another bite, but this time I'm listening harder when he mumbles, "Up at Beau's."

"Beau's?" I ask as I start putting hot dogs in the buns laid out in front of me. "Why would he be at Beau's?"

"Honey, Beau explained that it was just a kid argument 'tween him and Brittani. He wasn't really stalking her. Guess Beau's sister overreacted. Has some history with guys getting out of control. Pretty dramatic up there, I guess." He laughs and starts helping me fill hot dog buns.

"Are you telling me Bryan and Brittani are back together?"

He guffaws. "No, not at all. I mean…" He pauses. "I don't think so. Right?"

And I explode. "You're asking me? I wasn't there. Just yesterday we stood right here and said we needed to focus more on him. Remember? Hand me two spoons out of the drawer."

Jackson nods as he hands me the spoons. "I *was* concentrating on him. We were on the same softball team all afternoon. We had a great time."

I hand him one of the spoons back and say, "One is for you to use. Put onions on each hot dog." Reaching across him, I turn on the oven and add, "I like Beau, but you remember how it felt when her sister was ready for Bryan and Brittani to get married? How we were 'part of the family'? We got invited to Brittani's sister's wedding?"

He stops spooning onions. "We did? Did we go?"

I also stop spooning onions to stare at him.

He quickly adjusts. "No, we didn't go. And maybe they aren't going together anymore. Maybe he and Brittani are just friends." This time he doesn't look up to see my stare.

"Here, you do the mustard," I say as I hand it to him. "So what were they doing up at Beau's?"

"Cleaning up the trailers the floats were on. They belong to her cousin or something," he says as he concentrates on making trails of mustard on each hot dog.

I add the ketchup and fill him in on what happened at the Dollar Store.

As we wrap the last ones up tight in their individual sheets of foil, he frowns and asks, "What do you think? Seem like it's true? You know, him hitting her?"

Opening the oven door, I motion for him to put the pan with all fifteen wrapped hot dogs inside, then I shrug. "I don't know. I need to talk to Missus some more, and I want to check with Kimmy, too. See what she says."

He leans back against the counter and folds his arms. "Don't like Savannah being in the middle of all that. Be interesting to see what she says, though."

I pull his arms open and then lean against his chest, saying, "I'm glad I have you."

He folds his arms back, this time with me inside them. He

rests his chin on my head and murmurs, "World seems crazy sometimes."

Nodding in agreement, I burrow closer and let the tension in my body go. This feels even better than the couch.

There's a steady stream of traffic headed up to Laurel Cove. The two-lane road winds up and up, and the slow drive gives me the chance to see the vistas usually missed when I'm driving. Surrounding us is lush greenery, both the mountains and the valleys. There are no splotches of spring flowers from dogwoods or mountain laurels. No reds or yellows or oranges portending the season change into fall. All is green. And thick. And healthy. Summer.

All our chicks ended up at our house and are now riding in the back of the van like they did for years. However, there is no squabbling over window seats, kicking of chairs, smelly feet, or iPods turned up too loud. All three are staring out their windows, not talking. I'd say pouting, except it feels deeper than that. More serious. Even Bryan.

We tried talking at first, but none of them took the bait. So, I'm enjoying the view out my passenger window, and Jackson is listening to the Braves pregame talk on the radio.

This, just us five in the car together, was something I lamented the loss of when Will surprised us with his and Anna's elopement. We would never be this again. Now we are, and it's not all it's cracked up to be. That time is truly over.

I think I appreciated it, recognized it as special. I think I did, but really, is that possible? To understand, to grasp every bit while it's happening? Or can you only see something once it's a whole, not something you're in the middle of, which means it has to be in the past? Our family of five is a thing of the past.

Even if Anna and Will don't make it, she's part of our family. And there's the baby.

Strange to be on this side of things. Up until now, I was the one creating, forcing change. Bringing home a fiancé, a husband, then three babies. I was on the pushing, expanding, moving forward side of things. Now? Now I'm on the being left side. I'm on the holding ground, keeping traditions, letting go side of things.

Letting go. Letting go. Wonder if you get used to it?

"Here we are," I announce as we make the turn into the country club parking area. "Missus said there's a big area of grass for parking. And don't you all scatter. We need help carrying everything."

Parked, Jackson opens the back door, and we load up chairs, coolers, blankets, and bags. One cooler is cold for drinks, the other one has our hot dogs in it. The wide open area at the beginning of the driving range is where we park, but we have to cross back over the road to get to the picnic area. Down below that area a small lake sits, and apparently the fireworks are shot off behind the lake, as everyone faces it. Mountain peaks surround us, and a welcome breeze makes the summer temperatures more tolerable.

Jackson lays face down on the blanket, and I unfold one of the canvas chairs to sit on. I sigh and relax for the first time all day. Savannah sits down on the edge of the blanket, and Will rests on the bigger cooler. Bryan is digging through the bags.

"Now what?" Savannah asks.

"Are your friends here?" I ask, without opening my eyes.

"I guess," she answers. "Everyone said they were coming up here. Only thing to do, sounds like."

Bryan sets forth his first priority. "Can we eat? I'm starving."

That gets Jackson's attention. "Yeah, me too."

So much for relaxing. "Okay, fine. Bryan, hand out the

plates and napkins." I get up from my chair. "Don't need utensils. There are chips, whole dill pickles, and cookies for dessert. Canned tea, soda, and water in the cooler."

"Guess I'm eating with y'all?" I look up to see Anna standing at the corner of our blanket.

"Of course," I say. "Will, open her a chair. Bryan is handing out paper plates."

Jackson gets up and stretches. "What's everyone want to drink?" he asks as he begins handing out cans and bottles.

"Really?" Savannah sighs. "There are onions on all of them?"

When I turn towards her, I see she's opened up three of the foil wrapped hot dogs. "Yes, and quit opening them up, the steaming of the bun and all is the idea. Boys, eat those she's opened. What, you don't like onions, now?"

She rolls her eyes, "I've never liked onions."

I flop in my chair beside Anna and say, "Then scrape them off. You've always liked onions before." I try to share a smile with my daughter-in-law at my daughter's expense, develop some good will, but Anna's not having it. It's hard to do, but she's sitting stiff as a steel rod in a low-slung canvas chair. She has on the same clothes from earlier. A navy skirt and a short-sleeved white shirt. She even still has on her lanyard with her name and assistant manager trainee title under the Dollar Store logo.

Will is eating his second hot dog and hasn't said a word. He finally says sideways to Anna, "Who'd you ride up here with?"

"Missus and FM dropped me off. They're at the dinner in the clubhouse. She tricked me. I thought I was eating there."

"Oh," Will says. Then adds acerbically, "Sorry."

"Apology accepted," Anna says, and I tense. Jackson looks at me with raised eyebrows.

Will's voice gets harder. "So where's your boss? With his family? Bet his kids like fireworks."

Anna stares at him and then, with a small smile and superior tone, answers, "Mr. Kendrick is in the clubhouse at the dinner for the important people."

Will crumples up the foil in his hand and throws it across the blanket in the direction of the plastic trash bag. "So that's how they got you up here. Funny, you were just a stray we brought here from Athens, but now you're too good for the rest of us."

Stray? Yikes! "Okay, that's enough, you two." I reach out and put a hand on Anna's arm. "Anna, we're glad you are here."

She smirks. "Will's right. I'm only up here on this mountain because I hoped to keep Missus off my boss. She attacks him every time he turns around." Then she swings her head to Savannah. "Right, Savannah? You saw her today. She's completely out of control." Anna looks back over her shoulder. "I only hope she's under control in there. Kyle is just trying to do a good thing in Chancey."

Will stands up. He stands over Anna's chair, and he's livid. "Kyle? You call him Kyle? Who are you?" He stomps off and leaves the rest of us with open mouths.

Bryan tries to fix things by holding out the package of Oreos he'd just pulled out and offering them to Anna. "Want an Oreo?"

She shakes her head and smiles a bit, although it doesn't look much like a real smile. "Oreos? No, I don't want an Oreo. I don't eat chocolate, remember? Of course, why would any of you remember, or care? You didn't want me sticking around, anyway." She leans back in her chair and eats a chip from her plate.

"That's not true, Anna," Jackson says. "Remember, we took you in last year when no one even knew who you were."

There's that 'not real' smile again. "Oh, when I was a 'stray'? Guess I wasn't thankful enough. Didn't pull my own weight. You know I was free labor for all the things Carolina and Savannah didn't want to do."

I'm stammering now. I don't know who this girl is. "Anna, no. Never. You were just so helpful, and we loved having you there. We love having you in our family."

"Really? You're glad Will isn't heading off to law school? That he's selling cars and living back in your house?"

When I pause to try and say none of that matters now, she steps into the pause. "See, told you." She sets her full plate, minus the one chip, on the ground beside her, then stands up. "Thank you for dinner. It was... interesting." When she turns around to leave, Kimmy appears out of nowhere and marches up to her.

Kimmy's jean skirt is straight and tight. She has a navy blue sleeveless shirt tucked in and a silver belt around her waist. She has on silver wedge sandals and a silver clip holding her blonde hair up in back. She has on makeup, but not like it's hiding a bruise. It's actually done very well. She's small and doesn't exactly have a figure, but she doesn't look like the hillbilly I have in my memory.

She brushes some floating strands of hair to the side, then puts that hand on her hip and tips her chin at Anna. "There you are. Kyle said you offered to watch the kids. They're done with being cooped up in there. They're over in one of the bounce houses. Baby's in that red stroller there. I just fed him, so he should be good for a while." She leans toward me. "Hey, Carolina. Thanks for helping Anna out. Good to get to meet folks inside, where it's air-conditioned and there's a bar." She starts walking away, then turns back to yell, "Diaper bag is under the stroller."

Savannah stands up as we all stare at Kimmy's retreating

back. "Good luck, y'all. Those kids are a nightmare. I see Jenna and some others. Give me a couple Oreos, Bry."

She walks off in one direction with her handful of cookies, and Anna walks toward the bouncy house area and the red stroller. Bryan stands up and talks through a mouthful of chocolate and cream filling. "I'm going over there." He points with his elbow. "Will and them have a Frisbee. You want the Oreos?"

I present him an open hand. Yes, I want the Oreos. I *need* the Oreos. I *deserve* the Oreos.

Dark is taking way too long to get here. Until I found myself helping Anna, the kids play area hadn't registered with me. It's an actual carnival company they've hired. Not a carnival like at the fair, with full-blown carnies running the rides and the smell of sawdust and vomit. This looks like a church group hired to do face-painting and expensive rental games. Not our games, like the duck pond which still has mildew on it from being stored out behind the ballpark stands in a shed. The workers are young and friendly and all wearing collared shirts with a logo on the left breast that says, "Carnival Capers. We bring the fun!"

Sleeping baby Kevin and I wander around, and I'm realizing everyone here is from town. So, where are the Laurel Cove people? I walk past the last bouncy slide and look toward the clubhouse where things appear to be winding down. Noise level sounds like they thoroughly enjoyed the open bar and air conditioning. As I stand there watching the crowd of "important people" meander on the clubhouse lawn heading in this direction, Anna comes up behind me.

"They're done?" she asks.

"Looks that way. So, you volunteered to watch the kids?"

She sighs and crosses her arms. "I guess. For Kyle, not her. But anyway, I was kind of mean to y'all back there. Things just feel so stupid right now."

We turn and watch K.J. and Katherine get back in line to come down the slide again. There are two workers who have everything handled. "We really just want you to be okay," I explain. "Us and Missus and FM and Peter."

She shrugs. "I guess. But, well, I really like my job. I think I could be good at it." She turns and challenges me. "Did you know they have a whole manager training program? That I could become a manager of my own store? I don't need college or anything."

"Really? That's great, Anna," I encourage. "You are such a hard worker. They'd be lucky to have you."

"What do you mean 'they'd be lucky to have me'? They *do* have me."

Stammering, I say, "I mean in the management training program. Right now you just work there, right? You're talking about the future, aren't you?"

As K.J. dashes off the end of the slide and starts running in our direction, she flips around, facing me with her back to the little boy. "Why does it have to be in the future? The baby?" She looks down at the stroller. "A baby is not stopping me."

I reach out and grab her hand. "It won't. We'll help. Whatever you need. Okay?"

She looks out at the people coming from the dinner. Missus is there in a red dress with a white jacket. She's holding on to FM's arm and getting into a golf cart. As K.J. walks up and says he has to go potty, Anna doesn't break her gaze on her grandparents. When I see tears in her eyes, I pull her to me.

"Honey, don't cry. It'll be okay."

She pushes away from me. "How? Unless I do what my grandmother did and give my baby up for adoption. And look what a disaster that was. I'm stuck with it." She starts walking off and growls back, "C'mon, K.J. Let's go to the bathroom. Watch Katherine."

Oh, Katherine. When I turn back, I see just how much darker it's gotten facing away from the open driving range. Katherine is in line once again for the slide. The baby, Kevin, is beginning to stir, and I look for Kimmy and Kyle in the crowd near the clubhouse. I see them also getting into a golf cart with another couple. As they pull out, I watch where the golf carts are going. Walking around the big red bouncy slide I not only see the golf carts' destination, I find the Laurel Cove people. On the side of the lake, on a beautifully sculpted golf green, there are dozens of golf carts. They weren't there earlier, and now I understand the signs posted all along that side of the road about "No Foot Traffic" and "Members and Invited Guests Only."

"You didn't think they'd mingle with us commoners, did you?" a voice asks over my shoulder. I turn to see LaVada's granddaughter, whom I met at the hospital.

"Rose, oh, I don't know. It's my first time for Fourth of July here. Who all is down there?"

She smiles and says, "Laurel Cove residents and the special guests for the dinner. They invite us here for fireworks, and a picnic which we bring, then permit us to hang out over there. Keep the riffraff out of the way."

"But the games are pretty nice, right? They don't have to provide those," I say as I turn to check on Katherine again.

Rose shakes her head and laughs. "Yes, they are. They wouldn't have anything but the best for their Fourth of July celebration, which was earlier. This is all just leftovers."

As Kevin begins to cry, I lean over the stroller and pat his back. Then I straighten up and say, "Oh, that's why you didn't like me. You thought I was from Laurel Cove."

She looks down and nods. "Yes, ma'am. Grandmother set

me straight. Matter of fact I only came up here to find you and apologize. And to bring you this." She holds out a plastic grocery bag. As I look inside at the towel wrapped bread and small jar, she explains, "It's bread and a little jar of herb oil."

"Did LaVada make the bread? It looks homemade. Smells homemade."

"No, Ma'am. I did. Part of our deal, I do the cooking. She does the gardening. She's teaching me about herbs, though, so I enjoy using them in the oils and cooking. Well, I better get going. Getting dark."

"Come watch the fireworks with us, and then we'll give you a ride home. Just let me get Katherine. Guess her parents aren't coming for them. This is Kevin," I say as I begin pushing the stroller to the slide.

Rose follows me, making excuses, which I don't answer as they sound pretty weak. I don't think she's got a reason not to stay, but feels she has to try.

"Katherine, let's go watch the fireworks." The little girl takes my hand, then looks around. "K?" she asks me.

"K.J. is coming. Want an Oreo?"

With a quick bob of her head, she comes right along beside me and the stroller. Most times I might worry about feeding a child cookies, but these particular parents don't get a minute of my worry. Rose walks on the other side of the toddler, and Katherine reaches up to hold her hand.

"Oh! You want to hold my hand?" We walk along, and it's not the fast falling darkness making Rose stumble as she walks. It's her staring at Katherine.

I ask her, "Not used to being around children?"

She shakes her head. "No, I'm the youngest in my family. My brother and his wife don't have children, and my sister isn't married. She's getting her doctorate in Texas. How old is she? Katherine, I mean."

"Um, almost three, I think. The baby is about six months. There's our blanket."

As we make our way, an explosion and a burst of white light sends sparkles across the surface of the lake. Katherine jumps and starts to cry. "Take the stroller," I say to Rose as I bend down and scoop up the little girl. Just as we get to the blanket, Jackson and Will arrive from the other side. I make the introductions while digging the Oreos from the picnic bag. With another explosion and a burst of green up high in the sky, we all look up and settle down. Katherine looks around, a cookie in each hand, then plops onto Rose's lap.

"Oh, hi there," Rose says surprised, but in the fading green light, I can see she's delighted.

Kevin, however, is not. I pull him out of the stroller and just as he begins to settle down, another explosion sets him off. "I'm going to walk around with him," I say as I stand up. "Maybe I'll take him to his parents. Surely they don't want to miss his first fireworks show."

Jackson chuckles. "I bet they do."

Back over near the games area, where we aren't disturbing anyone, I take a seat on a bench and bounce Kevin on my knee. Being up and moving settled him down, so he's no longer jumping at every boom. K.J. comes running up and pokes his head in his brother's face.

"Hey, Kev!" He makes funny sounds and faces while Kevin reaches for him. Anna sits at the end of the bench. With another firework, both of the boys focus on the sky. Kevin on my lap, K.J. leaning against the bench seat.

"Did Kyle come by this way?" she asks.

I shake my head. "Not since he and Kimmy went off on the golf cart. Can't believe they left you with all three kids. But then, guess they're used to it with Zoe. Where is Zoe?"

Anna shrugs. "I don't know. Kyle complains about her being at Laney's all the time, but then he brags about how much money they're paying her. He believes work is very important."

"Work? Or money?"

Anna ignores, or just plain misses, my sarcasm.

"Both. Wish *I'd* known that earlier. My mom always talked about work like it was to be avoided at all costs. Whenever she had to work, she would get sick." She turns to look at me. "I love my job. And I'm keeping it." She swallows and lowers her voice. "I'll keep this baby, if y'all want me to, but I don't think I want to be its mama."

"And how do you think that's supposed to work?" I whisper back at her.

She shrugs. "Don't know. Guess that's for y'all to figure out. I figured out that I can't run off, have it, then give it up for adoption."

"Glad to see you realize that isn't a good plan."

She agrees. "Yeah, because I'd lose my job."

I sigh. Sometimes she's just so nineteen. "Oh Lord, yes. It's all about your wonderful job at the Dollar Store," I expel in a huff.

"I'm keeping my job. And I'm going to be a manager. If y'all, you and Missus and Will and Peter, all think this baby is such a great idea, then you can have it. I'll just be some kind of aunt."

"Anna, be serious. That's no way to raise a baby."

She leans back and takes a deep breath. "I am being serious. It'd be easier to just give it up for adoption, but everyone freaks out when I say that."

"Have you and Will talked about any of this?"

She looks at me and squints. "Will? Will's more confused than I am." She pauses. "You know, we really did think we loved each other, but I think we were both just scared."

"Having a baby, especially as young as you are, is scary."

She tilts her head off to the side and stares up at the exploding designs in the sky. "No, before the baby and all that. I was scared of being alone, and Will was scared of being a lawyer." She pulls her eyes back down and stares at the top of K.J.'s head, resting between us. "You know Will doesn't want to be a lawyer, don't you?"

"What? He's always talked about it."

She shrugs. "All I know is when I told him I was pregnant, he was mighty relieved. And first thing he said was, 'Now I don't have to go to law school.'"

My mouth hangs open, all the way through the finale's mass explosions. As I pull my mouth shut, I know she's right about Will.

And even though it rings true, I'm thoroughly, deeply disappointed. Jackson will be disappointed, too. Which tells me why our son didn't tell us sooner.

Well. Hasn't this been fun?

Chapter 30

"Hasn't he wanted to be a lawyer for ever?" I ask Jackson. Again. He doesn't answer me, as he gave up answering me about the four hundredth time I asked him that question last night and this morning. We are taking a walk down the hill to the river with our cups of coffee. There's only one church service today since it is actually July Fourth, and there are no Sunday School classes. The one service is at eleven o'clock and in the park at the gazebo. So, we are having a lazy morning, much needed after such a full day and late night.

Looks like we're in for afternoon storms the way the clouds are building. There's a stiff, warm breeze which is keeping the mosquitos by the river away from us. We stop beside a fallen log and sit down. It faces the river and you can see the train bridge, so it's our favorite spot down here.

Since Jackson is no longer answering, or seemingly listening to, my exhausting concerns this morning, I try a new tactic. "What did you think of Laurel Cove? Rose really seems to have a chip on her shoulder about it, doesn't she?"

He sighs. "Yeah, she does. But then she was explaining her grandmother's property matches up to it the whole way, and the Cove people continue to pressure her to sell. Guess there's a stream there they want for a horse trail."

I sip my coffee. "With all the curves in the road, I didn't

realize it was that close. Only took Will a few minutes to walk Rose home through the woods, though. But it was kind of strange how all the Cove people were on the golf carts on the other side of the lake. Oh, I didn't tell you. Susan is going to have a baby shower for Laney and Griffin, so you'll get to see their house. Everyone will get to see it."

Jackson stands up, "I thought Laney's on bed rest?" He says as he offers me a hand up.

I take his hand. "Apparently it's not total bed rest. She acts like it is, but it's more that she needs to rest throughout the day. Being on 'total bed rest' must feed that Southern Belle part of her persona. Plus, she got to order some lovely nightgowns and robes, Jenna says. For holding court."

Jackson keeps my hand in his as we walk out of the woods and begin up the hill. He swings it and laughs. "Also allowed her to hire herself an assistant. Shaw was telling me about the girl, Zoe Kendrick, right? That family just moved lock, stock, and barrel into Chancey. Did they apologize at all last night about leaving their kids with you and Anna?"

"Yeah, right." I scoff. "You've not met them. Both Kyle and Kimmy remind me of tough little mutts. Not much to look at, but so good at strutting around, you can't help but watch them. And as for keeping your distance, that doesn't work either because they'll march right up in your face. Pretty hard to ignore."

Halfway up the hill, I stop, face him, and take hold of his other hand, too. "But really, what about Will and Anna? Do we just let it go on falling apart like it is? Do we step in? Is a divorce the right thing for them? And what about the baby?"

Jackson looks down, then back up at me with squinted eyes. "Is there any chance that giving it up for adoption is the best option?"

I suck in my breath, and in that express my shock. Trying to cover it, I nod and say, "Okay, okay, we can talk about it."

He rushes to explain. "I mean, if she truly doesn't want to be its mother."

Tears fill my eyes. "Our grandchild? Never get to know him or her? It belong to another family?"

He pulls me into his arms and soothes me. "Here, I'm sorry. No, that's not a real option." He pauses, then I feel his arms tighten as he says, "I guess we're not too old to have another baby. Look at Laney and Shaw."

There. There's the thought that has kept pressing into my mind whenever I left a crack exposed. I close my eyes tight and let it form completely. My forehead rubs against his chest as my head shakes back and forth. Nothing in me lifts. No bit of joy surges in my chest. Instead there's a flutter of pure panic at my center, and the word "no" echoes back and forth from my heart to my brain to my mouth. However, it doesn't come out. Instead, I take a step back, force my head to nod, and say, "It's something we should at least consider."

Jackson nods once and turns toward the house. I walk beside him, but we're no longer holding hands.

Thunder more than worship keeps our eyes on the sky during the outdoor church service. It's an even smaller crowd than anticipated, and that crowd is only as large as it is because no rain has fallen yet and the thunder is distant. We mainly came because my plan for lunch is sandwiches from the Bistro. Peter and Alex had advertised they were running a special on Italian beef sandwiches today. They set up borrowed picnic tables on the whole sidewalk since the other shops, including Blooming Books, are closed today.

I'm not the only one having trouble concentrating on the service with the smell of beef and peppers wafting across the street, the threat of imminent rain, and the kids running around at the back of the congregation. Plus, no one remembered to set up a sound system. Or maybe they were afraid of lightning, but seeing as the audio/visual team has trouble inside the sanctuary on a weekly basis—I'm figuring a little lightning could only help.

My head lifts when folks around me echo, "Amen." Putting my hand on Jackson's arm, I stop him from standing, and he leans toward me. I whisper in his ear, "You help put up the chairs, I'll go order our lunch and get us a table." He nods and then we both stand up.

Apparently, I wasn't the only one coming up with that plan as each couple appears to have split duties as we did.

Susan and her mother are crossing the street beside me. "Good morning. Happy Fourth of July," I say to them. "Susan, didn't see you last night up at the fireworks."

She tugs on the front of her short linen jacket. The pale yellow makes her tan look even darker, and her ponytail isn't the jerked-up affair I'm used to. It's smoothed back into a simple gold clasp. She rolls her eyes. "Didn't know where to sit, with the Laurel Cove people or with y'all. So just skipped it and went over to Laney's. We got the shower all planned out."

"Y'all have a golf cart?"

Her mother laughs. "Of course they have a golf cart. Everybody in Laurel Cove has a golf cart."

Susan steps ahead of us a bit with a jerk of her head. "What is the big deal about having a golf cart? You can buy one, you know. They sell them to *anyone.*"

"Yeah," I say with a nod. "I guess they do. But I've just never known anyone that had one. So when's the shower? And how's Laney feeling?"

We slow down as we step up onto the sidewalk outside the Bistro. "Shower is Saturday afternoon," Susan says. "I want to have it catered, but Mother insists that isn't how we *do* things."

"Well, it's not." Mrs. Troutman puts her foot down, literally and figuratively, as she stomps her white pump lightly. She has on a soft green and pink dress, and her hair is done in her weekly style, fresh from her standing Friday appointment at Beulah Land. Friday hair appointments are left in wills in small towns across the south.

She continues. "And we are not eating on paper plates at my daughter's shower. If you don't want to wash a hundred luncheon plates and a complete punch service, then invite fewer people. And there will not be men present." She gives a tiny shake of her head—her hair does not move—and walks away from us.

Susan screws up her mouth and snorts through her nose. "There's the problem. Mother wants an old-fashioned shower, Laney wants a party, and I want to finally get folks off my back about the house."

I think for a moment. "What if we have two showers? First one can be like your mother wants with her friends, then one for the rest of the folks and the men, later?" We get in the line, which is snaking around the inside of the store.

Susan thinks while I add up how much food I need to order. She pulls her phone out of her skirt pocket and starts pushing and sliding things on the screen. "You know, that could work. Let Mother have the shower she wants to have and then a pool party-pig roast-shower later. Can we have Mother's shower at Crossings?"

"What? Just do them both at your house," I say, now completely distracted from the addition going on in my head.

"But your house fits my mother so much better than our place. It's so, not old-fashioned. Plus, it would be easier on Laney instead of one long day. And my mother and her friends will do all the work. We'll make it Sunday afternoon so the bookstore will be closed. A week from today." Her phone dings, and she looks down. "Oh, Laney likes that idea better, too. She says you are an absolute doll for thinking of it."

She slides her phone back in her pocket and turns to the counter we've made our way to. "Hey, Alex. I need eight sandwiches to go. Two without peppers, one with extra onions, four orders of the Italian pasta salad, four with bags of chips, which I have here. No drinks, but eight cannoli." To me, she adds, "Love this idea of an Italian meal. Oh, hey Angie. You working here now?"

Angie laughs, but looks around nervously. "Just on Sundays. I'm still working at the Pig." Then I see why she looked around nervously. Alex reaches over and kisses her cheek. Not just a peck, either. She blushes and looks at him through lowered lashes. Oh no, Alex and Angie? She *should* be nervous. Savannah will kill her.

"What can I get you, Mrs. Jessup?" Alex asks. As he asks, he bumps Angie with his hip, and she giggles.

Savannah and Alex and Angie. Susan and Laney and a baby shower at my house. Being a grandma, possibly a *very* hands-on grandma. There's no room in my brain for a lunch order. Susan prods me. "Carolina, you're getting lunch, right?"

My eyes lock on Susan, then shift to Alex. "I'll have the same as Susan ordered." I have no idea what she ordered, but it'll be fine. Of course it will be fine. Susan did it.

We get our sacks, and as I get my bags paid for and back outside, I see Jackson has us a table. Me and him. Yep, kids are nowhere in sight. That's right, they aren't eating lunch with us today.

"Whoa, that's a lot of food," Jackson says looking in the bags. "Where's our drinks?"

I throw up my hands, "Guess Susan didn't need drinks since they're going up to Laney's."

"Is this Susan's order? I thought I saw her leaving."

"She did. No, this is ours. Believe me, I paid for it. I messed up. Got confused. Guess we'll just eat Italian Beef sandwiches all week."

He gets up. "Kids will eat them later. I'll go get us something to drink. Water okay with you?"

"Sure." I open my sandwich and lean over to keep from dripping the fragrant juices on me. Um, this is delicious. I tear apart a piece of red cherry pepper and spread it around a bit better on the sandwich. Suddenly the sky opens up and rain pounds down. I wrap my sandwich up, grab the bags and dart to stand underneath the overhang. Setting the bags at my feet in the couple feet of dry space, I take another bite and feel the juice squeeze down the side of my mouth. Others jockey around in the small area like I am, but most dash for cover inside the store. By the time Jackson finds me, almost all my sandwich is gone. I exchange what's left of my Italian Beef for the water bottle he offers.

"Uh, thought you'd come inside. It's pouring out here."

"Yep, it is. But I, well, I don't know. I was hungry. Plus, I got soaked before I could gather everything up. Take a bite, it's really good."

So, he does take a bite. And another, then the final one. He leans against the dark warm brick, still soaked with Georgia heat. The rain is solid, only allowing us to look through it in part. The white gazebo, green leaves, colorful flower garden, even as a car splashes down the street, we only have a vague idea of what we're looking at. Like those impressionist paintings I like so much, where you can't really see what you're seeing. Scenery through a rain-soaked window.

Jackson leans over and kisses my cheek and whispers into my hair, "Want to share another sandwich?" Not only is the rain a visual curtain, it's so loud I can't hear any other sounds, except my husband's voice in my ear.

I laugh and turn to find his lips with mine. "Why, Mr. Jessup, you read my mind."

So we lean on the warm brick, let fragrant beef juice run down our chins and remember what's important. Oh, and we laugh. A lot.

CHAPTER 31

Steam rises from the street as I cross over to Blooming Books. There are puddles and sunshine everywhere. Rain all yesterday and last night left the puddles; the sunshine showed up all on its own this morning and is doing its best to send the puddles on their way. A day stuck inside has me feeling happier than I know I should feel. Nothing has been resolved with Will and Anna. Savannah retreated to her tower room and refused entry to others. (Like I wanted to go up there.) On the bright side, Bryan didn't stalk anyone yesterday, as he was in our basement playing video games all day. Jackson and I had a wonderful rainy day together, but he left this morning for the job site in South Georgia. And there is still a baby shower at Crossings on Sunday. Still, I'm happy.

And I have a good chance of staying that way since I brought my own cup of coffee from home and do not have to go into Ruby's or the Bistro this morning.

"Hey Shannon," I say as I set my purse down behind the counter. "Mmm, smells wonderful in here. What is that?"

From her work table, Shannon looks around the tall bucket of flowers in front of her and answers, "Stock. Just got in a new order. Finally done with red, white, and blue for a while. Patty and Andy are home. Hear them walking around upstairs?"

"Speak of the devil," I say as footsteps echo, coming down the back stairs. "Hey guys. You're home!"

Andy strides toward the front of the store with Patty not far behind. He stops and puts his hands on his hips. "This place looks great. Gotta get over there and see what my place looks like."

Patty has on a flowered dress, hot pink with big white flowers on it.

I exclaim, "Look at you!"

She blushes as she walks over to where we meet for a hug. "You like my dress?"

"Yes, I do. It looks great on you." And as I look closer, I prove to be even more right than my initial assessment. Its scoop neck isn't low, but lower than a T-shirt neck like she usually wears. The dress hugs her chest, but then flares out around her knees. The sleeves are tight and come to just above her elbows. Her skin has a little color, although it's more pink than tan, and her haircut, really just a trim, from the wedding is still holding its shape. "I don't think I've ever seen you wear a dress."

She shrugs. "Because I don't have any."

Andy comes up behind her and hugs her around her waist. "You *used* to not have any," he says. "Now you have a whole closet full."

Patty giggles and bends her head to the side to rub against his bearded chin. "Andy likes me in dresses."

Shannon says, a tad louder than necessary in my opinion, "But do *you* like wearing dresses? You should wear what *you* like."

Andy, Patty, and I all turn to stare at her. Andy takes a step back from his wife and pulls her around to face him. "*Do* you like them? I want you to be happy. I'm fine with whatever you wear."

Patty leans and kisses him. "Of course I like my new dresses. Shannon's just, well, she's just asking."

Shannon focuses on cleaning the flower stems in front of her and says, "I was just asking. No need to jump on everything I say."

Patty and I share a look that ends with us rolling our eyes. With his long strides, Andy is already at the front door, ready to go.

"Patty, come on! I can't wait." He sweeps open the front door. He yells "See y'all later" as the door closes behind them.

"I have so many books to go through," I say as I meander through the shop. Shannon doesn't say anything, so I keep talking. "People keep dropping them off. Surprising how many are current and in really good condition." Still silence.

Finally, I walk right up to her work table and stand there sipping my coffee. Shannon has on her work apron and bright purple Crocs. Buckets of flowers surround the area, while cut stems and stripped off-leaves surround her feet and her workspace on the table.

Maybe I should be a little more direct. "What's wrong with you?"

She acts like she didn't hear me, but I have three teenagers, I can wait her out. Besides, the alternative is to start working.

"My stepfather isn't taking us on vacation this year. He's just taking Mama. I needed a week at the beach. I counted on it. He's such a bully just changing everything without asking anyone else involved." She is so mad she stripped off a white blossom instead of a leaf.

"So, it's usually a family thing?"

She sighs and stares at me. "Of course. Every year. That's what families do, go on vacation together. I can't afford a week at the beach, and neither can my sister and her husband, I mean they have three children. Plus, my mother likes to be with her grandkids on her vacation. That's the only reason she even goes to the beach!"

"Your mother and stepfather were in here Saturday for the open house. They seem real nice." The couple isn't that much older than me and Jackson, and both were so proud of Shannon. "Matter of fact, you've never referred to him as your stepfather, I didn't know."

"He raised us. Mama and he married when we were preschool age." She drops her arm, and her hand full of flowers settles onto the table along with her sigh. "I just thought he saw us as his *real* children. But a *real* father wouldn't do this. Leave his kids at home while he goes on vacation."

"Sure he would, if the kids are adults. I mean, it has to stop at some point, right?"

She stares at me, mouth open and eyes incredulous. Eyes filling with tears. "That is so mean. Where could I afford to go on vacation? And by myself? And who would watch my sister's kids so we can go out and she can enjoy herself? And he doesn't care one thing about what Mama wants." She shakes her head and then wipes her eyes. "It's really going to be hard living with them, now." She sniffles as she goes back to working on her flowers. "I'd move out, but where to? I just never thought he could be so mean to my Mama and me." She turns her back toward me, so I go back to my work area.

I couldn't wait to get out of my parents' home. I love them, but after college I would've worked two jobs, heck, three jobs, to keep from moving back home. As I pull an empty box over to the stacks and boxes of donated books to begin sorting, I wonder why. Why did I resist moving home so much? Have we made it too easy for Will to move home? It's been such an upheaval with the wedding, the baby, and problems with Anna that we've not set any rules or looked at the future seriously. Maybe we're making it too easy for him and Anna to give up on each other.

If only I thought they could make it together. If only it appeared they were something more to each other than excuses. If only they weren't pregnant. If only I knew if we were helping them or hindering them. Flipping a page on the tablet of paper I'm supposed to be listing books on, I start a different list.

Rent, food, transportation, insurance. Jackson and I have to talk. We didn't mention any of this to Will, but he can't just assume we're going to take care of everything. But then, why shouldn't he? Why shouldn't he be just like Shannon, assuming things will go on as always?

For the second time today, my thinking about a person causes them to appear.

"Hey, Mom?" Will says over the tinkling of the door chimes. "Where are you?"

Standing, I wave and then walk towards the front. Will has dropped onto the couch. However, he only gets part of my attention as Rose is standing beside the couch.

"Hi Rose. Will, what are you doing? Don't you have work today?" I say attempting to keep my voice calm. *Why is he with Rose?*

"I don't go in until noon. Rose wanted to see your shop, so I offered to bring her by."

"This is wonderful," the young woman says. "Books and flowers. Oh, hi," she says as Shannon steps over from her worktable. Rose strides to my business partner on those long legs and puts her hand out. "I'm Rose."

Shannon does a look up and down the tall, slim young woman with her long cotton shorts and sleeveless tank top. I know that lift of Shannon's chin, defense mode. It doesn't make one any taller or thinner, but really, what else are you going to do? "Hello, I'm Shannon. Co-owner and florist of Blooming Books."

Oh yeah, lift chin and brag. She really is cleaning out the arsenal.

Will grins and says, "Hey Shannon. Y'all, this place looks amazing." He jumps up and goes to Rose. "Let me show you out back. These buildings are ancient." He places his hand on the small of her back and stands entirely too close as they maneuver around the shelves and tables. Bright sunlight comes in as he opens the back door and they step out. Then it's dark again.

Shannon tips her head at me and opens her mouth. No words come out at first, then she asks, "Who is she?"

"A friend. Her grandmother lives up towards Laurel Cove. LaVada? I introduced them at the fireworks Saturday."

When a flash of light from the back says they've come back inside, we both turn to look that direction. They look like a matched set. Tall, thin, young, healthy. What in the world is going on?

Shannon's voice is a bit higher, a bit more innocent. "So, Will, how's Anna liking her new job? Must be nice to have two incomes in the family now." Oh, yeah, lift chin, brag, and then drop an inconvenient truth bomb. No short dumpy woman's arsenal is complete without that.

Will ignores her—the only weapon a man needs. Didn't hear it, didn't happen. He grins at me. "We're going to get some coffee. Can I bring you one back, Mom?"

"No, thanks. Brought some from home."

He opens the door and again places his hand on Rose's back. "Okay, see you later. Bye, Mom. Bye, Shannon."

Rose semi-turns and says, "Shop is lovely and nice to meet you, Shannon." Then they are walking down the sidewalk. Heads tilted in towards each other, long legs matching strides.

I mumble. "I'm going to kill him."

Shannon harrumphs. "You won't get the chance if Missus is at Ruby's."

I brace myself on the counter. "Oh shoot, surely he's not stupid enough to go into Ruby's acting like that. I figured they'd go to the Bistro."

"They didn't head towards the Bistro," Shannon adds as she steps to the front window and looks down the sidewalk. "Don't see them."

"Shoot! I'll be right back." I rush out the door and toward Ruby's. Possibly it could be a disservice not raising our children in a small town; they don't understand how things work. That everyone is watching you and grudges formed in a minute can last years. Or that everything is personal. Everything.

At the door of Ruby's, I slow down and step in as calmly as possible after running for the first time in... well... running. Will and Rose are in a booth on the side, and Ruby is pouring them coffee. Wait, Ruby doesn't come out from behind the counter unless Libby isn't here, but Libby is at the next table watching them. That said, Ruby *does* come out if there is something she personally needs to handle.

Great, Will, you've qualified for attention from Ruby.

I walk to the table, ignore Ruby, and slide into the booth beside my son. "Thanks for getting a table. Any of the berry muffins from Saturday left, Ruby?" I ask with that light, innocent voice that says everything is fine, go back behind the counter.

"No," she answers. But after a quick look at me, she studies the young people. And she sees what everyone can see. They like each other. They aren't even trying to hide it. Will is an idiot, but Rose?

Ruby leans to the side where her wiry arm is bent and planted on her bony hip. "Where's Anna?" she asks.

I see Rose connect that name with who Shannon asked about. She looks at my son and asks, "Who's Anna?"

Ruby brightens and answers. "His wife, his baby mama." With a look toward the front, she adds, "Here, this is Anna's grandmother now. Missus, got a seat for you right here."

My back is to the front, but I can feel the frost forming as you-know-who nears. Will and I neither one look over our shoulders, but Rose's good raising surfaces. She smiles and scoots over. Oh, poor, poor Rose. The young woman offers her hand to Missus. "Hi, I'm Rose."

"Of course you are," Missus says, ignoring her hand and the one offering it. "Carolina." She barely nods at me before nailing my son with her gaze. "Will."

We sit in silence for only a couple beats. However, it's long enough for the Rose I met in the hospital, the one with the thorns, to appear. She pulls herself tall in the seat. "I don't know what's going on, but Will and I are only friends." Again, I only get a moment of her look, before she turns it on Missus.

Missus, however, smiles, "Oh, so you know his wife is pregnant?"

Rose handles it well. "Why would that matter to me? We are friends who just met."

Except none of the women in the booth miss Will dropping his head and letting a small groan escape. Yep, we did neglect a crucial part of his education. Small Town 101.

"I brought y'all some chocolate-chocolate muffins. And they're still warm." Ruby is serving our table and that is as odd as it sounds. Ruby and serving in the same sentence. "Honey, where do you live?" Ruby asks Rose.

Rose answers. "Up on the mountain on Webster Road. Can I get some more coffee? Muffins look delicious."

"Of course, sugar. Up on Webster Road? You mean Laurel Cove Road?" Ruby asks as she pours coffee into the girl's half-full cup.

Rose shrugs. "If that's what you want to call it."

Missus pulls back. "You're a Webster." It wasn't a question, and Missus doesn't wait for an answer. She lifts her cup and takes a sip. "Should've known. Websters think everything

252

belongs to them. The mountain, the road, other people's husbands."

"Wait, now," I interject. However, there's nothing to interject in to. Rose and Missus are calmly eating their muffins and drinking their coffee.

Ruby laughs and pats me on my shoulder. "Lord, Lord, things just never do change, do they?" She walks off, still laughing.

I look at Will, figuring we'll meet eyes and share a moment of confusion. But, no. He's eating his muffin and looking at his phone.

Missus speaks up. "Quit looking at Will. He doesn't know about any of this, and he can't help being attracted to a Webster woman."

Rose looks at me and grimaces a bit. "I'm not like that. I'm not like my mother."

"And grandmother," Missus adds. "Although she never acted on things like your mother did. I guess LaVada couldn't help being, well, a Webster. But now I know, I'll be watching. This boy here is married to my granddaughter and the father to my great-grandchild."

Rose chews for a moment and nods. "Okay, but we're just friends. I'm not interested in anything else."

Then Will blows it by looking up from his phone, and finally, *there's* that look of confusion. Missus closes her eyes and purses her lips. Rose widens her eyes at him and clears her throat. I elbow him into not being confused. Hurt, maybe, but no longer confused.

"Hey," he yelps. "That hurt."

"Good. I'm going back to work," I say and move out of the booth. I'm only one booth away when Will calls, "Mom?"

I turn around. "Yes?"

He's tilted around towards me and asks, "You got any money for this?" He waves his hand at the table.

"No," I answer and keep walking. We are most definitely overdue for a talk with our oldest son. He has too much time on his hands. You hate to see your kids scratching and clawing for a living, resulting in them being occupied and fearful.

But you know, that just doesn't sound that bad right now.

Chapter 32

"You invited Kimmy and her husband?"

I'm whispering, but I don't know why. This house is so big I could be shouting, and no one at the party would hear. Susan removes another tray from the shelf refrigerator. Not to be confused with the regular refrigerator. The shelf refrigerator is for platters of food. Like the platters left by the caterers earlier. Not to be confused with the caterers that are still on site and cooking on the deck in the outdoor kitchen.

See, this is why I can't be rich. I can't remember to clean out one refrigerator, and hiring a caterer makes me fear them actually looking inside that one refrigerator (which isn't cleaned out). Susan, however, seems to be handling it astonishingly well.

There are over a hundred people here for Laney and Shaw's baby shower. We have valet parking, which is how everybody in The Cove does it. (Obviously.) There are two sets of caterers, one for the BBQ and one for the platters of appetizers, veggies, and other finger foods. Then Alex has set up a dessert area with cookies and candies from the Bistro. Another entrepreneurial idea he's trying. He's as enterprising as he is good-looking. Angie's working the dessert bar with him, and Savannah is pouting. Oh, it doesn't look like she's pouting, she's much too Southern for that. No, she's playing croquet with the younger kids on the lawn below the decks (and well in sight of the dessert bar).

Some teenage girls willingly play with younger children, but most likely if they are attractive teenage girls they are making a play for a guy in the area. Yes, I know that sounds cynical. Have you met me? Better yet, have you met Savannah? Or any attractive teenage girl in the South?

Susan steps up to me and reaches for the dish towel I'm holding. "Here, let me dry my hands. Yes, I invited Kimmy and Kyle. Zoe has become Laney's right arm. Why did you ask? They behaving?"

I shrug and admit that they are. "They just don't seem right. She gets on my last nerve, and he, well, I think he's mean."

Susan leans against the wall next to me. "How does Savannah like working for him?"

"Yeah, right. Like Savannah tells me anything. But you're right. She hasn't said anything bad. Anna, of course, adores him." My scowl deepens and maybe I've found the true source of my annoyance at Kyle Kendrick.

Susan squints at me, reading my thoughts. "Anything on the Anna and Will front?"

"No. He's with that *Rose* whenever he's not working. I've been meaning to ask you. So Rose is a Webster, what's their story? Missus alluded to it Monday, but the week got so busy I forgot. Plus, I was waiting for Jackson to come home so we could talk to Will about everything. Who are the Webster's?"

Susan smacks me with the towel and exclaims, "No way, Rose is a Webster? I didn't know that. Oh my word, no wonder Missus has been so cranky. Does Peter know?" She pushes away from the wall. "How did I miss this? I did not put two and two together. I've got to tell Laney. Come on, let's find her."

I follow but say, "I don't know how hard it'll be to find her, she's sprawled out in your chaise lounge with her varied assortment of presents arrayed around her. Who knew she could be even more self-absorbed?"

Susan turns to me as we walk down a hallway lined with lit lantern fixtures and calls me the B word. Like, the whole word. Out loud. Who is this woman? First she moved up here on the mountain, out of her hometown, now she's talking like the Yankees that live up here. And I wasn't being a bitch, just honest.

Okay, maybe with a little b.

As we near the end of the hall, passing the sunroom off to the side of the front living room where Laney is, Grant comes running to us from off the deck. "Mom, Dad says it's time to eat. He wants you to tell Aunt Laney. See what she wants to do."

Susan stops and asks him, "Do about what?"

Grant shrugs, then adds, "I don't know. Dad said to 'Ask Laney if she wants to come outside to eat or should we bring the food in on a golden litter for her blessing.' But why would there be litter? We have garbage cans, right?"

Susan laughs and looks at me.

I shake my head and grin. "See? Told you."

Susan waves her son away. "Tell Dad to go ahead and start serving."

When we turn the corner into the living room we are brought up short by the stacks and stacks of gifts. Then an even more shocking sight causes us to catch our breath. Laney is crying.

"Laney! What's wrong?" Susan and I rush to her side. She's laying back in the reclining chair, perspiring so much that her hair is wet. Her face is red and shiny.

"Oh, Susan. I sent Zoe to find you and Shaw. My water broke, and I think I'm in labor. I forgot how much this hurts. I'm too old to have a baby. Why didn't I stay home like my doctor told me?"

Shaw runs into the room and hears that, and he roars, "What do you mean? You said the doctor said you were good to come."

She moans and reaches a hand to him. "I couldn't miss my party. Oh, Shaw, this is awful," she says as she begins sobbing.

Suddenly the room is filling, and I begin the sorting of who needs to leave. "Everyone just go on and eat. Shaw and Susan are here now." I herd folks in front of me and make my way to Jackson to whisper, "Call 911. She's in a lot of pain, and her water broke."

Grant sees Jackson dialing his phone and comes to us. "Are you calling 911? Want me to give them our address?"

Jackson explains the situation then hands the phone to Grant and we walk back towards the small group around Laney. Jenna and Angie are there and both look scared to death. Laney is never out of control, often dramatic and usually loud, but never out of control. However, now she's in obvious pain and her clothes are soaked through with sweat. This is not good.

"Girls," I say as I come up behind them. "Your mom needs a little air. The paramedics are coming. Why don't you move right over here?" I steer them to the loveseat to the side of their mom. They sit down, and Jenna starts crying as Angie wraps her arms around her sister while we wait.

Suddenly a man comes running in from the front entrance area. "Grant came down to the house and said you need a doctor?"

Susan exclaims, "Tom! Thank God. Yes, this is my sister."

The man enters their little circle, and Grant, along with Bryan, comes to stand with us. Grant explains, "He's our neighbor. He's a veterinarian, but I thought he's better than nothing."

Jackson pats his shoulder. "Good thinking. Let's move out of here and give them some room."

In the doorway, a woman I know from town meets us. "Need a nurse? Just heard there's a problem. Is it Laney?"

We all nod our heads as she moves past us.

In the same hall lined with lanterns, there's a bench that I sink on to. Jackson tells the boys to go on and eat, that everything is going to be fine. As they leave, he leans down to hug me and says, "I'll get you something to drink. You want any food?"

"No, but a drink would be nice."

Just as he leaves, Susan comes out of the room with Angie and Jenna and heads toward me. "Tom says we need to clear the room. Girls, you sit here with Carolina, okay?"

They sit huddled together on one side, and then Susan comes around to my other side and bends down to whisper in my ear. "Baby's coming. Paramedics won't be here for a bit. Pray."

The sounds from the living room get louder and scarier. When I hear Shaw start crying, I get up and force the girls to come with me into the sunroom next door. As we walk, I call Savannah on my phone. "Honey, can you and some of Angie and Jenna's friends come up to the sunroom? They need y'all."

"Sure, Mom," Savannah answers, then whispers. "I love you."

"I love you, too."

I look up to see Will. "Mom, is there anything I can do?"

"Yes, go out front and watch for the paramedics. Then direct them in here."

He starts toward the door then dashes back and gives me a hug. He looks in my eyes and says, "Mr. Conner is crying. Miss Laney's going to be okay, right?"

He looks almost as scared as Jenna and Angie, and I realize. He's next for having a baby. He's probably never given one thought to childbirth, and here it is in all its awesome glory. Tears, screams, 911 calls. It's scary even when things goes as planned.

Growing up comes to our kids whether they, or we, are

ready. So I'm honest. "I don't know, son. I just don't know."
We hug again and hold tight, then I push him towards the front
door. Just as he gets to it, it opens wide, and a woman in a
striped golf skirt with a matching pink sleeveless tank top,
wearing only ankle socks, comes in. She's small and has her
black hair in a ponytail. Great, one of the neighbors is coming
to the party late. Apparently straight from the golf course. I
rise to meet her and steer her away.

"Hi, I'm—"

She cuts me off. "I'm Doctor Yang. Mrs. Conner's doctor.
She's here?"

"Yes, in here," I say stepping back and directing her into
the living room. As she enters she tells us all that she was on
the golf course when the service called her. Just happened to
be the golf course at Laurel Cove. She laughs with an easy
confidence, which immediately relieves some of the tension in
the room, and lifts one of her sock-covered feet saying, "My
shoes are at the clubhouse, couldn't wear golf shoes in here.
Hey, Miss Laney. What are you doing? I was playing a great
round today!"

The veterinarian and nurse apprise her of the situation as
Will calls to me from the entrance.

"Mom, EMTs are here!"

They rush in, and I point them in the right direction. Then
Will and I go back to the bench and perch on its edge. We barely sit down before two of the EMTs come running back past
us. Will jumps up to hold open the door, and they race inside
again pushing a collapsible stretcher. Griffin comes out of the
living room and asks me, "The girls?"

"Sunroom," I say as I head there with him.

He steps into the room. "Girls, come with me. They're taking your mom to the hospital. We'll follow the ambulance."

In one long exhale of people and equipment, the living
room empties, then the driveway empties. Susan flew by at

one point saying, "I'll call you from the car and tell you what the doctor said."

Then all is quiet.

Will closes the front door and leans back against it shaking his head. He's still pale, and when I try to talk to him, he just shakes his head harder and walks into the living room. I follow him.

The beige recliner is ruined. The room is too warm, the air smells metallic and salty. And the fear is palatable. Will stands, still shaking his head. He finally speaks up. "I had no idea it could go so wrong. I mean, I know it can, but I guess…"

"It's not normal," I say. "Usually everything happens at the hospital, and it usually takes longer. But sometimes it doesn't."

He turns and tries to smile as he says, "This makes it all real." As my phone rings, he points to it. "That'll be Susan. I'll let you talk to her. I'm going out back."

"Hey Carolina, the doctor said things were looking okay for the situation. Thinks they'll get her to the hospital before the baby comes. Laney calmed down a lot when she saw her doctor and that helped. Can you believe she was on our golf course? Apparently, she lives up here. How's everything there?"

"Everything is fine," I say. "We'll take care of it all. Did you call your mom? Need someone to get her?"

"No, she and her neighbor are going to meet us at the hospital."

We're both silent for a few moments. Finally, I say, "Man, that was scary."

She agrees, but her voice is muffled and full of tears. After a deep breath, she finishes, "I'll let you go, now. I'll call when anything happens."

CHAPTER 33

"We're on our way home. Laney is resting, and the baby is doing okay. Will you still be there when we get there?" Susan asks.

"Yes, the boys are swimming," I tell her from my seat on her back deck. Only a few of us are still here. I'll make sure we have a bottle of wine chilled for you."

"Oh, perfect. See you soon."

Savannah comes over to where I'm seated with Jackson, Peter, and a couple others. "So Miss Laney's okay? What's the baby's name?"

"Yes, she's fine, and Susan didn't tell me his name. Have to wait until she gets here."

"Well," she says with a glance behind her, "I helped Alex clean up the desserts since Angie left. Think I'll go help him unload it all at the Bistro."

"Yo, Savannah, you coming?" Alex yells down from the upper decks. She turns and waves up at him.

"Yes, I'll follow you in my car." When she looks back down at me, she's already backing up towards the stairs. "Tell Miss Laney I'm glad she's okay. Bye!" She runs up the stairs, to Alex, in her flat sandals, khaki shorts, and black sleeveless shirt.

Mumbling so only Jackson and Peter can hear, I opine, "How convenient for Laney to have an emergency delivery to take Angie out of the picture for my daughter. When is Alex going back to New York?"

Peter shrugs. He's clearly over this teenage drama. "So Susan's headed home?"

"Yeah. I'm going to go set out some food. They'll be starving. Oh," I stop in the process of climbing up from the lounge chair. "What should I do about the shower at Crossings tomorrow?"

Nobody around me has any answers, so I follow Savannah's path up the stairs as I reason out loud. "Well, I'll talk to Susan about it."

As I turn onto the upper deck, which is outside the kitchen, I look down to the pool. While most everyone left in the past few hours, the Kendrick family is still having itself a regular pool party. Grant and Bryan are in the deep end, jumping off the diving board, but the shallow end belongs to Zoe and the younger Kendricks. The baby is playing on the wide first step, with Zoe sitting beside him. Kathryn and K.J. have on water wings and are staying where they can mostly touch, near the bottom steps. Kimmy and Kyle are standing near a table, when a sudden burst of movement attracts my attention.

Kyle's hand grips his wife's upper arm. Just as their movement caused me to look, the jerking of my head causes Kimmy to look up at me. Her eyes catching mine makes his eyes follow, and as he sees me watching, he drops her arm and backs away.

"Kids, time to go. Get out of the pool," he announces. Once. One time and the kids get out of the pool. That's not normal. We all know that's not normal.

Kimmy waves and shouts my name. "Carolina! Have you heard from Laney? So worried about her."

Waving back, I tell her that all is well and Susan will be home soon.

"Wonderful!" she exclaims and grins. "We sure have enjoyed her pool, but we're going to head home now. Maybe we'll see her on our way out."

I nod and stare at the back of Kyle's head, willing him to turn around so I can shame him with a stern look. However, he doesn't look in my direction at all. Pretty sure my stern look wouldn't stir up any shame, anyway. Especially the way Kimmy is rubbing his back and laying against his arm. What's he got to feel shame for? His wife is so obviously happy.

Obviously.

Susan lifts her wine glass for a refill, which I provide. Seated on the upper deck, the woods and mountain below us are in solid darkness now. It feels like we are on the prow of a spaceship. Muted lights from the house provide a soft glow behind us. The air is humid and close, but ceiling fans stir the air from open rafters above. It's down to me and Jackson, Susan and Griffin, Peter, and Scott, who is Susan and Laney's brother. Grant and Bryan are hunkered down in the basement with a plan to play video as long as anyone will let them. They'd already been told that as long as they know they have to get up in time to go to church, nobody cares how late they stay up.

I admonish everyone to wait before taking a drink. "We need to toast." We lift our glasses together, and I nod at Susan to do the honors.

"To Cayden Shaw Conner."

We all touch each other's glasses, take sips, and relax back in our seats.

Jackson releases a deep breath as he repeats what we've

all said so often in the short time Susan and Griffin have been home. "I was really scared. Can't believe they are both fine."

Griffin agrees. "She looked so pale and helpless when they loaded her in the ambulance, and I was really afraid of what we'd find once we got to the hospital."

Susan starts laughing, chokes on her wine, and has to sit up to cough. "Then to get there and find out she was delivering in the back of the ambulance at the curb. Instead of sitting in a waiting room like normal, we all ended up loitering in the parking lot."

Griffin reaches for her hand. Their eyes meet as he says, "Then we heard him cry. Shout almost. We were having a party right there at the E.R. entrance."

Scott tips his beer bottle at his brother-in-law and shares, "Yeah, I'm making like ninety running into the hospital, and then I hear my mother shout, 'Praise the Lord!' Stopped me right in my tracks. What was my mother doing having a prayer meeting in the parking lot? So I turn around and there y'all are. Hugging and laughing. Leave it to Laney to make a scene."

At the same time several of us say, "Laney does love a scene." We laugh, and then I stand up.

"Come on, Jackson, we need to let these folks get some rest."

Susan stands, too. "Thanks so much for cleaning everything up. And for making us these plates. We were starving. I'd figured on dinner from a vending machine and a long night at the hospital, but Cayden and Laney surprised us all. He's only six pounds, but they said everything was good. And Laney was placing her order for takeout when we left. Scott, you're welcome to stay the night here."

"Thanks, sis," Scott says, "but I'm going to get on home. I bet we all sleep good. Well, except for Laney and Shaw. Their long nights are just beginning."

We all groan as we enter the kitchen. Jackson says, "We all remember those days." And we laugh, until Peter speaks up.

"I don't. Remember those days, I mean. I always thought I'd enjoy being a dad."

Awkwardly, Jackson starts to apologize, but Peter stops him. "No, man, no. Don't apologize; it just kind of hit me." Then he smiles and tilts his head. "But guess it's not too late, me and Shaw are the same age, right?"

Scott claps him on the back. "That you are. You just gotta find a woman that wants a young'un. You might have to go younger for that." He winks. "Me and you will go out looking sometime."

The men walk on towards the front door. Susan and I hug, and she nods towards them. "Guess that means Scott and Abby Sue are on the outs again."

"Shannon has her hat set for Peter. You think they'd be good together?" I ask.

Susan wrinkles her nose and sighs. "She's so immature that I always think she's younger than she actually is. And who knows, her father might throw in a dowry to get her out of the house."

As we get to the foyer, I say, "Oh yeah, I wanted to ask you about that. It's her stepfather? She's really put out with him. He's refused to take her and her sister on family vacation this year. I guess he's kind of mean? He didn't seem like it, but I only met him once."

Susan twists her mouth into a frown. "Don't believe her. He's so sweet. He raised those girls just like his own. He might've been *too* good to them, pretty much spoiled them."

I nod as I open the front door. "That's what I was wondering. Guess he's putting his foot down finally, but it's making my life less fun. Shannon's been a pill."

Susan leans her head against the side of the door. "I bet if you get her and Peter together, she'll get a whole lot happier."

We laugh, and I wave to her with directions to get a good night's sleep. Griffin and I hug at our car, and soon Jackson and I are headed down the mountain.

The bugs drone outside and the air conditioner hums inside, and I don't even remember passing the country club because I was fast asleep.

Chapter 34

Sometimes I sit down in church, and I'm just happy to get to sit still for a whole hour. But not today. Today I can't stop fidgeting. My mind is whirling around, not like a spinning top, that would be too focused. More like a ballerina on a big stage—spin, then put a foot down to stop the spin, and leap over to another place to spin for a bit, then suddenly I'm lifted up and completely off the ground by some guy in tights. Only to end up somewhere completely different on the stage. One thought doesn't get good and started before another begins.

Peter. He's doing the scripture reading today, so he's sitting up front facing the congregation behind the pastor. Each time my eyes light on him, I look around to find a woman to match him up with. But then as I look for the single women, I wonder how Missus got Anna and Will to sit together. Then I replay the argument this morning getting Savannah to church, well, not exactly church, but this church. She wanted to go to the Catholic one in Collinswood today with Alex. Her obsession with him is over the top, and she's not going to use God to get a better grip on him. She's sitting next to me, almost as fidgety as I am. She never sits with me, must be she thinks she's punishing me. She's right, it's killing me to have to sit here mad at her and not be able to tell her about it. On the front row with the youth, where Savannah also usually sits, is Bryan. However, that's not a safe place for my thoughts to land because he's sitting with Brittani. No, wait, he's draped around her, and she's squished up under his arm. That can't be comfortable for either of them. Yet, do they move? Oh no, joined at the hip is a well-known description for a reason.

Then Susan gets my attention from the choir loft. Her eyebrows are high, and she's pointing for me to look at – Oh, Beau has a new beau? Beau is my hairdresser and friend, at least when her niece Brittani is not accusing Bryan of stalking her—and Beau has four children by four different men. Apparently she only likes men when she's in need of a baby daddy. Let's see, how old is her youngest? Okay, I guess it's time. The new boyfriend is quite good-looking. Wonder if he knows the deal? That he'll be pushed off the stage once he's done his part. Wonder how folks would react if she showed up for church with a girlfriend?

I stand because everyone around me stands. Jackson pushes the open hymnal at me, and I reach out to hold my side of it. We sing something, and before the last chorus is finished, I fold the hymnal back over to Jackson and turn to pick up my purse. My name being whispered gets my attention, and I look behind us. Two rows back is Laney and Susan and Scott's mother.

She give me a thumbs-up and smiles. When the last note of music stops, she says, "Everything still good for this afternoon?"

Oh, so we *are* still doing that. The shower. But I try. "Oh, Mrs. Troutman, are you sure it's still a good idea? Laney won't even be there."

She nods and waves a hand at me as she dashes my hopes. "Of course. Everyone is coming, and the food is all prepared. I will get there at 1:30."

I turn back to Jackson. "Shower is on."

He rolls his eyes at me and says, "Told you. You'll have fun once they all get there. I, of course, will make myself scarce."

Savannah slumps and bites her lip. "Is this that thing you wanted me to help with? I don't have to come, right?"

I nod firmly. "Yes, you said you would. Think it was last week when you were trying to make me forget about that late-night trip to Alex's apartment. Remember? And just because you're being punished doesn't give you the right to act miserable."

She pushes past me to get out of the pew and says, "I'm not acting."

When Jackson laughs at her, I punch him with my shoulder and growl, "It's not funny."

He pulls away from my shoulder jab and sighs. He points to the front of the church. "And neither is that."

There, standing just to the side of the altar, with people milling all around, Bryan and Brittani are locked in a fierce kiss. All that matching of pressure points during the sermon must've caused a flare-up. Jackson takes some long strides up there and jerks on his son's arm.

Bryan steps back, grinning. "Oh, Dad. Me and Brittani are back together." He loops an arm around her shoulders, and they walk up the aisle to the back of the sanctuary.

Jackson meets me in the aisle as the newly reunited couple pass. We begin walking behind them with the small remainder of the crowd.

You know, if I can't concentrate on the sermon because of what I know is going on in just a few lives of the folks sitting there, I bet God is plum exhausted with what all he knows is going on with the folks sitting in the pews each week.

"Well, you know why she feels that way, right?" Gladys Troutman says as she pours another cup of pineapple sherbet punch. Her crowd of listeners grows, and it's not for the sweet, cold punch laced with maraschino cherries frozen in a ring of pink ice.

I sip my cup and, well, listen. Yes, I'm in the crowd, and yes, I want to know what made Missus go off like that. When Jackson and I got to the front door of the church to leave earlier, we weren't only hit with the bright sunshine of a July noon, but the dressing down of Kyle Kendrick like only Missus can, or would, do.

"If I *ever* hear of you intimidating your wife or either of your daughters – for that matter your sons, and extend it to your employees, too – if I ever hear of it, you will know all the wrath a godly woman like myself can muster. And if you think I can't muster enough to scare you straight, you just take a good look around. Any man, any real man, and this town is full of them, would be delighted to teach you how to treat a woman. I'm counting on you not getting caught so far out of line that I need to call the police, which I would not hesitate to do. However, I'm pretty much counting on you stepping across the line I'm lying out for you right now in front of God and everyone here. And when you do? You will not fare well. You push or grab your wife, and one of these people will let me know. You shout at my granddaughter or one of your other employees, and I'll find out. You strut around like the cock of the walk you believe yourself to be and say the wrong thing to the wrong person. I have no doubt you will not learn your lesson from this little talk. Oh, no. You're far too arrogant for that. And you just be aware, I will call on the men of Chancey to put you in your place."

She took a breath, straightened up, and looked around at the crowd that had gathered. Men had stepped to the front, and they were all staring at Kyle. Some nodding. Jackson moved past me to fill a spot beside Griffin.

Kyle shrugged and turned away as he said, "You don't know what you're talking about."

Missus lifted her chin and said, "Prove me wrong. Quit being a bully, and you'll not have one problem with any of these folks. Now, your kids are in the car, as I asked Zoe to do, but your wife is standing there hearing every word." Missus then called out, "Kimmy? You have my number in your phone. Hopefully there will not be any trouble, but if there is, do not hesitate to call me."

Kimmy is standing with her back to us, as she leans on the hood of their car. Her head bobs a couple times at Missus' directive.

Kyle had been walking towards his car, but when Missus called his name he turned around. Her voice was softer, pleasant actually. "Mr. Kendrick, we are happy you brought the Dollar Store to Chancey, and we are all happy to shop there, right?" She looked around, just as she had only a moment ago, except this time she's smiling at everyone. "And as long as you live here peacefully, we will make your store a true success. Probably a bigger success than any other store you've ever opened." Around her heads nodded and people spoke their agreement with her. She took a step towards him and held a hand out to him. "We can all live here and be very successful. It's up to you."

Kyle's jaw clenched even tighter, then it relaxed. He lowered his eyes, then grudgingly took the two steps forward to shake her hand. As their hands met, I noticed Missus' white gloves.

I'm thinking I might just get me a pair of them.

My memory of the afternoon and contemplation of purchasing white gloves is interrupted by the Gloved One herself.

She's just arrived and is standing between the front door and the dining room, behind the crowd gathered at the punch bowl.

"Please, Gladys, do tell us why I feel as I do about men who bully women and children. Why I think a community has an obligation to protect the vulnerable and oppressed. We're all riveted to hear how you were planning on stepping in and resolving this issue. I'm—" Missus breaks off and turns away from the dining room where the food for the shower is sitting, and she goes straight into the kitchen.

Gladys has turned almost as red as the cherries floating in the punch bowl. She closes her eyes and screws her lips tightly closed. One of the other ladies says something about how delicious the punch is, and the others take their cue from that. Suddenly everyone is chirping, loudly, about the table of homemade cakes. It is impressive, and I give it one more look as I rise from my seat. A tall coconut layer cake with a sprig of blue tinted daisies centers the table on a blue cake plate. There's a caramel cake, a red velvet cake, cheesecake with strawberries covering the top, and a dark chocolate cake. All are arranged around nosegays of blue daisies. Some of the arrangements have propped-up pictures of Cayden, printed out today from texts Laney sent.

Instead of fighting through the crowd, I go back into the living room to enter the kitchen. It's a busy place, but no one is talking. Everyone is focusing on what they are doing and keeping their heads down. Yep, Missus has been here. But she's here no longer, and an older lady filling coffee cups finally looks up at me and motions with her head to the back deck. I smile and whisper thanks as I pass her and open the glass door.

Missus is standing in the backyard looking at my garden. She has on a lavender dress and white pumps with a sensible heel. Her white gloves are still in place on her hands, and her hat still sits on her weekly hairdo from Beulah Land Hair Salon. That tells me she had just come in the front door when she heard Gladys' comment. If only she'd been a minute or two earlier.

She cocks her head and looks at me from underneath the brim of her hat. "Who did all this?"

"The garden?" I ask.

She sighs because I'm so dense. "Of course the garden. You obviously didn't do this. Any fool can see that. Jackson travels too much and your children, well, your children have been too busy making fools of themselves this summer, so… who did this?"

"Why are you being so mean? I came out here to tell you how I admire what you did after church today, but now? Never mind." I cross my arms and intend to pout, but then she bends her head down and brings one hand up to cover her mouth. She turns away from the house and me, and I watch in horror as her back begins shaking like she's crying. Missus crying?

I step ahead of her and point to the far end of the garden. Softly I say, "Come down here. We'll be out of view of the house." A tall, full bush with shiny green leaves sits at the corner of the garden, so we stroll behind it. There's a skinny wooden bench from an old picnic set, so we sit down.

She sniffles and then takes off her gloves to wipe her eyes with her bare hand. I dig in my pocket for a paper napkin from the cake table. "Here," I say as I hand it to her.

"Thank you, Carolina. Please forgive me."

We sit in quiet for a few minutes. It's hot out here, but the bush gives a bit of shade and every so often a breeze comes our way. The river below us is blue-green, reflecting the trees and sky. High above it, buzzards swoop to and fro. We watch them and just as I start to get up—after all, I am the host of the shower—Missus puts her hand out and lays it on my knee.

"Carolina, can I tell you something?"

"Of course."

"I've never told anyone this. There's something about you

not being from Chancey that makes it easier. You didn't know my father or my mother. You won't find what I'm going to say surprising or contradictory to what you knew about my parents." She stops there and takes a deep breath.

It doesn't feel like she's waiting for me to say anything, so I don't.

"My father was abusive. At home. To my mother. With me it was merely demeaning talk and threats, which I'm coming to see is abuse as well. Unlike many men I've read about, he never regretted his abuse. My mother deserved it, he always explained. She caused his anger, and, well, I'm ashamed to say, I agreed with him."

She's dry-eyed now and staring straight ahead. Again, even though there is silence, I don't feel like there's anything she needs to hear from me. So I just take slow, steady breaths and pray for calm. And there is an unnatural calm, like a blanket around us. My heart isn't jumpy, and my thoughts aren't scattered or fearful.

She smiles. "Have you ever wondered how someone as nice as FM could be married to someone like me?"

My mouth opens, but should I say it? "Well, to be honest, yes. It's obvious you love each other and you make a good match, but…"

"But…" She stretches it out, matching me. "Yes, I wonder, too. When he says he fell in love with me when he saw me up there on the Miss Whitten County beauty pageant stage, that isn't exactly true. He was offered the same money to vote for me that my father offered to the other judges. As you can imagine, something like that doesn't exactly stay a secret. My father did that my whole life, paid for any success. However, when FM refused my father's money, my father tore into *me*, not him. In front of FM. About how he couldn't even *pay* for me to win. It was awful. And then FM—" She chokes up and has to clear her throat. She finally continues. "FM defended me. Spoke back to my father, like no one ever had."

She suddenly turns to me and looks into my eyes. "Remember when you moved here and you would say you 'accidentally sold your house'?"

"Yes," I answer. "It just happened."

Missus nods and twists her mouth as she does. Then she says, "I accidentally married FM. After the pageant, when I won unanimously, father crowed that he didn't even have to pay FM, just scare him into voting for me. Father was merciless as we were leaving the pageant." She shudders and looks away from me. "It was as ugly as I've ever seen him, and worse, my mother had started joining in on his verbal abuse. It was like she saw a way to align with him." Missus shakes her head as if to clear it.

"Anyway, when we got to the entrance of the building, FM was waiting. My father always knew how to cover and he started telling FM he was wrong to have offered him money and he went on and on. FM apologized, actually groveled, and then asked if he could court me. I was flabbergasted, so were my parents. FM asked if he and I could have a few moments to talk. In private."

I interject. "FM apologized? Groveled?"

She shakes her head and says, "Wait. He figured that would sooth my father. After all, everyone always apologized to him. Him asking to court me was what really shocked them. I had never had many suitors. Well, my parents were so stunned, they simply agreed and went on to the car. They told me they'd wait there for me." She laughs a bit and continues. "As soon as they were out of earshot, FM took my hand and started walking, fast. Around the corner of the building was his car. He gently laid both hands on my upper arms and looked at me. He said, 'We're going to South Carolina to get married. You are never living another day under that man's roof.'" She lifts her hands, palm up, and says, "And I didn't."

"What?" I'm incredulous. "You eloped with him, right then?"

"Yes, and oh, did I make him pay for his spontaneity. I'd never been loved, so I didn't recognize him trying to love me. And I had no idea how to love him. Matter of fact, I hated him for many years. When we came back to Chancey, I sided with my parents. Now, I never moved back home, I wasn't stupid, but FM was made to look like he had stolen the princess from the castle. He was so beneath me. So not worthy of me. I was horrid to him. Then, about three years later, my mother passed away and my father quickly remarried. She was a middle-aged widow from a very good family near Atlanta. Well," she swallows. "Well, one day in church I saw that she had a bruise on her cheek and marks on her neck." Missus snaps her finger. "And just like that it all came back to me."

She closes her mouth and shakes her head. Then she exclaims, "As hateful as I had been to FM, I knew he would never lay a hand on me, and I began to see him anew. Luckily, Father's new wife wasn't as helpless or scared as my mother had been. She divorced him. It was a huge scandal, but it was in no way his fault, of course. He sold our family home without one word to me and left town saying he'd never come back to Chancey. We would go visit him at his home in Atlanta, when he was there, but mostly he traveled and then after a few years, he had a heart attack and died while overseas."

She draws in a long, calming breath before she says, "That felt good. Of course, people know parts, as I'm sure Gladys was getting ready to share when I came into your house. However, I've never said it all out loud before."

She looks down at her hands clasped in her lap and finishes. "When I saw Kimmy's bruised face and began watching her and that husband of hers together, I knew what was going on. As I've thought back, I remember I would think when my parents and I were in public that if only people knew what was going in our home. Then I realized later that people did know, they just didn't say anything." She bows her head, then jerks it back up, saying, "Well, not on my watch. Not in my Chancey." She stands up and folds her gloves together lengthwise. "My favorite quote is from Edmund Burke, 'All that is required for evil to prosper is that good men do nothing.'"

I stand up, too, and lean towards her to hug her. Her back straightens and her hands come up. "Oh no, let's not." She steps away from the bench and asks, "Susan?"

Looking up at the house, I echo her. "Susan?"

"Is Susan here?" She merely points at the garden as we walk by it.

I roll my eyes and acquiesce, "Yes, Susan did it."

"Carolina, please do not try to be something you are not. It's not attractive or honest."

Wonder where I can get a sainthood application for FM?

CHAPTER 35

"You look great," Susan says as she sits down at my table in Ruby's. "Few days at the beach can work wonders."

I take a deep breath, close my eyes, and lean back in my chair. "Oh, yes. It was our first time to see Jackson's mom's new place. It's in this tiny little town, and the basement apartment is perfect for a couple. Savannah and Bryan stayed upstairs with Etta."

Susan waves at Libby and turns her coffee cup over. "Did they get happier about leaving once they got there?"

I roll my eyes. "Have you ever heard of teenagers that don't want to go to the beach? It *was* short notice, and I know I considered not going. I'm not good with spontaneity, as you well know, but so glad we made it happen."

Jackson got up on the Monday after the weekend of baby showers and Cayden's early arrival, with a notice that his job site was going to be shut down for a week due to a concern about some of the concrete they were to use. Another round of concrete testing was going to take the week, and suddenly, we had time for a trip to the beach. With him on the job site, we'd thought we wouldn't be able to get away. We checked with Jackson's mom, who in one fell swoop last Christmas left Jackson's dad who was having an affair with his younger assistant; used a recent inheritance to buy a house at the beach; and moved. We hadn't had time to make the trip to the South Carolina coast, but with free time and Etta being between visitors, we piled in the minivan and headed southeast last Wednesday morning. We got back late Sunday afternoon, which was yesterday.

Libby carries a full pot of coffee and a plate of muffins towards our table. As she nears she exclaims, "Why Carolina Jessup, look at that tan!"

I stretch out my arms. "We had beautiful weather all week. Me and Savannah don't burn, but wait'll you see Bryan and his dad. They are both red, despite applying sunscreen constantly. But then, we were outside every possible moment. Since we haven't been to the beach in a few years, we couldn't get enough of it. Or the seafood."

Libby sighs and rests one hand on her hip as she pours coffee with the other. She explains her sigh. "Bill and I wanted to get away this summer, but now Cathy needs us to watch Forrest for her while she gets her business off the ground."

"Why, Libby," Susan says, "I didn't know Cathy was starting a business. Where? What is it?"

Libby sighs again and shakes her head. "You know my daughter. You can sell makeup or candles or baskets from your home, but no. She decides to sell sexy things, lingerie and such. Her daddy is pert near embarrassed to death. Especially since she's put these magnet pictures on her car. Downright pornographic. Here," she digs in her pocket and brings out a handful of business cards. "I'm supposed to be handing these out for her, but I just can't. Look at that."

"Oh my," Susan says at the same time I say, "Oh, wow."

The cards are hot pink with shiny gold writing, and I have to hold it up to the light to read the words, "Sexy Belles – Make their heads ring." Then under that Cathy's name and phone number. On the back is a picture of Cathy wearing some of the merchandise, I assume. While the writing on the front might be hard to decipher, the picture gets the message across loud and clear.

Libby pushes my hand down and whispers, "Don't hold it up like that. My daughter might not have the decency to be ashamed, but I do. Be right back."

She dashes off, and Susan and I turn the cards over to the picture again. Susan laughs, "I've heard of ladies going to these lingerie parties, but I never have. Can't imagine trying stuff like this on in front of my friends."

"Oh!" I exclaim. "You try it on? With everyone there?" I put the card down and pick my coffee cup up. "No way. I barely had the gumption to wear my new swimming suit on the public beach. So what's been happening while we were gone?"

Susan starts picking at the muffin on her plate. "Well," she begins, "Laney came home on Tuesday, but Cayden had to stay at the hospital until Friday. Apparently, he wasn't as early as they thought. He passed all the tests and is eating up a storm. It's been pretty quiet around town. Lots of folks on vacation it seems. Bonnie is amazing, you sure got a winner there. She has Blooming Books running like a well-oiled machine. Shannon is still sulking and chasing Peter. There are rumors they actually had a date."

"Really?" Then I scrunch up my nose and say, "Still can't see them together. Can you?"

Susan nods as she eats. She's looking down at her muffin, eating bit after bit, and rocking back and forward. When she maintains that for more than a couple moments, I dip my head toward her and ask, "Are you thinking? Or what? You went quiet on me."

"Oh, nothing. Just…" She pauses and begins brushing up the crumbs around her plate.

"Nothing? About what? Shannon and Peter?" I suck in my lower lip and ask.

"No, not them, however, the Bistro is looking really good.

Alex and Angie have that place really rocking." She suddenly looks up and says, "Oh, Angie quit the Piggly Wiggly."

"For the Bistro?" I ask.

Susan grins. "Well, for the Bistro and Alex. Savannah might've been right that leaving Alex alone for that long would take her out of the running."

I roll my eyes. "Don't remind me. Longest six hours of my life listening to her and Bryan whine about not wanting to leave Chancey the whole drive to the beach. Told both of them if Alex and Brittani couldn't manage to not cheat just because they were out of town, they shouldn't want to be with them in the first place. Of course, they lamented how old I am and how I don't understand."

Susan finishes her coffee and picks up her purse to sit on her lap. "Well, remember all that sewing and design stuff she did when you were opening Crossings last fall? She's doing the same sort of thing at the Bistro. Alex is actually wanting to open a food truck to take to some of the area colleges or towns." She makes a clicking sound with her mouth and squinches up her nose at me before adding, "And Alex may not leave like we thought."

I slump. "What? No. He has to leave."

She shakes her head at me and stands. "Not sure, but that's what Susie Mae was telling me. I've got to get to work. Actually have an appointment to talk to Alex about a food truck out at the park at the times when the concession stand isn't open."

"See you later," I say glumly. "You've ruined my morning telling me Alex may stay. I was hoping Savannah could get him out of her system. However, with cheerleading camp this week and then practice starting when they get back, maybe she just won't have time to chase him around like before."

Susan waves and leaves as I get money out to leave on the table. Laying it down I notice Cathy's card and pick it up. Cathy has on a black lace nightgown. Her hair is messy and her lips a glossy red. If not exactly pornographic, it's definitely not something I have any interest in seeing one of my friends modeling. I pocket the card as I stand up.

Lingerie parties in Chancey—the South *will* rise again.

Not having seen Blooming Books for the past week, and with all the extra touches Bonnie has added, it's like walking into a whole new shop. As the door opens and the bell chimes, it feels like the street outside melts away. There's a hush, an atmosphere I associate with those la-di-da shops on the Marietta Square or in Downtown Roswell. Places where ladies shop before or after a nice lunch. Places where the prices are a tad high, but oh so worth it. This is my shop?

"Bonnie! Shannon! You two have created a miracle." Walking through the tables and merchandise, I see candles lit here and there. Up near the front window there's a coffee station with an assortment of china cups and saucers. "Oh my," I exhale as I pick up a cream-colored pillow with a copy of our logo on it. "Where did you get this?"

Shannon says from behind the sales counter, "Angie Conner. Look at the tag. She's started her own little business.

Bonnie walks up to me, and I open my arms to hug her. She hugs me back and says, "It's been such fun. I'm so relieved you like it."

"Relieved? It's wonderful." I turn the pillow over and see the tag, *AC Creations*. "And I hear Angie is now at the Bistro working her magic there, too."

Shannon bristles. I can hear it in her voice even across the store. "Well, she's employed there, if that's what you mean. Peter is in charge. It's his shop. His creation."

Bonnie and I meet eyes and share a tiny eye roll. Bonnie

says low, under her breath, "We have Peter Bedwell's fan club president in residence here."

I laugh and step past Bonnie. "And I love what you did to the bookshelves! Looks much better this way." Bonnie has left spaces and turned books out different ways, even making displays of similar books in the middle of the rows. It looks much more inviting than my lining everything up nice and tight. I suppose that's the difference between a librarian mind and a decorator mind.

"Whew," Bonnie says. "Of course this isn't how the books were arranged in my classroom, or the school library, but I wanted to try it. Glad you like it."

Walking through the shelves, I say, "In a library you get so used to trying to get all the books on the shelves that there's not the space, or the time, to do things like this. But more's the pity, as this looks so enticing." I turn back to Bonnie. "And thanks for letting me run off at the last minute."

"Oh, don't you apologize for that. That's what I'm here for. To give you more freedom. I loved being here instead of up in Laurel Cove waiting for Cal to come off the golf course. You may have saved my marriage by hiring me!" We laugh as we walk back over to Shannon at the counter.

She holds up a pad of paper as we near. "What do you think?"

On the top sheet is a layout of an ad. I ask, "Is this for the *Vedette*? Looks good."

Shannon nods. "Yeah, Charles is doing a back-to-school page of ads. He's giving us a great price, says with the Dollar Store putting a flyer in each week, he's got more leeway in advertising prices."

"Speaking of the Dollar Store," I say, "how's Mr. Kendrick been? Anything happened?"

Bonnie clucks once and flutters her hands. "Shannon filled me in on what that Missus did. Well played, I feel. So many times as a teacher in public school I couldn't step in when I saw things happening in families. That was one of the best parts about working at Darien Academy. We *could* step in since we were private and address things like this. Kudos to Missus."

Shannon agrees. "Pretty much how everyone in town feels. Plus, it made folks a bit braver. And it's not hurt business for the Dollar Store." She laughs. "Steady stream of Nosy Nellies and Sally Do Goods."

I sigh and complain. "I was hoping with us leaving town with no notice he'd fire Savannah. But no such luck. He said she could come back after cheerleading camp and work as few hours as she wants during school. Do y'all think we should let her still work there?"

Bonnie lays a hand on my arm and says with a chuckle, "Probably the safest place in town, or the entire county, at this point." She changes tacks as she tightens her grasp on my arm. "I need to show you something, and then I have that dentist appointment to leave for."

I nod. "Yes, you don't want to be late. Glad you were able to change it from last week."

We walk towards the table we had set up in the back, with a couple of old dining room chairs. Here was where we planned to mark books and do our paperwork. Shannon tends to be near the front at the counter, so this way we can keep an eye on the book side of the store and the back. When Shannon is busy at her work table, then one of us makes sure to be in the front of the store. The best part is that one person can truly run the entire place in a pinch.

As we sit at the table, Bonnie pulls out two spiral bound notebooks, and as she does she whispers, "And get used to hearing 'Peter says.' It precedes most of her sentences now. I don't even think Mr. Bedwell says half of the things she attributes to him."

I whisper back. "So are they dating?"

She shrugs. "Who knows? She's over there a lot, and I've heard they did go out. She talks about his house like she built it, but has she actually ever been in it?" Bonnie lifts her hands, emphasizing another shrug. Then she speaks louder. "So here, this orange notebook is for people's requests. I started it after I had people asking me to keep a lookout for certain authors or books. And the green notebook is a list of local authors. Did you know we have several authors in the area? A gentleman from over in Woodstock came by last week to see if we would be interested in doing a book signing with him. He said he'd bring the books, and we'd get a percentage of his sales. I think that could be a wonderful way to build interest. So, I started a notebook." She lays it down and smiles at me. "You'll find I have a penchant for spiral bound notebooks. Guess it's from being a school teacher."

We stand up, and I laugh as I say, "I could use a few more notebooks in my life. My problem is I think I'll remember everything, or I write it down in the margin of a magazine I'm reading or on a scrap piece of paper. I may take your lead and get some notebooks. Might make me feel like I'm back in school." I check my watch. "Now you need to leave. Good luck at the dentist."

She bustles around and as she's leaving, Missus comes in. "Hello Shannon. Welcome home, Carolina. Bonnie? Tell Dr. Hewitt, I said 'hello.'"

Bonnie stops halfway out the door and turns back. "How did…" is all she says before Missus, without even turning around says, "Hurry on, don't make him wait."

Funny, doesn't even strike me as strange any longer that Missus knows everything. "Good morning, Missus," I say. "Good to be home. How are things in Chancey?"

"Can we step outside?" she asks me, even though she's looking at Shannon.

Shannon beams and answers with a song in her voice.

"Why of course, Missus. Take your time. Everything is in good hands."

Missus smiles, well, if you can call it a smile. Her lips turn up at the ends, but they are tight against her teeth and her nose looks like she might be able to shoot fire from it. Then, just because she can, she changes her mind. "Oh, Shannon dear, maybe you should step outside to give us some privacy. It's awfully hot out there for me, don't you think?"

"Oh, absolutely," Shannon trills as she darts from behind the counter. "I'll just dash next door and get an iced coffee. Can I get either of you anything? Peter says the iced coffees are extremely popular."

Missus turns away from Shannon and merely lifts a hand in farewell.

I, however, speak up. "I'll take an iced coffee." Digging in my skirt pocket, I pull out a five dollar bill. "Here, I was going to get one in a bit. Hazelnut, please."

Shannon takes my money and then waits beside Missus for an answer. She waits like one of those servants on an English gentry show. Solid and silent. Missus finally chokes out, "Nothing for me."

Shannon bounces off. I mean really bounces – her long skirt is a ruffled peasant skirt in shades of bright blue and dark red. She's sporting an off-the-shoulder dark red blouse that hugs her upper body. I watch on the sidewalk as she shimmies the fabric on her shoulder so that more of her upper body, and ample bosom, is exposed. She then fluffs her dark shag-cut hair to hang more in her face.

"Dear God in heaven, please tell me my son is not actually interested in that girl," Missus says from behind me.

I turn and shrug. "Don't know. Has he said anything to you?"

"Why would he say anything to me? I'm *just* his mother.

I will deal with that later. Right now I need to know what is going on with your son and Anna."

Notice "my son" doesn't even have a name? "Missus, we just got home late yesterday. I haven't talked to Will. Has anything happened that you know about?" Walking past her, I don't look up. Want to hear what she has to say before I add my two cents.

"That Bonnie is a treasure, you are aware, correct?" Missus has sat down on the end of the couch and looks around. She nods as she says, "I wholeheartedly approve. Now, sit so I can talk to you before that imp returns."

I oblige, and she continues. "Anna has been much happier this week. She has actually been pleasant to FM and me. Your son has not been around our house, but then why would they come to town when Crossings was empty and very private?" She smiles and lets her shoulders fall. "Anna mentioned how pretty the river was one morning, and that got me wondering if she hadn't been up there in recent days. After all, they *are* married. Maybe they've just needed some alone time." She sighs. "Possibly, my desire to make their marriage work blinded me to the need for some privacy. I am ready to entertain the idea that they should not live in mine and FM's home. Would you agree?"

Scooting up to the edge of my chair, I agree both by enthusiastically nodding and by saying so. "Oh, yes. And I have to tell you, I think you are right about them spending time together this week while we were gone. There were two coffee cups left out on the front porch, like two people had been sitting there. And in the hall bathroom, someone had used the guest shampoo and body wash which was under the counter, but I noticed it was in the shower. Coconut shampoo and strawberry body wash." We meet eyes and smile at the feminine scents. Then I add the most important piece of information. "And when I picked up the laundry from Will's room this morning, on the bedside table was a copy of that book *What to Expect When You're Expecting*. Along with a camisole top mixed in the bedclothes."

When she grabs my hand, there are tears in her eyes. "Oh, Carolina, I've been so worried. I have an appointment at those little apartments up behind the church this morning. One is available, and after talking to you, I'm going to go ahead and put a deposit down on it. Peter agrees with us that they need a fresh, and private, start. He said he'd help them move as soon as possible." When she notices my eyes look above her head, she asks, "Is she coming back?"

"Yes, and Missus?" I stand and look down at her. "If Shannon and Peter are supposed to be together, don't get involved. Learn from Anna and Will."

Missus stands up and folds her arms across her stomach. "Please do not confuse love with lust." She turns as she hears the bells on the door.

Shannon is pushing in with both hands full. I weave past Missus to give my partner a hand. "Here, let me have those." I take both drinks, and Shannon shifts the bag she clutched under her arm to one hand.

"Peter sent us some of the homemade chips they are working on for the Bistro. They're still warm," she says.

As she pushes for some space on the counter, the notepad with the design for our newspaper ad falls to the floor. When I bend to pick it up, my eyes fall to the line after line filling the previous pages. Some fancy, some block, some formal, some casual, but all sharing one theme: "Mrs. Shannon Bedwell" or "Mrs. Peter Bedwell."

Missus laughs and takes the notepad from my hand. She scoffs, "I guess it's good to have dreams. Oh, and you got grease from the chip bag on your shirt." She hands the pad to Shannon, turns on her heel, and leaves.

I take the bag of chips and open it. Holding one perfect,

golden, thick-cut chip, still warm and smelling of salt and grease, I point it at the sad young woman and say, "Her for a mother-in-law? Dream, my foot. More like a nightmare. Now, have a chip."

CHAPTER 36

"Oh, Laney, he's so little. You forget how little they are!" Cayden is stretched out in my hands, sound asleep. He has tufts of dark hair and long fingers, but his helplessness is what strikes me most. Blooming Books closed at five, and I came here straight from work. I only saw him through a nursery window at the hospital before we left town, and I couldn't wait to get my hands on him.

"Isn't he the sweetest thing you ever saw?" Laney asks. She's sitting at her downstairs table, folding clothes. "I can't believe how much fun he is. With the twins I was just so tired and so confused about it all. This feels like I'm playing house."

"Yeah, right. With Zoe waiting on you hand and foot." I sneak a glance into the next room. "What are you going to do when she goes back to school?" I ask in a whisper as Cayden stirs at his mama's voice.

Zoe speaks up from the kitchen. "Oh, no, ma'am. I'm home schooled, remember? I'm doing an independent study so I can graduate from high school early and go to nursing school. So, I'll do that in between taking care of Miss Laney and Cayden. School's no problem for me. Kinda learn real easy. You need a refill on that iced tea, Miss Carolina?"

"No, thank you, Zoe." I turn to her. "But, honey, don't you miss being with friends? People your own age?"

She comes over to the table and picks ups Laney's empty glass, carries it with her. "No more tea for you, Miss Laney, too much caffeine. And Miss Carolina, I've found that kids my age don't really interest me. I've tried getting involved in homeschool groups or church groups, but they seem immature. I always end up in the kitchen cleaning up and talking to the adults. If the adults are interesting. Goodness knows, sometimes the adults are worse than the kids." She returns to the table with Laney's glass filled with ice water and sets it down on a square of paper towel for the condensation. "While y'all are good, I'm going to go put that load of clothes in the washer on the line."

Laney rolls her eyes. "Girl, I've told you, there's a perfectly good dryer sitting right beside the washer. Just put them in there. That clothesline was left from when Shaw's parents moved out. Or maybe his grandparents. Nobody hangs clothes on the line anymore."

Being of the clothesline persuasion, I bend down to kiss Cayden's little fingers and stay out of the conversation. However...

"Miss Carolina hangs clothes on the line all the time. Don't ya?" Zoe accuses me, then asks for validation.

"Actually, I do. Missed it in the suburbs where it's basically against the law."

Zoe lifts her chin and eyebrows in a "told-ya-so" maneuver. Then turns down the steps to the laundry room at the back of the kitchen.

With a shrug, Laney resumes folding tiny blue baby clothes and laughs. "Doesn't she give you energy? She gives me energy. I love having her here. I'd have her here every day if I could."

At my look, she says, "No, not just because of how hard she works, but she just seems to enjoy being here. She makes everything, more, I don't know, happier. Even the girls are easier to get along with when Zoe's here."

Cayden begins to squirm, so I raise him up to nuzzle on my shoulder and neck. He smells so good. I blurt out what I'm thinking. "Jackson and I have talked about raising Will and Anna's baby if they can't work things out."

Laney's hands drop to the table in front of her, still holding a onesie. "What? It wouldn't come to that. Surely not."

"I don't know. She's pretty adamant about not wanting a baby. They've both even talked about giving it up for adoption, but we can't let that happen." I sigh and close my eyes while I hold onto Cayden tighter. "I hoped I'd feel better about it after seeing you and this sweet thing. But... No, nothing. I don't want it to feel like a burden, but right now that's all I've got."

Laney thinks for a minute, then says, "Missus was here yesterday after church, and she said Anna and Will are doing better."

"Yes, and I think they are, too. Guess just holding Cayden got me to thinking. Need to stop borrowing trouble! Oops." Raising my voice startled the baby. He pulls his head back and starts crying. "Oh, I'm sorry, sweetie."

Laney reaches out her hands to me. "Here, we were on borrowed time anyway. It's time for his dinner. Can you give Zoe a ride home?"

"Sure. Can I do anything before I leave?" I ask as I stand.

Laney stands, too, slower than me, and walks with the unhappy boy toward the living room. "Thanks, but we're good. Well, we will be as soon as this boy gets fed. Thanks for coming by. I love the quilt and the Braves outfits you gave him."

I smile at her and wave. "Gotta get him started right. See you later, holler if you need anything." Outside on the porch, I walk toward the back side of the house and meet Zoe coming inside with the empty clothes basket.

"Oh, there you are. Laney asked if I can give you a ride home. You ready?"

"Yes, ma'am. Let me put this in the laundry room and grab my backpack." She swings into the house, and I walk down the side porch steps to the driveway.

The white, modernized farmhouse sits on the top a little rise, and all is green and thick in every direction. Kudzu covers one whole side of the hill on the other side of the driveway and threatens to take over a grove of old trees at the back of the property in that direction. The lawn looks like a carpet, and unlike most farmhouses, there is no garden, flower or vegetable. In many ways it reminds me more of a house in the suburbs than in this small mountain town. By time I reach my van, Zoe comes bounding out of the house and down the steps.

She jogs past me and opens the passenger door as I open mine. I grin because she does bring her own kind of energy.

"So," I say, "you seem to be thriving in Chancey. You like it here?"

She nods and furrows her brow. "Yes, but then I find things interesting wherever I am, so that makes it's hard to not like everywhere. You know?"

Laughing, I shake my head. "No, I don't know. But I'd like to learn. How's Kimmy doing without you around as much?"

"Okay, I guess. House is messier and the kids not as happy. But I can't be everywhere. Plus, she needs to get used to doing things on her own."

"Oh, because you are working at Laney's?" We are driving down the two-lane blacktop, and she rolls down her window letting in a blast of hot air. She takes a deep breath of it with her eyes closed and head leaned back, my question ignored.

As she presses the button and the window rises back into place, she sighs. "Don't you just love summer?"

"I do. Not as much as fall or spring, but more than winter," I answer.

She continues to stare out the window, and we are both silent. She's such a talker, but now it feels like she's not even here in the van with me. She feels far away. I reach to turn on the radio, and then stop. The silence is kind of nice. Peaceful.

At the stop sign at the foot of the hill up to our houses, I remember her comment about me hanging clothes on the line. "Hey, how did you know I hang clothes on the line?" I ask as I make the left turn.

She shrugs and seems to come back to the present. "Oh, I see them. I like walking at the train bridge. Well, not on it, more under it down at the river. I can get there through the woods from behind our house. And down there you can see up into y'all's backyard. Just noticed you have clothes out on it a lot."

"Oh, I didn't realize you walked down there. I've only been down along that part of the riverbank once. Right after we moved here." I pull into her driveway and put the van in park. "Maybe I'll come in and say hi to Kimmy."

Zoe looks at me from outside her door, shrugs, then slams the door. She darts ahead of me and is already inside as I close my door. Up on the porch, I look in the front window and see moving shapes. As I raise my hand to knock on the door, Kimmy appears.

"Hey," she says as she slips out the door, pulling it closed behind her.

"Just thought I'd stop in to say 'hi.' How are y'all?"

Kimmy laughs, "Tired. Glad I've got Zoe tomorrow, I can get a nap in. Money from her job is good, but she sure doesn't get her chores here all done."

"Maybe she needs a nap since she's working so much," I say. I can't keep my annoyance hidden. The girl is still only twelve years old.

This time Kimmy really laughs, "Haven't you noticed how she runs rings around all of us? That girl couldn't take a nap if you nailed her to a bed. She is definitely her father's daughter! Only other person I've ever met that had that much energy. Wish he were home more so it could rub off on me." A shadow crosses her face as she says this, and with the shadow I see that her eyes are puffy and red. She notices my look of concern and sniffs as she explains. "Summer allergies. Hoped they might be better here. Well, I better get the kids fed. Don't you know Zoe came right in the door and went straight to the kitchen. I didn't even realize what time it was."

She opens the door, and as Katherine pushes out it, Kimmy pushes her back in with the side of her leg. I wave at Katherine, but then the door closes and I'm alone on the concrete porch.

Back in the van, I put it in reverse and pull out of the driveway. Zoe may leave folks feeling good, but even a few minutes with any of the rest of her family leaves me feeling the exact opposite.

CHAPTER 37

"Don't pick up. Have ride home." is the text message from Savannah on Thursday afternoon that stops me as I'm crossing the front porch, headed to pick her up at the high school. The cheerleaders' week at camp over in Alabama is done, and now there's only two weekends before school starts. We're not on a year-round school schedule, because that causes parents to come out of the woodwork to yell at the school board meetings and write scathing letters to the newspaper. Charles says a good school controversy helps circulation more than any ad campaign.

However, it sure feels like year-round school. First day of school this year is Monday, August 2, which means there's only one full week of summer vacation left. Didn't it just start?

I take my purse off my shoulder and sit in one of our rockers with my phone still in my hand. No other messages or emails so guess everyone else's plans are unchanged. We have guests for the B&B coming this afternoon. I'd told them if I wasn't here when they got here, I'd be back soon. But now I don't have to worry about that. And Jackson will be home from South Georgia in a few hours, depending on Atlanta traffic.

Pushing my feet to get the rocker started, I take a deep breath. This week has been nonstop. Bonnie's dental appointment turned into an unexpected three days of procedures, so she couldn't work. Laney, of course, is still at home with Cayden. She's planning on going back to being in charge of the books for Crossings next week. But those two out of commission meant both places were run solely by me, without Savannah to help. Yes, I've come to realize she is actually quite a bit of help. Bryan, not a bit. Well, unless you count the garden, and guess I really should count the garden. He's out there every morning, so then the rest of the day he's on his own. Mostly up at Grant's in Laurel Cove or out at the Lake Park.

Will is less help, and actually more work, than Bryan, and I can't wait for him to move to the apartment with Anna. Missus has had the painting crew Gertie hired to do Blooming Books and Andy's Place painting the apartment this week. Every night Will has been with Anna at the apartment getting it ready, and I believe she's already moved in. Have to hand it to Missus, she did have a good idea this time. They are nesting and making a good starting place for their little family.

I'm so relieved to not be starting over with a new baby here, I'm not even upset about Will being stuck in Chancey anymore. Funny how your perspective can change so fast. When a white SUV stops on the other side of the track before slowly crossing into our driveway, I wave. There's our guests. It's a first for Crossings, a girls' trip. I booked them earlier this week, and it wasn't the trains that interested them, it was having three available rooms.

Five teachers, they just wanted a few days away before school starts, the one I talked to told me. As the SUV doors open, I can hear the laughing and chatter already. I stand up, wave again, and realize—this may be our loudest weekend yet.

"Susan has planned a School's Back cookout at the Lake

Park tomorrow night," I say to Jackson as he eats a big portion of the Mexican casserole me and the kids had earlier. We're sitting out on the deck and the smell of bug spray mixes with the smell of the seasoned ground beef and the hot sauce he's poured liberally over the melted cheese topping. He's strewn a handful of lettuce and chopped tomatoes over the plate of spicy food—a small handful. He hit Atlanta right at rush hour, so he got home later than he planned.

A swell of laughter comes from down the hill as we watch our guests slowly make their way back to the house. The ladies are a little older than Jackson and me, and they will be easy, once we get used to the noise. But it's fun, happy noise, so the only one it really bothers is Savannah. Not a problem. Right?

"I'm working from home tomorrow. Still doing the wine and cheese?" Jackson asks between bites.

"Yep, then we'll go to the lake. Glad you'll be here for all of it. I'm kind of sad the summer is ending, but it'll be good to get back into a routine. It's great we were able to work in the trip to the beach."

"Mother sure has a sweet place there. Did I tell you I talked to Dad on my way home?" Jackson looks up at me, and when I shake my head, he sighs and says, "Hate to say it, but he got what he deserves. He doesn't complain about Shelby, but she's got his Hillbilly Hank schedule maxed out and has ordered workers to fix up the house."

I just shrug and stand. Shelby's move to the master bedroom from the back bedroom has given her just the confidence she needed to take control. But I'm not mentioning that to Jackson. The less said about Shelby is best. I hold my hand out for his plate, "Can I get you some more?"

"Naw, I'm good I think." He stands up, too, and asks, "So when does Will get home? I tried calling him this past week, but he never answered. Guess he's working a lot?"

We enter the dimly lit kitchen. "Yeah, at the car lot and at the apartment, too. I haven't seen him but for a few minutes as he's come through to change, leave his dirty clothes, then make a mess getting something to eat in the kitchen." Disgust in my voice is clear, and I don't even say everything I'm thinking; his moving out means I never did have a talk about him becoming more responsible. Let Anna fix him. They're the ones who were in an all-fired hurry to get married.

Jackson stops at the garbage can to clean his plate off and tilts his head up at me. "So he and Anna are good? Just like that?"

"I told you that she was here with him while we were at the beach, didn't I?"

He nods and lets the garbage lid close. "Yeah, you mentioned you thought that was what was going on. Have you seen Anna?"

"No. First of all, she was working extra since Savannah was gone, and honestly, I think too much family was part of the problem. So I've been avoiding her. Let them work it out together. How can I tell Missus to stay out of it if I'm getting involved? Besides, I've been so busy this week. Thank God Bonnie will be back tomorrow at Blooming Books."

When we hear the ladies nearing the deck, Jackson dips his head at me and gives me a distracted kiss. "I'm going to go on up and take my shower. Tell the ladies I'll meet them tomorrow." He slides out of the kitchen just as they open the back door. The noise level covers his running up the stairs. And believe me, he was running.

CHAPTER 38

"Did you hear Alex is staying?" Savannah asks as she folds her legs up underneath her on the couch in the morning. I only hear her because there was a pause in the laughing and talking coming from the dining room where our guests are having mimosas and muffins. I'm sticking to coffee and muffins, but thinking I might want to add champagne to our wine and cheese afternoon. The ladies really seem to like the bubbly, judging from the empty bottles in the trash.

Not that I'm judging.

I click my tongue against my teeth. "Yes, I did hear he might stay." Judging from the look on my daughter's face, she didn't get over him, despite the beach and cheer camp. Great.

Okay. Now I'm judging. Kind of my job as a mom.

She stretches back and rests against the couch cushions, then lifting the remote, clicks on the TV. "Can't believe I told Anna I'd come to work today. It's like my last day of summer with practice starting next week." She speaks up to be heard over the ladies and now the TV. "But I'll be off early enough to help Alex at the party tonight at the Lake Park. He's trying out the food truck."

I raise an eyebrow. "He already has a food truck?"

She turns up the TV some more and shrugs. "Borrowed it." Then she gives me a side look. "I'm trying to watch this."

Getting up, I throw a couch pillow at her. Jackson is working from home today, but not sure he knew it would be this loud. I fix him another cup of coffee and take it upstairs where he's set up a little office in the corner of our bedroom.

He's on a call, so I set the cup down beside him, kiss him on the top of his head, and go look in my closet. Of all the things I knew would change with this move, my wardrobe never crossed my mind.

Library work requires stooping and bending and climbing, so I wore pants all the time. Black pants usually. Though they show the dust that gathers in libraries, they don't show the dirt. And with so many people, especially kids, there's always dirt. That left just shirts to worry about. And they couldn't be low-cut, since I did a lot of bending over, or too short, because ditto. Not sleeveless because, upper arms, you know, and air conditioning. As we've already established, I'm not a big shopper, so I had a bunch of basically similar shirts in different colors and patterns. Easy.

But not so easy now. I'd die of heat stroke wearing long black pants running around this house, inside and out, and then at work the air isn't that great with such a high ceiling. Plus, they look too dressy, too business-like to me. My shorts are for fun times. Can't wear them to work. I have one blue jean skirt that I tend to overwear and a couple pairs of capris, but I'm wearing out the few shirts that go with them.

I push to the back of the closet and gaze. Yep, today's the day.

I'm going to wear a sundress.

A sleeveless sundress. A pink, sleeveless sundress. There are three of them (not all pink, of course) shoved behind everything else. My mother and I bought them when they visited for Will's graduation. His *high school* graduation. I wore the pink one to the graduation but felt so out of place, I buried them. For four years I've ignored them, but now it's time. On vacation I remembered these dresses were hanging in my closet and wished I'd thought to pack one of them. I made myself a promise I would wear them once we returned home. It's taken me all week to work up to it (and to work through all my clean shirts that go with my capris).

Jackson is still on his phone call and facing out the back doors to the rickety porch outside our bedroom. We have to get that fixed so we can actually go out there. Dressed, I slide into the same white sandals I bought with my mother for the graduation, and then pull the spread up over the bed as I hear Jackson winding up his call, then hanging up.

"Well, I'm going downtown, but I'll be back to get things ready for wine and cheese time. It's all in the fridge," I say. "Then the Back-to-School thing at the Lake Park is later."

Jackson stands up and stretches out his back. "Okay, I'll be done here by lunch. What are the kids up to today?" He picks up one of the throw pillows from the floor to place on the bed.

"Will's at work all day, I guess. Didn't see him this morning. Did you talk to him last night? When's he officially moving into the apartment?" I ask as I walk over to pick up another throw pillow, which, when Jackson is traveling, never get put back on the bed.

Jackson, hands pillow-free, holds his arms out for a hug. As I settle into them, he says, "No, I saw him for just a bit last night. Like you said, he was just passing through. I asked about the apartment, and he said it was all coming together. Maybe they're taking their time." He pulls back to smile at me. "Which would be a welcome change for them. I like the dress. Pretty."

We hug again, then with a quick kiss he excuses himself. "Have a conference call starting. Love you. See you later."

Swaying down the stairs, I repeat his words to myself. Pretty. Yes, I feel pretty. Pretty good. Pretty cool. Pretty happy.

My dress matches Blooming Books. I feel light and classy, just like the store. Bonnie is back, and she's happy to be back, sans tooth pain. Shannon is busy with a weekend wedding order, so her area of the shop is exploding with flowers, pink and green and white everywhere. The pink perfectly matches my dress. Our chatter reminds me of the ladies staying at Crossings, and when they show up to look around midmorning, the place practically vibrates with their oohs and aahs. Then Peter brings us all trials cups of a new frozen coffee drink, and it really is like a party.

One of the B&B guests finally stands from the couch, saying, "We want to go check out that Andy's Place. On Facebook and TripAdvisor it's listed as a 'must-see.'"

"Andy's is a 'must-see'?" I ask.

Another of the teachers agrees. "Oh yes, he has quite the eclectic collection of things apparently."

As they move to the front door, Shannon and I look at each other and shrug. Then Shannon speaks up. "But don't forget to stop in and see Peter next door at the Bistro, right? He did bring those delicious drinks."

They all say, "Of course" and "Next stop." The last one leaving says with a wink and a laugh, "And Carolina, you tell your Jackson he better keep a close watch on you, that Peter couldn't keep his eyes off you in that dress."

The door closes behind her, and Shannon marches back to her work table. And it wasn't a happy march.

Now it's my turn to shrug with Bonnie, who says, "I have heard good things about Andy's Place. Up in Laurel Cove it's all the talk. Antiques, collectibles, but then just the right amount of junk. Even the husbands enjoy shopping around in there. Every room is full, both floors and even the basement. Have you been over there?"

I shake my head. "No, but how did they get it so full so quick?"

Bonnie waves a hand. "Look at this place. Gertie gets more done in a morning than most folks do in a week!"

And all the talk at Wine and Cheese at Crossings? Andy's Place. And a lot of giggling. Even Jackson started looking confused. The teachers kept making funny eyes at each other and laughing. The ladies from up at Laurel Cove just looked smug, like they were in on the secret. Laney ignored them as she had Cayden sleeping in the little office off the kitchen. She was excited to be having a glass of wine, since she'd given up on breastfeeding.

"Carolina, I do like that dress on you," she says from her seat at my kitchen table. Everyone has left, or gone off to take a nap in the case of our guests. She holds up her glass and adds, "And that's not the wine talking. Although it could be. I might need a ride over to the Lake Park. Y'all are going, aren't you?"

"Yes, did you hear Alex is trying out the food truck tonight?" I ask as I sit down across from her.

"Of course. Angie is very excited about it," she says. She nods her head at the old ice cream churn still sitting on the counter. "Is that the mystery ice cream maker that showed up? Susan told me about it."

"Yeah, you didn't leave it?"

She looks up at me through half-lowered eye lids. "Oh, yes, I wasn't busy doing anything else the last few weeks." She laughs and shakes her head. "Not me." She then starts digging around in the diaper bag beside her. "Where is Zoe? She said she'd meet me up here." She pulls out her phone. "Oh, she texted me." Laney reads for a minute, then sighs. "More drama with Kimmy. That woman is her own reality show. Zoe is going to meet me later at the Lake Park, so I'm on my own for another hour." Then she smiles up at me. "Except for you. You'll watch Cayden while I take a little nap, won't you?"

"I guess," I answer. "Where are you going to nap? The rooms are all full."

She stands up. "You forget how tiring having a baby is. I can sleep standing up, but I have my eye on the recliner in the living room." She yawns and heads out of the kitchen. "His bottle is right there, and he doesn't need it warmed. Thanks."

CHAPTER 39

First thing we see as we pull into the parking lot is the food truck. It's tall, and there are people crowded around it. Plus, it's painted bright orange.

Hanging on the side of it are banners, and the logo looks familiar. Laney sees them, too. She mutters, "What's going on?" and I just respond with a shake of my head. We park, and then try to gather everything that goes with Cayden. Everything that goes with Laney. Everything that goes with me.

Finally, I say, "Just leave some of it. When Jackson gets here he'll bring the rest of it in, or I'll send Bryan out to get it."

As we get closer to the food truck we see we weren't mistaken about the logo. A big AC in a circle, the same logo on the pillows made by Angie when we opened Crossings. Angie and Alex are framed, elbow to working elbow, in the serving window, and the smell of the food is spicy and enticing. They are both wearing blue jeans and black T-shirts with the AC logo and some fancy artwork that matches the truck signs.

Neither Laney nor I have said anything because we're not sure what we're looking at. Then we hear someone that *always* has something to say. Savannah.

"Alex, I'm here to help you out. This looks like fun! Oh, hey, Angie. Aren't you burning up in that black shirt and those jeans?" Savannah obviously changed from working at the Dollar Store. She has on a white peasant blouse and jean shorts. Short jean shorts. Very short jean shorts.

Alex looks up, sees her, and stops working for a minute, then waves a spatula at her and goes back to work saying, "Think we've got it."

Angie doesn't look up at all, but as Savannah weaves her way to the steps at the end of the truck, Angie does lean out the window and look at her friend. Then, she speaks up loudly and clearly, none of the usual Angie quiet mumbling. "He said we're good, Savannah."

Savannah rolls her eyes, laughs, and marches right on up the steps. She opens the door, and as she begins to step inside, she's met by Angie.

Angie pushes out and causes Savannah to back down to the ground. Angie points around the truck's side. "Do you see that sign? AC? We're a team. It's Angie Conner and Alex Carrera, get it? We work together and are together. Like as a couple. I tried to tell you, but you just won't listen."

My mouth is not the only one hanging open. Savannah's is for a moment, then she swivels her eyes to Alex, who has stepped up behind Angie. He also looks a bit stunned. His mouth is hanging open and his eyes are wide. Angie cocks her head at him, folds her arms, and closes his mouth with one word, "Right?"

Alex looks at Savannah, looks back at Angie, then nods. "Yeah, we're a team, a couple." He shrugs at Savannah, lays one hand on Angie's shoulder, then with the other hand, reaches out for the inside handle on the door. With a quick smile at my bare-shouldered daughter, he says, "Sorry."

The door shuts, and Angie shows back up in the serving window talking to the customers standing there. Savannah tosses her hair and walks—no, sashays—toward the Lake Park entrance pavilion. Only her mother sees that everything in her wants to retreat to her car.

Laney and I ask each other, "Did you know?" at the same time. We both answer with shakes of our heads.

I say, "She's been working at the Bistro lately, but what's this about being a 'team'? Never dawned on me they had the same initials. Some reason I thought his last name was Moon, but he is Diego's sister's son. *Are* they dating?"

Laney just keeps shaking her head, then says quietly, "She's never dated anyone. Anyone. And he sure doesn't seem like the type a girl starts with."

We push the stroller along the path through the pavilion and just as we come through the other side, Laney starts laughing. She stops and rests her arms on the stroller handle. "I'm sorry, I know Savannah is your daughter, but that was funny."

I smirk. "It was, just because we know Angie and Savannah, and that was so out of the blue. Angie said she's tried to tell Savannah, but my daughter has had tunnel vision when it comes to Alex." Then I laugh with an eye roll. "Bet this cures that!"

We follow the path down the hill to a picnic table near the edge of the water. As she lifts a fussy Cayden from his stroller, Laney says, "Gotta say, I might've seen Jenna doing something like that, but Angie? My Angie? However, that is how you keep a man like Alex. Make everything nice and clear."

Then she stops and gasps, "Oh no. It's me that has to worry about him having his own apartment now. Shoot." She looks down at Cayden who is really starting to cry. "With you not sleeping, and Jenna being Jenna, Angie was my *easy* one."

Dusk, with its blues and purples, has settled in over the lake. Everyone is full of food and praise for the food truck. Cayden is sleeping soundly in his stroller, and the older teens have left to go to the movies over in Canton. Bryan and his friends are congregated out on one of the docks, and Brittani, in that tiny blue bikini, is sitting on Bryan's lap. Makes me wish he would sneak around more so I wouldn't actually have to see things like this.

The one disharmonious note is Kimmy's table. The Kendrick clan only got here about twenty minutes ago, and Kimmy has been shrieking most of that time. Zoe is there, mostly dealing with the kids and ignoring her stepmother. Finally, I can't stand it any longer. (I used to never get involved in things like this, but I guess it's the Chancey effect.)

"Hey, guys," I say in a nice, sing song voice as I walk up. "What's going on?"

Kimmy's allergies must be on overdrive as her eyes are red and swollen, and she's sniffling between shrieks. "These kids are driving me crazy. Look at 'em! Just bought them all this expensive food, and they won't eat. Can't I get a minute's peace?"

Zoe shrugs and explains. "I told you they wouldn't eat the tacos. They're spicy and have green stuff on them."

Katherine and Kevin are crying while K.J. pulls on his mother's arm whining about going swimming. Looking around I see they don't have any bags or coolers with possibly more kid-friendly food. "Hey," I offer quietly to Kimmy, "I have some crackers and peanut butter and some grapes, if they'd like that?"

Zoe brightens up and nods at me. Kimmy throws her hands in the air and exclaims, "Sure! Throw all this food away! Just let them have their way. Everyone but me gets to do whatever they want. Sure, whatever!" She begins grabbing the food from off the table, and now the kids cry harder.

Laney, bless her, has apparently been listening and comes up at that moment like Lady Bountiful. "Here we are! Crackers and grapes. Yum." She's laying the food out and smiling at the kids, who immediately quit crying and start filling their mouths. Another mom hands me some juice boxes and quietly backs away. While another sets a bag of cookies on the table as she slips past. This is not a scene folks want to be a part of, because now that the kids are happy, Kimmy is sitting at the end of the picnic table wailing. She's buried her face in her hands, and her long, dirty blonde hair hangs like a curtain to the tabletop.

Laney and I look at each other, then at Zoe. Zoe comes up close to Laney and whispers, "Dad moved out."

You know, I didn't really think it was allergies after all.

CHAPTER 40

"So what are you and Grant going to be doing at the golf course today?" I ask as Bryan and I wind up the sunny mountain road toward the Laurel Cove clubhouse.

"I think we're going to caddy for Grant's dad and a couple other members. He said we might get paid."

"Do you even know how to caddy?" Dawns on me having non-golfing parents might be a handicap if you lived somewhere like Laurel Cove.

Bryan shrugs and says, "That's why we might *not* get paid. It's kind of an experiment."

Jackson and I weren't up when Bryan knocked on our bedroom door saying he was ready to go. I'd completely forgotten I'd told him I would drive him to Laurel Cove this morning. Jackson offered to bring him, but figured he needed to relax a bit and try and sleep in. Plus, I want to talk to Susan. We're going to have coffee at the clubhouse.

Car rides provide the best opportunity for learning what a kid is up to. So I ask, "Saw you and Brittani last night. Guess you're back together?"

I wait for the shrug and noncommittal *yeah*. But he gets still. Very still. Then he starts tapping his fingers on his thigh. So I wait.

"There's this other girl…" he mumbles. "She kind of likes me, and I kind of like her."

"But last night Brittani was sitting on your lap. You were holding hands."

He looks over at me with wide eyes and sighs. "Yeah. I know."

"Son, if you like this other girl, you need to break up with Brittani."

He screws up his face and whines, "But she'll be mad. I didn't think she still really liked me, but last night she was all about how we were going to be a couple at school this year."

Exasperated, I pull into the parking lot, and as I put the car in park, I say, "Boys are awful at breaking up, and I understand it, because you will be the bad guy. So, you ignore the girl or make her mad so she'll break up with you. Well, you missed your chance earlier this summer. Now you are going to have to break up with Brittani, or you'll end up two-timing her." I look over my sunglasses at him and speak sternly. "And that's not allowed."

He scowls and opens his car door, and says just as he gets out of the car, "But you don't know Brittani. I don't think she'll *let* me break up with her." He slams his door and jogs over to the grass where Grant waits with his mom.

By time I get to Susan, the boys are around the corner headed to the golf course. We walk towards the outside café area to find a seat. On the way, I relay Bryan's conversation.

Pulling out chairs at a small table on the edge of the patio, she sits down and waves at a waitress, then says, "He's right about her not letting him go. The Bennett women don't actually get broken up with."

"For crying out loud, they're kids! Anyway, he can figure it out. He got himself into this mess without my permission, so he can get himself out." I hand my menu back to the waitress. "Just coffee, please."

"Me too," Susan says. "We had breakfast before I left this morning."

"Not us. I left Jackson in bed, and we're having breakfast when I get home. Nice lazy day for us." I close my eyes in a cringe and ask, "So, did you hear all about Savannah and Angie last night?"

She laughs. "Every last word, several times. But, hey, you wanted her to get over Alex."

"Well, did you know your niece and he were an actual item, *and* a business partnership?"

It's her turn to cringe. "Yeah, you know, I did. I've been working with them on the food truck idea, and I just assumed everyone knew. They didn't really hide it. They've done everything under the AC logo that Angie came up with. But it seems to have really thrown Laney for a loop, she isn't sure what to think. As different as she thinks Angie is from her, she's really so much like her mother. Jenna looks like Laney, but Angie acts like Laney."

I think back and smile. "You know, you're right. But with the dyed hair, black makeup, and sullen attitude, I didn't see it."

Susan leans toward me. "And Shaw was every bit as much of a player as Alex ever hoped to be. That is until my sister jerked a knot in his tail one time after they were in college."

"Just like Angie did!" I say, then after a pause, I add, "Boy, Kimmy was a mess. You heard Kyle's moved out?"

Susan nods. "Yeah, can you imagine being left with all those little kids? And the good one, Zoe, isn't even hers. Thank God for Zoe, though. I don't think Kimmy could manage without her."

Thinking about the sad little family puts a pause in our conversation until Susan clears her throat. I look at her. "What?" I ask.

She chews her bottom lip and then takes a deep breath. "We're putting Grant into Darien Academy."

My shoulders slump. "No, Susan. Really?"

"Yeah. He's excited, and well, it's such a good school and so close to us. Much closer than Chancey High now. He's going to tell Bryan today, so I wanted to let you know. We had to make sure he could get in."

I scowl. "So he did get in? I guess, congratulations. I'm sure it'll be good for him." I fake grin. "It makes my life suck, but don't worry about that!" Laughing, I lay my hand on her arm. "But really, congratulations and I'm sure it'll be fine. Now, that's my stomach growling, so I need to get home and make some breakfast."

Up on top of the mountain, it feels like I can see forever. It's a clear summer morning, and the air is so clean and fresh. As I pull onto the road down the mountain, I make a mental note to see if Miss LaVada's rosebush is still in bloom. It would be wonderful to fill the house with them again. On the way up, I was distracted by Bryan's relationship woes.

With the windows down and the warm breeze in my face, I slow down near her curve and prepare to pull off the road. But there's no room to pull off as there is a car parked in the only open spot. The UGA window sticker catches my eye.

It's Will's car.

There's no one behind me so I slow down to practically a stop, and as I do, the front door of the tiny house opens. I lift my hand to wave at Miss LaVada, but it's Will coming out the door with Rose beside him. As I start to shout his name, he leans Rose against the doorjamb and kisses her. And he keeps kissing her. A car horn startles me, and I look up into my rearview mirror. As I wave in apology and put my foot onto the gas pedal, Will sees me. We lock eyes and then I'm gone. Driving down the hill. Headed home. Alternating between two thoughts:

I'm going to kill my son.
Poor Anna.

Chapter 41

My phone rings as I pull into the driveway, and I see that it's Shannon. "Hi, what's up?" I say.

"Bonnie's temporary crown came out, so you need to come to the shop. I have the wedding today. Bonnie's dentist is coming in just for her, so she needs to leave as soon as possible."

I groan and get out of the car, saying, "I'll be there in just a few."

Shannon is either still mad at me because she thinks Peter was watching me the other day or it's just stress from the hillbilly wedding she's trying to pull off. She's complained about this wedding for weeks, and now it's finally here.

"Jackson?" I call as I cross the threshold. No fear of waking up our guests as I can hear them on the back deck. Sticking my head out the back door, I greet them and look around for my husband.

"Your hubby is down at the river. We might've been a bit loud for him." This brings more laughter.

Another of the teachers says, "And that pretty daughter of yours, the one who got an earful at the lake last night? Well, she might not be feeling that well this morning." The ladies, all mothers of grown kids, raise eyes at each other, and then one nods at me and finishes. "We were on the porch when she came home last night and, well, it looked like she had a... a

317

full night. We wouldn't say anything, but well, we know how it is to have a houseful of teenagers. It's always something, and it's better to know, right?"

I sigh and thank them. Not that I wanted to thank them, but, you know, manners.

Up the stairs, I don't even stop at my bedroom, but plow on ahead up Savannah's staircase, too. Needless to say, by time I got to the top I couldn't breathe, much less talk. But there's nothing to say as she's not in her bed. Then I hear her commode flush, and by time she walks out in her cami and pajama pants, I'm actually standing up straight and not sucking wind.

She screams and that makes me scream. "You scared me!" she accuses as she moves past me to fall onto her bed.

"Are you okay? The ladies said you didn't look that great when you came home last night."

She speaks into her pillow. "They scared me, too. Sitting there watching me stumb—walk up the sidewalk."

I put my hands on my hips. "You were drinking, weren't you? And you drove yourself home?"

She coughs and then raises up on one arm. "No, I wouldn't do that. Terry drove me home."

Then I think back, so her car wasn't in the driveway this morning and I didn't even notice? My phone rings in my pocket and makes me jump. It's Shannon. I don't know why I'm answering. Manners again?

"Hi, I'll be there soon," I answer.

"Tell me you are on your way! That you are parking as we speak!" She's yelling, so I hold the phone away from my ear. Then my manners completely disappear, and I hang up on her.

Savannah appears to be back to sleep, but I step over and nudge her. "I have to go to work, but we'll talk about this later." I turn away and start down the stairs. Then I remember and ask, "Terry drove you home? Who's she?"

Mumbling from the bedclothes I hear, "*He*. You know, Terry. Air-conditioning Terry."

I take a step back up. "The Terry that fixed our air conditioning? The man that works with your brother? That Terry?"

My phone rings again, and I decline Shannon's call. Even with the yelling and phone ringing, soft snores tell me my daughter has fallen back asleep. Or she's faking it. Either way—I've got to go. But this is not the end of this discussion.

Things are lively downtown, and I can see why Shannon was so upset. The parking places are full, and people fill all the tables in front of the Bistro. There are people on the lawn of Andy's Place, and Ruby's looks to have a line out the door.

What in the world is going on?

When I stride in the front door of Blooming Books, Shannon throws up her arms and shrieks, "Finally! Bonnie had to leave, and this awful wedding is only four hours away."

She turns back towards her worktable and then plunges into her cooler, yelling behind her. "You are in charge of it all."

At the counter, I look to see the notepad, which is full of purchases from this morning. There are two ladies shopping in the store, one browsing the books and one looking in the cooler of nosegays and small arrangements Shannon keeps stocked for immediate purchase.

As she brings a small bouquet up to me to purchase, she says, "That piece in the newspaper was right about y'all."

Wrapping her flowers in a cone of light gray paper, I ask, "What piece in the paper?"

She pulls out money and takes her flowers. "The Thursday local travel piece in the Atlanta paper. It always has nearby places to visit. And when today turned out to be such a beautiful day, my husband and I decided to take a little ride."

I'm shocked to hear about our free publicity. "Oh, okay. That explains why we're so busy, I guess."

She tucks her purse back on her shoulder. "Of course, my husband isn't much interested in the rest of the town. He's holed up at that Andy's Place, wouldn't you know it?" She laughs and walks to the door. "Thanks, and I'm sure we'll be back!"

The day was so busy, I didn't have time to think about Will or Savannah or Anna. I did get the chance to talk to Jackson and fill him on the happenings with our kids, though. He couldn't get off the phone fast enough when he heard who brought Savannah home last night. He said he was going to handle that, and I could hear him stomping up the stairs when I hung up. Finally, he's home when something happens.

I call the Bistro, and Angie answers. She fills our orders for sandwiches and brings them over herself.

As I pay her, she pauses and takes a breath. "Miss Carolina, I hope you weren't upset about what happened last night with Savannah."

"With Terry? Were you with them, too?"

She squints her black-rimmed eyes so that I can only see the black, no eye at all. "With who? I meant at the Lake Park."

"Oh." I shake my head at her. "Oh, no. I'd already forgotten about that."

She continues. "I tried to tell her. Honestly, I did. We work so well together. Me and Alex, I mean, and well, things just progressed." Her face hardens. "Don't think Savannah believed he could prefer me over her. She and my sister are like that."

As an older customer comes near the counter with a handful of paperback books, Angie steps to the side, but asks, "Did you say Savannah was with Terry? Terry Minns?"

"Yes, why?" I ask as I reach for the books to ring up.

The girl shrugs and shakes her head. "No reason. Just wondering." But she has a reason, I can see it in her nonchalance. "Well, I better get back to work."

After that customer there is a break. Shannon leaves for the wedding with a rented van loaded with flowers. She takes her sandwich to eat on the road, and I move back to her workspace to eat where I can see the front door, but also have a bit of privacy.

Just as my mouth is full, the door opens and Missus comes storming in. Oh no, I bet she's heard about Will and Rose. She is sputtering mad, but I don't hear anything that sounds like my firstborn's name in her sputtering.

"A speakeasy, a bar, a joint right next door!" she says when she finally spots me in the work area. "That woman is going to get us all arrested!" She's barely got that out when FM comes barreling in the door.

"Now, Missus. It's all going to be okay. No need to get all riled up. Hey Carolina, can you believe all these people coming to Chancey? Must've been some amazing article. Have you been busy?"

Missus draws up and squares her shoulders. "Carolina, do you know what's going on in that Andy's Place?"

"No," I answer. "I mean I guess a lot of stuff folks like looking at. Is that where you're talking about there being a bar?"

FM hangs his head. "Missus, you're going to ruin it all."

She turns to her husband, "It's illegal. Of course I'm going to ruin it!" She turns back to me. "That Gertie Samson is selling moonshine in the basement. Has a bar set up there! Next door to my home!"

I turn to look at FM, hoping he'll laugh and explain how ridiculous this crazy notion of his wife's is. However, he just grins and shrugs. "Well, you know, that was her family business here a ways back. And she's not 'selling' it, she's giving out samples. That's all."

Missus sits down on the stool near her. "FM, samples or shots, whatever you want to call it. There's a fee to go to the tasting room, correct?"

He nods and then turns as the door opens. Zoe comes through the door and holds it open for Laney and the stroller.

"Hey, y'all," Laney says. "We decided we'd come to town and see what all the fuss is about." Laney heads toward us, but Zoe meanders over to the bookshelves.

I look around FM and Missus and ask, "Laney, did you know what's going on at Andy's Place?"

Laney laughs. "Oh, the tasting room? Isn't that a great idea? Wish I'd thought of it."

Missus sniffs. "Well, of course, the accountant who thought gambling away our very town was a *brilliant* idea would approve."

"But, Laney," I try to explain. "It's completely illegal. I mean, I *guess* it's illegal, and she could get in so much trouble!"

Zoe comes around the table with two paperback books. "Hey, Miss Carolina, how much are these?"

"You can have them for free for being such a big help to everyone. How's Kimmy doing?" I ask.

The young girl leans against the worktable. "She's okay. It's happened before."

It's obvious from the looks Missus and FM give each other that they've heard the news about the K family's drama. The awkward conversation drags a bit, and we all watch Laney bend down and pick Cayden up from his stroller.

As she straightens up, she puts a burp cloth on her shoulder and says, "He seems gassy today. Can't get him settled down."

I finally have to ask. "Zoe, what do you mean it's happened before?"

She leans over to rub Cayden's fuzz-covered head. "Dad moving out. He'll get to missing the kids and Kimmy and come back." She coos to the baby, then says to Laney, "Let me try."

Laney hands him over explaining, "Zoe is the baby whisperer. She's got such a way with him."

We watch as Cayden begins almost immediately to settle down, then Missus stands up from the stool. "FM, let's go. Carolina, I can't get a straight answer out of Anna. Since I paid the deposit and first month's rent, the least I should be able to expect is a simple answer, but I'm assuming Will is moving into the apartment today?"

The picture of Will and Rose kissing comes to mind, and my face grows warm, so I turn it down and take a drink through my straw. But my head snaps up when Zoe says, "Isn't Will going with that pretty girl with the braid?"

Missus inhales. "Who? I don't believe he's *going with* anyone except his wife. Maybe you've got Anna confused with someone else."

Zoe bounces with the baby and speaks quietly, confidently. "No, Anna works at the Dollar Store with my dad. It's that girl, Rose, who stayed at your house when you were on vacation, Miss Carolina. I saw her pretty much every day when I'd walk down under the bridge. They'd snuggle on the front porch or have picnics on the hill. I wasn't spying, they just didn't know I was there."

"But…" is all I can say. Missus and FM don't even get that much out.

Then FM lets out a long breath and laughs a bit. "No, I saw boxes being moved into Anna's apartment this morning on my walk. She even waved as she was holding the door open for the moving man. Will's definitely moving in."

Laney has moved behind Zoe and is lifting her sleeping baby back into her arms.

Zoe rubs her arm like it's fallen asleep. She nods at FM. "Was he a big, bald guy? That's Jim J. He works for my dad, too. Drives a truck and helps set up new stores. Dad said he was going to help him move this weekend."

And then—I put my hand on the girl's shoulder and try to get my breath. With a swallow I squeeze out, "Where is your dad moving to?"

Zoe curves one side of her mouth up in apology and says it. "In with Anna."

CHAPTER 42

"I thought Missus was going to throw up, right there," I say to Jackson.

We're standing on the front porch watching evening clouds gather over the river. We went outside to sit in the rockers, but the image of Rose and Will in them stopped that.

I sigh. "I've often read the description of someone 'blanching,' but never actually witnessed it. All her color drained in an instant."

Jackson hits his palm on the porch railing. "How did this happen? Our son has lost his mind. Explains why we've seen so little of him lately."

"I know. I thought he was at the apartment with Anna. And Rose knows Anna's pregnant." I stop and turn when I hear a car coming across the tracks.

"It's Will," Jackson breathes and we steady ourselves. Our son parks on the other side of the driveway and takes his time getting out of the car. Between the thickening clouds and the lowering of the sun, the porch is in heavy shadows by the time he comes up the steps.

"How was work?" I ask with an edge. "Do you even still work at the dealership?" At the sharpness of that line, Jackson puts his hand on my arm.

"Work was fine. And yes, I do still work at the dealership."
Will looks at the rocking chairs. "Can we sit down?"

Jackson moves to sit down, but I shake my head and say,
"No. I'll stand. Do you want us to ask questions, or do you just
want to tell us what's going on? Like we can believe anything
you say."

Will's shoulders are sharp, with his elbows on the rocking
chair arms and his head hanging down. He stares at the floor,
and I stare at him. I'm so mad right now, I'm shocked I am this
controlled. My arms are folded like a straitjacket across my
chest, and my tight fists are burrowed into my ribs. I had too
long this afternoon at the store to think and stew and worry.
Now the words press against my skull, but I can't find any to
come out of my mouth. Okay, that might be a good thing, so
we'll go with it.

Jackson looks in my eyes, and I blink at him. He turns toward Will. "Son, what's going on?"

Will shakes his head and then shrugs. "I'm in love with
Rose. It makes no sense, I've just met her. Oh, and she feels
the same way." He smiles and that makes my heart hurt even
more. Every young person deserves to be in love. But...

My lips unseal. "But, that's exactly what you said about
Anna."

His smile fades. "Yeah, I don't know what happened there.
We, uh, well, we thought..." He lifts his arms, and nothing
comes out of his open mouth.

Jackson asks, "So she's with this Kendrick, a married man?
With four kids?"

Will jumps up and starts pacing. "Yeah, can you believe it?
He's scum. I tried to tell her, but she doesn't see it. He's got
her under his thumb. She believes anything he says. Craziest
thing I've ever seen!"

"Maybe this is just a woman's perspective, and a *mother's*
perspective," I say, "but maybe she felt left alone when you

decided to play around with Rose and ignore her. Maybe she felt she didn't have a choice, that she needed someone on her side." Oh, now I'm finding all those words I practiced all afternoon.

Will has his back to me, then he turns slowly. His voice is sad and slow when he says, "Maybe. And I've thought of that. I've apologized to her. I didn't mean to fall in love with Rose. But Anna says 'no.' That she sees I'm just a boy, and she doesn't want a boy." His disgust takes over any sadness.

Jackson speaks up. "Well, what about wanting the father of her baby?"

Our son's laugh is hollow. "Can you believe she thinks this will be easier having the baby, with us being apart? Honestly, that's what she's saying."

Jackson, ever the logical engineer, scoffs. "Is she crazy? What is easier about that?"

"That we'll share the baby. I'll have it half the time, and she'll have it half the time. That way she says there's always someone to keep it when one of us has to work or wants a weekend off."

I twirl around and shout. "For crying out loud, you people are idiots! This is a baby, not a pet goldfish!" I walk down to the end of the porch and look out at the river. There's one little sliver of bright sunshine at the horizon underneath the layer of clouds. Humidity and the smell of rain wrap around us. I slap at a mosquito and turn back to face my son and husband.

Jackson pats the rocker where Will was sitting. Will takes his seat again. His daddy says, "We've only got a couple more minutes before the mosquitos arrive to carry us away." He laughs a bit, but he's alone in finding any humor. He continues. "So you are planning on having the baby and keeping it. How's that going to work?"

Our oldest leans forward on the edge of his seat. He puts his elbows on his knees and brings his hands together. He looks at both of us and says, "I want to teach. Talking to Rose, I've decided that's what I want to do and with just an extra year of school I can. History. You know how much I've always loved history and there's courses in Georgia that use your degree, even if it's not in teaching, to get licensed. Like I said, it'll take about a year." He's nodding and smiling, like we've not seen this movie before.

I mumble, "I can't," and turn away from him. He looked just this earnest and excited when he told us about law school and again about marrying Anna.

Behind me, I hear Jackson saying exactly what I'm thinking. Then he adds, "And where will you live while you go back to school?"

My eyes close as I wait for the answer, because I know what it is.

And he says it. "Here. I'll keep working, and then we can all help with the baby when I have it. Rose still has another year of grad school, so it's not like we can get married now."

"And the little fact that you're already married might be a problem, too," I say with a lilt in my voice, but it's a mean lilt. Accompanied by rolling eyes, which he can't see in the darkness.

Proving he's no longer in possession of his God-given senses, he answers me. "Of course, but we'll just get a divorce. Shouldn't be a problem, right?"

I slap my arm again. Not because there was another mosquito, but because I've got to get away from this and mosquitos give me an out. "I'm going inside," I say. As I pull open the screen door, a car pulls across the crossing and lets Bryan out. Griffin waves as he turns the car around. Bryan walks up the steps as Griffin's taillights disappear.

We're all standing as Bryan walks through and leads us into the living room. He heads to the kitchen, and we follow him there. No one says anything, but each of us start looking for something to eat or drink. I guess it is dinner time, but I know *I* don't feel like eating. Jackson pulls a frozen pizza out and says, "I'm going to pop this in if anyone wants to join me."

Bryan has taken a couple slices of cheese from the lunch-meat drawer. He sits down at the table, eating them while I try not to look at his grimy hands holding the cheese. Will settles for a bottle of water. When the congestion clears in front of the fridge, I'm going straight for the wine.

Between pieces of cheese, Bryan tells us he made twelve dollars, and he's decided he wants to be a professional golfer. Will rolls his eyes, and when Bryan catches him, he growls at his brother to "Shut up!" He then looks at me through narrowed eyes and asks, "Miss Susan tell you? Grant's going to Darien." He sniffs. "Just so you know, I'm not going to Chancey High without Grant." Jackson and I sigh in unison, but the front door opening distracts us.

The front door slams closed, and the lack of noisy chatter says it's not our B&B guests back from their dinner yet. Savannah comes in and looks around the kitchen. She has on her Dollar Store work clothes, which are wrinkled and dirty. Her face is puffy and her eyes are surrounded by dark circles. Standing to the side she looks around at us for a minute before walking to the snack cabinet. She pulls out a Little Debbie Nutty Bar and opens one end. She leans against the counter and pulls one of the pieces out.

As she takes a big bite, she surveys our cozy family scene while she chews. Then, puffing out pieces of chocolate, wafer, and peanut butter, she says, "Don't know about y'all, but I'm kind of sick of this summer."

Amen.

Don't miss...

Next Stop, Chancey
Book One in the Chancey Series

Looking in your teenage daughter's purse is never a good idea.

After all, it ended up with Carolina opening a B&B for railroad buffs in a tiny Georgia mountain town. Carolina knows all about, and hates, small towns. How did she end up leaving her wonderful Atlanta suburbs behind while making her husband's dreams come true?

Unlike back home in the suburbs with privacy fences and automatic garage doors, everybody in Chancey thinks your business is their business and they all love the newest Chancey business. The B&B hosts a senate candidate, a tea for the County Fair beauty contestants, and railroad nuts who sit out by the tracks and record the sound of a train going by. Yet, nobody believes Carolina prefers the 'burbs.

Oh, yeah, and if you just ignore a ghost, will it go away?

Chancey Family Lies
Book Two in the Chancey Series

Holidays are different in small towns. You're expected to cook.

Carolina is determined her first holiday season as a
stay-at-home mom will be perfect. However...

Twelve kids from college (and one nobody seems to know)
Eleven chili dinners (why do we always have to feed a crowd?)
Ten dozen fake birds (cardinals, no less)
Nine hours without power (but lots of stranded guests)
Eight angry council members (wait, where's the town's money?)
Seven trains a-blowin' (all the time. All. The. Time.)
Six weeks with relatives (six weeks?!?)
Five plotting teens (again, who is that girl?)
Four in-laws staying (and staying, and staying...)
Three dogs a-barking (who brought the dogs?)
Two big ol' secrets (and they ain't wrapped in ribbons
under the tree, either)
And the perfect season gone with the wind.

Derailed in Chancey
Book Three in the Chancey Series

Should she jump?

When the train is headed for disaster, the engineer can jump out, right?

Carolina knew moving teenagers from the Atlanta suburbs to a small Georgia mountain town was a horrible idea. She knew opening a B&B was an even worse plan. She can't see around the next curve, but…

Should she jump?

Oncoming headlights aren't only aimed at her family, the town of Chancey is being set up for a collision that could change everything. And as that unfolds, Carolina's husband Jackson is smack dab in the middle of it all, his hand on the throttle, going full steam ahead.

Should she jump?

Would you?

Chancey Jobs
Book Four in the Chancey Series

Aren't small towns
supposed to be boring?

Overnight, a shiny new business opens on Chancey, Georgia's Main Street, with a manager straight from New York City who doesn't find the South charming, at all. Carolina's bookstore is also opening on Main Street. *If* she can keep Patty's mind on books instead of a new romance.

Then, when a secret wedding catches everyone off guard, a springtime tornado in Chancey just seems like icing on the cake. (Wedding cake, that is.)

Trains still run by Crossings, the B&B for rail road enthusiasts. Ruby still sells coffee and muffins. And kids still get out of school for the summer.

However, even in a small town, change is constant.
New jobs mean a move for long-time Chancey residents. Cancelled plans lead to moves across the state—and broken hearts. Graduations mean new chapters. And babies mean…well…

Babies mean nothing will ever be the same again.

You can find out more about Kay and her books
on her web-site, kaydewshostak.com

www.ingramcontent.com/pod-product-compliance
Lightning Source LLC
Chambersburg PA
CBHW031150120726
47905CB00006B/1883